Ansley sped up. So did the dark SUV.

Are you really doing this? Both Maribelle and Harrison had made her question herself, hinting that she wasn't going to like what she found out. Telling her that they were only trying to protect her. What if they were right and she couldn't handle the truth?

She let up on the gas. The fear was still there. What if there was something horrible they were trying to shield her from? *Are you doing this or not?*

Ahead, there was a wide spot on the right, a turnoff onto a dirt side road on the left. The highway continued but in a curve, quickly hidden by the pine trees growing close to each side. There was no other traffic this morning on this two-lane highway outside the city. There was just her and whoever was in that black SUV.

B.J. Daniels is a *New York Times* and *USA TODAY* bestselling author. She wrote her first book after a career as an award-winning newspaper journalist and author of thirty-seven published short stories. She lives in Montana with her husband, Parker, and three springer spaniels. When not writing, she quilts, boats and plays tennis. Contact her at bjdaniels.com, on Facebook or on Twitter, @bjdanielsauthor.

Books by B.J. Daniels

Harlequin Intrigue

A Colt Brothers Investigation

Murder Gone Cold
Sticking to Her Guns
Set Up in the City
Her Brand of Justice

Cardwell Ranch: Montana Legacy

Steel Resolve
Iron Will
Ambush before Sunrise
Double Action Deputy
Trouble in Big Timber
Cold Case at Cardwell Ranch

Visit the Author Profile page
at Harlequin.com for more titles.

B.J.

NEW YORK TIMES BESTSELLING AUTHOR

DANIELS

HER BRAND OF JUSTICE & WEDDING AT CARDWELL RANCH

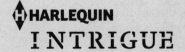

HARLEQUIN
INTRIGUE

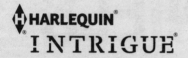

Recycling programs
for this product may
not exist in your area.

ISBN-13: 978-1-335-44979-5

Her Brand of Justice & Wedding at Cardwell Ranch

Copyright © 2023 by Harlequin Enterprises ULC

Her Brand of Justice
Copyright © 2023 by Barbara Heinlein

Wedding at Cardwell Ranch
First published in 2014. This edition published in 2023.
Copyright © 2014 by Barbara Heinlein

For questions and comments about the quality of this book,
please contact us at CustomerService@Harlequin.com.

Harlequin Enterprises ULC
22 Adelaide St. West, 41st Floor
Toronto, Ontario M5H 4E3, Canada
www.Harlequin.com

Printed in U.S.A.

CONTENTS

HER BRAND OF JUSTICE

If you have ever felt as if you didn't belong in your family and suspected that the babies were switched at the hospital or your parents stole you from your real parents, this book is for you.

Chapter 1

It wasn't the first time Ansley Brookshire had noticed a black SUV following her after an argument about finding her birth mother. It was, however, the first time she'd seen her adoptive father leave his office to rush home. What was different about this time? she wondered as she saw his driver pull into the estate. Her mother—*adoptive mother*, she mentally amended—must have called him. Which meant this time, because she'd threatened to hire a private investigator, it was serious. How far would they go to stop her?

The thought made her nervous—as if the black SUV now tailing her wasn't enough cause for concern. It only made her more determined. Her adoptive parents should know that once she decided to do something, she did it.

Except that she'd never felt they knew her. She'd spent most of her twenty-eight years feeling as if she didn't belong. An only child, she'd always been looking for someone who resembled her. Both Maribelle and Harrison were blond, fair skinned with dark blue eyes. Then there was Ansley, their only child, hair so dark it was almost coal black, eyes a washed-out blue like old denim and her skin olive instead of fair like her adoptive parents'. She'd never looked anything like them.

Now she knew why. Neither of her parents could have been responsible for her conception. At first she'd thought that she must have been adopted and they had just never told her.

But now she suspected that her whole life was a lie wrapped in secrets. When she'd asked for the truth, they'd lied to her. When she'd gone to public records to find details about her adoption, they weren't there. Had they stolen her as a baby? She still wasn't sure that hadn't been the case, even though Maribelle said it had been a private adoption and that's why she couldn't find any record of it.

Even private adoptions had records, which led her to believe that if she had been adopted, it had been illegal. Otherwise, she must have been stolen. Why else would Maribelle and Harrison be so adamant that she not look for her biological mother?

That's when she decided she would find out the truth no matter what.

Except the most recent "no matter what" appeared to be her father's bodyguard, Lanny Jackson, following her in the large black SUV he drove. What was it her adoptive parents were so afraid of her finding out? She felt a shiver of trepidation. Since her discovery, they'd done everything they could to keep her from learning the truth—or had they?

She glanced in the rearview mirror again. If they thought she could be intimidated, they were wrong. Maybe before all this began, she would have turned around, gone back to town to her apartment and waited for another day to follow the only lead she had as to who she really was. But she no longer felt safe even in her apartment. Since she'd discovered the big lie, she hadn't been able to shake the feeling that she was constantly being watched.

Never one to back down from a challenge, Ansley wasn't waiting another day. She finally had a lead. She wasn't going to put off chasing it. Even so, she'd tried again this morning to reason with her mother before she was forced to hire a stranger to help her.

That's why she'd gone to Brookshire Estate this morning, as it was commonly known, determined to give her mother one more chance to tell her the truth. Had she really thought that if she asked this time, it would be different?

Earlier she'd found Maribelle upstairs in the massive house where she'd grown up, standing in her huge walk-in closet, holding up one dress after another in front of her as she considered each in the full-length mirror. Clearly, she was getting ready for one of her many luncheons. Ansley had lost track years ago of how many boards her mother served on.

"What do you think, dear?" Maribelle asked, flashing her daughter a smile before returning to her image in the mirror. She hadn't seemed surprised to see her, even though Ansley had moved out of her room in the far wing right after high school and seldom showed up without calling. "I'm afraid the navy one says the wrong thing, don't you?"

"I've found a private investigative firm I'm going to hire," Ansley said, getting right to the point. It had been something she'd decided after running into nothing but dead ends on her own. "I'd hoped it wouldn't come to this."

Her mother met her gaze in the mirror. This was far from the first time this discussion had come up since she'd stumbled across at least part of the truth.

Yet her mother looked genuinely perplexed. "Whatever for?"

"I need to know who I am."

"You know who you are," she said with a dismissive scowl. "Ansley Brookshire. Do we really have to go through this again?"

"I'm going to find my birth mother with or without your help." The look her adoptive mother gave her said it would be without her help, as usual. She recalled the fear she'd seen in Maribelle's eyes the first time she had confronted her after finding proof that she wasn't related to either of her parents.

"Why are you so afraid of what I'm going to find?"

"*I'm* your mother," Maribelle had said with finality. "I think the coral dress. It wouldn't hurt to stand out today," she said flipping her chin-length blond hair back as she returned her attention to the mirror.

Ansley moved to stand next to her until they were reflected side by side in the huge mirror. The contrast between them was startling. Maribelle was a natural blue-eyed blonde, a former beauty queen, tall and leggy. Ansley stood five foot five, with her obsidian-black hair, the palest of blue eyes and an athletic build. No one had ever believed that they were mother and daughter—not that her mother's social circle would have ever mentioned it, at least not to Maribelle's face.

How she'd come to live in this house as their daughter was only one of the many lies and secrets, she thought now. For years, she'd wondered why she was so different from her parents—and not just in appearance.

"I like the navy dress," she said to her mother, who smiled distractedly at her in the mirror.

"You would," Maribelle said. "You've always had that stubborn streak—just like your father."

"My birth father?" Ansley asked, making her mother's mouth form a thin, straight line of disapproval.

"What can I say to you to make you change your mind?" Maribelle asked with a sigh as she tossed the navy dress aside. "Your father and I were discussing buying a place in the Bahamas just this morning. We'd need you to do the decorating. You have such a good eye for that sort of thing. It would mean a lot of work, but I'm sure you can close your little jewelry shop for a few months while you're away."

Her *little jewelry shop*. Neither Maribelle nor Harrison had ever taken her jewelry making seriously—even when she'd turned it into a very successful business that more than supported her.

"I'm not closing my shop, and I'm not going to the Bahamas," she said. They'd already tried to buy her off. This was just another stalling tactic in the hopes she would change her mind. Or was it about giving them time to cover their tracks?

When she'd first confronted them with what she knew, Maribelle had offered her anything she wanted to drop this obsession. Then had begun issuing threats when bargaining and bribing didn't work. But since she was no longer dependent on them financially nor interested in inheriting their wealth, the monetary threats hadn't worked.

"You know I love you and appreciate everything you and my father have done for me," she'd said. They hadn't been a normal family—at least not like her friends' parents, who often ate together at the kitchen table in a roar of voices and laughter as everyone tried to talk at once.

Ansley had grown up eating in the kitchen with the cook and a nanny. She'd seldom seen her parents except in passing. They would give her a kiss as they left for this event or that. She'd thought when she was young that her father always wore a suit and her mother a fancy dress. She remembered the smear of her mother's lipstick on her cheek, the smell of her perfume lingering in the air as they rushed out into the night.

Not that she sincerely wasn't grateful for the advantages she'd had. But there had always been a hole in her heart she hadn't understood, as if she'd lost a missing piece of herself somewhere. Just as she had always felt there was some secret, something she hadn't been told, something important that had been left out.

She glanced in her rearview mirror again. The dark SUV was still back there. Harrison wouldn't pay his bodyguard to physically keep her from the truth, would he? She remembered seeing his driver pull in through the gate at the estate as she was leaving. She'd gotten only a glimpse of her adoptive father in the back with Lanny. Just from his expression through the tinted window, she'd felt a sliver of fear. For him to drop everything and come home at this time of the day… And now, if she was right, Lanny planned to follow her all day and night if that's what it took.

Ansley sped up. So did the dark SUV. *Are you really doing this?* Both Maribelle and Harrison had made her question herself, hinting that she wasn't going to like what she found out. Telling her that they were only trying to protect her from disappointment. What if they were right and she couldn't handle the truth?

She let up on the gas. The fear was still there. What if there really was something horrible they were trying to shield her from? *Are you doing this or not?*

Ahead, there was a wide spot on the right and a turn-off onto a side road on the left. The highway continued ahead but curved, quickly disappearing behind the pine trees growing close to each side. There was no other traffic this morning on this two-lane highway outside the city. There was just her and whoever was driving that black SUV.

Ansley put on her blinker to pull into the wide spot and turn around. She didn't have to do this today. Going by the estate had been a mistake. She should never have told Maribelle her plans.

As she came to a dust-boiling stop beside the highway, the black SUV sped on past. She couldn't see the driver's face, but from the large, bulky shadow behind the wheel, she knew she'd been right. It was Lanny Jackson, her father's personal bodyguard.

The moment he and black SUV disappeared around the curve, obscured by the trees, Ansley gunned her vehicle across the highway and onto the dirt road bordered by pine trees. She knew it wouldn't take Lanny long to turn around and come back. Ahead she saw yet another narrow dirt road to the right. She slowed just enough to take the turn and kept going.

She took the next road to the left and then one to the right. She had an idea where she was, so she wasn't surprised when she finally hit the paved two-lane highway miles to the north. She took it. The traffic was sparse in this part of Montana once you got out of the city.

No black SUV appeared behind her as she wound her way north toward Lonesome, Montana, and the only lead she had. She could see a spring squall building in the mountains. An omen that this was a mistake? She kept driving north, even though she knew that once Lanny reported that he'd lost her, there would be an even worse storm at Brookshire Estate.

Chapter 2

"This had better be an emergency, Maribelle," Harrison barked as he stormed into the house. "I was in the middle of an important meeting."

"You are always in the middle of an important meeting," she snapped back. She could see through the front window that his driver was waiting by his car, the engine running. Where was that obscenely large bodyguard of his?

"Maribelle?"

Any minute he'd be checking his watch, she thought bitterly. "It's about our daughter."

He groaned, rolling his eyes. "You told my secretary it was an *emergency*. I had Jackson follow her. What more do you want? Not only is it a waste of time and money, but also I now have no security other than

Roger, and we both know how my driver would react in a real emergency."

She hated the way he talked down to her. It didn't help that he was nine years older. She'd been his child bride. He still treated her like a juvenile. And him acting like there was always someone waiting around the corner to rob him, kill him… She should get so lucky.

"This *is* an emergency. Ansley is hiring a private investigator to track down her biological mother." He stared at her, nonplussed. "She can't do that. We can't allow it."

With a sigh, he said, "Once she learned that we weren't her parents, this was bound to happen. So what if she finds her birth mother?" The question hung in the air. He narrowed his eyes. "What the hell have you done, Maribelle?"

She swallowed, feeling small and afraid, a feeling she abhorred. She was Mrs. Harrison Brookshire. Everyone wanted to be her. "I'll fix it. But I'm going to need Lanny's help—and money."

He shook his head. "You're the one who just had to have a daughter. At all costs. I let you take care of it, just giving you the money and staying out of the details, and—"

"Yes, I know all that," she said. She'd heard this lecture many times. He hadn't wanted a child and had made it clear from the beginning that it was her deal and not to involve him in any way. She'd had this picture in her mind of having a daughter just like her—matching dresses, people stopping them on the street to compliment them.

The fact that Ansley was nothing like her had been a huge disappointment. Nor had she realized how much work children were, even with nannies and boarding schools. "I might need a lot of money."

Harrison glared at her. "Since you have a purse full of credit cards and your own checking account that I refill monthly, I know you're not talking about money for new dresses or shoes or spa treatments or expensive trips." He looked as if he were grinding his teeth. For all the money the man made, he was crass and cheap about things that were important to her, and it annoyed her to no end. "How much, Maribelle? How much this time to undo whatever it is you've done?"

Buck Crawford considered the weather for a moment before he parked his pickup in the alley behind Colt Brothers Investigation just off the main drag of Lonesome, Montana.

Snow in May? He'd awakened to sunshine only to have the clouds roll in, followed by rain, then sleet, and now he was watching the flakes fall, the wind whipping them around outside the warm cab of his pickup. Well, this *was* Montana, he reminded himself. Yet this winter was hanging on way too long.

Snowflakes had begun accumulating on his windshield before he snugged his Stetson down on his head, pulled his sheepskin coat around him and climbed out. With luck one of the Colts would have a pot of hot coffee going this morning.

Wind whirled icy flakes around him as if he'd stepped into a snow globe. He squinted through the blur of white as he hurried toward the back door of the narrow brick building that housed Colt Brothers Investigation.

But before he could reach to open the door, it was

flung outward as a woman dressed in a long red wool coat came flying out. He glimpsed shiny black hair and startled pale blue eyes before he collided with her.

Instinctively he grabbed hold of her shoulders to steady her—and keep them both from going down. Their gazes met for an instant before she broke free and rushed down the alley, disappearing into the falling snow as she turned the corner and was gone.

Buck looked after her for a moment, still startled by the encounter—and what he'd seen in those eyes. Fear. As he considered going after her, he noticed that she'd dropped something in her hurried escape. Reaching down, he picked up what appeared to be a used envelope. The top had been sliced open, and it was now empty. It was addressed to Colt Brothers Investigation. There was no return address.

He turned it over and saw that someone had written what appeared to be a list of names and dates on the blank side. Was this something important that she needed? The writing was starting to blur from the wet snow landing on it. The woman long gone, he quickly tucked the envelope under his coat, opened the door and stepped in out of the cold.

As he entered the back of the Colt Brothers Investigation office, he pulled out the envelope and waved it in the warm air to dry it before the inked names and numbers ran. To his surprise, he recognized the names—all of them Colts, all the way back to his friends' great-grandfather Ransom Del Colt, who'd been a famous Western movie star in Hollywood back in the '40s and early '50s.

Their grandfather RD Colt Jr. had started his own Wild West show and traveled the world ropin' and ridin'.

All the Colts had followed in their famous predecessors' footsteps, riding the rodeo circuit, including the brothers' father, Del, who later quit the circuit to start the PI agency.

It seemed the woman had picked up a discarded envelope and hurriedly written down not just their names, but dates associated with each. Why her interest in the Colt family? He didn't like the bad feeling this was giving him. Who was that woman?

Maybe more important, why, when she'd crashed into him, had she looked scared? He'd thought at that instant it was from the shock of not expecting to open the door and see a man there.

But after finding the envelope, he realized that something had happened inside the office that had made her look pale and shaky—and had her tearing out the door. Had one of the Colts told her something that had upset her? Didn't explain the envelope with their names and dates on it.

"James?" he called out. "Tommy? Davy? Anyone?" No answer. As he moved deeper into the main office, he kept seeing her face, those washed-denim blue eyes that had looked almost familiar, even though he would swear he'd never seen her before.

He stopped in the center of the main office. He'd been so deep in thought that he hadn't realized how eerily quiet the office was. Where was everyone?

Pushing open a door to one of the private offices, he saw with a start that it had been ransacked. Desk drawers stood open, and papers were strewn on the floor. A filing cabinet had been broken into.

"Hello?" he called tentatively as he pocketed the envelope and reached for the sidearm on his hip, only to belatedly remember he wasn't armed, no longer law enforcement. Nor was he a rancher raising rough stock for rodeos. Right now, he was in limbo, but those cop instincts had him on edge.

He moved stealthily through the building, checking each private office, finding them empty, all having been ransacked. As he did, he mentally kicked himself. He should have gone after the woman. All his instincts told him she had just brought trouble to Lonesome—and the Colt brothers. Just his luck that he was the first to cross her path. At least he could give them a description of her. Hopefully she hadn't taken anything.

Buck did wonder, though, what she'd been looking for as he pulled out his cell to call Sheriff Willie Colt, the oldest Colt brother. Before he could, James walked in through the front door holding a shallow cardboard box, the smell of cinnamon and sugar quickly filling the room.

He realized that James must have opened the office, then popped next door to the sandwich shop that his wife, Lori, used to own to pick up cinnamon rolls.

"What's going on?" James asked, glancing around as he carefully put the box down on the scarred old oak desk that had been his father's and now sat in the main office as reception.

"The offices—"

"They're ransacked," James said.

Buck nodded. "I think I might know who did it. As I was coming in the back door, a dark-haired young woman with these really pale blue eyes was rushing out in a hurry. It appears she had a look around before she left."

"Attractive young woman?" James asked, tongue in cheek. "Thanks for clarifying that."

"Seriously, she was...striking and somehow familiar." He frowned and saw his friend shaking his head.

"You make one heck of a witness. Any idea what she was looking for?" James asked as he quickly checked the offices.

"No idea, but she dropped this before disappearing down the alley." He handed James the envelope with the writing on it as the PI moved to the large old oak desk again. The family story was that the desk was the first thing Del Colt had bought used when he'd started Colt Investigations.

Del hadn't lived long enough to see each of his sons also leave the rodeo circuit to return to Lonesome, Montana. Three of them had taken over the PI business while Willie had turned to law enforcement, having recently been elected county sheriff.

"If I'm right and that's her handwriting on the envelope, it would seem she has an interest in the Colt family," Buck said as James sat down behind the desk.

"Let's try that description again," James said as he pulled out a notebook and pen. Buck drew up a chair and described her as much as he could remember to his friend.

"She doesn't sound familiar," James said, surveying his notes. The top of the desk was clean. He opened his desk drawer. "It appears she sorted through things, but nothing seems to be missing. She didn't take the business checkbook or the spare change I keep in here," he said, closing the drawer.

"She didn't seem like a woman who needed your spare change," Buck said almost to himself as he gazed at the wall with the posters of Colt ancestors. There was a framed movie poster of James's great-grandfather Ransom and numerous photos from RD Jr.'s Wild West show, along with action shots of Del's sons trying to ride bulls and broncs in local rodeos as boys.

"I take that back," James said with a curse as he followed Buck's gaze. "She did take something." He pointed to the wall where a small, faded rectangle showed where a framed photo had hung.

"Which photo was that?" Buck asked, frowning. He'd studied the wall many times but couldn't remember that exact print. Growing up helping his father and brother raise rough stock for rodeos, he'd been as infatuated with the sport as anyone. It was something he and the Colts had always had in common.

"It was one of the four of us out on the ranch," his friend said. "It was my dad's favorite of us boys."

Buck remembered it now, the brothers looking as if they'd been wrestling in the dirt, their jeans as filthy as their faces, Western shirts torn and askew, the knees of their jeans caked dark with mud, their cowboy hats pushed back on their dark heads with all four of them grinning from ear to ear.

"You might have a problem," Buck said. "There was something about the woman I couldn't put my finger on, but I felt as if I'd seen her before. More of concern, she looked shaken when she came flying out the back door. Whatever she found, it scared her."

Ansley was still in shock by the time she reached her SUV parked down the block on Lonesome's main drag. She climbed in, hurriedly started the motor and turned on the wipers to brush away the snow that had accumulated in the short time she'd been gone. But she couldn't drive right now. Her hands were shaking too hard, her heart a thunder in her ears as she fought back tears.

She couldn't believe what she'd just done after finding the investigation office unoccupied. She'd known whoever had unlocked the door must have just stepped out. They would be back soon. She'd planned to have a seat and wait, but she'd been so nervous that she couldn't sit. Instead, she'd noticed the wall of photos and posters and had been drawn to it.

She'd found herself searching the faces. Her eyes had widened in surprise, shock and then alarm. Even now she couldn't believe what she'd been thinking. What she was *still* thinking—that the answer had been staring her in the face? She'd grabbed a used envelope off the large reception desk and a pen and had furiously written down names and dates as she'd tried to make sense out of what she was seeing.

The envelope. She looked around for it now, searching her coat pockets and groaning as she realized that she must have dropped it in her hurry to escape. She'd been frantic to get out of there after she'd heard a noise upstairs. It had sounded as if someone was rummaging around up there. That's when she'd noticed one of the office doors ajar and had seen the mess. Someone had done this, and now they were upstairs and could be coming down the steps at any moment.

She'd taken off out the back, realizing that when one of the Colts came back, he'd think she'd made this mess. It was bad enough that she'd impulsively taken a framed photo off the wall. What had come over her?

She dug again for the envelope she'd written on, hoping she hadn't dropped it. But given the way she'd torn out of there, she wasn't surprised that she must have. What would the Colt brothers do when they returned? Call the sheriff? What about the cowboy she'd crashed into on her way out?

As she pulled her hand from her empty coat pocket, she realized that she had cut her finger enough to make it bleed. When she'd taken the photo? She vaguely remembered catching her finger on the nail. Pulling out a tissue from the glove box, she frowned as she wiped away the blood, then turned up the heater, feeling chilled in a way that had nothing to do with the Montana spring weather. The wipers were barely keeping up with the falling snow, and yet to the south, at the end of the main street, she could see blue sky on the horizon.

She should get out of town. People could already be looking for her—and not just the men from Colt Brothers Investigation. She thought of the cowboy she'd nearly knocked down. If he hadn't grabbed her... They'd looked at each other, but only for an instant. She'd half expected him to chase after her and had been relieved when he hadn't. She told herself that she wouldn't recognize him even if she saw him again.

With the snow falling, the flakes so large and lacy, she could barely see across the street. She shouldn't drive until she got control of herself. Maribelle was right about one thing—she wasn't herself. Her actions today proved that.

Guilt nibbled at her. She'd been relieved when she found out that Harrison and Maribelle weren't her birth parents. She'd always felt not just alone and lonely, but like an outsider. Her life might have appeared charmed, since it appeared that she'd never wanted for anything.

And yet she'd ached for what she'd thought of as a real family. Her true family, she believed now.

As her heart rate began to drop back to normal, she felt her resolve returning. She wouldn't turn tail and run. Not now, especially. The answer *was* in Lonesome. A few days ago, she'd tracked down her original nanny and questioned her. If there had been any evidence of where Maribelle and Harrison had gotten her, she figured Gladys Houser might know.

Gladys had been in her fifties when she went to work at the estate, a matronly spinster who seldom smiled. She'd been her nanny until Ansley was five and entered preschool.

Now over eighty, Gladys had been reluctant to talk to her. She'd pursed her lips when questioned and said, "I don't like talking about former employers."

"Please. Anything you can tell me might help me find my birth mother."

As if seeing how badly Ansley needed to know the truth—and that she wasn't going to stop until she did—the former nanny had said she couldn't help, because she knew nothing about the adoption.

She said she'd heard about the employment opportunity through a friend who thought she'd be perfect for the job because she'd taken care of newborns before. She'd gone to the estate, met with Maribelle and been told that she would be living in the wing farthest away from the couple so their sleep wouldn't be disturbed.

"It was clear that Mrs. Brookshire wasn't pregnant, so I was to wait until the baby arrived," Gladys had told her. "A few days later, Mrs. Brookshire came in with a newborn. She carried you into the nursery and put you down in the crib and left. You were crying, and your diaper needed changing. I took over and spent every day with you until you were walking. Mrs. Brookshire hired a second, younger nanny to keep you busy during the day. I stayed in the employment until you went to preschool, taking care of you at night and on the other nanny's days off."

"What about how I was dressed or what I was wrapped in the first time you saw me," Ansley had asked. "Any clue as to where the adoption had taken place?"

She had waited, seeing that Gladys knew something. Just from what the nanny had said, she hadn't been a fan of Maribelle and her parenting.

"You were wrapped in a knit blanket. It had a tag on it that read 'made with love,' but quite frankly, the knitting was very amateurish," she said, turning up her nose.

"As if a teenager might have made it?" Ansley had suspected her birth mother might have been too young to keep her. Gladys had shrugged. "What happened to the blanket?"

"Mrs. Brookshire told me to dispose of it in the trash, along with a plastic bag with some disposable new-born diapers and what appeared to be clothing someone had bought for you." Ansley had felt her heart sink. "I couldn't bring myself to throw any of it away. Someone had obviously cared. I took it to a friend whose daughter could use the clothing and the blanket. I found a receipt in the bottom of the plastic bag. The yarn had been purchased in a store in Lonesome, Montana, some months before Mrs. Brookshire brought you to the house."

Ansley had started to ask about the family who'd

taken the blanket that her birth mother might have knit herself, but Gladys had already been shaking her head.

"The family moved. I have no idea what happened to the blanket. I'm sorry. I shouldn't even be telling you this much."

"What color was it?"

"Pink. A pale pink. But she'd also bought enough yarn for a blue one as well, according to the receipt."

"As if she didn't know if she was having a boy or a girl," Ansley had said, more to herself than to Gladys.

She had thanked her, tears in her eyes as she'd left. Her biological mother had loved her. Why else had she knit her a blanket "made with love"? But why had she given her up? If she had willingly.

Ansley had followed that thin thread of a lead to Lonesome. When she'd researched online, she'd seen that there was a private investigation business in the small Western town. She'd told herself she would hire them to find her birth mother. That had led her to Colt Brothers Investigation.

After years of yearning for someone who resembled her, everything had gone as planned—until she'd walked into the PI office and had seen a wall full of photographs of people who looked so much like her that she'd been swamped with emotion. That's when she'd heard the noise upstairs and panicked, grabbed the small photo of the boys from the wall and run.

All the time, she kept thinking, what if Maribelle and Harrison had been right? What if she couldn't handle the truth?

Chapter 3

Maribelle fumed. It was clear that she couldn't stop Ansley. Nor could she depend on Harrison to do anything. His idea of help was throwing money at the problem. Too busy with his empire to run, he'd always told her to handle things and then complained about the way she'd done it. Had he gotten her a baby daughter? No, she'd had to do it herself. Just as she was going to have to take care of this matter herself.

She made the call, not surprised that the woman's landline phone number hadn't changed in twenty-eight years. "I need to see you."

A cough, then a gruff "Who is this?" in that husky voice she remembered.

"Don't even pretend that you don't know," Maribelle snapped, wondering what she'd been thinking to ever get involved with this woman. As much as she hated to admit it, Harrison had been right. Getting a baby had been a bad idea. Worse, now that baby had grown up and was threatening to destroy everything Maribelle had accomplished in life. If what she'd done ever came out…

She thought of the night she'd met Judy Ramsey, one of the servers working for the catering service at a party she attended. The woman had been on her knees in the bathroom heaving up her guts. Maribelle had just hoped it wasn't something she'd eaten in the kitchen that the caterer had brought.

"Morning sickness," the woman had said as she'd flushed and risen.

One look at Judy Ramsey and she'd seen an opportunity. "You don't sound happy about the pregnancy." Judy had merely mugged a face in answer as she'd rinsed her mouth out under the faucet at the sink. "Is it a girl? Or a boy? Or is it too early to tell?"

Judy had studied her for a moment. "Girl." That had been the magic word—and the answer to Maribelle's longing for a daughter. It had only come down to how much money Judy would demand.

"We need to meet," Maribelle said now and heard the woman cough again. In the background it sounded like the television was on one of those daytime stories. She silently groaned to herself. She could imagine the woman's face, the greed in those beady eyes—she could see her calculating how much a meeting would net her. The thought of giving this woman another dime turned her stomach.

"Is that so?" There was a teasing, mocking quality to her tone that made Maribelle grind her teeth. Had she already heard that Ansley was searching for her?

"Meet me on the old river highway at that motel and café tomorrow evening. Seven. Don't be late." She disconnected before she could change her mind. Harrison would definitely not approve of what she was planning to do. But then again, he seldom approved of what she did. Worse, she might make matters worse.

But she had no choice. She stepped to her walk-in closet–slash–dressing room, opened the bottom drawer and reached in the far back, past her expensive negligees, to the box she kept there.

Drawing it out, she opened the box and took out the gun, even though she told herself that she had no intention of using it. The gun had been her father's. He was the one who'd taught her to shoot. She'd never told Harrison about it. Nor did he know she knew anything about weapons. There was so much about her he didn't know. Lack of interest, she thought. He'd taken one look at her long legs and her long blond hair and big blue eyes and had seen everything he'd wanted in her. Which had worked in her favor. He'd married the woman he thought she was, the fool. He never would have made such a mistake when it came to business.

She tucked the firearm into her designer leather shoulder bag next to the envelope of cash Harrison had grudgingly removed from the safe in his study. That done, Maribelle walked into her closet to go through the process of deciding what to wear tomorrow. It was very important to choose the right outfit—maybe especially to meet a woman you were probably going to have to kill.

Sheriff Willie Colt was on a mission of his own after returning recently from a case out in Seattle. His life had been a whirlwind since then. He'd fallen in love and gotten married—something he'd thought he would never do—to a very attractive attorney in Seattle who'd stolen his heart. Now he and Ellie were building a house on Colt Ranch.

He'd also found a girl's gold necklace in the wrecked pickup his father had died in almost ten years before.

While he'd never been this happy, or this busy, he was still determined to find out what had really happened to his father the night he died. When he'd originally joined the sheriff's department as a deputy, he'd thought it was temporary. The only reason he'd taken the job was to try to get to the truth about his father's death. Del had died when his pickup had apparently stalled on the tracks. Struck by the train, he'd been immediately killed and his pickup totaled. The sheriff back then had closed the case, declaring it an accident.

But Willie and his brothers had never believed that. Unfortunately, he was never able to find any evidence that proved otherwise—even as a deputy in the sheriff's department.

Instead, what had happened was that he realized that he liked law enforcement—just not the sheriff at the time. So he'd run for the office against him—and won. It hadn't stopped him from looking for answers. After returning from Seattle, he'd gotten lucky and found his father's pickup in a wrecking yard, miles from Lonesome. On the floorboard behind the seat of the king cab, he'd found the small, tarnished gold necklace with the name *DelRae* engraved on it.

Since then he'd been even more obsessed with finding what had happened that night on the train tracks. His father had warned his sons about crossing where there were no bars, no flashing lights, and yet Del had gone to that very spot and been hit by a train that night almost ten years ago. It made no sense. Where had he been going on that dirt road that led up into the mountains? Had he been meeting someone tied to one of his PI cases?

The only clue they had—other than the necklace—was a report called in to the sheriff's department from an anonymous source who said she saw Del Ransom Colt arguing with a woman in front of a downtown bar in Lonesome not long before he died on the tracks. Unfortunately, the sheriff at the time hadn't gotten the woman's name. The crooked sheriff also could have made up the story to make it look like Del had been coming from the bar and was drunk.

Online, Willie had found there were dozens of Delraes but no DelRae, the way it was spelled on the necklace. Since he had no idea how old DelRae had been or would be now, he had nothing to go on.

His cell phone rang. He saw it was his brother James and quickly picked up. Things had been relatively slow at the sheriff's department lately. It wasn't quite tourist season in Montana. Kids were still in school for a few more weeks. The only excitement was the upcoming high school graduation, which brought out most of the town since so many people in the county were related.

This latest snowstorm had a couple of deputies out because of fender benders, but other than that, Willie had found himself digging through the mountains of paperwork that went with the job.

"Something strange happened here at the office this morning," James said without preamble. He went on to tell Willie what had been taken and how Buck Crawford had seen a young woman escaping.

"That's all that was taken?" the sheriff asked. "Just a photograph of us?"

"I know that doesn't seem important, but that was Dad's favorite. I want it back."

Willie smiled at the anger he heard in his brother's voice. "And this criminal mastermind was a woman, a young, good-looking woman, given Buck's description. Sounds like he was taken with her."

"I'm serious. Maybe you could come take fingerprints, *Sheriff.* We have an envelope we believe she wrote on, but I figured the desk and drawers would produce a better print."

He couldn't believe what he was hearing. Before he could argue, James said, "Davy just found some blood. She must have cut herself on the nail when she took the photo. We need to run DNA on it."

All this over a stolen photo, even his dad's favorite? "I think you're overreacting, but I'll be right over. Don't touch anything else." He disconnected, chuckling to himself. James knew that most people's fingerprints weren't in the national database—not to mention how few people even had their DNA on file.

But if it would make his brother feel better... And it was a break-in and something had been stolen and he *was* the sheriff.

Buck Crawford left the Colt brothers to their work. He was at loose ends. An injury had forced him to leave his job as a state highway patrolman. While he'd healed, at least physically, he didn't want to go back to being a patrolman. Nor did he want to join his father and brother out on the ranch raising rough stock for rodeos. He didn't know what he wanted to do with the rest of his life—and he was only thirty-five. Except thirty-five often felt old. His future appeared to be a long, dark, endless tunnel—unless he took the advice of the psychiatrist he was required to see after his injury and let it go. He chuckled. If only it was that easy, he thought.

As he walked down the main drag of Lonesome, he knew he had to make a decision about his life. He'd never been in this state of mind before. Almost dying did that to a person, he thought. But he knew it was much more than that. He'd been told that he had trust issues.

The snow had let up, and as usually happened in the spring in Montana, the sun peeked out through the clouds. What snow had stuck was now melting, the icy water running down the street.

Like a lot of small Montana towns, this one had that Old West look with the usual: a courthouse, post office, jail, bank, an old movie theater, a hardware store, a clothing shop, grocery, several cafés and an assortment of touristy shops that sold everything from T-shirts and Montana curios to quilt fabric and antiques.

There was a damned good steak house outside town, near the fairgrounds. If a person wanted more, they could drive to Missoula or one of Montana's other larger cities. There weren't that many. Buck had seen enough of cities. When at home on the ranch, he seldom even drove into Lonesome.

But today he'd been more restless than usual. If he hadn't been, he realized, he wouldn't have come into town today. He wouldn't have run into the woman fleeing the PI office. He'd been thinking about her when he noticed a white SUV pull out of a parking space up the block and head in his direction.

He caught a glimpse of the woman behind the wheel. His heart rate kicked up. She wore large sunglasses, and while she didn't look in his direction, he was positive it was the same woman. The collar of her red wool coat was turned up.

As she passed, he tried to read her license plate number under the road grime but only got the last three numbers. He wanted to run back to the alley where he'd left his pickup and give pursuit, but knew he couldn't reach his truck quickly enough and catch her, since she was headed for the highway out of town.

Nor did he have any business chasing after her. He reminded himself that he was on an extended leave from the highway patrol—a tenuous position at best. He was just a plain old civilian without any authority to chase down the woman. Best to leave chasing this particular criminal to the Colts.

Yet, as he watched her white SUV disappear down the highway, he couldn't help wanting to go after her. Just as he couldn't help being intrigued. What had she been looking for in the Colt office? More important, what was her interest in the Colt family? Wasn't that what worried him the most? He felt protective of his friends. They'd gotten him through some tough times in his life. He owed them.

He texted James with the three numbers he'd gotten off the license plate and a description of the vehicle's make and model.

The sheriff considered the spot where the missing framed photo had been, bagged the envelope in question, attempted to get prints off the desk drawer handles and had his lab tech take a blood sample for a DNA test. Then he stopped to study the photos and posters on the wall. He'd looked at them a million times growing up, but he still enjoyed studying them. The Colts had one hell of a legacy, he thought with no small amount of pride.

For so many years, growing up just outside Lonesome, he and his brothers had had free rein. His father hadn't believed in running roughshod over his sons. No wonder a lot of people in these parts called them "those wild Colt boys." Willie knew his brothers thought their childhood had been magical and wouldn't have changed it for the world. As the oldest, Willie had known a darker side, one he'd made sure his brothers had been spared.

His gaze fell on a photo of his father on the back of a bronco just moments before it had dumped him in the dirt. The look on Del's face was priceless. Willie knew that kind of wild happiness. He'd felt it many times while on the rodeo circuit—and recently having fallen in love.

Now he wondered—as he had ever since finding the girl's necklace in his father's wrecked pickup— had there been someone in Del's life after he lost his wife and his sons' mother? If so, he'd kept it a secret, which made the girl's tarnished gold necklace and their father's death even more of a mystery. As he studied his father's photo, he promised himself again that he wouldn't give up until he knew what had happened that night on the railroad tracks.

"Thanks for doing this," James said as he joined him. "I can't imagine what the woman was looking for. Why would she steal a photograph of the four of us boys as kids?"

"Because we were so dang cute?" Willie joked.

His brother pulled a face. "I'm serious. It's...weird." Willie couldn't argue that. "Buck just called. He saw her leaving town. He got a partial plate number on her white SUV. Said it's a newer Escalade and the plate was framed with a dealer's name in Bozeman."

Willie took the information his brother had jotted down and promised to get back to him. He didn't hold out much hope on fingerprints or DNA coming back with a hit. But they just might get lucky with the license plate numbers and vehicle description. He couldn't help being curious about this female mastermind, he thought with a chuckle.

Chapter 4

After picking up a few supplies for the ranch, Buck headed out of town. He'd thought about sticking his head in at Colt Brothers Investigation to see if they'd learned anything about the woman but changed his mind, knowing that one of them would have called if they had any new information.

He was only a half mile out of town when his stomach growled. He realized he should have at least gotten something to eat since it was still a long way to the ranch. Ahead, he saw the sign for the steak house. Several cars were parked out front. One thought of the restaurant's burgers and fries and he couldn't help himself. He swung in.

It wasn't until he'd parked that he noticed a white SUV parked on the side of the building that looked a lot like the one he'd seen the dark-haired woman driving.

His heart bumped up a few beats as he got out and walked over to it. Same model SUV, same framed license plate from Bozeman. He pulled a glove from his coat pocket and wiped off the plate so he could read all the numbers. Same last three numbers he'd given James Colt.

It was her.

He looked up, hoping she wasn't watching him from one of the front windows as he headed for the door. As he caught a whiff of something frying, the hot-grease smell making his stomach growl even louder, he considered how he was going to handle this.

It wasn't until he pushed open the door and saw his mystery woman sitting in a booth by the front window that he made up his mind. She looked lost in thought, with what appeared to be a cup of coffee growing cold in front of her. It appeared that's all she'd ordered. He wondered how long she'd been sitting here. If anything, she looked paler than earlier and possibly just as scared. *Striking* was the only way he could describe her.

As he approached her, he warned himself that she was going to be as skittish as a wild horse—and even more challenging to get a rope on if he handled this wrong. She'd had her hands in her lap but raised them to the table, palms down. Her hands were pale, with finely shaped fingers and perfect nails painted a demure pale pink. But what caught his eye was the glint of the ring. He hadn't noticed it when they'd collided with each other earlier in the alley.

Now, though, he couldn't miss the pear-shaped diamond on her left ring finger. It was large enough to put an eye out. The woman was engaged.

He felt a strange mix of emotions. Of course, he'd been attracted to her instantly in the alley. She was beautiful, and he hadn't been that close to a woman in quite a while now. He swore he could still smell the faint hint of her perfume on his sheepskin jacket. For so long, no woman had even made him turn his head. So why the interest in this one? Just to get the Colts' photo back?

Chuckling to himself, he hoped that's all it was. It would be just like him to be drawn to a criminal, he thought with self-deprecation. Yet he couldn't deny her allure, which, upon seeing her again, was stronger than ever. Who was this woman?

For just an instant, he tried to talk himself into walking on past her table and letting her be. *This is not your rodeo.* But he knew himself too well. He would always regret it. He wanted to know her story. He was also the only one who could positively identify her as the woman he'd seen running scared out of the ransacked office.

Now he had her dead to rights.

But as he neared the table, his common sense argued again for him to let it go. Let *her* go. She was trouble. All his cop instincts, the ones he thought he'd also packed away for good, wouldn't let him. Damned if he wasn't still a lawman at heart.

His fear was that this disturbingly attractive woman with her big blue eyes was a con artist—and the Colt brothers were now her marks.

"Excuse me, Miss."

Ansley hadn't heard the cowboy approach her table. She looked up, startled, but even more alarmed when she recognized him.

"Mind if I join you?" He didn't wait for a reply as he slid into the booth across from her and removed his

Stetson. He set it on the booth seat beside him before returning his gaze to her.

She'd thought that their encounter had been so brief that neither of them would remember the other. Clearly, she'd been wrong. She remembered the blond hair that curled at his neck under the cowboy hat, the intensity of his blue-gray eyes, even the feel of his large, strong hands on her shoulders as he'd steadied her in the alley. Several days of stubble added to the strong jawline, but it was the way he looked at her that welded her to her seat and stole what little breath she had managed to take.

After a few moments, she finally found her voice. "I'm sorry. I was just about to leave." She reached for her purse and coat on the seat next to her. Earlier, she'd stopped at the steak house needing a cup of coffee, needing time to think. She'd figured she was far enough out of Lonesome that she was safe. Wrong again.

"I think we should talk."

There was nothing threatening in his tone. She turned back to him, studying him as intently as he was her. She saw now that his hands were calloused, the hands of a workingman. His voice was deep and yet gentle, almost soft. He was handsome in a rough and rugged way that she thought she would never have found appealing.

For a moment, she felt lulled into believing that this man meant her no harm. But given the way they'd first met... Common sense told her to get out of the restaurant, out of town. Even if she hadn't had the shock of her life earlier, she didn't feel up to a confrontation with this cowboy.

Yet wouldn't it make her look guiltier if she walked out now? Worse if she ran? She replaced her purse and coat on the seat and, taking a breath, let it out slowly as she waited. *Hear him out. See what he has to say.* They were in a public place. What was the worst that could happen? Well, he could be trying to keep her here until the law arrived to arrest her.

"I didn't come in here to give you a hard time," he said quietly, as if sensing her uneasiness. "Actually, I'm hungry. You don't mind if I order something, do you?" He really wasn't going to drag this out, whatever it was, was he? She started to tell him that she needed to be going, but he cut her off. "I appreciate you not pretending that we didn't cross paths earlier in the alley."

Out of the corner of her eye, she saw the waitress headed in their direction. Ansley knew that she could use the distraction to leave. She didn't think this man would try to stop her. She didn't think he would make a scene. If he planned to have her arrested, he would have already called law enforcement, wouldn't he? She glanced out through the window, but she didn't see any patrol cars.

She could feel him watching her. He was expecting her to make a break for the door. She sat back, determined to prove him wrong, reminding herself that it wasn't as if she'd broken into the PI office. Nor had she been the one to ransack the place.

If she hadn't impulsively taken something on the way out, she would have been able to claim her innocence. Not that she probably would have been believed. If she hadn't been so nervous earlier, she might have realized that someone had ransacked the offices before she'd walked in. Or realized that she wasn't alone—that whoever had done it was still in the building.

She considered him for a long moment wondering what he wanted from her. Maybe more to the point, what he planned to do, since he'd caught her leaving Colt Brothers Investigation earlier—and while innocent of ransacking the offices, what she'd stolen was in her shoulder bag on the seat beside her.

"Whatcha goin' to have, Buck?" the young gum-chewing waitress asked, all smiles as she reached the table.

"Hey, Susie. I'll have a burger and fries," he said and looked across the booth at Ansley. "How about you? Have something more than coffee. I hate to eat alone. You don't want to just sit here and watch me eat."

She felt Susie's quizzical gaze on her. Buck had made it sound as if they were old friends who had purposely met here today for an early lunch.

"Bring her the same," Buck told the young waitress and waited a beat to see if Ansley was going to argue before he added two colas to the order.

"Sorry for being presumptuous," he said after Susie left. "But I really do hate to eat alone, and I thought you might be hungry. Thought maybe you'd had enough coffee, since I suspect you've been sitting here for a while."

Ansley studied him with growing interest and foreboding. Who was this cowboy? Had he followed her here? She was still so shaken by what she'd seen in the PI office that she wouldn't have noticed. Was he stalling until backup arrived? Surely this man wouldn't need to wait for backup.

"We haven't properly met," he said with a smile that lit up his handsome face but didn't quite meet those eyes. "Buck Crawford. My family ranches outside town. Raise rough stock. For rodeos. I tried to ride most everything we raise. Thus the scars." His smile wasn't quite as bright, giving her the impression he had other

scars—those harder to see. There was something be-
guiling about him.

Under other circumstances she might have appreciated this cowboy's attention.

But she was still too shaken by what she'd found inside the PI office, let alone the shock of running into
this man on her way out. Him showing up here had her
feeling even more off balance. He would want an explanation, and right now she didn't have a believable one.

The smell of frying grease was making her nauseous. She couldn't imagine eating a bite. Why hadn't
she gotten up and left the minute he approached her?
She needed to put an end to the suspense.

"What is it you want from me?" She was surprised
how calm she sounded even as her heart raced.

"The truth might be nice." Funny, she thought, she'd
come to Lonesome in search of the truth. "But how
about just your name to start." He was no longer smiling, but his tone was gentle, like his demeanor. "First
name will do if that's all you want to share."

She took a breath and let it out. His apparent kindness
was making this harder for her, and yet she was sensing
an undercurrent of suspicion. He said he raised stock
for rodeos, but his manner felt more like that of a cop.

Ansley swallowed, giving herself a moment. Buck
Crawford wasn't wearing a sheriff's department uniform, but he could be off duty. Nor had he come here
to arrest her, or he would have already done it.

"It's Ansley," she said, wondering if she was making a mistake even talking to him. Normally, she was
levelheaded, both feet firmly on the ground, but this
day had knocked her catawampus. She felt as if she
couldn't trust herself—especially around this cowboy.
"Ansley Brookshire."

"Brookshire?" he repeated, frowning. "Brookshire Oil and Gas?"

Everyone in Montana knew the name, because her adoptive father's name turned up in more than just the oil and gas business. Harrison Brookshire invested in anything that made money—and quickly slapped the Brookshire name on it.

She could feel the cowboy's speculative look. No doubt he was wondering what would have brought her all the way to Lonesome—let alone the Colt Brothers Investigation office.

"You're probably wondering what I was doing at the PI office this morning," she said, her voice not quite as steady. She'd never imagined when she came to Lonesome, Montana, to hire a private detective that she would walk into the office and see all those photographs of people who looked like her.

But it was that one photograph of the Colt brothers—their faces so much like her own at that age—and their happy smiles… Impulsively, she'd taken the framed photo. Why had she never realized that finding her biological parent might mean finding a family that had grown up entirely without her? A family that had been happy and full of siblings, something she had yearned for her whole life?

"You seemed upset as you were leaving," Buck Crawford said, encouraging her to continue.

Upset? She felt a distraught laugh rise up her throat. This cowboy already thought the worst of her. She didn't need to make it any worse by laughing and not being able to stop. Her emotions were too close to the edge right now. *Upset?* She'd been shocked, gutted, elated, terrified, furious, heartbroken. Her emotions had run the gamut—and still were.

"Yes," she said as she fought back the erratic emotions. "I *was* upset." Even as she thought about it, she reminded herself that she was probably wrong. It could just be a coincidence that the boys in the photo looked so much like her at that age—sans the grins. She'd come to Lonesome looking for family. Her only lead had brought her to Lonesome, Montana, and Colt Brothers Investigation.

But had she really found them? Or was she as delusional as Maribelle thought she was for doing this?

Susie came back with their lunches then, balancing the plates in her hands before putting them down, then pulling ketchup, mustard and hot sauce from her large apron pockets with a flourish. "Anything else I can get you?"

Buck Crawford looked to Ansley. She shook her head and thanked Susie, and the young woman left.

In the silence that followed, Ansley said, "You're a cop."

He seemed surprised that she thought that before he said, "I used to be. Now I'm just a rancher, like I said."

"Then I'm confused by your interest in what I was doing in Lonesome this morning," she said.

"I've known the Colt brothers all my life. I won't let anyone hurt them." He softened his words with a smile. "Let's eat while it's hot." He dived in with relish, but she'd heard the threat, seen the granite-hard glint in his eyes. She didn't doubt he meant it.

She told herself that she wouldn't be able to eat a bite even as she picked up her burger. Out of the corner of her eye, she watched the man across the table. He wasn't just trying to protect his friends. Somehow this was personal for him.

Chapter 5

Willie couldn't believe that they'd actually gotten a decent print from Colt Brothers Investigation office. Even more surprising was that when they'd run it through the system, they'd gotten a hit. "Lanny Jackson?"

His deputy beamed. "Got a rap sheet as long as my good leg. Mostly when he was younger, but we're looking at assault, intimidation of witnesses, breaking and entering... He's done little time behind bars, though. Probably where the intimidation of witnesses comes in."

"What was he doing in Lonesome?" Willie said, more to himself than to Deputy Chris Fraser.

"Been employed for seven years as a personal bodyguard by Harrison Brookshire," Chris said.

"*The* Harrison Brookshire?"

"The one and only."

Willie shook his head, surprised that a man like

that would employ a criminal as his bodyguard. Then again... "I don't get it. We know a woman matching the description Buck gave us was in the office. Could Jackson's print be an old one?"

The deputy shook his head. "Doubtful. James said no one has been in that office for a while, with Davy on a case down in Wyoming."

Leaning back in his chair, Willie considered this. Buck had said the woman had looked scared as she'd rushed from the office. What if she wasn't the one who'd ransacked the place? What was she doing here to start with? And which one of them had stolen the photo of the four Colt brothers?

He felt a chill. A man like Harrison Brookshire didn't get where he was without bending a few rules—hiring Jackson as his bodyguard seemed proof of that. He told himself that Brookshire might have hired Jackson to rehabilitate him. If so, it didn't appear to be working. So what had the man been looking for in the office—and had he found it?

"As for the blood that was found where the photograph was taken," Chris was saying, "we're waiting on the DNA test results. Think they were in it together?"

Was it just a coincidence that while James was next door getting cinnamon rolls, two people with no connection were waiting in his office—one looking for something, the other...? That's just it. They had no idea what the woman had been doing there. Yet they had an envelope with their names on it that she'd dropped after running into Buck.

Willie had to admit it made him worry now that they knew Lanny Jackson was involved—not to mention that

Harrison Brookshire might be, too. "I'm just wondering who took the photo from the wall—and why."

Buck had told the truth—he really had been hungry. He put away the hamburger and fries in record time. Not that he hadn't been studying the woman across from him as he ate. He put her in her mid-to late twenties. Well-dressed, she exuded confidence even though he'd caught up with her. She was a Brookshire, after all. Knowing she had her daddy's money and power behind her would give any young woman confidence.

He'd been trying to get a read on her beneath the veneer of privilege. He was better with wild horses then women, he thought with a silent chuckle. Always had been. Thus his downfall, he thought.

Still, he got the feeling that she didn't have it together as much as she pretended. He'd seen fear in her eyes when she'd come tearing out of the Colt Brothers office. She'd been running from something. Weren't they all, he thought as he pushed away his plate, glad to see that she'd eaten some of her burger and fries. He'd always found that getting some food under his belt seemed to steady him. Right now he needed steady, and he suspected she did, too.

"You don't have to tell me what you were doing in the office earlier," he said as he leaned back in the booth and settled his gaze on her. If she got up and left, he wasn't going to try to stop her. He had her license plate number, the make and model of her car—and if she was telling the truth, he had her name, a name that would make even their new sheriff think twice about taking this questioning any further.

She pushed away her plate as well and straightened in the booth to look at him. She had the palest blue eyes—even more dramatic because they were fringed with dark lashes. He still couldn't shake the feeling that they'd met before. But he wouldn't have forgotten a woman who looked like this, he was sure of that.

"I came to Lonesome to find my birth mother," she said, her voice stronger than earlier.

"Why Lonesome?"

"I didn't have much to go on, only a receipt that was found in a bag of baby clothes, according to my original nanny." She looked down at her hands resting on the edge of the table for a moment, then back up at him. "I had decided that I was going to hire a private detective to find her. Colt Brothers Investigation seemed the logical place to start."

He nodded. "The only PIs in town."

"When I found the office door open, I decided to go in and wait. I was looking at the photos and posters on the wall when I heard someone upstairs. It sounded as if they were frantically looking for something. I panicked and left."

His gaze locked with hers. "But why take the framed photo of the Colt boys?" He saw her swallow before she dragged her eyes away.

"You're going to think I'm delusional. I certainly do," she said quietly. "That photo, the boys, their faces at that age… There is a photo of me on the mantel in the house where I grew up." Her gaze came back to his. She swallowed before she said, "Our faces. We look identical. Except for the grins." Her voice broke. "I came to Lonesome looking for my biological mother, hoping to find my true family, and when I saw that one photo…" Her voice broke. "I realized that I could have found them."

There it was, he thought with a start. Why she looked so familiar. She was right. The washed-out denim blue of her eyes, the almost coal-black hair. But while the

Colts were handsome in a rugged way, this woman was a dark-haired beauty.

Could it be true? He told himself that there had to be dozens, hundreds, maybe even thousands of people that she might resemble. What were the chances she was related to the Colts? If that was really why she'd taken the photo.

"So you're thinking they could be cousins? Even…" Brothers? The thought shocked him. "How old are you?"

"Twenty-eight."

"When's your birthday?"

"Fourth of July. At least that's what I was told and what it says on my birth certificate, which I now know isn't original."

Same age as Davy almost to the day?

He could feel her staring at him.

"Like I said, I know it sounds delusional," she said.

"You must have been shocked." He was shocked at what this could mean—if true. But if this was some kind of scam…

Those big blue eyes filled with tears. "I *was* shocked. I can't describe how I felt knowing that I could have grown up with them if my mother hadn't given me up. That is, if I'm right."

He saw now why she'd written down the names and dates on the envelope. She was trying to figure out how she fit in—if she did. "Do you still have the photo you took from the wall?"

She looked embarrassed as she reached into her shoulder bag lying next to her on the booth seat and brought it out. Carefully she laid it on the table between them and their dirty dishes.

Buck picked it up, remembering the Colt brothers at this wonderfully innocent age. What wild boys they'd been. Del had raised them alone after losing his wife. Maybe *raised* was the wrong word, he thought, unable not to smile, since he'd been only a little older than Tommy and had often come home just as dirty and scraped up as the Colt brothers after a day with them.

"I see the resemblance," he said looking from the photo to her, wondering what she'd been like as a girl. He quickly reminded himself that he was jumping to conclusions, just as she had. Until they had some kind of proof...

He tried to hand the photo back, but she didn't take it right away, so he set it down where she had earlier.

"I just wanted to compare it to the photograph of me at about the same age," she said. "I wanted to see if they match as closely as I think they will. I wasn't thinking or I could have simply taken a photo with my phone. It was just impulsive, something I'm usually not."

"You should keep it for now. Just hang on to it. It has sentimental value to the Colts."

She hesitated, but only for a moment before she picked it up, studying it before she put it back into her purse. She seemed to be waiting to see what happened next.

What *did* happen next? Buck cleared his voice. "I'm not one to usually dispense advice, but if I were you, I'd come back to Colt Brothers Investigation office with me. You can tell them what you told me. A DNA test will quickly clear up whether or not you're related to the Colts in any way. If you are..." He tried to imagine how his friends would take the news. If she was their half sister, then that would mean that Del Ransom Colt, the father they'd idolized, had a child they'd never known about.

He reminded himself that he was putting the cart before the horse. All this was speculation. Or worse, if this woman was running a con. For all he knew, she wasn't even the daughter of Harrison Brookshire. Maybe nothing she'd told him was the truth. It wouldn't be the first time a woman had deceived him.

"If you're related," Buck said. "I suspect the Colt brothers will want to find out the truth about your birth mother as badly as you do."

"You sure they won't have me arrested?"

"For stealing a photograph?" He shook his head. "Even if you aren't related, I think you'd be smart to hire them as you originally planned. If your biological parent has a connection to Lonesome, they'll find it—and her." He could see her making up her mind. If she hedged, then it would certainly appear that nothing she'd told him was the truth.

"All right." She nodded. "I've come this far. I need to see this through."

He wasn't quite sure, surprised it had been that easy. "Good," he said as he picked up his Stetson from the booth seat. "Let's take my truck. I'll drive you back to your car afterward just to make sure you're safe."

"You don't trust me."

Chuckling, he said, "I've been told I have trust issues."

She cocked her head, a half smile on her lips. "But I should trust you?"

He shrugged. "Up to you. I'm just trying to help."

"Why is that?"

"You need help, and right now, I'm kind of in between."

"In between what?"

He grinned. "Jobs. Just in an odd place in my life that I never thought I'd ever be. It's a long story and not one I'm going to bore you with. You want a ride? Great. Otherwise…"

Chapter 6

James had figured he'd never see the mysterious woman Buck had run into leaving the office earlier—or the missing photograph—again. So he was more than surprised when his old friend walked into the office with the woman shortly after noon.

He'd just hung up from a phone call with Willie about a hit on the fingerprint found in the front office. He was trying to get his head around what the sheriff had told him when they walked in.

Buck had described the woman well. He saw at once why his friend had been taken by her—she was strikingly pretty. As he offered them both chairs, he quickly assessed her. Somewhere in her late twenties, educated, nicely dressed and with an air of privilege about her.

Once seated, she introduced herself. Ansley Brookshire, daughter of Harrison Brookshire. That got his attention. The fingerprint had belonged to Lanny Jackson, bodyguard to Harrison Brookshire. So she hadn't come alone?

Yes, she had been in the office earlier. Yes, she had taken the photo, which she pulled out of her expensive shoulder bag but didn't offer to return. Yes, she had left in a hurry. Her story was that she'd heard someone upstairs searching frantically for something and hadn't noticed before then that the offices had been ransacked. So she didn't know her father's bodyguard had been in the building ransacking the offices? Was that possible?

"I want to hire you to find my birth mother," she said in conclusion. "I have little to go on, other than a receipt for yarn bought in Lonesome months before I was born. It's what brought me here, and since you are the only private investigators in town…" James saw her glance at Buck, who nodded, before she turned back, swallowed and seemed to brace herself. "Also, I think I might be related to you."

Okay, that he hadn't seen coming. There was a resemblance, yes, but… "In what way?"

She shook her head. "I think I might be your sister. Half sister. Or at least cousin?"

James was at a loss for words. "Based on what evidence?" A receipt for yarn in a bag with baby clothes from a shop in Lonesome?

"You could do a quick DNA test," Buck said. "Should answer that question, right?"

"DNA test results aren't quick," he said, already knowing that Willie had taken the blood sample and was having the lab run it. It wouldn't take much to see if it matched any of the brothers. Willie's DNA was already in the system because of his job. "We are already running your DNA. When you took the photo, you cut yourself. I put a rush on it." There was no way she was their half sister, was there?

She didn't seem surprised or worried that they might have the results of the DNA test sooner rather than later. He glanced at Buck. He knew his old friend too well—Buck wasn't completely convinced. But then, the former law officer wouldn't be in a situation like this one.

What Buck didn't know about was the girl's necklace Willie had found in their dad's wrecked pickup with the name DelRae engraved on it. Hard not to jump to conclusions. He knew when Willie met this woman and heard her story, he would instantly think the same thing now whirling in James's own mind. Except this young woman's name wasn't DelRae. There might not have ever been a connection between the necklace and their father. All this could be conjecture.

But that didn't mean that she wasn't the little girl who'd been given the necklace. Or that she wasn't Del Ransom Colt's daughter—and their half sister. Wasn't that why he was hesitant to take on this case? Because he didn't want to believe his father had had another child? Or worse—that his father had had another child he'd kept secret?

Yet James couldn't brush this under the rug just because he didn't want to believe it. "Like Buck said, there is one way to prove it. We'll know when we get the DNA results if we're related. In the meantime..." He studied the woman. Damned if she didn't resemble him and his brothers. "I'd like to see the photo of you when you were about the same age as me and my brothers in the one you...borrowed from the wall."

"I'll get it and bring both of them back to show you.

You'll take my case?" she asked. The hope in her voice alone should have decided for him.

"Your parents told you that you were adopted?" James asked.

She shook her head. "I found out by accident. I was looking for something in my father's study and I found a letter from a local physician that made it clear that neither of my parents had been capable of conceiving a child and that adoption was recommended. The physician said he would put them in touch with an agency if they were interested."

"Did he mention the agency?"

"I already checked. They didn't go through an agency," she said. "When I brought it up with my... adoptive parents, they refused to talk about it. From what I've been able to find out, they didn't go through any of the legal adoption procedures. I've searched adoption records. As I understand it, Maribelle passed me off as her own after lying that it had been a home birth. How else could she have gotten me a birth certificate?"

James thought about that for a few moments, then asked for her date of birth. He couldn't hide his surprise. He supposed the Brookshires could have managed it given their financial situation. "Do you have anything else to go on besides the receipt that brought you to Lonesome?"

She shook her head but then hesitated. "There is one thing I should tell you. My adoptive parents are so adamant about me not finding my birth mother that they have tried to buy me off, threatened me and even had me followed."

"*Followed?* Did they know you were coming here?"

"My mother knew. I suspect she called my father, because he came home from work as I was leaving. But I was being followed before that. I lost the tail, though."

"Do you know a man named Lanny Jackson?" he asked and saw her expression change.

"He works for my father as his…bodyguard. He's the one who followed me when I left the estate."

"His fingerprints were found in the front office this morning."

Her eyes widened, and for a moment, he saw his brother Davy. Hell, maybe she *was* their sister. "He'd been following me earlier, but I was sure that I'd lost him."

"Why do you think your adoptive parents don't want you learning the truth about your birth mother?" James asked.

"It was a private adoption, they said. But I suspect it was illegal. I've even thought that they might have stolen me. I suspect they're afraid I'm going to learn the truth and that it will come back on them." She frowned. "If Lanny was in your office looking for something earlier…" Her blue eyes widened again. "Then he reached Lonesome and your office *before* me." She shook her head. "I have no idea how that was possible. I looked up Lonesome on my computer and found your office…" Her voice trailed off, and a knowing, shocked look came into her expression. "What if they haven't just had me followed? Is it possible they've been somehow tracking everything I do?"

"It's possible. Jackson might have been trying to find a connection to your birth mother and our PI agency," James said. "He could have just been fishing." Or he could have been sent to destroy any evidence he found.

James couldn't bear the thought of a cover-up by his own father. If there was a cover-up, he should have found evidence of it by now, wouldn't he have?

"We'll take your case," he said, realizing that he needed to know the truth as much as she did. He could see that his longtime friend Buck looked worried as well. If he took the case, he would be going up against Harrison Brookshire's power—and his muscle. That alone made him want to take on the case, even though he knew it would be dangerous.

"Where can I reach you?"

She gave him her cell phone number and her apartment address. "I'd like to keep this photograph of the four of you until I retrieve the one of me from the house where I grew up. If that's all right with you. I want to compare them. I promise to bring it back."

James nodded, although a photo wouldn't prove anything. The DNA sample now being processed would tell the tale. He needed to know what it was her adoptive parents didn't want her to find out. He told himself it could be merely the possible fallout if an illegal adoption came to light. There could be any number of reasons the Brookshires didn't want their daughter to find out the truth.

He studied the young woman, unable not to see the resemblance—and just as unable not to be worried for her. She didn't look afraid. She looked angry and even more determined. "You're sure you want to go forward with this?" he had to ask.

"Yes," she said with authority. She reached for her purse. "You'll want a retainer—"

"I also need a copy of your birth certificate, Social Security number and any other pertinent information to the case." She nodded. "You're sure you're twenty-eight, born on the Fourth of July?"

"I'm not sure. According to my former nanny, my adoptive mother brought me home on July fifth—the day after I was allegedly born. So it definitely wasn't a home birth."

"I'm sure you realize that your father...adoptive father and mother...have a powerful reach. But they might not be the only ones who don't want the truth to come out." He hated to even mention this but knew he had to. "Your birth mother might not want to be found." He saw her surprise.

"Maybe she doesn't want to be found, but I really don't believe she would harm me to keep me from finding out the truth," Ansley said.

Had she really not considered this? He admired her optimism, but at this point they had no idea what they were going to find. "If you're determined to do this... I'd be very careful if I were you."

If Lanny Jackson was any indication, she was already in danger. What if her birth mother really didn't want to be found? Also, if any of this were true and she was related to them, then this case could rewrite their family history. If she was their half sister, then the news could be devastating to their father's memory.

Meanwhile, they were all now—including Buck Crawford—in the crosshairs of whoever was determined to keep the truth about Ansley Brookshire's birth a secret.

Buck told himself to walk away. He'd done what he could by bringing her back to the PI office. James and the rest of the Colts would take it from here.

Yet as he drove her out of Lonesome toward the steak house, where she'd left her vehicle, he didn't want to walk away. Nor did he want to dig too deep into why he felt that way. It wasn't just because he was worried about this woman, although he was.

Ansley had been quiet after they left James. Was she having second thoughts? He doubted it, given the set of her jaw. "If you're still determined to go back to your adoptive parents' house for that photo, why not stay in Lonesome and go in the morning?"

Ansley seemed to consider. "It has been quite the day."

Buck nodded. "And a long drive back to Bozeman. Often best to sleep on it."

She smiled. "I won't change my mind."

"I can see that. But I agree with James about the danger. Isn't there someone who could go with you tomorrow to collect the photo you're after?" *A witness*, he thought but didn't say.

Meeting his gaze, she said, "I really doubt that's necessary, but I can call my fiancé." She was silent for a few moments. "I know I haven't handled this well, so I can understand why you'd be concerned about me. But I'm much stronger and more capable than I look. I've just had a shock today and I'm not myself."

"I don't doubt that you're plenty strong, but like you said, you've had a shock. Also, I've known James Colt all my life, and if he's worried that you're in danger, then there is reason for caution. You said you were planning to come back to Lonesome once you got the photograph, but I'm betting you plan to show the photo of the Colt brothers to your adoptive parents." Ansley didn't deny it. "That would be dangerous for everyone concerned—including the Colts."

"Dangerous? Over a photo?"

"There's a lot more at stake here, I suspect," he said as he pulled in next to her SUV and put the truck into Park before turning to her. "Lanny Jackson was sent to Lonesome to the PI office. This time he was searching for something. Next time, he could be sent to make sure the Colt brothers don't find out the truth. I know you want to compare the photos for your own assurance. But it will prove nothing. Once the DNA test results come back—"

"You sound as if you're hoping I'm wrong and that the results will prove it," she said, locking her gaze with his.

He couldn't deny it. "I just know that if true, it opens a whole can of worms for my friends, who want to believe the best about the father they lost almost ten years ago."

"You're saying they would rather believe the best of him than know about a half sister?"

He shook his head. "If you're related, the Colts will welcome you into the family. They'll move heaven and earth to find out the truth for you—even if it tarnishes the memory of their father. I'm saying that it will be hard to watch them go through that, but nothing will stop them."

"I don't want to hurt them," she said quietly. "Is it wrong to hope just the opposite of you? I've always dreamed of a family, but I never imagined I might have four brothers—half brothers."

"It's not wrong, and I have to admit, the first time I laid eyes on you, there was something so familiar, I would have sworn that we'd met before. I can see the resemblance." The more he was around her, the more he could see so much of the Colt genes in her, but he kept that to himself. Maybe because he hated to see her get her hopes up as much as he hated to see his friends go through this ordeal. "Never doubt that they will make you part of the family if you really are Del Ransom Colt's daughter."

She looked out at the shadows forming in the nearby pines. "When I realized I was adopted, I thought maybe there was someone out there like me." She shook her head. "I know. I can't let myself think that until we have proof. In the meantime, I need to compare the photos. But…" she added with a smile as she turned back to him, "you're right. It can wait until tomorrow."

"The motel in town isn't too bad for a night," Buck said. "Then tomorrow, do me a favor and take your fiancé with you to the house. What can it hurt?"

"Thank you. For everything." Opening the pickup door, she stepped out, met his gaze for an instant and then closed the door and walked to her SUV. He sat, engine running, as she climbed into her vehicle and pulled away.

He watched the SUV until it disappeared down the road, and then he followed at some distance back to town, telling himself he was a damned fool. This had nothing to do with him. He'd done all he could. He needed to back off.

But he couldn't. Just as he couldn't shake the feeling that this woman didn't realize what she'd set in motion and where it might lead.

And here he was getting in deeper.

Remember the last time you got involved with a

woman in trouble? He had the scars to prove it, including the one that ran diagonally from just below his breastbone down to where the knife had plunged into his torso.

It wasn't until she reached the motel and entered the office to check in that he turned around and headed home to the ranch. He doubted he was going to get any sleep.

Chapter 7

"We have a new client," James said, then cleared his voice. He could feel his brothers' gazes on him, expectation in their expressions, just as he could feel their growing concern. It wasn't like he called a meeting every time they had a new client. Also, Willie was here. As the county's newest sheriff, Willie had little interest in new PI clients.

"Why aren't we going to like this?" Willie asked, cutting to the chase as usual.

James raised his head, not surprised his oldest brother was the one to ask. Willie probably already knew where this was headed. It was what made him a good officer of the law. "Her name is Ansley Brookshire, and yes, her father is the Harrison Brookshire."

"I guess we won't have to worry about getting paid,"

Tommy said and then must have realized neither Willie nor James smiled at his joke.

But before he could speak again, Davy piped up from the Zoom connection on the open laptop nearby, "What am I missing?"

"Buck came back by with our new client earlier. We talked." He didn't say that Buck had made a convincing argument. If they didn't take the case, Ansley Brookshire would hire another agency. The truth was going to come out, one way or another. "She's looking for her birth mother. I told her we would take the case, since she suspects the woman might have lived or still lives in Lonesome."

He saw Willie cross his arms impatiently as if to say, *spit it out.* "What aren't you telling Tommy and Davy?"

"Here's the thing," James said. "Ansley Brookshire thinks she's related to us. She thinks she's our half sister." The dead silence that followed didn't last long.

From the monitor, Davy asked, as if he'd heard wrong, *"What?"*

"You can't be serious," Tommy snapped. "Our half sister?"

"Seems you left out something. This is the woman who ransacked your offices and took the photo of the four of us, right?" Willie asked.

"She ransacked our offices?" Davy demanded.

"There's more to the story," James said quickly. "I'll get you all up to speed as soon as I can. In the meantime, we have a blood sample that has been sent to the lab for testing. Once we have that, we'll know if she is even related to us."

"How old is this woman?" Willie asked.

James looked down at the information he'd taken

from her, even though he didn't need to check her age. He'd never forget what she'd said. "Twenty-eight." She would have been conceived about the same time as Davy—if her birth date was correct. But he didn't point that out. He didn't have to.

"It's bull," Davy snapped. "Dad would have never cheated on our mother." Davy had never met their mother. James hardly remembered her and doubted Tommy did, either. She hadn't been well, in and out of hospitals. She'd been like a ghost in their young lives, here and then gone. "I don't have time for this." Davy was gone in a flash of the screen.

Willie reached over and closed the laptop before sitting down on the edge of their father's huge oak desk with a resigned sigh. "What does she have for proof?"

"She's gone to collect a photograph from when she was about the same age we are in Dad's favorite photo." He saw Tommy look to the wall and open his mouth, no doubt to ask where it was. "She's going to bring both photos back. She says that when we see the resemblance..."

"Sounds like a scam," Tommy said. "I just can't see what she hopes to gain. Can't be money."

James was looking at his older brother, waiting. Willie had to have jumped to the same conclusion that he had. "Her adoption apparently was private and not necessarily aboveboard. Tommy, I want you to look into adoptions. You should know that her adoptive parents are dead set against her finding her birth mother—let alone, I would think, her birth father."

"You think she's DelRae," Willie said as if it was a no-brainer.

"Truthfully, I don't know what to think," he said as

Tommy swore and reached into the bottom drawer of their dad's desk. He pulled out the blackberry brandy and the paper cups. His hands were shaking.

"Dad would have told us," Tommy said.

"Unless he didn't know until the night he died," Willie pointed out. They'd all heard about the alleged confrontation with a woman in front of the bar that night. The eyewitness said the woman had thrown something at Del. He'd stooped to pick it up as the woman stormed away. Otis Osterman, the sheriff back then, hadn't gotten the eyewitness's name. Since Willie had found a little girl's gold necklace in their father's wrecked pickup, they'd assumed that's what his father had picked up from the ground that night—if any of the story was true.

James swore. "If the child was his, how could he not have known about her? There's the damned necklace that we're all assuming he bought for her. Also, we have only a crooked sheriff's word that a woman saw Dad and another woman arguing on the street that night."

"But what if it's true? Maybe it wasn't Otis concocting the story to insinuate that Dad was drunk," Willie argued. "The coroner said he'd had a drink but wasn't over the legal limit."

James couldn't believe that they were having this same argument without any evidence. "We don't know that this woman even exists. According to Otis, the alleged woman said Dad staggered to his pickup. Otis has always wanted us to believe that Dad had been drunk or on drugs and that's why he'd stopped on the railroad track with the train coming."

"The autopsy report doesn't lie," Willie snapped. "Whatever happened that night, it wasn't because he was drunk or on drugs. Did this Ansley Brookshire say anything about a necklace?"

James shook his head. "Of course, I didn't say anything about it. We'll keep that to ourselves. Once the DNA test results come back... The whole issue might be moot."

"Or not." Tommy handed them each a paper cup. They usually didn't drink the blackberry brandy except to celebrate. There was nothing to celebrate now. Unless finding out your father might have had an affair the same year your mother was dying was cause for celebration, even if you got a half sister out of it, James thought.

"You think it might be true?" Tommy asked after he'd downed his brandy.

"She resembles us, no doubt about that." James looked at Willie. His brother had been convinced for almost ten years that their father's death had been foul play. He'd just never been able to prove it. Was it possible this woman, Ansley Brookshire, held the key that would finally reveal the truth?

"I want to meet her," Willie said after finishing his brandy and balling up the cup in his large fist. He tossed it in a perfect arc. It rimmed the trash basket for a moment before going in.

"You'll all get the chance," James told them. "She's coming back with the photo. At least she said she was. Buck called earlier to say he talked her into staying at the motel in town for the night and going down tomorrow to get the photo. He's worried about her going to the Brookshire Estate by herself."

The brothers shared a look. It was only Willie who mumbled the obvious. "Damn fool. I thought Buck had learned his lesson."

* * *

After a night of weird dreams, Ansley awakened worried. Had she done the right thing hiring Colt Brothers Investigation? What if she really was their half sister? It all felt like too much for her to grasp. One moment she was filled with excitement at the thought of finding the missing part of her life, of having siblings, of having a family that felt like a real family.

So why was she scared? Because it was clear to her that James Colt was hoping she was wrong. Maybe Buck didn't know the Colts as well as he thought. What if they wanted nothing to do with her? She couldn't imagine finding the family she'd wanted her whole life, only to have them push her away.

Was this why her adoptive parents had tried so hard to talk her out of her search? Maybe they knew something she didn't. What would they do when she told them that she'd hired Colt Brothers Investigation? She thought about what Buck had said. If she told her adoptive parents, would they harm the Colts? They'd tried bribing her, threatening to disown her and even having her father's bodyguard follow her. But she didn't really believe they would do anything beyond that, did she?

A shudder moved through her. She reached for her phone. That was the problem: she had no idea what the secret of her adoption was—or how harmful the truth might be to any of them. "It's Ansley," she said unnecessarily as her fiancé answered her call.

"Where are you?" Gage sounded impatient. "I've been trying to reach you." She glanced at her phone, surprised to see that he'd called a half dozen times and apparently left her messages. She remembered turning her phone off last night, exhausted and desperately needing sleep. She'd been glad that Buck had talked her out of making the drive until this morning.

"I had my phone turned off," she said as she looked around for her purse before heading to her SUV parked outside her motel room. "Why? What's going on?"

Buck hadn't slept well, either. With his life at loose ends, he worried that he was getting too involved in Ansley Brookshire's quest to find her birth mother. Why else was he up so early and now parked across the street from the motel?

Her SUV was still parked in front of one of the rooms. He hoped she'd gotten more sleep than he had. He also hoped that she'd changed her mind about driving all the way back to Bozeman to pick up a photo at her adoptive parents' house. Given the time, he was beginning to think maybe she had changed her mind.

But just then, he saw her come out of her room and head for her vehicle. She was on the phone. He slid down behind the wheel a little. The last thing he wanted was for her to think he was stalking her. He watched her climb in and start the SUV.

Was she still going back for the photo? If so, he worried what would happen when she showed the one of the Colts to her adoptive parents. If they were really that determined to stop her from finding her birth mother, they certainly weren't going to be happy about her thinking she was related to former rodeo cowboys turned private detectives, he suspected.

As she pulled away, he caught movement out of the corner of his eye. An older-model pickup pulled in after her. Buck sat up, realizing that the truck had been idling across the street. He hadn't noticed anyone behind the wheel and didn't get a good look as the truck went by, sun glaring off the windshield.

Buck told himself that he was just being paranoid. The driver of the truck hadn't been watching the motel and wasn't now following Ansley out of town.

But as he made a U-turn, he swore. He couldn't seem to shake off the suspicious cop in him as he watched the driver of the pickup match the white SUV's speed as both headed south of town. Damned if the driver wasn't following her. Only, whoever it was, they weren't someone her wealthy adoptive father had hired, his gut told him. Not in that old pickup.

No, unless he was mistaken, this was someone else with a dog in this fight.

Ansley held the phone away from her ear for a moment. Gage sounded angry. "You didn't get any of my messages?"

Obviously not, Ansley thought as she drove south out of Lonesome. "Well, I've called now. What's wrong?"

"I came by your apartment last night. Your SUV was gone."

"I stayed in Lonesome."

"Lonesome?" Gage demanded. "So this is about that ridiculous quest of yours? Your mother called me, frantic with worry about you. She asked if I knew where you'd gone. Of course, I didn't. The fiancé is the last to know, apparently." She'd stopped telling him about her search for her birth mother after he'd made it clear that he thought it was a bad idea.

"She knew where I went. I told her yesterday morning when I stopped by the house."

"She was beside herself with worry, saying that you'd

argued and then taken off. She feared in your state of mind that something terrible had happened to you."

Maribelle, beside herself? Not likely, she thought. "I'm fine."

"Did you really threaten to hire a private detective? Ansley, you're breaking their hearts, and mine, too. What is it you think is missing in this fairy-tale life of yours?"

They'd had this conversation before. Of course, he couldn't understand. He knew who his biological parents were and could see no reason for her to find hers. He also really believed that she'd lived a magic life just because of the Brookshires' wealth. He'd said many times that he would gladly trade places with her, even though his father owned a thriving business and did well financially. Just not as well as Harrison Brookshire, but then, who did?

"I really don't want to have this argument again," she said. "Anyway, I'm driving. I'm on my way to the house now. I thought you might want to meet me there. I'm picking up a photo of me when I was five."

"A photo? Whatever for?"

She really didn't want to get into it with him, and yet she couldn't help being excited. "There's a chance I've found my family, and the photo will help prove it." She described the small, framed photo that sat on one end of the mantel at Brookshire Estate. Maribelle liked the shot because Ansley had been in a pretty dress, her hair fixed with a bow, her cheeks pink, her blue eyes staring straight ahead at the photographer. She looked precious, Maribelle often said. No grin, but if Ansley remembered the photo as well as she thought, then she did look exactly like the Colt brothers at that age.

"You're joking. You want me to leave work to pick up some photo of you?"

"I don't think there will be trouble, but I could use the emotional support, if nothing else."

"I'm at work. I can't leave. I don't understand you." She could imagine him brushing back his perfectly coiffed head of salon-blended blond hair in frustration. It made her think of Buck Crawford and his imperfect, darker sun-streaked natural blond shade.

"I know you don't understand. Never mind. It was just a thought," she said, shoving away the reminder of Buck irritably. It wasn't fair to compare Gage and the cowboy. They were nothing alike in so many ways. "I'll talk to you later." She disconnected and took a deep breath, letting it out slowly. Was it Gage who'd changed? No, she thought. It was her. As he said, he didn't understand why she had to do this. When they'd met, she'd been the daughter of Maribelle and Harrison Brookshire. The owner of a successful jewelry business, a seemingly contented young woman with her life on a fairly straight, paved highway ahead of her and no speed bumps in sight.

They'd met at a conference at Big Sky. Gage's father had a beverage distribution company in Bozeman but did business all over the Northwest. Gage had taken over the business after his father fell ill and died, and he made no secret of the fact that this wasn't what he wanted to do the rest of his life. He couldn't sell, though, without his mother's agreement. So far, he hadn't been able to convince her.

Ansley thought about how he'd been impressed that she'd made a viable business out of designing jewelry using Montana gems. He'd asked her out soon after Big

Sky, and they'd started dating and he'd been the perfect attentive boyfriend. It hadn't taken him long to ask her to marry him. He'd proposed after a dinner at the Brookshire Estate in front of her parents—all before she'd discovered they weren't her birth parents. She'd seen their delight at her engagement to Gage. Her father thought Gage had promise.

Recently, though, her fiancé had become more unhappy with his family business. Then Ansley found out that she was adopted and had become determined to find her birth mother, alienating herself from her adoptive parents—and Gage.

"If you don't stop, they are going to disown you," Gage had said. "Where is that going to leave us?"

Us. Wasn't that the moment when she began to realize that he wasn't as enamored with her as he'd claimed? He'd fallen in love with the Harrison Brookshire empire and what that much money could do for his life. Not that she could blame him. He wasn't the first boyfriend who'd had dollar signs in his eyes.

She pushed the thought away to consider the Colts. What if they really were her family?

The driving time passed quickly. As she neared the exit that would take her to the estate, she realized she would have to face her mother alone. More than likely her father would be at work—as usual. She doubted he would come home early again, even if Maribelle called him when Ansley arrived at the house. Still, she couldn't imagine that her adoptive mother would object to her taking the photograph.

As she turned into the drive to the estate, she didn't notice the older-model pickup behind her that pulled over just outside the gate. Ansley was thinking about the framed photograph she'd taken from the Colt Brothers Investigation office—and the one she wanted to compare it to. What would Maribelle say when she saw how much Ansley resembled the Colts in the photo?

Her heart thumped against her ribs. Was she about to find her family? Or blow up her entire life, including Gage and their engagement with it?

Buck saw the pickup pull over as Ansley's white SUV turned into a paved drive that led up through the pines to a monstrous brick structure. He'd been debating how to handle this after impulsively following both the pickup and Ansley. He had no doubt that this was the Brookshire Estate she'd mentioned.

True to her word, she'd gone straight there to get the photograph that in her mind would prove everything.

Meanwhile, Buck needed to deal with whoever had been following her. He pulled in front of the truck, blocking the driver's quick escape. Jumping out, he headed for the driver's side of the truck. As he approached, he could see a shadow behind the wheel wearing a Western hat pulled low, though he couldn't tell if it was a man or a woman driver.

Before he could reach the driver's side door, the pickup's engine revved, just as he'd feared. The truck roared backward, then jumped forward, almost clipping him as it sped away. All Buck could do was get the license plate number. It wasn't nothing, but he didn't get the satisfaction of seeing who was driving that pickup and finding out why the person had been following Ansley Brookshire.

Back in his own truck, he considered chasing down the pickup or heading back to the ranch or going on up to the house. He had a bad feeling about just leaving. Ansley had said she wouldn't go alone, but it darned sure looked as if she was doing just that.

He knew he'd be welcomed like ants at a picnic, but that had never stopped him before, he told himself. *You should just let this go. This isn't your business. Don't be a damned fool. She isn't going to appreciate you following her down here.*

Buck realized he'd never been good at taking advice, even good advice, from anyone, let alone himself. He had become involved the moment the woman rushed out the back door of Colt Brothers Investigation and into his arms.

Starting his truck, he drove up the paved road to the house. There was a gate, but it was open. Fortunately, there was no guard station, except there were plenty of security cameras and what appeared to be a laser beam across the road. He drove through it, realizing that someone now knew he was coming. Ahead he could see Ansley's SUV was parked outside. There was no sign of her. Or anyone else. Yet.

Chapter 8

Tommy did a crash course in adoption in Montana by calling the county attorney. He told Attorney Frank Edwards a little about the case he was working on—a woman had discovered she had to have been adopted because neither of her parents could have children. They'd confessed it was true, and now she was interested in finding her birth mother.

"There are a lot of hoops to jump through in any legal Montana adoption—lots of steps that end with two hearings," Edwards said.

He explained that Ansley's adoptive parents could have done a direct parental placement, meaning they didn't go through the Department of Public Health and Human Services but dealt directly with the birth mother.

"So the birth mother could have simply signed away

her parental rights to the child and consented to the adoption."

"Not that easy," Frank said. "Under Montana law, she was supposed to have completed three hours of counseling, disclosed the birth family's medical and family history, and reviewed a preplacement evaluation of the adoptive family.

"That's just the first step," he continued. "After the adoption, there is a six-month waiting period where a licensed social worker visits the family and files a report to the judge. At the end of the waiting period, there is a second hearing."

Tommy was nodding to himself. "What you're saying is that there would be a record of the adoption—if it had been legal. What about the birth father?"

"Under law, the birth mother would have to provide information on the location of the other legal parent and any others who were legally entitled to notice of the adoption proceeding. That would include any spouse who the birth parent was married to at the time of conception."

"Unless all of this had been done under the table, so to speak," Tommy said. "So what about a home birth?"

"All you have to do is apply for a birth certificate. It would have been even easier twenty-eight years ago," Edwards said.

"So the so-called adoptive mother could have put anything she wanted on the birth certificate," Tommy said. "She could have passed off the baby as her own. The question is, where did she get the infant?" He checked to see if any infants had been kidnapped about that time in Montana. None.

Where would someone get an infant if they weren't going to steal one? *You buy it*, he thought.

Buck wasn't surprised by the grandeur of the house. It was massive, brick, stone and glass, a monument to Harrison Brookshire's success. Multimillion-dollar homes had once been unique in the Bozeman area. Not anymore. Not since a classic three-bedroom house in town now went for almost a million with the influx of people with money looking for a simpler life.

Yet as he walked up the stone front steps, he wondered what it had been like for Ansley growing up here. He couldn't imagine.

It didn't appear that the Brookshires were home. However, there was a five-car garage. He couldn't tell what was parked inside it.

He knocked and waited. A breeze sighed in the nearby pine trees. Beyond them, he could see the tops of the mountains that surrounded the Gallatin Valley. Nearer, he could smell the Gallatin River close by and hear a jet passing over after leaving the busiest airport in Montana just miles away.

The massive wood door was opened by an older woman in a pale blue uniform. She seemed distracted, her attention on whatever was going on behind her. He heard Ansley's raised voice from deep inside the house.

Removing his Stetson, Buck said, "I'm here to see Ansley," and stepped past the distracted woman. She called after him in obvious frustration. He had no idea where he was going—hopefully this was the right direction. He heard the housekeeper close the door, her shoes squeaking as she hurried after him.

He glanced around as he went, finding all the lav-

ish furnishings cold and uninviting. It felt as if someone had staged the house for a potential buyer and none
of the furniture had ever been used. A stone fireplace
took up almost the entire back wall of the living room.
He spotted Ansley off to one side of it. She was going
through some cabinets on a nearby wall and had apparently been arguing with the housekeeper.

"Don't tell me you don't know where it is," Ansley
was saying as she dug in the cabinet. "Nothing gets
moved around here without you knowing about it, Ingrid. Where did my mother put it?"

"Miss," the housekeeper said impatiently as she
caught up with Buck. "*Miss!* You have company."

Ansley looked up then, straightening in obvious surprise. *"Buck?"* Those blue eyes widened. "Did you follow me?"

"We should talk about that. In private," he said.

She gave him a look that said, yes, they would be discussing it, before turning again to the housekeeper. "I'm
not leaving without that photograph. I'd hate to have to
tear this house apart to find it. But I will."

Ingrid sighed heavily. "Perhaps your mother did
move it. I'll find out." She seemed to hesitate, as if
afraid to leave Ansley alone with the cowboy who'd
pushed his way in. With another sigh, she headed for
the stairs at a trot.

"She's gone up to tell my adoptive mother on me,"
Ansley said with a shake of her head. Her gaze settled
on him. "You're about to meet Maribelle Brookshire.
Brace yourself." She sighed. "How am I going to explain you?"

"What? You've never brought home a cowboy before? I thought it was every woman's dream."

Her laugh was a nervous one, and yet he heard a lightness in it that he liked. Just as he liked her smile. Because of that, he hated to be the one to wipe it away.

"You were followed after you left the motel," he said quietly. "And not just by me. I couldn't see the driver of the pickup, but I did get a plate number. I'll give it to James. Just as I feared, your adoptive parents aren't the only ones who might not want you finding your birth mother."

"Ansley?" A woman's voice floated down the stairs, followed by an elegantly attired blonde woman. "Ingrid says we have company."

"Did she also tell you that I'm looking for that small, framed photo of me when I was five?"

Maribelle Brookshire swept into the room, all smiles. She was a woman who'd done everything money could buy not to look her age. It had worked. "Oh, my," she said when she saw Buck. Smiling, she extended her hand. "I don't believe we've met. I'm—"

"Maribelle Brookshire," he said, taking her limp, cool hand for an instant.

"My reputation must precede me," she said and glanced at Ansley, as if suspecting what he'd heard about her hadn't been nice. Her look, when she returned it to Buck, said, *Don't believe anything my daughter tells you.*

"I just want my photo," Ansley said, crossing her arms over her chest and holding her ground.

"Aren't you going to introduce me to your friend?"

"Buck Crawford," he said. "It's nice to meet you, Mrs. Brookshire." He saw the question in her gaze. She was wondering if he was the PI her daughter had hired and, if so, what he was doing here.

"Mother?"

Maribelle dragged her gaze from him to look at Ansley. "What's this about a photo?"

"You know the one I'm asking about, the one that was on the mantel yesterday when I was here."

The two stared at each other for a full minute before her mother sighed and walked down a short hallway. He heard a door open, then close. When she came back, she handed a small, framed photo to her daughter. Buck could feel the tension between the two.

"I hope you know what you're doing," Maribelle said under her breath before excusing herself. "Is your friend staying for lunch?" she asked before starting back up the grand stairway.

"No, and neither am I," Ansley said, holding the photograph tight to her chest until her mother disappeared from view.

Ansley was almost afraid to look at the photo. What if she remembered it wrong? What if she looked nothing like the Colt brothers? What if it had all been in her imagination and now she'd dragged the Colts into her delusion? Dragged them into a wishful dream of a family that looked like her?

She held the photo to her chest for a moment longer before she finally looked. Tears rushed to her eyes as she was overwhelmed by emotion. It was just as she remembered. She was one of the Colts. It had to be true. It couldn't be only wishful thinking, and yet the look in her young eyes broke her heart. She remembered that little girl and felt that old pang of loneliness in this big house with only passing glimpses of her parents. She'd wanted a family, her real family, as far back as she could remember. That desire had been heart deep, as if she'd known all along that she didn't belong here. But had she really found it in the Colts?

Buck took a step toward her, no doubt anxious to see the photo, but he didn't get the chance as the front door slammed open. They both turned as Lanny Jackson stormed in. He was a large man dressed all in black with a face that matched his bad disposition. Ansley clutched the framed photo, determination making her rigid. She had to show this to the Colts, especially James. He had to know that she wasn't delusional. She couldn't wait for the DNA test results. The photo would make him understand why she believed she was one of them.

"I suggest you put that back," Lanny said, dismissing Buck with a brisk wave of his hand as he focused all his ire on her. "I've already alerted your father of an intruder on the estate."

"I'm not an intruder," she snapped. "I have more right to be in this house than you do."

He grunted in answer to that, an ugly grin doing nothing for his face. So far Lanny hadn't acknowledged Buck and continued to ignore him, his gaze on her as he spoke. "As of this afternoon, you aren't allowed to take anything from the house without your father's expressed permission."

She shook her head as if in disbelief. "My mother knows I'm taking the photo. She gave it to me."

Lanny held his ground. "That may well be so, but I work for your father. I can't let you leave with—"

Buck stepped in front of him. "Lanny Jackson, right? The not-too-smart felon who left his fingerprints at Colt Brothers Investigation yesterday when you ransacked their offices?"

"I don't know who you are or what you're talking about, but this is none of your business," the thug said. "I suggest you leave while you still can."

Ansley could see where this was headed. "Buck, don't—" She didn't want trouble. She especially didn't want this cowboy to get hurt because of her.

"You're really threatening to physically keep Ansley Brookshire from taking her own childhood photo from this house?" Buck asked Lanny, as if he hadn't heard her try to stop him.

Just as she feared, both Buck and Lanny looked ready for a fight.

Buck had known there would be trouble. Ansley had said she would call her fiancé to come to the house with her. So where was he? And would it have done any good if he'd been here now? He doubted it, unless her fiancé was a cop or an NFL football player or carried a weapon.

He met Lanny Jackson's scowl, saw a twinkle in the man's dark eyes and knew the bodyguard was hoping for a showdown.

"You need to back off." Lanny cocked his head, his hand snaking around to his side. Buck had already noticed the telltale sign that the man was carrying. But just in case he didn't get the hint, the bodyguard brushed his jacket aside and turned just enough so Buck could see the holstered Glock.

Buck smiled and said, "Show me yours and I'll have to show you mine. You sure you want a shoot-out here in this nice house?" He shook his head. "I didn't think so. Ansley, it's time for us to leave." She moved up beside him. He didn't see the framed photo. He figured it was resting next to the one of the Colt brothers in her large purse on her shoulder.

Clearly the bodyguard didn't want to back down. They were about the same height and weight. Buck had grown up wrestling with the wild Colt boys. He knew he could hold his own—unless Lanny Jackson fought dirty. Looking into the man's sneer, Buck knew instinctively that he did.

As he and Ansley stepped forward, Lanny moved to block their way. Buck had to question if this was really about a photograph—or was this man just protecting his turf?

"You need to mind your own business, cowboy," the bodyguard said, getting in his face.

Buck really doubted Lanny would pull his gun—let alone use it here. "You think your employer would appreciate what's about to go down in his living room? How much do you think this rug under our feet costs? Doubt your boss will be able to get the blood out of it. I would hate for any of the fancy furnishings to be destroyed when you and I go at each other. But why don't you call your boss first, because I'm betting whatever we break will come out of *your* wages."

Lanny's jaw tightened. It took a moment or two, but he finally stepped aside to let them leave. "This isn't over."

Buck didn't doubt it. He could tell that it took all the man's self-control to let them go. Lanny wasn't the kind who backed down. Which meant Buck would be seeing the man again. Only next time, it would be an ambush—and there would be blood.

Chapter 9

"We need to talk," Buck said the moment he and Ansley stepped outside her adoptive parents' house. He watched her turn to look back at the balcony on the second floor. Maribelle Brookshire was standing at the railing, watching them. There was no sign of Lanny Jackson.

"Not here. We can talk at my office in Bozeman," she said. "Do you mind following me? It isn't far."

He thought about the last woman in trouble he'd thought he was saving. Hadn't he learned anything? But after seeing what had transpired at the house earlier, he couldn't walk away now, no matter how dangerous. Maribelle Brookshire had given her daughter the photo that she'd obviously hidden before they'd arrived. Had she really been afraid Ansley would tear the place apart to find it, as she'd threatened the housekeeper?

Clearly she hadn't wanted Ansley to take it. Why else would she call Lanny to stop her? What mother would do that? One who had a whole lot to hide, he thought.

On the way into town, Buck called Willie and told him about the pickup following Ansley to the estate. He gave him the plate number of the vehicle. It took the sheriff only a few minutes before he called back.

"The vehicle matching that description and with those plates belongs to Mark Laden of Mark's Used Cars." Buck knew the fly-by-night business north of Lonesome. "Mark said he saw the pickup missing this morning but just assumed someone had taken it out for a test drive. He was going to check with his wife before reporting it stolen. Apparently, it's a vehicle she loans out occasionally."

"Great, so we have no idea who was driving it."

"Not yet," Willie said. "You followed her to Bozeman? You sure you know what you're getting into?"

Buck laughed. He was in way too deep to stop now, he told himself. "I'll have to get back to you on that." He disconnected as ahead he saw the parking area in front of Ansley Brookshire's jewelry shop and the woman herself waiting for him.

They didn't say a word to each other as they went upstairs to her office. The room was bright and airy, filled with artwork and photographs of interesting jewelry, the windows overlooking busy downtown Bozeman's Main Street. "Your designs?" he asked, intrigued by the jewelry. She nodded. "I haven't seen anything like them before."

That brought a smile. "Thank you."

Buck took the chair she offered him. This woman was talented. She had her life together. At least she had until she'd found out that the Brookshires had lied to her. Now it was as if she'd climbed onto a runaway train. He wanted to pull her off, protect her, because he could feel the heartbreak coming for her.

But one look at the determination in her eyes and he knew he couldn't stop that train any more than he could the one that hit and killed her possible biological father, Del Ransom Colt, ten years ago.

Worse, he'd climbed aboard and was now racing headlong with her—into something that could get him killed this time.

Ansley studied the man sitting across the desk from her. She was still furious over everything that had taken place back at the estate. Buck had taken off his Stetson and now balanced it on his knee. He'd come to her rescue. Again. He was starting to make a habit of it. And worse, she felt herself starting to depend on him.

"I appreciated your help back there at the house, but this was a mistake," she said. Because of her, he'd crossed Lanny and was now in the man's crosshairs. "I've put you in danger. And I'm concerned that you followed me."

Buck chuckled. "Don't worry about me. I can hold my own. When I saw someone following you out of Lonesome, I had to follow them. It's a fatal flaw of mine."

"Like that trust issue you mentioned." She was just starting to realize what she'd done. It was as if she'd thrown a stone into a quiet pool and now the ripples were growing wider and wider, threatening to drown anyone in its path. "I never dreamed that looking for my birth mother would cause this much trouble or get so many people involved."

"You've kicked over an anthill, that's for sure," Buck agreed. "Hard to say who else wants to keep your adoption a secret. But word seems to be out that you're looking for your biological mother. Apparently more than your adoptive parents don't want that to happen."

She listened as he told her what he'd learned from the sheriff after he'd called him with the license plate number and make and model of the vehicle. "The sheriff is looking into it. I didn't get a good look at the driver. Sorry."

"You've already done so much for me." Ansley studied this soft-spoken, good-looking cowboy, remembering how he'd handled Lanny. There was more to him than he let most people see. It seemed almost fateful that their paths had crossed. But should she be worried that he always seemed to be around when she needed him? Or worry that he might not be? "I don't know anything about you."

He grinned, a glint in his eyes. "Not much to know. Raised outside Lonesome, got my butt kicked as kid growing up with the wild Colt brothers, spent my youth helping my dad break horses when we weren't raising rough stock for rodeos." He shrugged. "Decided it wasn't for me after college and joined the state police highway patrol. Left that a while back. Now I'm figuring out what's next. Told you—not much to tell."

"Do you always come to the aid of a woman in trouble?"

His grin faded. "Tell me about you."

"Even less to tell. I grew up believing I was a Brookshire, graduated from college in the arts, followed my dream of designing jewelry. To my surprise, it took off online, so I opened a storefront and had to hire jewelry makers to keep up with the demand." She smiled, hoping she didn't sound as if she were bragging. "It was a dream come true." Her smile faded. "Then I found out that everything I'd thought I knew about myself and my life was a lie."

Her heart ached at the memory of that confusing and yet enlightening moment. "I had no idea wanting to find my birth mother would be met with so much opposition on so many fronts." Ansley shook her head. "I don't understand what's happening or why."

"Neither do I," Buck said, "I'm guessing your fiancé isn't on board?"

She glanced away. "Why would you say that?" When he said nothing, she was forced to look at him.

"Just seems someone tipped Maribelle Brookshire off that you were coming for that photo, giving her just enough time to hide it." He held her gaze. "Hard to know who's trying to stop you. Or who you can trust."

That one hit home, hard. She couldn't trust Maribelle or Harrison. Both had lied to her. Now Gage?

"I know I said I'd call him about going with me to the house for the photo," she said, looking away again. "I did call him, but I changed my mind about asking him to go with me. Truthfully, it seemed silly. I really didn't think there would be a problem."

"Did you happen to tell him what you planned to do?"

She let out a nervous laugh. "You really think my fiancé warned my mother?" But she could see that's exactly what they both thought.

"Sorry, you know him, and I don't," Buck said. "I

guess you were lucky that Maribelle didn't have time to get rid of it."

It was clear that her adoptive mother had been warned, and they both knew it. They also knew who had given her the heads-up—the only person she'd told where she was going and why. Gage had betrayed her. As much as she hated to admit it, she couldn't trust the people closest to her.

Instead, she was now depending on strangers. One stranger in particular, she thought, as she met Buck's gaze again.

Buck could see how upset she was, having come to the same conclusion he had. Her fiancé had sold her out. He hoped he got a chance to meet him. He told himself that he wouldn't punch him in the face. Unless the guy asked for it. Ah, hell, he'd punch the man just on general principles.

"After hearing about Lanny Jackson reaching the PI office before you—" he began.

"You think he knew where I was going before I did," she said, nodding. "I only told Maribelle, and I didn't mention Colt Brothers Investigation."

"You'd looked it up online?"

He saw her eyes widen. "How would Lanny— Unless he had access to my phone…" Lanny probably didn't have access, but her fiancé no doubt did. He saw her expression harden as the pieces of the ugly picture began to fall together.

"Someone could have been tracking your internet searches," Buck said. His money was on the fiancé putting the device at least on her phone and probably her computer. "They also could have put other devices on your car." She looked sick as realization settled in. "You sure you want to keep looking for your birth mother? What about your business?"

"My assistant is more than qualified to run things. I've already let her know I won't be in the office for a while. I booked the motel room in Lonesome for a week. I'm not changing my mind. If anything, this only makes me more determined. Whatever everyone is hiding, I plan to expose it, no matter who is involved." She took a breath and let it out slowly as she met his gaze. "But I can't ask you to risk your life for me."

"You're not asking," he said, feeling his chest tighten at her look, his breathing catch. "I've been involved from the moment we collided in the alley. You're actually helping me. In between careers right now, remember. I need the distraction."

She eyed him. "So, I'm a *distraction* and this is just about you amusing yourself between careers?"

He chuckled. "A lovely distraction." No way did he want to believe it was anything but that—as drawn to her as he was. "Seriously? If I can be of help to you and the Colts, all the better."

"James is right. This is more dangerous than I first thought. You met Lanny. I hate to think what could have happened back at the house if you hadn't been there—or worse, if you hadn't talked him down." Her blue eyes shone with worry. "You forced him to back down. He won't forget that. He'll come after you. That was what I was trying to avoid."

He knew there were some much more dangerous ways he could get hurt. "Let me worry about that." He leaned forward, telling himself he'd gotten into this to protect his friends. If she was wrong about her connection to the Colts, then that part would be moot. She'd just be another client. Would he still be so willing to risk his neck for her? He held her gaze. Yep, he'd risk his neck for her, and that should have worried him more than it did. "Mind if I see the photograph you took from the house?"

She reached into her shoulder bag and pulled out the framed snapshot of the Colts, then the one of herself. She put them side by side on her desk, turning them to face him. He could feel her watching his expression as he compared the two.

He studied the photos for a moment, then looked up at her. She'd already seen the same thing that he now had. She was the spitting image of the Colt brothers at that age.

She nodded. "You see why I can't stop now. I have to know."

Harrison Brookshire paced the floor of his office, his cell phone held away from his ear as Maribelle yelled obscenities at him.

"Some bodyguard you hired," she snapped. "He let her and that cowboy just walk out of the house with the photo."

"What photo?" he asked, trying to understand what had happened, and, more important, what any of this had to do with him. She knew better than to bother him at work.

"The photo Gage called me about. He warned me that she was coming to get it. You know, the one taken when she was… I don't know what age, little, just a kid. She wanted it, because she thought it proved who she was. At least that's what Gage said. She plans to show it to the private investigator she hired in Lonesome."

Harrison couldn't believe what he was hearing. "What in hell's name have you gotten us into, Maribelle?" he demanded. "I never wanted a child. I told you that. But you just had to have a daughter, and like everything you've just had to have, you lost interest right away. And now she's turned on us."

"Not this again. I don't need another lecture from you," she snapped. "What are you planning to do about her?"

"What would you have me do?" he yelled back. He could feel his blood pressure rising to a dangerous level. If only he had stopped her all those years ago. Had he really thought that a daughter would make his wife happy and keep her out of his hair?

"I don't care what you do as long as you stop her before she ruins us. Our daughter has lost her mind. I seriously think she needs help—maybe to be admitted to an institution until she comes to her senses. Now she's hooked up with some cowboy who even your so-called bodyguard was too afraid to stop."

He groaned inwardly. "What cowboy?"

"I think he said his name was Buck Crawford."

"Is he the private investigator?"

"I don't think so. I have no idea where she picked him up. Gage was beside himself when I called and told him about it after she left with that man. Dear, sweet Gage—he said he's done his best to dissuade her from this foolish quest of hers, but not even her fiancé seems to be able to reason with her. He agrees with me that if Ansley doesn't change her mind, something awful might happen to her. I don't think he'll break off the engagement. But I can't bear the thought of that bit of information hitting the news, not to mention social media—"

"Embarrassing you is the least of my worries," Harrison snapped. "I thought you handled this with the money I gave you."

"I'm working on that end, but unless Gage can stop Ansley—"

"Maribelle," Harrison said, talking over her. As if things weren't bad enough, she seemed determined to stir the pot by bringing Gage into whatever this was. "Don't wind Gage up. She's lucky to have a man like him. Let me handle this. You go on about your business and leave it to me."

He disconnected and walked to his office bar. He poured himself a shot and downed it, afraid of what Maribelle had done. At this point, he just had to deal with it, and as quickly as possible, from the sounds of it. He hadn't gotten to where he was in life by backing down when things got tough. He wouldn't this time. Yet although he knew there was only one way to handle this, he hesitated. He'd learned in business that sometimes it took a drastic move to get the outcome he wanted.

Pulling out his phone, he made the call. "This has to be handled very carefully and even more quickly and quietly." He disconnected and poured himself another shot. Downing it, he told himself there was no other way. He certainly couldn't afford to grow a conscience at this point in his life.

Chapter 10

James couldn't help being frustrated with this case. Finding Ansley's birth mother was proving to be like looking for a needle in a haystack. Tommy had researched everything he could find out about adoption in Montana. Even if the adoption had been legal and aboveboard, under the law, the birth mother could keep her offspring from contacting her or learning her name.

If this was a back-porch adoption like he suspected, then even if money had changed hands, it would be hard to prove. They might never know the truth.

Ansley hadn't been adopted legally. That much they knew. Where to go from here— He felt discouraged as his cell phone rang.

"Hey," he said, seeing that it was his wife. He waited for the sound of Lori's voice, needing to hear it right now.

When she finally spoke, there was an edge to it that

he knew too well. "I want to meet her," she said, getting right to it. "Invite her to dinner."

James cursed his baby brother, Davy. Newly married, Davy had confided to his bride, Carla, about Ansley Brookshire. Davy knew better than to talk about their cases, but James was sure this had hit too close to home to for Davy keep it from Carla and for Carla to keep it from Lori.

"I don't talk about cases, you know that," James said. "And I sure as the devil don't invite clients to dinner."

She made a dismissive sound. "This woman might be your sister and you don't think we should meet her?"

"Half sister, but we don't know that for a fact and won't until the DNA test results come back, so I don't see any reason to—"

"Well, I do. I want to meet her," Lori said definitively. "I heard she's staying at the motel, paid for a whole week. Even if she isn't your sister, she thinks she is, and that's good enough for me. Family is family. Invite her to dinner. In fact, I want the whole family here." He started to argue, but she cut him off. "I've talked to the wives, and we all agree. Our house tonight."

"What is the rush? We could have the DNA results any day—"

"Please?" He could almost see her giving him that look he knew so well. It was a look he couldn't resist— even just imagining it over the phone. "Please, James. If there is any chance she's your sister… Don't disappoint me."

"Never," he said and had to smile as she disconnected. He knew how his wife felt about family. Add that to the pregnancy, and you didn't argue with a woman running on hormones. He could have called her back and argued his case, literally, but he was too smart for that. Also, she was right. If there was a chance that Ansley might be family… He still didn't want to believe his father had kept something like this from them. If Del Ransom Colt had, then they hadn't known him at all. James wasn't ready to go there.

He picked up the phone. "Do you have plans for dinner tonight?" he asked, clearly catching Ansley off guard. "I know it's short notice. The whole family will be there. Buck's coming." He hadn't yet asked him, but that didn't stop James. He still had hopes that his friend would be joining the agency. "I'm sure he'll give you a ride out to the ranch. Seems everyone wants to meet you."

After he hung up, he called Buck's number, not surprised to learn he was with Ansley in Bozeman. Buck told him what had been going on. He listened, shaking his head. Someone had borrowed an old pickup from Mark's used car lot and followed Ansley to the Brookshire Estate.

"She got the photo," Buck was saying. "Lanny Jackson tried to stop her. I'm pretty sure I'll be seeing him again."

"Buck." The news didn't get better. "Her fiancé ratted her out to Maribelle Brookshire?"

"Looking forward to meeting the fiancé one day," Buck said. "I'm willing to bet he's responsible for the tracking devices on Ansley's car, phone and computer as well as inside her condo. I removed all of them I could find. I told her to hire someone to sweep her office as well."

James groaned. "You realize what you're saying,

don't you? The people around her are determined to stop her. Stop you. Stop us from finding out the truth."

"And she's just as determined to keep going. I'm going to follow her back to Lonesome. She's taken a room at the motel for a week," Buck said. "She got the photo from the estate. You're going to want to see it, James. If she isn't related to you, I'll eat one of my lucky boots."

"The leather on your lucky boots is thin enough. With some steak sauce, you'll probably enjoy it. Seriously, Buck, be careful. Also, I don't know if Ansley mentioned it or not, but Lori is having the whole family over tonight for dinner at our place at seven. I told Ansley you'd bring her. After dinner, I was hoping we could talk."

"Sure. But James, the Brookshires are serious about not wanting her to find her birth mother. I'm afraid of what they'll do next."

"I'm afraid of what you'll do next," James said but realized his friend had already disconnected.

Judy Ramsey had never expected to hear from Maribelle Brookshire ever again. She told herself that she would have been fine with that. For years she'd tried to put what they did behind her. Nasty business, her mother would have said. She'd felt dirty, as if she had blood on her hands, giving a woman like Maribelle Brookshire a baby.

She never would have done it except that almost thirty years ago, she'd been desperate. Not that that was a good excuse. It was just the truth. Had she been able to do it again, she would have never let Maribelle talk her into it.

So why was the woman calling her now? Judy considered her current situation and tried to assure herself that it could be good news. Maribelle would want something from her, that was a given. But there would also be a reward, and let's face it, the years hadn't been that good, Judy had to admit. She was getting too old to wait tables. Her legs had been bothering her. Her back, too.

How much money could she get out of the woman this time, though? Would it be worth it to meet her? With a shudder, she reminded herself who she was dealing with. Maribelle wasn't like normal people. She made up her own rules. That's what too much money and power did to a person.

As Judy sat on the back steps of her house smoking, she kept wondering why the woman wanted to see her now, after all these years. It couldn't bode well, could it?

For a moment, she thought about not going to the meeting. But she knew that wouldn't stop the woman. She felt torn, but she needed to know what this was about. Best to find out what she wanted. And if there was money involved, well, she'd take it.

She felt a chill as she crushed out her cigarette. The last thing she wanted was to get involved with this woman again. The last time, she hadn't felt as if she had an option. Did she really this time, either? Judy had kept their secret for more than twenty-eight years. She lit another cigarette. Whatever Maribelle wanted, she'd better bring a lot of money tonight, because this was going to cost her.

James was just about to call it a day and go home and help Lori get ready for the dinner tonight when Ansley Brookshire walked into the PI office. He hadn't expected to see her until later at the ranch.

She headed right for his desk without preamble. She pulled a small, framed photo from her shoulder bag and laid it down in front of him. She then pulled out the framed photo that had graced the Colt office wall for as long as James could remember and set it next to the first.

With the photos side by side, he looked down, first taking in the one of him and his brothers. He really would have been heartbroken if he hadn't gotten the photo back, because he had no idea what had happened to the original or the negative. The photo had been taken before digital snapshots on cell phones.

His gaze shifted to the girl in the other photo. He felt his heart do a whoop-de-do in his chest, stealing his breath, before he looked up at her.

"Yeah," he said. That was the best he could do. He felt as if he'd been punched. "I'm told we should have the preliminary DNA test results soon. Then…there won't be any doubt." Not that there was much doubt now, he thought as he met her blue eyes. So familiar, just as Buck had said.

Meanwhile, he had to tell Ansley that so far he hadn't learned much on her case and neither had Tommy. By whatever means Maribelle Brookshire had gotten baby Ansley, she'd done a good job of covering her tracks.

James explained what the agency had been doing since they'd last talked. She listened, appearing not surprised. Davy was still tied up in a case down in Wyoming, so it was just James and Tommy doing the legwork. "Tommy is following the money trail, seeing who came into unexplained money about twenty-eight years ago. He's also checking on births in town and nearby and trying to find midwives from that time, since we don't believe you were born in the hospital. Twenty-eight years ago in Montana, the birth mother would have been required to fill out the birth certificate before leaving the hospital. So there would have been a record. Except there's none."

Ansley wasn't surprised. She'd done enough research to know that Maribelle hadn't gone through proper channels. The only thing that had surprised her had been the dinner invitation. The family wanted to meet her? The thought scared her and, at the same time, filled her with hope. They were taking this seriously.

"My searches have reached the same conclusion," she told James. "What can I do to help?" The thought of just hanging around every day waiting was killing her. She wanted this over with, and as quickly as possible. "Please. I've taken a room at the motel in town, and I'm staying as long as it takes. Tell me what I can do."

James glanced up as Buck came into the office. "You could talk to anyone who worked for the family at the time you were brought home as an infant. Gardeners, housekeepers—anyone who knew that your adoptive mother wasn't pregnant before you arrived at the house. They might have some idea where she got the baby, especially if she had to leave for any length of time to pick you up."

She nodded. She'd talked to her first nanny but hadn't thought about the other staff. She knew how household staff liked to gossip. Also given how many Maribelle had fired over the years, she thought some might be more honest with her and less afraid to talk.

"I also plan to visit the yarn shop," she said. "I know it's a long shot that someone there might remember a woman who bought yarn nearly thirty years ago, but I have to try."

James agreed. "Toni might be more apt to talk to you than me."

"I'll go with her," Buck said.

Ansley saw a look pass between James and Buck. "I just want to be sure that she's safe," Buck said. "So, if it's all right with Ansley…"

"I'm hoping Buck will be joining the investigation," James said. "With his background in law enforcement, we could really use him—at least on this case." Another look passed between them. One she couldn't read.

She smiled at Buck, who'd been standing by the door, already proving that he planned to keep an eye on her. She told them about what she knew regarding the pink baby blanket believed to have been made by her birth mother.

"Why would she buy both blue and pink?" James asked. "Wouldn't you find out the gender if you were going to all the trouble of knitting a baby blanket?"

Ansley had to smile as she imagined her birth mother making two blankets because she didn't want to know before her baby was born. "Maybe she didn't want to know because she couldn't keep me." She looked to Buck, to see if he understood, and got a nod.

"She would have gotten more attached otherwise," he said. "I get it. So she was ready with both blankets when the baby was born."

Except Ansley couldn't imagine how hard it must have been for her birth mother to go home empty-handed with only the blue blanket that she'd knit.

* * *

Judy wasn't looking forward to a clandestine meeting with Maribelle Brookshire, but she was curious. Something must have happened to shake the woman. Why else were they meeting? That thought brought a smile.

She was feeling better by the time she pulled onto the old river highway. She dodged potholes and tried to convince herself that meeting Mrs. High and Mighty was a good thing. The woman must need her help again.

Judy told herself that she could put up with Maribelle looking down her nose at her just fine—as long as it paid well. It had the last time. This time, she'd demand more—after all, she knew Maribelle Brookshire's darkest secrets, didn't she?

It wasn't like she'd treated the woman as if she was a bottomless well that she could tap whenever she needed a decent drink. She'd kept her mouth shut and never asked for more money. But to have Maribelle call her asking to see her? This was one of those times when the sky could be the limit. The woman had sounded desperate, which made Judy wonder why. What if the cops had gotten wind of what they'd done? Maybe Maribelle was looking for a fall guy and this was a setup? The woman could even be wearing a wire.

No, Judy decided. The last thing Maribelle wanted was the cops involved. With her money, she could keep that from happening. It was something personal, something about the girl. Judy realized that the baby she'd given Maribelle was a young woman by now. Had it really been that many years?

Maybe it was time to make a major withdrawal from that well—just in case there was any chance of it going completely dry.

Pulling off the old river highway to the spot where Maribelle had said to meet, she stopped short. The old motel and restaurant looked abandoned. She spotted a for-sale sign propped up in front of the dirty front window of the café. How long had it been closed? Probably since the new highway had passed it by.

What she hadn't expected was for the area to be so isolated. A car hadn't passed since she'd turned off onto the decaying asphalt. She felt a shiver of trepidation. The entire place was miles from anything, in the middle of Montana, on a road that clearly didn't get much traffic anymore.

For a moment, she thought about hightailing it out of there before Maribelle arrived. She could call her, suggest somewhere a little less spooky to meet. But at the sound of a car pulling in next to hers, she realized it was too late. Maribelle had arrived. Best to just get this over with, since Judy definitely could use the money. If she put it off, Maribelle might change her mind.

As she looked over at the fancy car and the person sitting behind the wheel, she was surprised the woman had come alone. She'd expected to see some huge bodyguard. She'd just assumed Maribelle would bring one with her. She had brought backup the last time they'd met at some off the beaten path. But that had been almost thirty years ago. Maybe Maribelle Brookshire trusted her this time.

Judy pushed aside her earlier trepidation. The woman wouldn't have called her unless she needed her help. Still, she waited. *Let her come to me.* The driver's side door of the expensive car opened, and Maribelle stepped out wearing a suit and high heels. Maybe that's all she owned, but she looked ridiculous all dressed up like that out here. She'd mostly seen Maribelle's photo at some social event in the newspaper or society magazines. Judy had made the newspaper only once—for a DUI when she was younger.

Maribelle flung a large designer purse over one shoulder as if she was on her way to a board meeting. If she hoped to intimidate her, the woman didn't know her very well.

Maribelle didn't know her at all. Their brief acquaintance had been more of a business arrangement. Money exchanged hands and so did a baby, Judy reminded herself—as if she could ever forget.

The first time she'd laid eyes on Maribelle had been on the Brookshire Estate, as it was known. Judy had been visiting a friend in Bozeman. "This wealthy woman is throwing a party," her friend had said. "The caterer needs more servers. The money is really good. I'm working it. I could put in a good word if you're interested."

Judy hadn't wanted to be impressed when she'd seen the place, but she was blown away by the opulence. She couldn't imagine having that kind of money, let alone throwing a party like that one. The pay had been really good, and there was plenty of leftover food and champagne. She had indulged as she helped clean up the kitchen, even though she knew she shouldn't.

And later, throwing up in the guest bathroom, that's when she'd met Maribelle Brookshire. She'd expected a tongue-lashing. Instead, the woman had been sympathetic. She'd handed her a warm, wet washcloth as Judy had apologized.

"Pregnant?" Maribelle had asked.

She remembered blinking in surprise. It wasn't like

she was showing. She'd only suspected the previous week. It was why she was in Bozeman. She was hoping her friend would tell her what to do, since the father didn't even know. Wouldn't have made a difference, anyway. He wasn't available. She was on her own.

That night, all those years ago, the woman still dressed in her fancy party clothes had sat down on a teak bench she'd pulled from the shower and told Judy how desperately she wanted a baby. No, not a baby—a daughter. "Is it a girl?"

Judy had said yes, hoping it was true, because she'd seen the gleam in the woman's eyes and realized what this could mean for her. The answer to all her problems. And if she was having a boy? Well, the woman would just have to be glad to get a baby of any gender.

Now, all these years later, Maribelle didn't even glance in her direction before walking over to a worn wooden shelter over a weathered picnic table, its green paint peeling off in clumps. Apparently the woman just assumed she was going to follow her, Judy thought, still sitting behind the wheel of her car.

For a moment, she considering starting the engine and driving away, imaging Maribelle's shocked expression. She shoved away the impulse and got out to follow her. *This had better be worth it.*

Chapter 11

The shop where her birth mother had purchased both pink and blue yarn also sold baby clothes, some maternity wear, and a few bolts of fabric. As in most small Montana towns, businesses had to diversify to keep the doors open. The shop itself was located inside a larger building that had been divided into smaller commercial spaces.

The sign in the window read simply Toni's. That was another thing Ansley had noticed about small Montana towns—signage was often sparse if it existed at all. If you lived in Lonesome, you knew what Toni's sold. If you didn't, well, then, you probably weren't going to shop there.

When she commented on this to Buck as they entered the shop, he laughed and said, "For some old-timers, their attitude is that if you don't know where you're going, then you have no business here."

Toni turned out to be a tiny woman with short gray hair and a huge welcoming smile. Buck had told Ansley that Toni had started the shop years ago, so there was the chance that she'd known the woman who'd bought the yarn.

They both knew it was a long shot, though, that she would remember a purchase all those years ago.

"Buck Crawford, I declare. I don't think I've ever seen you in my shop." Toni grinned as she shifted her gaze to Ansley. "What brings you in today?"

"Actually, I have a strange request," Ansley said. "I'm looking for a pregnant woman who bought yarn from you in the spring almost thirty years ago."

Toni's eyes widened. Ansley rushed on. "The woman bought both pink and blue, as if she wasn't sure what she was having."

"Honey, I barely can remember what I had for breakfast. Why would you be looking for someone who bought yarn all those years ago?"

"I believe she was my birth mother. I'm trying to find her."

Toni seemed at a loss for words. She looked at Buck, then back to Ansley. "Oh, honey, I wish I could help. Even if I kept records of all purchases, I wouldn't have any that far back anymore."

Ansley couldn't help feeling crestfallen. She knew it had been an incredible long shot, and yet she'd still gotten her hopes up. "Thanks, I understand. I just thought you would have...remembered her. A beginning knitter. Maybe she asked for help." She could see that nothing she could say was going to trigger a memory. "Thank you for your time, anyway."

"Wait," Toni said as Ansley started to turn away. "I

remember a lot of my customers. Pink and blue yarn. What did she make?"

"A baby blanket. My nanny told me it was quite a simple pattern. That's why she thought my mother was just learning to knit."

Toni raised an eyebrow at the word *nanny* but said, "Leave me your phone number. There aren't that many knitters in town, although this sounds like it might have been a onetime purchase. If I think of someone who could help you, I'll give you a call."

Ansley thanked her and left her number.

"Sorry," Buck said as they walked out.

"I knew it was a long shot. But for a moment there…" Ansley thought she'd seen a flash of recognition, as if the shop owner had remembered something.

Once outside, she glanced back and saw Toni talking on the phone. She looked excited and turned her back as if keeping her voice down.

Ansley knew the call might have nothing to do with her, but she didn't believe it. Had Toni called her birth mother to warn her?

If so, her mother didn't want to be found. She couldn't help feeling defeated. With so many people trying to keep her from it, did she even stand a chance of ever learning the truth?

Willie had the day off. He'd spent his morning calling engraving shops in the area around Lonesome. Each call took time, as most businesses almost thirty years ago hadn't gone to computers. He'd waited while an employee dug through the files. No engraving with the name DelRae with that spelling.

He was about to widen his search area when a young female employee came back on the line.

"I found it." She sounded triumphant. "DelRae." She spelled it out. "That it?"

His pulse pounded. "That's it. Was the necklace purchase there at your store?"

"It was. Looks like the engraving was free."

"Who purchased it?" He held his breath.

For a moment, there was no answer. "Sorry, looks like the person paid cash."

No, he couldn't get this close and then find out nothing. "But didn't they have to wait for the engraving? Didn't they leave a telephone number or a name?"

"Looks like they said they'd come back to get it."

He groaned silently. "So we have no way of knowing if it was a woman or a man." He had another thought. "Did the person have to fill anything out?"

She seemed to brighten. "They had to put down the name they wanted engraved on the piece and sign the form. You can't believe the people who come back and say, 'That isn't the engraving I wanted.' This way we have proof."

"Good for you," he said, meaning it. "Can you read the name?"

"Sorry. It's pretty sloppy and faded."

"That's okay. Can you take a photo of whatever is written on the form and send it to me?" He would recognize his father's handwriting anywhere. He gave her the information and thanked her while he waited for the text.

Antsy, worried about this dinner with the Colt family and with no desire to go back to her motel room, Ansley told Buck that she was going back to the PI office.

"James suggested I try to contact former Brookshire employees who might remember something about the time I was born," she told him. "I need to keep busy."

He nodded as he understood. "I want to help, too. Tell me what I can do."

While Ansley tracked down former Brookshire employees from the time Maribelle brought her to the estate, Buck checked to find out if any babies had been stolen during that same time period in the state and the surrounding states.

They took separate offices at Colt Brothers Investigation, promising to holler if they found something. Ansley tracked down the gardener who'd worked for the Brookshires about the time Maribelle brought her home. Les Owens had sounded surprised by her call.

"Why would you be asking questions about that?" he asked in a grating, impatient older voice.

"Because I'm that baby now grown. You were working there when Maribelle brought me home?" A grunt. "Do you remember seeing my mother pregnant with me?"

"What kind of question is that?" he snapped.

She decided to be as direct as he was being. "I know she didn't give birth to me. Do you know where she got me?"

Silence, then, "Maybe a stork brought you to her."

Ansley sighed. "I really could use your help."

"Maybe she found you somewhere."

"Stole me, you mean?" she asked, heart in her throat.

"Or got a good deal on you."

She tried to form the next sentence carefully. "From whom?"

More silence. For a moment, she thought he'd hung

up. "Where are you looking?" he asked, almost whispering.

"Lonesome, Montana." She heard the office door open a crack and saw Buck. "Is that where she got me?" She glanced at Buck and saw that, like her, he was waiting for the answer.

"I'd be real careful if I was you about crossing the Brookshires. If you really are the daughter, you should already know that." With that he disconnected. She put down the phone and told Buck about their conversation. "He suggested that she bought me. When I mentioned Lonesome, he told me to be careful."

Buck shook his head. "No record of any infant being kidnapped or taken during that time. I checked for both years since we don't know exactly when you were born, necessarily. Nothing. Sorry."

"He could have just been toying with me," she said with a sigh.

"How about lunch?" he suggested. "There's a diner down the street."

Her cell phone rang. She didn't recognize the number. For just an instant, she thought it might be Les Owens calling back from a different phone. Maybe he hadn't been able to talk freely earlier. But it was a female voice. It took a moment for her to recognize it. "Toni?"

"Can you stop back by the shop? I think I might know who you're looking for."

"We'll be right there," she said.

Toni was waiting for them when Buck and Ansley reached the shop. She motioned them back into her office, closing the door behind them and clearing away boxes of yarn that hadn't been unpacked to make room for them to sit on two plastic chairs she dragged up.

Ansley noted that the woman seemed nervous. "You thought of someone who might have purchased the yarn?" It seemed such a long shot, she still didn't believe it possible. But that didn't keep her from hoping.

"I wouldn't even have remembered someone buying yarn so many years go except for the pink and blue—and you mentioning that you thought she might be new to knitting," Toni said and took a breath before continuing. "It rang a bell. I called the woman who used to work for me part-time. We had laughed that day because of who came in to buy the yarn, a how-to-knit book and knitting needles. But that's not why we remembered. She was the last person on earth we thought would take up knitting, let alone buy a pattern for a baby blanket."

Before Ansley could ask why that was the case, Buck spoke up. "Someone local, then?"

Toni looked at him and whispered, "Judy Ramsey."

Ansley looked from Toni to Buck and back. "Why would that be so strange? Who is Judy Ramsey?"

"There are just some people you don't expect to take up knitting," Buck said, as if to remind Toni that they might be talking about Ansley's birth mother.

"We had no idea she was pregnant," Toni said. "We just never thought she'd actually knit a blanket, but you said she did—if it's the same woman. Who knew? Just didn't seem the type. She'd never been in the shop before—or after."

"But you saw her that day when she bought the yarn, and she was pregnant?" Ansley asked.

"She wasn't showing, if that's what you're asking," the shop owner said. "We didn't see her again, because she didn't return to the shop. We were trying to remember, but we think she was working in an old folks' home down in Lincoln. When she came back to Lonesome to go to work at the café, she didn't look pregnant, and she didn't have a baby."

"So it could be her?" Ansley asked hopefully, her voice cracking as she looked over at Buck. "Do you know where we can find her?"

"I do," Buck said. They thanked Toni and left the shop.

"What is it about Judy Ramsey that you were trying to get Toni not to say?" she demanded once they were outside and alone on the street.

He seemed to hesitate. "She had a hard life. Made some poor choices when it came to men, I think. As far as I knew, she never had any kids. Twenty-eight years ago she would have been in her late thirties, early forties. Her being pregnant would have been a surprise, that's all."

It wasn't all. She waited giving him a look that finally made him speak.

"It's just that Judy had kind of a reputation around town. She tended to be attracted to other women's husbands," he said.

"And she might be my mother." It wasn't a question. "Buck, I had no expectations when I started this." That was mostly true. "I know I might not like what I find. I just have to know. I can't let this go until I do. Where can I find her?"

"I'll take you. She lives close by. We can walk if you want."

It was a short walk. They left the business district behind and walked into the older residential area. As they did, the houses got smaller and so did the yards. Before long they were in an area where most of the houses needed paint and repairs. The yards were filled with junk or the parts of vehicles, kids' bikes or rusting motorcycles.

Judy Ramsey lived in a small house with several cluttered vacant lots between her and her neighbor.

"Her car isn't here," Buck said—nor was the pickup that had followed Ansley to the Brookshire Estate, he added.

Still, Ansley went up to the door and knocked. Someone had put plants out at the edge of the porch but appeared to have forgotten to water them. She peered in through a crack in the curtained window of the door. It was neat enough inside, but she caught the smell of old cigarette smoke and saw an overflowing ashtray next to one of the porch plants.

Was this the woman who'd given her life and then given her up? She kept thinking about the knit blanket. She'd cared. Ansley held on to that like a life raft in the rough sea of her emotions.

As they were heading back to the office, Buck took a call. "You're sure about that? Okay." He disconnected and looked over at her. "Sounds like someone from the mayor's office borrowed that pickup that followed you to the Brookshire Estate." He glanced at the time. "Too late to stop by today. In fact, we'd better get ready for dinner." He smiled and added, "It's going to be fun—you'll see."

Fun? She doubted that, as she tried to ignore the butterflies already flitting around her stomach. She would feel like she was on trial. They would be trying to decide if she was one of them.

* * *

Maribelle waited, her irritation growing. Why didn't the woman get out of her car? What was she waiting for? She was furious that it had come to this. She'd sworn she would never see the woman again—as long as Judy Ramsey kept her mouth shut.

But with Ansley determined to open this can of worms, she'd been left little choice. She just hoped to remind Judy to keep her mouth shut now more than ever.

But first she needed to find out if the foolish woman had ever told anyone—and if there was anything the PIs could find that would lead them to her.

At the sound of a car door opening and closing, Maribelle pulled herself together. She didn't want to come off as desperate—even though she was. Judy would smell fear and try to rob her blind.

In the mood Maribelle was in, that would be bad for Judy's health.

She hugged her large, expensive leather purse, feeling the weight of the gun inside. She'd promised herself that she wouldn't use it. She would just pay the woman off like last time. She'd make it clear there wouldn't be any more money in the future—once she was sure that the woman had kept her mouth shut all these years.

As Judy Ramsey walked toward her, she noticed she was limping a little. The woman had aged, and not in a good way, Maribelle thought. Maybe she was the desperate one. It gave her hope that this could be handled without any bloodshed.

The spring sky had filled with clouds that obscured the sun and darkened the pines all around the old motel and café not far from Lonesome. Squalls were building along the horizon. They'd be lucky if they didn't get caught in another snowstorm, she thought.

"What's this about?" Judy asked with a sigh, hoping to rush along whatever it was as she faced Maribelle. The woman had had work done. She didn't look all that much older than the last time she'd seen her. "I need to get to my job. Some of us have to work." It was a lie. She had taken some time off after injuring her leg on the job.

"I'll make this brief," Maribelle said from her high horse. "My daughter found out that she was adopted."

Judy felt her eyebrows arch up. *"You never told her?"* Maribelle gave her an impatient look. "You didn't tell her because you never wanted her to know that someone else carried her for nine months, through morning sickness and weight gain, before spending hours pushing her out of her womb and going through all that pain."

"Before giving her away without a second thought for money?" Maribelle snapped, "No, I didn't. Maybe I should have told her that her mother didn't want her—sold her for fifty thousand dollars." She made it sound like that wasn't even that much money.

Judy saw contempt in those eyes and felt anger burn in hers. She'd provided this woman with the daughter she just had to have. The woman had no idea how hard that had been or what she'd had to go through to pull it off. Maribelle should be grateful to her. "What is it you want from me now?"

Maribelle recoiled. "I don't want *anything.* I just never want my daughter to know about you."

Judy couldn't help being insulted. "Let's not start throwing stones, okay? I have a few I could fling back at you. Just spit it out. What did you get me out here

for if you don't want anything? You want *something.*
It's just a matter of how much you're willing to pay for
my silence this time."

Maribelle's blue eyes darkened, her body going still.
Judy realized that she'd overstepped, but she didn't care.
This woman couldn't treat her like this. Judy was the
one with all the knowledge—thus all the power here.

Maribelle took her time answering. "My daughter
has been asking questions about her birth mother," she
said without looking at her. "She's determined to find
her."

Judy couldn't hide her surprise. The girl had grown
up in the lap of luxury. Why would she care about the
mother who'd given her away?

A meadowlark sang close by. The breeze whispered
in the new green leaves of the nearby aspen trees. In
the distance, she thought she could hear the hum of vehicles on Interstate 90.

"I need to know how many people knew about your
pregnancy." Maribelle's voice sounded calm—maybe
too calm.

"I told you, no one. I went to the place in the mountains I told you about. Everything went as you planned.
I called you when the baby was born, we agreed on a
spot to meet and you picked her up. We never saw each
other again. That was it." She didn't know how Maribelle had gotten the baby a birth certificate. She should
have assumed the woman had passed the baby off as
her own. She hadn't cared. The money had been badly
needed, Maribelle had taken care of all her expenses
for those months, and she hadn't had to deal with the
woman ever again. Things had worked out satisfacto-
rily for them both.

"Look, I told you I'd keep my mouth shut, and I have. So what if your daughter wants to find her birth mother? She won't. If somehow she finds me, I'd deny it." She shrugged. "You have nothing to worry about."

"I wish that were true. I need to know if there is anything, anything at all, that she could find."

Judy frowned. "Like what?"

"Did you tell anyone, leave a trail, anything that can come back on me?"

She raised a brow, noticing the way Maribelle clutched the large leather purse hanging from her shoulder. "We had a deal. I promised you I wouldn't."

Maribelle scoffed at that. "Promises are often broken."

That was true enough, but Judy was still insulted. "I don't break *my* promises." Didn't Maribelle realize that Judy would never want any of this coming out, either? "Something else is going on here. What is it?"

The woman took her time answering, clearly not wanting to tell her. "My daughter has hired Colt Brothers Investigation to find her birth mother."

Judy felt gutted. She knew the Colt brothers. They'd already proven they would turn over every rock to solve other cases, including one cold case.

"You promised that no one would ever know," Judy said between clenched teeth.

"And I've tried to keep my promise. Don't you think I've done everything I could to stop Ansley? She is a stubborn young woman, mule headed and unyielding." Maribelle glared at her as if putting the blame on her. "So I ask you again, is there anything these PIs will find that will lead them to you—and ultimately to me?"

"Ansley?" Her name was Ansley? "I thought you promised to name her after her father like I asked?"

Maribelle waved a hand impatiently through the air. "Just answer the question. I don't have all day."

Judy felt sick to her stomach. Promises get broken? So it seemed. She was suddenly fueled with anger. This horrible woman. Why had she ever given her that precious baby? Guilt knifed into her heart. Money. Desperation. Greed. She swallowed down the bile that rose in her throat.

"I don't feel like I can trust you," she said, feeling as if she'd sold her soul to the devil.

Maribelle looked shocked. "Trust *me*?"

Furious and scared, she told herself she didn't want anything from this woman. If money changed hands, the Colt brothers would find out once she started spending it and come looking for her. One of the wives used to be a loan officer at the bank. They might already be looking for her, checking up on where she got the money to buy her house—money she'd said she inherited back then.

"Why should I tell you anything?" Judy demanded. "Our…arrangement is over. You didn't keep your promise—why should I?" She started to turn away. "Maybe I'll save the Colt brothers the bother of trying to find me and tell them what they want to know."

"I brought money."

She stopped and closed her eyes, her back to Maribelle. *Magic words*, she thought with so much pain that it almost doubled her over. Her life hadn't gone anything like she'd planned. Karma? Payback for what she'd done?

She'd sold her soul once. Was she really going to do it again?

Judy turned slowly, avoiding even looking at the woman. With enough money she could leave town and not look back. "How much money?" When Maribelle didn't answer, she finally faced her.

The gun surprised Judy. She hadn't been expecting it, but the experienced way Maribelle handled it surprised her even more. Judy looked from the weapon to the woman holding it. "You don't want to do that. I took out some insurance in case you ever—" But that's all she got out before she felt the hard slam of the bullet hit her chest. The shock of it made her tumble backward off the picnic table bench. As she fell, she grabbed for the edge of the table and felt a sliver slice into her hand. Her head hit the cracked concrete slab hard; lights flashed before her eyes as she fought to breathe.

As if the words she'd spoken had just now registered, Maribelle moved to stare down at her. "Insurance? What are you talking about?"

Judy tried to smile, not sure if her lips were moving or not. A strange coldness was seeping into her. Her words came out slurred as darkness intruded into her vision. "You're screwed." She didn't even feel the second shot or any of the others as Maribelle kept firing, screaming in frustration and fury, as she emptied the weapon into Judy's lifeless body.

Chapter 12

Ansley thought she'd feel like a bug under a microscope at James and Lori's dinner that night. While she was anxious to meet the rest of the family, she couldn't help being nervous about the invitation. She figured the wives were curious. She was curious about them as well, but she was also distracted even before Buck picked her up at the motel.

Before they'd headed out of town toward Colt Ranch, Buck had, at her request, swung by Judy Ramsey's place again. Still nobody home. Ansley feared the woman had heard she was looking for her and taken off. At lunch at the diner where she worked, they were told that she'd taken a few days off.

"You'll like them," Buck said as if reading her mind as he drove out toward the Colt Ranch. "They're nice people."

"James doesn't want to believe that I'm his sister. Even his half sister."

"He doesn't want to believe that his father had a child with a woman they'd never met, and he kept it a secret from them," Buck said.

"Even if I'm their half sister, I still have no idea who my birth mother is."

"That's why you hired the Colt brothers." He glanced over at her. "They're good. If anyone can find her, it's them."

"Maybe we already have found her and that's why she isn't around," Ansley said.

"Let's not go there until we know for sure. By the way, you look beautiful."

His last words made her glance over at him in surprise.

He grinned. "I wanted to say something when I picked you up. Didn't want to make you feel uncomfortable. Now I probably have."

She shook her head. "Thank you for the compliment." He went back to his driving, but she let her gaze linger on him a little longer. Surprisingly, she didn't feel uncomfortable in his presence. In fact, she was glad he'd be at the dinner tonight. She couldn't imagine facing the family alone. It wasn't like she could invite Gage.

Just the thought of him brought both regret and anger. He'd called her mother to warn her. He was in on it with them against her. Why was it that a complete stranger understood and was trying to help her when the man she'd agreed to marry had betrayed her?

Buck slowed the pickup and turned down a narrow dirt road. The truck's headlights cut a swath through the pines lining each side of the road. They hadn't gone far when the road climbed and a house, aglow with light, appeared against the mountainside.

The log-and-stone house looked so warm and inviting that she felt herself relax a little. As Buck parked and shut off the engine, he glanced over at her and said, "It's going to be fine."

She wasn't sure if he was referring to this dinner or all the rest, but his words helped. "I hope so," she said, surprised when he jumped out and went around to open her door for her as if they were on a date. It was so sweet and gentlemanly that she couldn't help but smile.

Maribelle was surprised to find Lanny Jackson waiting for her in the living room when she got back to the estate. "Where's Harrison?" she asked, looking around for her husband.

"He's still at work."

The man looked nervous. Had Harrison told him what she'd said about his bodyguard skills? Did she care? "Here." She thrust the box with the gun inside at him. "Get rid of it."

He started to open the box, but her words stopped him.

"You know what's inside. Just make sure it never turns up," she said and handed him a scrap of paper. "You'll need this."

He looked down at the address she'd written down for him and frowned. "What am I supposed to—"

"You'll know what you're supposed to do when you get there. Get rid of the body, and not a word to my husband or you'll be next."

Lanny looked as if he might balk. Or worse—go to Harrison.

She reached into her shoulder bag, glad she hadn't given the money to Judy. She pulled out half of the cash. If Lanny wanted more, she'd have it ready. If he dared. She thrust the bills at him as her cell phone rang. Waving him away, she turned and started for the stairs, leaving him standing in the foyer staring after her. "Oh, and if you tell my husband, I'll have your eyeballs cut out before I kill you." She glanced back and smiled. The scary thing was he smiled back.

She dismissed him from her mind as she took her husband's call.

"Where have you been?" Harrison demanded.

"Out. Is this about Ansley? Maybe you should talk to your lawyer—you know, be ready. You'll need to buy us a compassionate judge—"

"We don't have enough money to buy a judge for this, Maribelle," he snapped impatiently.

"I'm sure a lawyer will be able to advise us. Maybe I'll call the one that Charlotte Dryer got for her son."

"Please, let me handle it," he said. "I was afraid when I couldn't reach you and Lanny said you weren't home that you might have taken things into your own hands, as you often do."

"I don't want to argue. Could you ask around about sympathetic judges?"

"Maribelle." He apologized for raising his voice. "Please, just trust me."

"In other words, you're going to wait to see what happens. Honestly, Harrison, if this gets out and I'm ostracized by all of our friends, I'll never forgive you. Do you hear me?"

"All our friends?" he said with a sigh. "Who all

would that be? We don't have any real friends, Maribelle."

"What are you talking about?" she demanded as she
reached the second-floor landing and stopped to catch
her breath.

"Nothing. I'm just saying, let me handle it. I've gotten us this far, haven't I?" Silence then, "Mari?"

He hadn't called her that in years. She felt herself
soften. "What?" For a moment, she thought he was
going to say that he loved her. Did he still love her?

On the other end of the call, she heard him say, "I
have to go. I'm taking care of everything. You have to
trust me and do nothing. Can you do that?"

A little late for that, she thought as she glanced after
Lanny, hoping she could trust him. "Of course. I'm so
glad you're handling it."

In front of James and Lori's house, Buck offered
Ansley a hand as she climbed from the pickup, but as
he did, he noticed that she was no longer wearing her
engagement ring and froze for a moment. He saw her
flush as he raised his gaze to her face. Had she broken
off the engagement after what she'd learned about her
fiancé? It would be too bad if he didn't get a chance to
meet Gage.

He wanted to ask but was afraid of her answer.
Maybe she just forgot to put the ring back on. Although
he couldn't imagine her going through with a marriage
to the man after such a betrayal.

Lori met them at the door, all smiles, and ushered
them into the house. He could tell she was doing her
best not to stare at Ansley and make this any more uncomfortable than it was.

"Come on in," she said cheerfully. "We're all in the kitchen. Isn't that the way it always works?"

Within moments of entering the house, Ansley didn't know why she'd been nervous. Everyone was so welcoming. James's wife, Lori, introduced her to Tommy's wife, Bella, who handed her a glass of wine.

"This is Carla, Davy's bride," she said. "I'm sure they told you that Davy is on a case down in Wyoming. But you'll meet him soon."

Bella stopped and laughed. "One of us just has to say it, so I guess it's me. You have to be a Colt. The resemblance is just too much."

"I guess we'll see," Ansley said. "Once the DNA report comes back."

"Doesn't matter." Lori put an arm around her shoulders. "We've already made our decision. You're one of us."

The entire dinner was filled with laughter and stories about the Colt brothers as boys. It fascinated her, the kind of childhood they'd all had. They'd gotten to be kids, something she'd missed. With her, it was always, "Now don't you dare get anything on that dress!" Or if she had even a smudge, "Clean up this child—she's disgusting," on her mother's way out the door.

"What hellions they all were," Carla said. "Raised like a pack of wolves."

"We had the perfect childhood," James said.

Tommy agreed. "Just because we had a lot of freedom…"

"To get into trouble," Bella said.

"You should know," her husband said. "You were right there with me."

Ansley could see the love between Tommy and the

pregnant Bella. Same with Lori and James. "When are your babies due?"

"I've got months to go," Bella said. "But Lori could pop out those twin boys at any minute." They all laughed.

"Soon," Lori said. "At least, I hope it's soon. It's crowded in there, and they've been kicking up a storm."

Ansley felt as if she'd always known these people. More than ever, she wanted to be part of this family. She feared it would be a mistake to get her hopes up, though, knowing she would be crushed if their DNA wasn't a match.

Willie got the call in the middle of dinner. He excused himself and stepped away from the table, mouthing it was work to his wife. Ellie, as he'd always called her, even though her name was actually Eleanor. She nodded and smiled to him, clearly used to this by now as he left the dining room.

He went outside into the spring night. It was early enough in the season that the air was brisk and smelled of pine and new pasture grasses. The sky overhead had filled with stars that now sparkled against an endless, deep blue backdrop. The rising moon rimmed the jagged, dark silhouette of the mountains to the east with gold, while to the west he could see dark clouds. Another spring storm.

"A group of teenagers found a body in a ditch out on the old river road," his deputy told him when he returned the call. "They recognized her. It's Judy Ramsey. She's been shot. A bunch of times, from what I could see. Coroner took her down to the medical center morgue. Pete said the body had been dumped there. Definitely not the crime scene. No tracks other than the ones made by the teenagers. He's going to do the autopsy in the morning."

"Thanks for letting me know," Willie said. "Come daylight, we'll search the area." Though he wondered what good it would do. The teenagers would tell their friends, even though he was sure the deputy had warned them not to. By now, half the town could have driven out there to see the spot.

He shook his head as he disconnected. Judy Ramsey. Lonesome was small enough that most everyone knew each other. Judy had worked as a waitress for years down at the diner. She lived in a small, older house on the west edge of town.

Nothing more he could do tonight, he thought as he went back inside. Still, he wondered who would want to kill Judy Ramsey and dump her body out there off that old highway.

As he started to pocket his phone, he saw the text from the jewelry and engraving store. His day off had gotten crazy after that. He'd forgotten the woman had promised to send the information to him.

He stopped walking to stare at the printing on the form and the signature. The clerk had been right. It was impossible to read. But someone had scribbled in a blank space at the middle of the receipt. *Call...* with a number.

Willie felt his heart rocket in his chest. He knew that number, even though he hadn't seen it in ten years. It was his father's. Del Ransom Colt had bought a necklace for his daughter before she was born and had it engraved with the name DelRae.

Ansley couldn't remember enjoying a night more. The Colt family had been so welcoming, the food delicious, and Buck, well, he'd been sweet and supportive. He didn't glance at his phone once—unlike Gage, who was usually glued to his mobile screen.

She stole a look at him, amazed at the circumstances that had brought this cowboy into her life. They'd grown close in a matter of days. She realized that she would trust him with her life and quickly reminded herself that she was just a distraction. She shouldn't read more into it than it was.

Yet she'd never been more aware of a man. The cab of his pickup felt intimate, the darkness beyond the headlights making her feel as if they were the only two people in the world. She fought the urge to lay her head on his broad shoulder and close her eyes as she savored this night.

"Did you have fun?" Buck asked as he drove down the narrow road bordered by tall pines, the boughs black against the midnight blue of the sky overhead.

"I did." She couldn't help smiling. She'd been so nervous, and for no reason, as it turned out. "They are so nice." Her voice broke.

He reached over and took her hand, squeezing it. "I know. I always wanted to be a Colt, too. Fortunately, they adopted me into their family. They're all pretty amazing."

She nodded, afraid to speak for fear it would come out a sob. She'd tried so hard not to get her hopes up. But after tonight, she wanted more than ever for the DNA test results to prove that she was right about what she was feeling. That these were her people. She knew it might not be anything more than wishful thinking on her part. But if she could wish upon a star tonight and make it come true…

"James told me that he's put a rush on the DNA test," he said. "I know the waiting is rough, but we'll know soon."

A part of her wanted to put it off as long as possible for fear that the results would show she was wrong, she thought as he pulled up in front of her motel room door. The night was dark, only a few stars peeking out of the low clouds. The neon motel sign on the highway buzzed, several letters burned-out. It did little to hold back the darkness.

Buck parked and got out, going around the front of the pickup to open her door. It had felt like a date all night. She'd felt such a rush of warmth whenever she looked at him and found him looking back, smiling. *Don't get attached*, she told herself. *Not to the Colts, definitely not to Buck Crawford. Your life is miles away, and when this over, even if you are a Colt...*

As he opened her door, he took her arm. She stepped out and directly into his arms. She looked up into his eyes in surprise. What she saw there made her heart hammer in her chest and her breath catch. It happened so quickly, she wasn't sure who initiated the kiss—just that she found herself pulled even closer, her lips parting, her whole body wanting this.

"Buck." The word came out as a breathless plea as she looked into his eyes and drew back, shaken by her body's reaction to the kiss.

Buck immediately held up his hands in surrender as their gazes locked. "I'm sorry. I don't know what I was—" He let out a curse. "No, I'm not sorry." Before he could stop himself, he closed the space between them again and pulled her into his arms. This time there was nothing tentative about the kiss. It was all passion, all desire, all need.

He felt her open up to him, heard a whispered groan as her body came to his with a need almost matching his own. He deepened the kiss, drawing her up against him, feeling her soft, full breasts against his chest, desperately wanting to sweep her up and carry her inside and make love to her.

But she wasn't his. Not yet. He drew back from the kiss. "I've wanted to do that almost from the moment I laid eyes on you." His gaze bored into hers. But now, after having her in his arms, feeling her respond to his mouth on hers, he wanted a damned sight more, and that scared the bejesus out of him.

He could see her trembling, as if she was as unsteady on her feet as he was. But he could also see the heat of desire in her eyes, even as she took a step back. "I'm the one who's sorry. I shouldn't have let myself get carried away like that. I'm *engaged*." The last word sounded strangled.

"Are you?" He glanced at her bare finger. "Are you still planning to marry him?"

Ansley took a breath and let it out slowly before her gaze locked with his again. "So much has happened so fast. I... I feel as if I can't trust any of my feelings."

He cocked his head at her and then laughed. "Boy howdy. I'm the one who should be pulling back the reins, yelling whoa." He dragged off his Stetson and raked a hand through his hair. "The last woman I fell in love with turned out to be a psychopath. She damned near killed me. I swore..." He didn't finish that thought. "I should get you inside. I can feel a storm coming."

"Buck." What had she planned to say? Hadn't the

way she'd kissed him said it all? She moved toward her motel room, still seeming unsteady on her feet. He had felt her passion, seen it in her eyes. He mentally kicked himself for his impulsive behavior. It wasn't like him.

He watched her open the motel room door and go inside. She hesitated for a moment at the door, as if wanting to say something, but then quickly closed it. He heard her turn the lock.

Turning, he walked back to his pickup, fighting the mix of emotions coursing through him. He'd thrown caution to the wind. What had he been thinking? Of course he was attracted to her. She was beautiful. He'd wanted to kiss her and make love to her, but that hadn't been coming from his head. She was the last thing he needed. To make matters worse, his future was up in the air right now. What would a woman like her want with an unemployed cowboy with a saddlebag full of baggage from his past?

Chapter 13

Ansley stepped into her motel room, closed the door and leaned against it. Her whole body tingled. She could feel the weight of her breasts, the nipples hard and aching. The kiss had taken her by surprise, but not just because it had been unexpected. She felt her face heat at the memory of how she'd kissed him back.

The passion she'd felt. Where had that come from? She'd never felt that kind of intensity, that kind of need with Gage. But then, he'd never kissed her like that. She closed her eyes, remembering the feel of her body against Buck's. She'd never wanted anyone the way she had the cowboy.

Just the thought of his words… His confession, his desire for her. How had she let this happen? She was still engaged. She barely knew this cowboy. She couldn't trust the emotions raging through her right now.

Yet no one had ever kissed her like that. No one had ever made her feel like that.

Ansley told herself that she needed sleep and blamed the magic of the night for her confused feelings. Dinner with the Colts had been so enjoyable. She couldn't remember when she'd had that much fun. That's how she'd ended up in Buck's arms. She'd been caught up in all these new feelings.

She still felt so worked up, she doubted she was going to be able to sleep even after her shower. She kept going over the night, wrapped in the warmth of the Colt family. As she got ready for bed, she reminded herself that she might not be a Colt. That when the DNA results came back, it could burst this bubble she was in right now. Climbing into bed, she tried not to think about what would happen if she wasn't really part of the Colt family.

Realizing she was trying to think about anything but Buck Crawford, she turned her thoughts to the mystery woman she was searching for. She still didn't know who her birth mother was. Or her father, for that matter. Del Ransom Colt? Maybe not. She thought about Judy Ramsey. Was she her birth mother? Tomorrow, she would go by the woman's house again.

Maybe she was getting close to solving this, she thought as she lay in the darkness staring up at the cracked ceiling of the old motel room. Her thoughts kept circling back to dinner tonight, though, and the Colts and Buck and his kisses.

Had he been caught up in the magic of the night as well? Was that why he'd kissed her, why he'd said what he did? She told herself that he would feel differently in the morning. They would probably both pretend the kisses had never happened.

Just as she was starting to drift off, she heard footfalls outside her door. She froze as they were followed, closer, by a whispered noise. As the footfalls retreated, she turned on the light and saw that someone had pushed an envelope under her door.

Buck found James waiting for him at the office. He'd said he needed to talk to him but privately after dinner. He'd suggested they meet at the office. Kissing Ansley still simmering in his blood and his brain, he took a chair across the big oak desk from James. He felt as if he'd taken a beating today. He should go home to the ranch, but he had to know what was up. "Any word on who was driving the pickup borrowed from Mark's lot?"

"He said he talked to his wife. She lent the pickup to Penny Graves down at city hall. You know her?"

Buck nodded. "Why would she borrow it?"

"Said her rig was broke down and needed it to get to work. Said she left the keys in it, parked outside city hall, because she thought Mark was going to pick it up. Sounds like someone borrowed it. Mark says it's back on the lot."

"Why would Penny Graves follow Ansley to Bozeman?" he asked, more to himself than James.

"Doubt she would. Could have been anyone driving it, even some kid just screwing around."

"I suppose," Buck said. "Unless she borrowed the pickup for someone else."

James rose. "I'm glad you stopped by. I wanted to talk to you," his friend said. "Come on." He led Buck upstairs, stopping just long enough to pull a couple of beers from the apartment refrigerator before taking the stairs to the roof.

James handed him a beer and motioned to one of the folding beach chairs. Only a few lights lit the main drag of Lonesome. Residents often joked that the sidewalks rolled up early in the evening when they described Lonesome. Behind the town, the dense pines added their scents to the night breeze.

Buck had to smile as he opened his beer, took a seat and stared up at the darkening night sky filled with stars. He and his friends had come up here often as teens. He'd missed those nights. He pulled off his Stetson, set it aside and leaned back as he took a drink of the cold beer. After the day he'd had, it tasted wonderful. And it was clear that James had something on his mind.

"As you know, when I came back to town, mostly to heal from my last rodeo ride, and got involved with Dad's last investigation, I didn't have plans to be a private investigator," his friend began. "Even when I got hooked on the job, I never thought I could make a go of it. Then Tommy wanted in and then Davy..."

Buck started to speak, but James cut him off. "The point is, Colt Brothers Investigation has taken off. We're getting calls from all over the Northwest. We could use help from someone who is more qualified than any of us."

"You know someone like that?" Buck asked, tongue in cheek.

"I'm serious. You don't want to raise rough stock, even if your dad and brother needed your help, and I suspect you don't want to be a highway patrolman again. Am I right?"

Buck looked down at his boots. "I appreciate the offer, but—"

"You'd be doing us a favor. I did save your life that time." His old friend looked up and grinned.

"I was wondering how long it would be before you cashed in on that," Buck said.

"How about you try it out for a while?" James suggested. "See if you like it. See if you like working with us." He shrugged. "Either way, no hard feelings. Debt paid." He grinned to let him know he was kidding about the debt. "I was hoping you'd work the Ansley Brookshire case with us." He gave Buck a side-eye. "Unless you aren't interested."

Buck chuckled. "I admit it's tempting, but maybe that's why I should give it a wide berth."

James shook his head. "You need to forgive yourself for falling in love with the wrong woman."

He snorted at that. "If anyone should have known better, it was me."

It was James's turn to laugh. "What makes you so much smarter than the rest of us when it comes to women?"

"Because I was a cop," he snapped. "A damned good one, I'm told. I should have seen it. I should have sensed it. I should have heard it the moment she opened her mouth."

"Yep, psychopaths have such obvious tells."

Buck took a drink of his beer, licking the foam from his lips. The midnight blue canvas was alive with stars. A breeze stirred his hair. When had he let it get so long? Not that it mattered. He'd come home to the ranch, his safe place, and yet the woman of his nightmares had followed him, reminding him that he would never be free of her. Look how suspicious he was of Ansley Brook-shire. How could he ever trust his judgment when it came to anyone—especially women—ever again?

"You'll get past it," James said quietly, his gaze sky-ward.

Buck didn't express his doubts. He didn't have to. His friend knew him too well.

"Why do you think Willie never wanted to fall in love? Then he met Ellie. You think I wasn't terrified of the feelings Lori stirred up in me?" James chuckled. "Everything about it was wrong, and at the worst time of my life, I thought." He glanced over at Buck. "You're dealing with a lot. Almost dying does something to you, no doubt about that. Willie almost drowned twice. Who knows if he'll ever go back in the water." He laughed. "But he loves the hell out of Ellie. That he'll never re-gret."

Buck shook his head, unable to imagine surrender-ing to that kind of love. "I thought we were talking about a job."

"We are. You need something to challenge you. But we also could use your help with this case, especially going up against Harrison Brookshire. You know Lone-some and this county. We're pretty sure that Ansley wasn't born in a hospital. That means either a home birth or a midwife. Someone in this town knows."

"By the way, Ansley and I talked to Toni down at the yarn shop again. She thinks Judy Ramsey bought the yarn. We went by her house. She wasn't around. You want me to keep beating the bushes?"

James shook his head. "I want you to make sure An-sley is okay. She trusts you. I have faith in you keeping her safe until we get to the bottom of this."

That made him want to laugh. He wasn't sure she was safe at all around him. He knew damned well that he wasn't safe with her. "After tonight, you have to know there is no getting rid of her—even if it turns out your DNA doesn't match. The wives all loved her. They've already adopted her into the family," Buck said.

"The women definitely did take to her," James said. "Ansley Brookshire is quite captivating, but then, I don't have to tell you that, do I."

Buck stared up at the stars, enjoying the Montana spring evening even though it was far from warm. He drank his beer and thought about Ansley in his arms, his mouth on hers. He was already in over his head, in deep in this when it came to the woman—and that worried the hell out of him.

Ansley froze for a moment at the sight of the white envelope lying just inside her door. She listened but heard no sound outside her motel room. Why hadn't she jumped up, run to open the door and tried to see who'd left it? Because she was wearing nothing but one of the large, worn T-shirts she slept in—not to mention that she'd been too surprised to react.

It might be something from Buck. Apologizing for kissing her? Seemed unlikely. Or something from one of the Colts. Maybe news.

Frowning, she stepped toward the white envelope and bent down to pick it up. She felt a shiver and knew it wasn't from Buck or the Colts about her case. It was something else, something she felt instinctively that she wasn't going to like.

She turned the envelope over. It wasn't sealed. She slowly lifted the flap. There appeared to be a single sheet of note paper inside. She carefully pulled it out, trying not to leave her fingerprints. As it fell open, she caught sight of the words inside. The letters appeared to have been cut from a magazine.

GO HoMe bEfORe iTs ToO lATe

She stared at the words, her heart in her throat, before she carried the note over to the small desk and dropped both the note and the envelope. Her first instinct was to call Buck, but she'd relied on him too much already. James? She glanced at the time. Too late. It would keep until tomorrow. But she had to admit she was scared. She'd never dreamed that looking for her birth mother would elicit this kind of response.

What she couldn't understand was who was behind this—and why. Judy Ramsey? Had Toni or someone else warned her that Ansley wanted to see her? There was no way Maribelle would take the time to cut out each letter and glue it to a sheet of note paper—let alone drive to Lonesome to shove it under her motel room door. In the first place, her adoptive mother wouldn't know where she was staying.

But someone did. Lanny Jackson? Didn't seem his style. Then who?

She closed her eyes for a moment, unable to accept that maybe her birth mother didn't want to be found. She'd given up her baby to Maribelle. That alone told Ansley that the woman might have cared enough to learn to knit and make her a baby blanket and buy a few clothes, but ultimately, she hadn't wanted her. Was she now worried that her daughter was about to expose her secret?

Ansley realized she had no idea who was threatening her or how serious they might be. She checked the lock on the motel room door and shoved a chair under the knob. There was no chance she was going to get any sleep.

On the drive home to the ranch, Buck got the call. He'd been mentally kicking himself, not just for kissing Ansley but for telling her how badly he'd want to kiss her. He wouldn't be surprised if she wanted nothing more to do with him. He was a bigger fool than even he thought if he lost the job with the Colt brothers. He wanted it—at least temporarily.

"Didn't you tell me that Toni's sure the woman who bought the yarn was Judy Ramsey?" James asked. Buck could hear Tommy and Davy arguing in the background, with Willie trying to break them up.

"She's pretty sure, why?"

"Willie's here. Judy Ramsey was found murdered earlier tonight. Shot, and more than once."

Buck slowed the pickup as he took in this information. "You think it's possible that she's Ansley birth mother and this is somehow connected?"

"I don't know. But I'll tell Willie and the others what you told me. If Ansley really is our half sister…" James sighed. "Dad and Judy?" In the background, Buck heard Willie telling him not to jump to conclusions. "Talk in the morning."

"Yeah, and James…? I'll take the job. At least temporarily. If it's okay with Ansley."

"Right. Glad to hear that."

He had a bad thought. "I left Ansley at the motel. She should be safe, right?"

"I'll ask Willie to have a deputy drive by during the night," James said.

He disconnected, his thoughts whirling. Judy Ramsey was dead. Murdered. He thought of how Harrison and Maribelle Brookshire had been one step ahead of them thanks to the tracking devices they'd put on their daughter's phone and SUV with the help of her fiancé.

Had Judy Ramsey been killed because he and Ansley wanted to talk to her? If so, they'd had Lanny Jackson take care of it, he told himself. He wondered when he and the burly bodyguard would cross paths again. Soon, he figured, hoping he would be ready as he drove the rest of the way to the ranch.

As he parked and climbed out of his pickup, he spotted his father sitting in the dark on the porch. "Have a nice night?" Wendell Crawford asked as Buck climbed the steps to join him.

He nodded and sat down in one of the porch chairs next to him to look out at the darkness. He could smell the coming thunderstorm on the night air and feel the chill.

"You've been spending quite a lot of time in town lately," his father said. "Makes me wonder if there's a woman who's caught your eye."

Buck chuckled. His father could read him like an open book and always had. "I'm helping James with a case, and yes, there is a woman involved." Out of the corner of his eye, he saw the older man nod and knew he must have heard the scuttlebutt.

"I suspected it might be something like that," his dad said. "Heard a little about it from a breeder who stopped by. A young woman looking for her birth mother."

Still, he couldn't believe the way news traveled in this county. Ranches could be miles from town, and yet word managed to get there. He wondered how much his father had heard. "James offered me a job. Temporarily, while I figure some things out." He knew his father had been worried about him. "I've taken it."

"To work on this case." Wendell Crawford nodded and picked up his iced tea from the small table next to his chair to take a drink. "There's more tea if you're interested."

"I'm fine. Not sure how much you've heard, but she could be related to the Colts." Silence from his father. "You were friends with Del Ransom Colt," he said, not sure how to ask what he needed to know. "After his wife died, was there someone else?"

"He was pretty busy raising four boys."

Buck gave him a side-eye. "*Raising* might not be the right word. You didn't deny that there might have been a woman."

"Not necessarily. Some of us, when we've had the best, we know we can never love another woman like that again. So we don't try."

Buck would love for his father to find someone again. His mother had been gone for seven years now, but while he couldn't see his father marrying again, Buck would have liked for him to at least have a female companion.

"This woman thinks she's your friends' half sister, I heard," Wendell said.

"We're waiting on the DNA test results, but the first time I saw her, there was something so familiar about her. There's something else." He hesitated. "You'll hear about this soon enough. Judy Ramsey was found murdered tonight. There's a chance she's the birth mother."

His father took a sip of his iced tea, seemed to give it some thought before he put down the glass and said, "My first instinct is that Del wouldn't have gotten involved again—especially that quickly. Isn't this woman claiming to be their sister about Davy's age?" Buck nodded. "But maybe I'm going with my own feeling after I lost your mother." His father shook his head. "No one could replace her. But as for Del…" He chuckled. "Can't see him with Judy Ramsey, though. But then I couldn't see him with Penny Graves, either."

"Penny Graves? The woman who works at the mayor's office?" Interesting, since whoever had followed Ansley to Brookshire Estate in the borrowed pickup had been from the mayor's office, apparently.

His father nodded slowly. "I don't like spreading rumors, but if I hadn't seen them together myself… I guess he and Penny were seen together more than a few times." Buck heard the hesitation in his father's voice and waited. "If they had a relationship, it was a rocky one, from what I saw. You think Penny could be this young woman's mother?"

"That's just it—we have no idea at this point." He sat for a few minutes, listening to the night sounds. "I suppose there are always women who are interested in a widower," Buck said, thinking of his father now more than Del.

Wendell laughed. "Some believe they can make you love again, heal your heart, fill that place. They bring pies and casseroles. They do their best to catch your eye. Most are just lonely. Believe it or not, there were even some who set their sights on me, and I'm not half as good-looking or exciting as Del Colt."

Buck laughed. "I've seen how Angie Fredericks always saves you a spot next to her at church and Emily Larson brings your favorite bars for after the service. You've still got it."

His father chuckled to himself. "None of them can hold a candle to your mother. Not their fault. Just not interested. But Del… His wife was sick for so long, in and out of the hospital. He was sole guardian to those boys. He had to have been lonely, though, needing someone. How far it went, who knows."

"Can you think of anyone else Del might have been involved with?" Buck asked, seeing that his father had someone in mind.

Wendell shook his head before turning to him. "I'm more worried about the woman in your life than Del's," his father said changing the subject. "Just be careful. Mind your heart, son. Since you were a boy, you always tried to help anyone in need, anyone in trouble. You brought home everything from birds with broken wings to stray dogs and cats that looked hungry."

"If you're saying I'm a bleeding heart… Ansley Brookshire is far from a stray cat. And I don't have designs on her."

His father laughed. "I'm just saying you're a wonderful son with a big heart and a lot of compassion for others. Those are not shortcomings." He finished his tea and rose, taking the empty glass with him. "But like you said, until you get the DNA results, you can't even be sure who this woman is. She might not be related to anyone in the county—maybe especially the Colts." He felt his father's gaze on him. "But that isn't going to make a difference to you, is it."

Chapter 14

Ansley came out of a deep, dark sleep filled with nightmares. She sat bolt upright in bed. Scared, she frantically searched the small motel room before she realized her cell was ringing and that's what had awakened her.

She glanced at her phone next to her bed and the time. Who would be calling this early? Buck? James? Had something happened? "Hello?" She felt a jolt as she heard Gage's voice.

"We need to talk."

She couldn't help think about all the messages she'd left him and her attempts to reach him yesterday. "At this hour? What's wrong?"

"How can you even ask that?" he demanded. "Do you know what you're doing to me?"

She groaned inwardly. Seriously? This was about her

finding her birth mother? This really wasn't the time, not after her scare last night with the threatening note.

"This really has nothing to do with you." The moment the words were out of her mouth, she regretted them. Buck had made her question Gage's loyalty to her. Not that she hadn't worried that he'd called her mother to warn her about the photo. She hadn't wanted to believe it. Still didn't. It was just a photo. A photo that wasn't even proof.

"Nothing to do with me?" He sounded both shocked and hurt.

"You know what I mean."

"No, I don't think I do. Just open the door so we can talk face-to-face."

Open the door? She glanced at her motel room door. "Where are you?" she asked, her voice strained at the thought that he was out there.

"Right outside."

Had he been out there last night, shoving an envelope under her door?

"You tracked me down?" Now fully awake, she felt a rush of anger.

"Ansley, please. Just open the door. I drove all the way up here to talk to you—and not through a motel room door."

She disconnected. He'd tracked her down without the help of the tracking devices Buck had removed. Or were there others he'd missed?

Still stunned and upset, she slid out of bed and quickly pulled on clothes before going to the door and throwing it open. Gage stood just outside, looking impatient and out of sorts. "What are you doing here?" she demanded.

"Hoping to talk some sense into you," he snapped as he pushed past her and into the room.

Ansley felt her hackles rise as she closed the door and turned to face him. Fiancé or not, she felt bullied, and she didn't like it. "You could have called before driving up, and I would have saved you the trip."

His expression softened. "I'm sorry. I've just been so worried about you." He glanced around the sparse furnishings of the motel room. "This was the best you could do?"

"Gage—"

He held up his hands. "Sorry, but could we at least get out of this depressing room and go across the street to that café? I could use some coffee. We can talk. You can tell me what's going on with you."

She took a breath and let it out. Coffee right now sounded good. She also felt strangely uncomfortable in this motel room with him—as uncomfortable as he looked. "Just give me a minute. You can wait outside if it makes you feel better." He nodded, and she went into the bathroom to freshen up.

All she could think about was that she'd kissed Buck and now Gage was here. She felt disloyal, and yet she wasn't sorry about the kiss, which made her feel worse. Gage was *here*. She was trying to get her mind around that. She thought about the note pushed under her door. Had he driven up this morning? Or did he come up last night?

She hated even thinking that he might have lied about that.

As she stepped out of the bathroom, she was surprised to see that Gage hadn't gone outside. He was standing next to her bed, holding the framed photograph of the Colt brothers. "What are you doing in my purse?"

"I saw the edge of the frame sticking out. I was curious." He held it up, then reached for the one of her that he'd also taken out of her purse. "This is the photo you just had to have from the house?"

"If you compare the two…"

Gage frowned. "Compare them why?" He swore. "You think you're related to these…these…boys?"

She instantly felt the need to defend the Colts. "They're successful men now."

"I hope they discovered soap." Shaking his head, he met her gaze. "You don't really want to be related to some backwoods cowboys rather than accept Maribelle and Harrison Brookshire as your family, do you?"

"I want to know the truth." She stepped to the end table where she'd left her shoulder bag. Picking it up, she reached for the framed photos. "Do you really not see the resemblance from the photo when I was five?" He shook his head, looking at her as if she'd lost her mind. "Then why was it that you and Maribelle were so determined that I not take it?"

He stared at her blankly. "What are you talking about?"

"That photo in your hand of me. It's the one I told you I was getting from the house. But when I arrived, the photo wasn't where it was always kept. Maribelle had hidden it right before I got there. You called her and told her I was coming, didn't you?"

"I don't even remember you mentioning a photograph. I was at work. I was busy. I certainly didn't remember some photo of you when you were five. You think I called your mother?"

She heard the answer in his voice, in his overworked denial. She glared at him. "Give me the photos."

He did, though reluctantly. "You don't know what

you're saying. You know how you are before you have your coffee in the morning. Come on—I didn't come here to argue. I really wanted to see you and find out what's going on."

Ansley ground her teeth. She'd just bet he did, since Buck had removed the tracking devices from her phone and vehicle. It wouldn't have been that hard for him to find her, since her SUV was parked right outside and the motel was on the main drag.

But she told herself that he was right about one thing. Coffee. She needed it before she said what she really thought.

Neither of them spoke again until the waitress put two cups of coffee and menus in front of them at a booth in the corner of the café. They both drank, avoiding each other's gazes for a few minutes. When she finally looked at him, she saw the truth on his face as clearly as she saw it in his rumpled suit. "You lied about calling my mother about the photo, and you didn't drive up this morning."

He started to argue, then seemed to change his mind. "Everything I've done was for your own good." He rushed on as he saw her angry expression. "I don't think you realize the damage you are doing to your life. You have two amazing parents who wanted you and gave you everything. How can you throw all that away for some fantasy family? How can you afford to?"

"I started my business without any help from them." She'd begun making jewelry at a young age, selling it to friends. The business had kept growing along with her skills. "I made a success out of it on my own. I can afford to do whatever I want."

"Yes, yes, I know. You're a self-made woman. You've

told me that enough times. Whereas I work for my father. You must think I'm a real sellout, huh."

"I'm not the one telling you how to live your life."

His face flushed for a moment as the waitress refilled their cups and left. He took a drink of his coffee, setting the cup down a little too hard and splashing some on the table. He grabbed a napkin and began to dab at the spill. "Maybe I don't want to always work for my father. Maybe I haven't had the privileges you have taken for granted. Maybe someday I'd like a helping hand up, since I'm not as…talented as you are."

She took a sip of her coffee before she said, "Let's be clear, you're talking about my inheritance."

He met her gaze, both hands wrapped around his coffee cup. "See, that's exactly what I mean. You've always had anything you wanted, so it's easy for you to scoff at a fortune."

"I didn't have everything I always wanted. I actually wanted a family like yours."

His laugh was laced with bitterness. "You don't have a clue."

"Maybe not," she agreed after consuming more coffee. She could feel the caffeine doing its job. She was waking up more—and not just from a night's sleep. "But I am starting to see a lot of things more clearly." She held his gaze, seeing the real Gage Sheridan. He'd always been impressed by the Brookshire lifestyle. Clearly, he wanted it more than he wanted anything else—her included. "As a matter of fact, I've needed to talk to you, so I'm glad you drove up. Slept in your car, did you?"

He didn't deny it. He must have been parked down the street, waiting for her to come back from her dinner. Had he seen the kisses between her and Buck? Or had he fallen asleep and that's why she hadn't known he was here until this morning? No, she thought, he'd woken up just long enough to slide the envelope under her door. He must have had his assistant at work cut and glue the letters from the magazine, though. Unless it really had been from someone else.

She reached into her purse, dug to the bottom and pulled out the engagement ring. "All of this has made me realize—"

"What the hell?" He seemed to start as he stared at her left hand, then at the ring she put down on the table between them. "When did you stop wearing your engagement ring?" His gaze flew back to her face. "Is this about that cowboy? I saw the two of you last night."

"Seems you have been keeping track of me for some time," she said. "That cowboy is a former law officer. He found the tracking devices on my SUV and on my phone. But you wouldn't know anything about that, right?"

"No." He shook his head, his Adam's apple working furiously. "You are not breaking up with me. Your mother's right. You've lost your mind and need professional help. She wanted to get you locked up, but I told her I would try to talk some sense into you—"

"My mind is just fine." She realized with a jolt that she hadn't seen the threatening note where she'd left it on the desk back in the motel. "Did you take that note that was in my room?"

He frowned. "Why would I take—"

She cursed under her breath as she got to her feet. "You can tell Maribelle that I'm just fine. As for you... The engagement is off. Please don't ever contact me again."

He glanced at the ring, then at her, and shook his head. "You'll change your mind. You'll see that everything I've done was to save you. You wouldn't be happy with some cowboy."

"Not that it is your business any longer," she said, thinking of Buck's kiss. It wasn't about the cowboy. The kiss had only made her more confident that Gage wasn't the man for her. She just hadn't admitted it to herself after he'd been against her finding her birth mother. She'd known then that he didn't understand her need—or care. He'd only been worried about her getting cut out of the Brookshire inheritance.

Her cell phone rang. She saw it was James.

"Don't answer it," Gage snapped. "We aren't done here."

"Hello, James," she said into the phone, stepping back as her ex-fiancé tried to take the phone from her hand. She turned her back on him. "The DNA test results are back? I'll be right there." She disconnected and turned to look at Gage.

He had his phone out but now pocketed it. He looked flushed, as if she'd caught him texting someone behind her back.

"I'm sure you've already let them know, but just in case you haven't, I'm going to find out the truth," she said. "You and Maribelle and Harrison are going to have to accept it."

He shook his head. "You're making a huge mistake."

"No, I did that when I agreed to marry you," she said and walked out.

Willie entered the local medical center, anxious to talk to the coroner. The center served the community with limited staff and also provided a morgue and autopsy room in the basement.

He nodded to the physician's assistant who was busy stitching up a teenage boy in the ER and headed for the basement. He found the coroner standing in front of a metal table on which Judy Ramsey's body now rested. Was this woman Ansley's birth mother? It sure looked that way. Earlier, Tommy had called to tell him that nearly twenty-nine years ago, Judy Ramsey had come into enough money to put a down payment on the old house she lived in on the edge of town.

"Mornin', Pete," he said as he stepped into the room, but kept his distance. He didn't want to have to suit up unless necessary. "Gunshot wounds?"

"Looks like five from a .45. I've been able to retrieve one." He pointed to a small metal dish with a blood-coated slug lying in it. "All the shots were close range. No defensive wounds."

"So more than likely she knew her killer," Willie said. "Any idea where she was killed?"

"Outside. There was caked dirt on the bottom of her shoes, different from the soil where the body was dumped." The sheriff raised an eyebrow. "I know my dirt," Pete said. "She was killed closer to the river." Willie didn't doubt that Pete knew what he was talking about, since he'd trained in forensics before moving to Lonesome to semiretire. "She wasn't dressed for an early-spring swim in the river. Had she been to work that day?"

Willie shook his head. "She'd injured her leg at work, was off for a while."

"She was wearing makeup—more than she usually wore at the café," Pete said.

Willie took that in as he marveled at how observant the man was. "A date out by the river?"

"Could be." Pete picked up a small glass dish. "She had a splinter in her hand. The wood is weathered but has some old green paint on it, like from a picnic table."

"I'll have my deputies look for old, weathered once-green picnic tables down that way," the sheriff said. "What else can you tell me?"

"She broke her arm when she was young, after all these years on her feet, she has varicose veins, and she's been through menopause and had a terrible diet."

Willie shook his head, chuckling. "Can you tell me if she gave birth? There's a woman looking for her mother." He'd been joking so was surprised when Pete looked up.

"This woman has never given birth to a child."

He stared at him. "You can be that sure?"

The coroner nodded. "Sorry, but she's not the woman you're looking for."

Willie's cell phone rang. He excused himself and took the call out in the hall. Deputy Chris Fraser sounded excited. "We have her DNA. Judy Ramsey's. From when she was arrested for a DUI. Do you want me to let the lab know?"

"Thanks, but it won't be necessary now." He told him to take another deputy and drive along the old river road looking for a weathered once-green wooden picnic table. "There's a good chance it's the murder scene."

His phone rang. Willie got as far as his patrol SUV when a call came in from Chris. He was anxious to get to Bozeman, worried about Buck and Ansley.

"Judy Ramsey's neighbor says Judy left a letter with her years ago," the deputy told him. "She thinks it might be important—thinks Judy was worried about someone killing her. I didn't open the envelope, just put it in an evidence bag. I'm at your office."

"I'm on my way," Willie said and drove the few blocks to the sheriff's department. As he walked in, the deputy held up an evidence bag with a yellowed envelope inside. Taking it, he saw that Judy had apparently written "In Case I'm Dead" on the outside.

The deputy said, "Didn't even touch it. I had her drop it into the bag."

Willie nodded and took it into his office. Taking gloves from his drawer, he pulled them on and opened the bag to take out the letter. The handwriting was sloppy, as if she'd been hurried, many of the words misspelled. But still, he didn't have any trouble understanding what was written.

The first two lines sent his pulse pounding.

DelRae, if you red this, I'm so sorry. I shoold never have gave you to that woman. There is a place in hell wating for me. After what I did. Things didn't go rite. I thought it was the best thing. No one wood get hurt—until I found out I wasn't pregnant. Female promblems.

I was despurate. She'd given me $50,000 for a baby girl. What was I goin todo? I coudn't tell her the truth. I did what I had to do. I told meself I was helpin out someone in trouble. That I was savin the baby.

Now I'm scard. I don't trust her. I swor I'd nevr tell, but I don't think she beleeves me.

That's why I'm writin this down. Mariblle Brookshire will kill me to keep the secret. But the laugh is on her. She don't even no that the baby I sold her want even mine. No one nos.

His heart hammered against his ribs as he reread it. No mistaking the words. Judy Ramsey had sold a baby to Maribelle Brookshire, a baby she'd called DelRae. But if she hadn't been pregnant, then where did she get a baby? And why name the infant DelRae—after her father?

There was a large missing piece of this puzzle—Del-Rae's mother, the one who'd given birth to her.

Meanwhile, Willie had to deal with the information he had. Judy Ramsey was dead and had named Maribelle as her killer. But why kill her? Because Ansley was searching for her birth mother and Maribelle was determined that Ansley never find her. He thought about James saying that Judy's name kept coming up in the investigation. It was just a matter of time before they ended up at her door to question her. Maribelle must have realized that.

Judy's fears had apparently been warranted. If Maribelle had killed her. Willie let out a curse. What the hell was he going to do with this? He knew that the letter wouldn't be enough evidence. Not against Mrs. Harrison Brookshire.

He thought of Ansley and how she was going to take this news. Willie pulled out his phone and called the county attorney. "We have a big problem. I'm on my way over." He bagged the letter again, afraid none of this would hold up in court against a Brookshire.

He'd barely disconnected when he got another call. He saw it was his brother James. "What's up?"

Ansley felt the tension in the room the moment she walked in the Colt Brothers Investigation office. James was sitting behind the big oak desk. Tommy and Davy had pulled up five chairs in front of it and taken two of them. Buck had been waiting by the door. As Ansley sat down in one chair, Buck took the chair next to her.

After a few moments with no one speaking, Willie came through the door. James motioned to the last empty chair, but he shook his head and opted to stand against the wall near the door.

James cleared his throat before explaining that the lab had tested Ansley's DNA taken from her blood sample and compared it to Willie's, which was on file. "I asked for confirmation in writing," he said. "I haven't opened it. I thought we should all be here when I did."

"Just get on with it," Willie snapped, crossing his arms as he leaned against the wall.

Ansley swallowed as she looked from one face to another, suddenly terrified that she was wrong. After the other night at James and Lori's house, she felt like part of the family. What if they'd all been wrong about that? To find four brothers and their wives, only to lose them all again, would be a crushing blow. Her eyes burned. She blinked to hold back tears as James picked up the letter opener.

Holding her breath, she watched as he hesitated. She wanted this too badly, she thought as she looked at the official envelope lying on the big oak desk.

Beside her, Buck took her hand and squeezed it. He'd said that no matter what she found out, she already felt like part of the Colt family—and his own. But they both knew it wouldn't be the same. The disappointment would be excruciating.

"Just rip off the bandage," Willie said with a groan.

James picked up the envelope. He sliced the edge open and, taking a breath, pulled out the report. He read silently for a moment, Willie moving to read over his shoulder.

Ansley watched James's face. He was the one who'd been most skeptical about her being his half sister. But she also knew why he was hoping that she was wrong, because of his father. Possibly *their* father, Del.

When he looked up at her, he broke into the first genuine smile she'd seen on his face when he looked at her. Her heart dropped. *I'm not his sister, I'm not his blood, I'm a fraud, just as he's always suspected.*

"Welcome to the family, sis," he said.

For a moment, she thought she'd misunderstood. This time there was no holding back the tears. "It's true? I'm a Colt?"

He nodded, still smiling, as he opened the desk drawer and pulled out a bottle of blackberry brandy and some small paper cups.

Buck was squeezing her hand as they all rose to their feet. Tommy hugged her, Willie gave her a high five, Davy congratulated her and James handed her a paper cup half-full of brandy.

"We try to only drink this when we have something to celebrate," James said as he passed out the other cups, then held his up. "Welcome, although a lot of people wouldn't think finding out that you're related the wild Colt brothers is anything to celebrate."

They laughed, held up their cups and all drank.

"Now, we just need to find your mother," James said as the room turned more somber. "At least now we know who your father is."

Chapter 15

Ansley felt as if she were in a dream. She had family. Four half brothers and their wives. James had called home before she'd left the office. Apparently, Lori, Bella, Ellie and Carla had been waiting for the news. She heard cheering as James held the phone away from his ear.

She realized that she couldn't be happier. James had said that Bella was planning a party to celebrate out at the ranch. Ansley was still trying to take it all in. She'd fought so hard not to get her hopes up. Yet she had, and now it was true. She was a Colt. Del Ransom Colt had been her father.

There was only one piece missing—her birth mother. As she walked toward her motel room just down the street, she couldn't help the feeling that her mother was here in Lonesome and had been all these years.

"Ansley?"

She turned instinctively, a smile already curving her mouth upward before she realized who it was who'd called after her. "Gage, I thought you left."

"We didn't get to finish our talk." He eyed her. "So the news must have been good."

"I'm a Colt. The Colt brothers are my half brothers."

He laughed. "I don't know what to say."

"How about 'I'm happy for you' to start with? I've found my family, and I couldn't be happier."

He stared at her, shaking his head. "Where does that leave Maribelle and Harrison?"

"They're still my adoptive parents, and I'm grateful for everything they did for me. But it doesn't change my need to find my birth mother. So you can report back to them and tell them that I'm not quitting my search." She started to turn, but he grabbed her arm. She jerked free, turning to glare at him. "It's over, Gage. Maybe Maribelle will adopt you. Goodbye."

She started down the street again when she heard the roar of an engine followed by the screech of brakes as a white van pulled up next to the curb. Before she could move, two men in white coats jumped out. She tried to scream for help as they grabbed her, but one of them had covered her mouth with his gloved hand. She felt the jab of a needle in her arm as she was lifted off her feet and into the open side door of the van.

Just before the drug she'd been injected with began to knock her out, she looked back and saw Gage standing on the sidewalk. She could tell from his expression that this had all been planned, and he'd been in on it. The last thing she saw was his smug face as her body went limp on the van floor and the door slammed shut with the same speed as her eyelids.

* * *

After Ansley left, Willie asked Buck and his brothers to stay. "Judy Ramsey isn't Ansley's birth mother. I didn't want to hit her with the news yet." He quickly filled them in on what the coroner had told him, and the letter Judy had left with a neighbor.

Buck couldn't hide his shock. Judy Ramsey was dead, murdered, and now it looked like Maribelle Brookshire was behind it. He was glad Willie hadn't broken the news to Ansley. He'd seen how happy she was to find her biological family.

"If true," he asked, "why would Maribelle Brookshire kill Judy? To keep Ansley from finding her. What was she afraid Judy might say? Even if the adoption wasn't legal, why add murder to your list of crimes?"

Willie swore. "How did Maribelle Brookshire even know about Judy Ramsey, let alone that she was having a baby? Judy was definitely involved in the illegal adoption. So where is Ansley's mother? They had to have known each other."

"Maribelle somehow knew Judy Ramsey, who knew Ansley's birth mother," Buck said. "She had to be the one Judy was buying the yarn and knitting book for."

"Judy got paid fifty thousand dollars for the transaction," James said.

He glanced at Tommy, who said, "I'm already on it. She never deposited the money in the bank so she must have gotten cash. If there was a money trail, I would have found it."

"That note isn't enough to arrest Maribelle Brookshire, though, is it," Buck said, realizing how hard it would be to get justice.

Willie shook his head. "We'd need a smoking gun to take on that family."

"I doubt Maribelle would have done it herself. Probably had Lanny Jackson do it," James said.

Buck had to disagree. "I've met her. I'd say she is capable of just about anything."

"I'm still dealing with Ansley being our half sister," Davy said. The celebratory mood from earlier was gone. Realization had set in. "How could Dad keep something like this from us?" The brothers exchanged looks.

"I've got some errands to run," Buck said, reaching for his Stetson and heading for the door. He knew they'd want to talk about this among themselves.

"Why would Dad have kept it from us?" Davy repeated after Buck left.

There was a general shaking of heads before Tommy said, "There's a chance he didn't know about her."

But Willie shook his head. "He knew. I was going to tell you… I found the jewelry store that did the engraving of the necklace from Dad's pickup. To have engraving done, you're required to sign a form with what you want printed on the item." He looked up. "Dad's phone number was on it. He bought the necklace with 'Del-Rae' engraved on it thirty years ago. If Ansley is right about her birth date, he bought it before she was born."

"So what happened?" Tommy demanded. "Why are we just learning about this now?"

"It wasn't like our father to keep secrets, was it?" James said.

The room fell silent again as if this last piece of evidence destroyed the last shred of doubt. Their father had known that he had a daughter.

Willie's cell phone rang. He checked the screen and

frowned as he said, "It's Buck," before picking up. "What do you mean, Ansley's missing? Hold on, I'm at the office. I'm putting you on speaker."

Buck's worried voice filled the room. "I just went by her motel room. Earlier we'd agreed to meet for lunch to celebrate the news. She's gone—didn't check out. A maid saw a man drive away in her car. The man's description matched that of Lanny Jackson."

Willie swore, looking at his brothers. "Pretty clear who's behind it. I'll let law enforcement in Bozeman know that she's missing. Let the law handle this, Buck. Don't do anything rash." He swore as Buck disconnected.

"Wherever Ansley is, she doesn't know about Judy Ramsey's murder or that she definitely isn't her birth mother," Tommy said.

"When I got James's call about the DNA report, I'd just learned that Judy wasn't the birth mother and about the letter naming Maribelle her killer," Willie said. "After finding out that Ansley is our sister, I figured the news could wait."

James tried her number. It went straight to voice mail. "Buck's right. She's in trouble. We have to find her."

"I'm headed to Bozeman and the Brookshires now," Willie said. "Keep looking for her birth mother. All of us storming Brookshire Estate isn't going to help. I would imagine Buck is already on his way there. I'm not sure who's in more trouble right now—Ansley or Buck."

Buck drove too fast. It would be just his luck to get picked up by one of the state highway patrol officers he used to work with. But traffic was light, as usual, and he reached Brookshire Estate in record time.

As he pulled in past the gate, he noticed the cameras again. It didn't matter, he told himself. They would know he was coming, anyway. He roared up the road, coming to a dust-boiling stop in front of the house. No one rushed out to stop him as he climbed out of his pickup and headed for the front door.

The same housekeeper answered the door as last time. "I want to see Maribelle Brookshire," he said, pushing past her.

"She isn't here," the woman said, chasing after him as he strode into the living room. "No one is here. The family has gone on vacation."

He swore as he spun on her. "Vacation? Where?" He could see she was about to say that she couldn't reveal where they'd gone. "Where?"

"I don't know. I honestly don't."

Buck was surprised, but he believed her. "Was Ansley with them?"

The woman hesitated but only for a moment. "I believe they were meeting her. That's all I know. Please, you should leave."

He glanced toward the stairs and considered searching the house. "What vehicle did they take?"

"Mrs. Brookshire took her SUV. I believe Mr. Brookshire was meeting her after work. His driver was taking him, I think."

"Did you see Ansley?"

She shook her head. "Please don't get me fired. I need this job."

"I won't." He headed for the door but stopped. "One more question. Did Mr. Brookshire's bodyguard go with him?"

"I wouldn't know. I haven't seen Mr. Jackson."

Climbing back in his pickup, he considered where they might have gone. He didn't believe for a minute that

Ansley had agreed to this, let alone that she was meeting them at their destination. She'd been taken. Why else was Lanny Jackson seen driving her SUV away from the motel?

Buck slammed his palm against the steering wheel. He'd known they were going to find out that her so-called adoption had been illegal. He just hadn't thought the Brookshires would go to this extreme to keep it from coming out. But he should have, he thought as he started the engine and drove back down the road.

He'd just turned out of the gate when he caught a flash of light off to his right. Before he could react, his side window exploded. His foot came off the gas as glass rained down on him.

Dazed from the impact, Buck watched, blurry-eyed, as Lanny Jackson reached in, unlocked his door, flung it open and shoved him over. He tried to reach for the gun in the holster at his back, but his movements were slow and awkward from the blows to his head. He barely felt the needle prick his shoulder. The lights dimmed and went out, but not before Buck saw Lanny climb behind the wheel of the pickup and a man he suspected was Gage Sheridan get behind the wheel of Lanny's black SUV.

Ansley opened her eyes with a start. She'd been asleep? Must have, because in the nightmare, she'd been calling for help, but there was no one listening. She blinked, seeing what appeared to be a hospital room. No, this room was more sterile and apparently only furnished with a bed.

Her brain felt fuzzy as her eyes focused on a figure standing in the shadows. "Gage?" His name came out garbled. Her tongue felt too big for her mouth. She tried to sit up, but with a bolt of terror, she realized that she was strapped to the bed. Her eyes widened in horror as she fought the restraints.

"Don't," Gage said as he quickly moved to her. "You'll hurt yourself."

"What—" She tried to swallow, but her mouth was cotton. "Wha—"

"Water," he said. "Just relax. I'll get you some." He moved out of her view and returned a moment later with a paper cup. A bendy straw stuck out of it. He navigated the end to her mouth.

She drank, sucking down the lukewarm liquid as if she'd been lost in the desert for days. All the time, her gaze was on Gage as bits and pieces of memory began to come together. The moment he drew the cup back as it ran dry, she tried to speak again. "You lousy son of—"

"I did what I had to do," he said, talking over her.

"Where am I?" She looked around again, terrified she already knew.

"We just wanted you safe."

"We? You and my mother?" Her heart was racing. "Get these restraints off of me."

He took a step back. "I'm not sure that's a good idea. The doctor will be in soon. You need to calm down. You've been acting…delusional. We were afraid you would hurt yourself."

"You and my mother were afraid I'd learn the truth about both of you," she said. "Believe me, I've learned enough to know I can't trust either of you." He moved toward the door. "Go, coward. You can't keep me here, and when I get out of here, you won't be able to hide. Not even Maribelle's money will protect her from what I'm going to do to her—and you."

"See, it's this kind of talk that's got you in here, for your own good."

She growled deep in her throat, and he hurriedly pulled open the door and rushed out. As the door clicked closed, her eyes filled with tears. She told herself that Buck would find her. Her half brothers, too. They wouldn't let her rot in here.

Ansley held on to that hope and tried, as Gage had said, to settle down. She would have to hide her anger if she had any hope of getting out of these restraints.

Buck felt himself begin to surface. He lay perfectly still, concentrating on his steady breathing and ignoring his blinding headache. He was on his side, lying in the remains of a building. He could hear two male voices. He recognized one of them. Lanny Jackson's. He was arguing with someone, someone with a more cultured accent, although rather whiny. Gage, he thought.

"All you have to do is keep an eye on him," Lanny was saying. "He isn't going to wake up for a while—not as hard as I hit him. Also, that drug should keep him under."

"But what do I do if he does wake up?"

He *was* awake. He could tell without opening his eyes that his wrists were bound in front of him. Zip ties. That was good, because anyone with a computer knew how to get out of them. He tested his legs. Not bound. Even better.

"Here, take this, Sheridan," Lanny was saying.

"I'm not going to shoot him!"

"He doesn't know that," Lanny snapped. "We just need to keep him here until we can get Ansley moved to somewhere safer. Take it, Gage. You want to get her back, don't you? Then do what I say. I won't be long."

Gage Sheridan must have taken the gun, because Buck heard footfalls, then a vehicle engine start up, the sound of gravel under tires and then a sound much closer.

Gage had come into where Buck was lying on a crumbling floor, musty and moldy smelling, but he could feel fresh air on his face. Not that it mattered. From what Buck could tell, it was now just the two of them.

Ansley's fiancé moved closer.

Buck could hear him breathing hard, scared. He knew when he made his move, he needed to waste no time or effort. Gage had a gun, and he might be just stupid enough to pull the trigger without even realizing it.

He felt a finger poke in his side and didn't react. Another poke. Gage was right next to him, close. The time was now.

Buck rolled over, swinging out both legs at where he estimated Gage had been hunched down next to him. The man tried to get up before Buck kicked his legs out from under him. Too late. As expected, Gage pointed the gun at him as he started to go down.

But Buck was too fast for him, too trained in just this type of thing. He grabbed the gun, wrenched it from Gage's hand with both of his and kicked again. Gage fell on his rear as Buck launched himself to his feet. Tearing his wrists free of the zip ties, he swung the gun around to aim it at Gage, who was trying to crab crawl away.

"Don't shoot me!" Gage cried as Buck stepped closer. He placed a boot to Gage's chest, shoving him back and pushing the muzzle of the gun against the man's forehead as he warned him not to move.

"I'm only going to ask you once, so think long and hard about your answer," Buck said. "I can shoot you right here, or you can tell me the truth right now. Where is Ansley?"

Chapter 16

James found himself pacing the office, anxious to hear from Buck. "Bella's asking a lot of questions about our mother," Tommy said. "Why don't I have any memory of her? She died right after Davy was born, so I can understand him not remembering her. But shouldn't I be able to? I've never really known anything about her." He looked from one to the other of his brothers. "I've never even seen a photo of her. Why did Dad never talk about her? Don't you think it's odd?"

"She was sick a lot and not around when we were growing up and then she died," Willie said.

"So we've been told, but that's about it," Davy said. "You must remember her." When Willie said nothing, he moved his gaze to James.

"She wasn't well," Willie said. "I was busy helping raise you bunch, so no, I don't remember much."

"Have we ever been to her grave?" Davy asked.

Willie shook his head. "I think Dad had her cremated. I was ten. I don't remember a funeral. I just know that Dad never wanted to talk about her."

"And about that same time Davy was conceived, he knocked up some other woman?" Tommy demanded. "And kept that a secret, too?"

Willie got to his feet. "I don't have time for this. Ansley is our sister, DelRae. It's a fact. Let's deal in facts until we know the rest. Right now she's in trouble, and if I know Buck, he is, too." He walked out.

The air in the office felt thick and hard to breathe in the silence that followed. James broke it. "Buck will be fine." He had to believe that. "Ansley's birth mother is the key. We have to find her, and not just for our client. We have to know the truth. We need to know for certain if it was Penny Graves who borrowed that old pickup from Mark's lot. What's interesting is that her grandmother used to be a midwife. Didn't the grandmother have a cabin up in the mountains?"

"You think Penny could be Ansley's biological mother?" Tommy asked.

"If she is, then the cabin could be the perfect place to hide a pregnancy—and even have a baby you didn't want anyone to know about," James said.

After Buck tied up Gage so he wouldn't be warning Lanny, he took the man's keys and cell phone and double-checked the address for the institution. Outside, he took his own pickup—missing side window and all.

He drove fast, still shocked at how far Ansley's adoptive parents would go—let alone her fiancé. Gage had confessed that it had been Harrison who'd had her com-

mitted. His heart pounded. Lanny had gone to the institution to move her to a "safer" place. He hated to think
where that might be. That's why he had to get there and
stop this abduction, no matter what he had to do. He
called James to tell him where he was going and why.

"Why is it so loud?" James asked.

"I'm missing the driver's side window, thanks to
Lanny Jackson." He didn't mention that he was still
trying to overcome whatever drug the man had used
on him as well.

"They put her in an institution?" his friend said when
he told him the whole story. "I can leave now and meet
you there."

"No, I'll handle it one way or another. Harrison got
a judge to commit her. You might have to get me out
of jail."

"There's something you need to know," James said.
"Willie told me that Judy Ramsey left a letter that im-
plicates Maribelle Brookshire. He's going down there
to question her. This could be over soon."

Buck had his doubts about that. "I was at the house
in Bozeman. Maribelle was gone, supposedly on vacation. I got the feeling she wasn't coming back. I'm almost to the institution. Wish me luck."

"Be careful. I don't want you risking your neck."

"Too late for that." It was his heart he was more worried about, Buck thought as he turned down a narrow
road. Ahead he spotted a two-story white building. A
black SUV was parked in front. He roared toward it,
wondering how he was going to find Ansley—let alone
get her away from here.

Even if he and Lanny were on better terms, Buck
knew the man couldn't let him take Ansley without a

fight. He hoped to avoid bloodshed but worried that there was a good chance it would come to that as he swung into the parking lot, coming to a stop next to Lanny Jackson's big black SUV.

As much as he wanted to go inside the facility guns blazing, he knew he'd be better off to wait out here in the parking lot. Lanny had said he was moving Ansley to somewhere safer, which meant harder to find. The way Buck had parked beside the big SUV, Lanny wouldn't see him at first when he brought Ansley out.

He'd never been good at waiting, but this time, it was the smart thing to do. He checked the weapon he'd taken from Gage and his own that he'd retrieved as he'd left the hog-tied fiancé. Then he removed his Stetson and waited.

Buck didn't have to wait long. From where he sat, he could see the side of the building through his window and the black SUV's. There was a garden with benches closed off by a short wrought iron fence. He saw Lanny first. He came out, looked around, then disappeared for a moment before he appeared again, this time with Ansley. Buck could tell at a glance that she was heavily medicated. She leaned into Lanny, the large bodyguard practically carrying her along the sidewalk to the gate. She slumped against him as he opened the gate and led her out, closing it behind them as they made their way toward his waiting SUV.

"Bastards," Buck said under his breath at the sight of Ansley, eyes half-closed as she stumbled along, dragging one leg behind her.

Lanny struggled to keep her upright as he approached the SUV to open a back door. He swore, clearly having trouble opening the door and not dropping Ansley.

"They were supposed to make you compliant, not co-matose."

Buck eased open his pickup door and jumped out. The SUV was blocking Lanny's view until he rounded the front of the vehicle, coming at the bodyguard from the back. But before he could reach him, Buck saw Ansley suddenly come alive. She kicked out, slamming a foot into the big man's ankle before she kneed him in the groin, dropping Lanny to his knees.

She saw Buck when he came up behind Lanny and smiled as Buck hit him hard in the back of the head with the butt of his gun. The man toppled over onto the asphalt. Buck rolled him under the SUV and looked up at Ansley.

"Nice to see you," she said, her eyes bright.

"You, too."

He reached for her, and she stepped into his arms. He could feel her trembling and didn't want to think about what she might have been through inside that place. He held her for a few moments, worried that Lanny would come to and try to stop them. He didn't want to shoot the man, but he would if he had to. "Let's get you out of here." He led her around to the passenger side of his pickup.

"I'm fine. I didn't take the pills they tried to give me," she said as she climbed in without any help. As he brushed his fingers over her arm, he realized she was trembling with rage. "This was Maribelle's doing," she said through gritted teeth. "I want to see her."

He closed the door, checked to make sure that Lanny was still out and went around to climb behind the wheel. "Not a good idea. Harrison got a judge to commit you. All Maribelle has to do is make one phone call and you will be locked up again. As it was, Lanny was taking you to another institution, the next one more isolated, with more security. It sounded like they intended to keep you there indefinitely."

Tears filled her eyes, and she turned away. "All this because I wanted to find my birth mother?"

"Apparently so." There was so much he needed to tell her, and yet he hesitated. She'd been hit with enough. "I'm taking you to my family ranch. You'll be safe there."

He'd expected her to object, but all she did was nod and turn to glance out the side window. He could see that whatever had happened back there, it hadn't taken away her determination or her spirit. She just looked tired, beaten down—but only for the moment.

Buck was glad when she leaned back, closed her eyes and fell asleep.

It was late by the time they reached the ranch. Ansley stirred when he lifted her out of the truck but didn't wake as he took her inside. He'd called to have his father make up the guest bedroom.

Wendell met them at the door, glancing at an exhausted Ansley, then at his son. Buck could see the worry in his eyes. Earlier he'd told him that it might be dangerous bringing her to the ranch, but his father hadn't hesitated.

"She'll be safe here," the rancher had said.

Buck carried her into the guest room, laid her down on the bed. She let out a sigh and rolled over. He studied the peaceful look on her face for a moment, then covered her with one of his mother's quilts, turned out the light and left the room. His father was waiting for him out on the porch.

"I'm sorry about this," Buck said as he sat down to look out at the darkness, wondering how much time they had before all hell broke loose.

"If the law comes, we'll handle it," Wendell said without looking at him.

"It won't be the law." The Brookshires had gotten the commitment order from a judge, but it was Lanny Jackson who did the real dirty work. He'd failed to get Ansley to another asylum. When Lanny came for them, he would be looking for vengeance this time. "The Brookshires will send their hired thug, Lanny Jackson." He described the man for his father. "He'll be looking for me to settle a score as well as take Ansley. I can't let him do that."

His father was silent for a long moment. "I assume the Colts are working through legal avenues to stop all this."

"The Brookshires have apparently left the country, but that won't stop Jackson. Even if they tried to call him off, he won't let this go."

Buck expected his father to ask him about Ansley, but maybe there was no reason. He'd brought the woman home to the ranch. Didn't that say it all about how involved he was with her? "I don't like you being here alone when Jackson comes looking for me."

"I won't be. Your brother gets back tomorrow with stock from the latest rodeo. He and the ranch hands will be more than enough. Don't discount your old man, either. I can still handle myself."

Buck smiled over at this father. "I'd never do that." He felt such love for this man who'd taught him so much about life.

"But we'll be leaving again in a few days for another rodeo," Wendell said.

"Lanny will make his move before then."

They were quiet for a few minutes. "Any closer to finding her mother?" his father asked.

He shook his head. "But we're not giving up."

"I figured as much." Wendell nodded, but the look in his eyes was one of worry as he went inside.

Buck sat for a few more minutes listening to the frogs down at the pond, the hoot of an owl in the distance, the sound of the wind in the nearby pines. He grew up with these sounds. They comforted him even when he knew trouble was coming. Still, he felt safer here than anywhere on earth.

Rising, he went inside to check on Ansley.

She woke to darkness, and for a moment she thought she was back at the institution. She let out a cry of anguish before she realized she was no longer strapped down. Sitting up, she shoved off the quilt, still disoriented as she frantically tried to see in the blackness. At the creak of a floorboard, she turned to find a large, dark figure standing in the doorway.

For just an instant, her breath caught in her throat and she felt her eyes go wild with terror.

"Ansley?" Buck quickly stepped into the room to turn on the small lamp next to her bed.

She blinked as the room came into focus. Buck. She was safe. Her memory came back—Buck carrying her in from the pickup. She'd been so exhausted but also fighting the drugs they'd injected her with while she was captive. Yet her heart was still thundering in her chest.

"You're safe," he said as he sat down on the edge

of the bed. He reached for her, and she came to him, letting him gather her up again in his arms—the only place she felt safe.

"Buck," she whispered as she drew back to look into his eyes. He'd saved her from that horrible place. He'd saved her from Lanny. Also, from Gage. He'd saved her in so many ways. She felt such a surge of emotion. This cowboy, she thought, shocked by the raw, primal need she felt for him. It was beyond desire. She wanted this cowboy for keeps. "Buck."

Cupping his handsome face, she kissed him—at first tentatively and then with passion as he responded in kind. Her fingers worked at the snaps on his Western shirt, releasing one, then another until she could touch the bare skin of his chest.

She pulled back, frowning with surprise and concern as her fingers felt the rough edge of a long scar that ran diagonally from his breastbone down across his abdomen.

"It's a long story," he said.

"The woman who almost killed you."

He nodded.

Her heart ached for what he must have gone through. "I'm so glad she didn't," she said, then bent to leave a trail of kisses across the scar. He groaned and drew her closer to kiss her passionately, deepening the kiss and then pulling back to look at her in the glow of the bedside lamp.

She answered his questioning gaze by slowly beginning to unbutton her blouse. He rose to close and lock the door and was back before she reached the third button.

Later, lying in his arms, Ansley sighed. She'd never felt this sated, this content. She thought about how his hands, his mouth had explored her body. The touch of his tongue, the quickening of her heart as he bent to take her aching, rock-hard nipple between his teeth. Her legs had trembled as he'd stroked her to a height she'd never reached before.

She shivered at the memory of their lovemaking, and he pulled her closer, kissing her temple. "You can tell me," she said quietly. "I overheard Lanny talking to Gage, so I know a little."

He hesitated, but only for a moment. Ansley listened as he told her about Judy Ramsey being murdered, but that she definitely wasn't her birth mother. Then he told her about the letter Judy left and how Willie was meeting the local sheriff down in Gallatin County before they headed out to talk to Maribelle and Harrison.

She took it all in, sifting through the parts that hurt to reach the news that buoyed her. "I was supposed to be named DelRae?"

"It seems so. After your father, Del Ransom Colt. Apparently, your birth mother made Judy Ramsey promise, and Judy made Maribelle promise."

She made a disgusted sound. "So like Maribelle to break that promise."

"Ansley, there is a good chance that Maribelle either killed Judy Ramsey or had her killed to keep her quiet. Now more than ever, your adoptive parents want you under lock and key. You have to trust that we're all still trying to find your birth mother and keep you— and her—safe."

"I trust you and my brothers," she said, her voice breaking. "But there isn't enough evidence to arrest Maribelle and Harrison, is there?"

He shook his head. He didn't have to tell her that the

justice system was weighted toward those with money and power. "I believe both Lanny and Gage are getting their orders from Maribelle or Harrison. That's why I wanted you here, where I can keep you safe." He looked at her as if expecting her to argue.

Instead, she nodded. "I know now what they can do to me. That place… I was strapped down…" Tears welled again. She wiped at them furiously. "I want them to pay for this."

"If I'm right, Maribelle didn't know about the letter Judy left as insurance. It might not be enough to convict her, but it's a start. In the meantime, we might be getting closer to finding your birth mother."

"How, with Judy Ramsey dead?"

"James thinks the two of us need to talk to a woman named Penny Graves." She listened as he told her about what they'd learned and how it led back to city hall. "The one thing we know is that Judy knew your birth mother well enough that she was the one who brokered the deal with Maribelle," he said.

"Why the intermediary? Why wouldn't my mother make the deal?"

"Good question." He hesitated. "She might not have known what Judy was up to or that she was paid fifty thousand dollars."

"So that's what I was worth. Fifty grand?" Ansley said and shook her head. "That amount is nothing to Maribelle. She must have thought she got a real deal— until she realized her mistake. I was never the daughter she wanted."

"Her loss." He drew her close. This time they made love slowly. Ansley told herself that she never wanted to leave this bed—or this man.

But when she woke the next morning, she was alone.
She rose, showered and went to find Buck. Not surprised to find him in the kitchen making pancakes. He
poured her a cup of coffee as she sat down at the island.

All he had to do was smile at her, and she felt the
heat rush again through her body. As she slipped her
coffee, though, she knew this couldn't last. Lanny was
still out there. He'd be coming after Buck—if not her—
again. As for Gage… She pushed the thought of him
away and thought instead about the woman who'd given
birth to her.

Would she ever find her?

It didn't take his deputies long to find the murder
scene. Willie sent forensics out to the abandoned motel
and café to see if they could find any evidence that Maribelle Brookshire had been there.

In the meantime, he decided he had time to stop by
the city office and check on who had borrowed the old
pickup from Mark's lot. James had called just as he was
leaving the sheriff's department to tell him what Wendell Crawford had said about Del and Penny possibly
having dated way back when.

"No way. Dad and Penny? Not a chance." But even
as he said it, Willie had to agree with his brother. Del
Ransom Colt was proving to his sons how little they
knew about him. He glanced at the time as he entered
the courthouse. Later today he would be meeting with
the Gallatin County sheriff for a visit to Brookshire Estate to talk to Maribelle.

Penny Graves wasn't at her desk, so he stuck his head
in the open door of the mayor's office. "Did I catch you
at a bad time?"

"Willie!" Beth Conrad burst into a smile. "I was just going to call you. I have some great news. I just got confirmation from the railroad. We're getting crossing bars and lights. *Finally.* I wanted you and your brothers to be the first to know. It's been an uphill battle. But we finally won."

He knew how hard Beth had worked on it. "Thank you for doing that," Willie said. Not that it would bring back their father. But it might save a life in the future.

"I'm sorry it took so long. If only that rail crossing had crossing bars ten years ago..." Her blue eyes shone with emotion. "Anyway, I was thinking maybe we could have a ceremony in Del's name."

"I don't know. I can ask my brothers what they think."

"I know it's too little, too late."

"No, it's amazing that you got the railroad to finally act. Dad would have been happy. It might save someone else the same fate.

"While I'm here," Willie said. "I heard that someone from your office borrowed a pickup from Mark's used car lot. Would you know anything about that?"

She looked surprised. "I don't, but I'll look into it if it's important," Beth said. "I'll have to get back to you. I did send Penny out to the RR crossing to shoot a few photos. We want to do some before and after shots once the work begins."

"Any idea why she would borrow a truck from Mark's lot?"

"Now that I think about, Penny's been having car trouble with that rig of hers. I didn't remember that when I asked her to get the photos. She's good friends with Mark's wife."

Willie nodded. He needed to get to Bozeman. He

was anxious to confront Maribelle Brookshire. He'd known better than go alone. Having the county sheriff and a few deputies with them would at least get her attention—if not get her to break down and confess. "Thanks, Beth, and thanks again for working so hard on the crossing. Also, the former sheriff told me that you put in a good word when I applied for deputy." He waited for her to say something. When she didn't, he said, "Thank you. Let me know what Penny says."

They'd finished their breakfast and Ansley had helped with loading the dishwasher when she heard the sound of tires on gravel and froze.

"It's just the Colt wives," Buck said, seeing her instant distress. "They're determined to help you find your mother."

Before she could reach the door, the women had piled out and were headed for the porch. Ansley stepped out, and they instantly surrounded her like a flock of geese in a protective huddle.

She realized how happy she was to see them as they entered the house.

"I'll be out at the barn," Buck said after greeting the women.

"We're all from here, and we know this town, this county," Lori said once they were in the living room and all seated.

"Also, we're women, and the PI agency is looking for a woman," Bella said. "We can find her while the men do what they can to keep you safe."

Ansley smiled. "Your husbands are all right with this?"

Bella seemed to give this some thought, making the

others laugh. "I was thinking of us working behind the scenes…so to speak."

"If your mother was a local," Carla said, "then how was it that no one knew she was pregnant?"

"She could have hidden it," Bella said, glancing down at her own flat stomach. "At least for a while, but then she'd have to hide out until the baby was born."

"Having Judy Ramsey buy pink and blue yarn and knitting supplies isn't really hiding it," Ellie pointed out.

"She could have said she was making the blanket for a friend and didn't know the sex of the baby yet," Lori said, waving it off.

"That's if someone caught her knitting," Carla said. "Why the secrecy? Like Lori said, she could have said she was making it for a friend."

"For some reason, she didn't want anyone to know she was pregnant," Ansley agreed.

"Because she was married to someone else?" Bella cut in.

"Or because a pregnancy would have cost the woman her job?" Lori said.

"That's a thought. Or just cost her her reputation?" Ellie said.

"Whatever the reason for keeping it secret, isn't it more likely that if her intent was to give up the baby, she would have gone away, had the baby there and returned without the infant? She might have been gone only a few months if she was able to hide her pregnancy."

"So why make the baby blanket if she had no intention of keeping me?" Ansley asked.

"Something changed," Lori said. "She wanted to keep you but couldn't. That's why she made you the blanket, to let you know that she loved you."

"Okay," Bella said. "If she went away, then that would have been noticed—even for a few months. With all the busybodies we have in town, someone had to have speculated, especially if your mother was a long-time resident."

"You're leaving out a key part," Carla said. "The father of the baby, Del Colt. Nearly thirty years ago, his wife was having Davy about the time Ansley's mother was having her."

"No getting around it," Bella said. "Del impregnated his wife at about the same time as Ansley's mother."

"According to my husband, Del wasn't that kind of man," Lori said.

As they talked, Ansley realized that she knew little about her father except that he'd rodeoed, quit to start the investigative business and died in a train accident ten years ago. She recalled the photograph she'd seen of him at the office.

But she told herself that she would get to know him through her brothers—and her birth mother.

"What we're missing here," Ellie said, "is our husbands' mother. Why is it we know so little about her?" They all nodded in agreement.

All Ansley knew was that Mary Jo and Del had married young and she'd died young, leaving Del with four rambunctious boys to raise alone. There'd been no other woman in Del's life—that the brothers knew of, anyway. Ansley wanted to believe that Del had cared about her mother, even loved her. But if her birth mother and Del Colt had been in love, then how was it that no one knew about them—let alone that the child they created was given up for adoption? No wonder James, and probably the other Colts, too, didn't want to believe their father would have given up his own child to keep his affair—if that's what it had been—secret.

"What do you know about Del's wife?" Bella asked Lori, who shook her head.

"James said he really doesn't remember his mother."

"Same with Tommy," Bella said.

"And Davy, obviously because she died soon after his birth," Carla said.

"Willie's the only one who must remember her," Ellie added. "But he doesn't seem to. As the oldest, he would have been ten when she died. Anyone know what caused her death?"

There was a general shaking of heads. "That's odd, isn't it?" Bella said.

"Makes me think there is more to the story," Ellie said. "All Willie has said is that Del raised them from the time they were little. I guess their mother was always sickly. Willie said he thinks his mother was in the hospital most of that time. He hates to talk about any of this. He just knows that she wasn't around. I suspect the pregnancy with Davy wasn't planned, since she died not long after giving birth."

The room grew quiet for a few minutes. "So there could have been another woman in Del's life," Bella said to Ansley. "If you're twenty-eight, born on the Fourth of July, then Del must have been with your mother about the same time Davy was conceived. But that doesn't mean they hadn't known each other, hadn't been in love, but that Del couldn't leave his sick wife."

They all grew quiet. "He already had three young boys and another one on the way," Ansley said. "I wouldn't imagine he would have wanted another child."

"I think we need to find out what happened to our

husbands' mother," Bella said. "I've never even seen a photo of her. Isn't that odd? Lots of photos of the boys growing up, but none of her with them."

"That is odd," Lori agreed. "Do we even know her name?"

"Mary Jo. I got that much out of Willie. I think he knows more than he's willing to share out of loyalty," Ellie said. "That alone makes me think something was very wrong with that marriage."

"We started talking about how to find Ansley's mother," Bella said. "But I suspect that once we know Mary Jo's story, it will lead us to Ansley's birth mother." There was general agreement.

How to do it, however, was debatable. But Ansley loved that these women wanted to help her. She really did feel part of the family.

The conversation turned to how she was doing and finally to Buck.

"He seems to have put some color in your cheeks," Bella said and chuckled.

"He was looking pretty happy before he headed to the barn," Lori said, and they all laughed. "We couldn't be happier for the two of you."

Ansley tried to tell them that it wasn't like that. "We barely know each other." But the women all giggled.

"We know Buck," Bella said. "Trust us. This is serious."

Chapter 17

"They're going to come for her again," Buck said when he made the call to James from the barn. "I have her out here at the ranch."

"Not sure you having Ansley at the ranch is a good idea. If a judge really did have her committed, then what you've done is against the law. But you know we'll have your back."

"I doubt they'll go the legal route. I suspect they'll send Lanny Jackson. Hell, he'll be looking for me even if they don't send him to get Ansley."

"I don't like you having a target on your back," James said. "When I asked you to work with us—"

"It was my choice. We never knew it would go this far, but now it has. I can keep her safe here better than anywhere else. With the Brookshire money and power, there is no place safe for her right now except as far away from them as possible. I'll do whatever I have to in order to protect her."

"I know you will."

Buck broke the silence. "I probably should warn you that all the wives are out here. They're determined to help find her birth mother."

James groaned. "Lori already warned me. By the way, Willie called to say that he spoke to the mayor. She said her assistant, Penny Graves, might have borrowed the pickup from Mark's lot as we were told. Apparently she was having trouble with her car. Any chance it's not the same pickup?"

"None," Buck said and told James what his father had told him about Del dating Penny Graves. "Wendell saw them together. He said he thought their relationship had been contentious."

"Penny and my father?" James sounded as disbelieving as Buck himself had. "But you know, the way things have been going, why not? If I've learned anything, it was that I didn't know my father."

Willie had a bad feeling even before the housekeeper opened the door at the Brookshire Estate. He and the other law officers with him flashed their badges. If the woman who'd answered the door was surprised, she didn't show it.

"We're here to see Maribelle Brookshire," the Gallatin County sheriff said.

"She's not here," Ingrid said. "She and Mr. Brookshire have left for a vacation abroad."

"Then you won't mind if we have a look around," Willie said and handed her the warrant. That didn't faze the woman, either, as she took the warrant and, without looking at it, allowed them to enter.

It took a while to search the place. When they finished, they found the housekeeper sitting on a chair near the front door waiting.

"Do you know where your employers went abroad?" the local sheriff asked.

"I'm afraid not," the woman said. "Nor do I expect to hear from them until they call to tell me to get the house ready."

"When they call, I need you to call me," the Gallatin County sheriff said and handed her his card.

"It could be a while. I got the impression it would be a long holiday," Ingrid said.

Willie swore as he left the estate. Maribelle and Harrison had made a run for it. The local sheriff promised to let him know if he found out where they'd gone. Not that it would do any good, since at this point, Maribelle was only wanted for questioning. But once Lanny Jackson was picked up for abducting Buck, there was always the chance that he might enlighten them for a lesser sentence.

As Willie drove back to Lonesome, he told himself that finding Judy Ramsey's killer would have to wait. In the meantime, his brothers were still looking for the woman allegedly seen throwing something at their father in front of a bar downtown—just before he left in his truck and was struck and killed by a train.

Willie had tried once before to get information out of the former sheriff, Otis Osterman, without any luck. But as he neared Lonesome, he pulled off down a road by the river, determined to give it one more try—for their father's only daughter's sake. If Otis knew who the woman was, Willie was going to get it out of him.

Otis lived in a small shack-like cabin on the river where he'd retired after being sheriff for years. Willie parked and started to climb the steps that led up onto the porch. He could hear the whisper of the river off to his right, the sigh of the pines as the breeze moved restlessly through the trees around the cabin and the unmistakable sound of shells being jammed into a shotgun just before the double barrels were snapped closed.

"Mornin', Otis," Willie said as the grizzly old former sheriff stepped from the pines just below the front porch. His gray hair stuck out from his head. From the white whiskers covering the lower half of his face, he hadn't shaved in weeks—if not longer.

"You're trespassing," Otis said in a gravelly voice.

He flashed his badge. "I'm here on business. My office knows I came out here. Still thinking about shooting me?"

"Sure as hell is tempting," Otis said under this breath, but he lowered the shotgun. "What do you want? Make it quick. I got things to do."

"You've probably heard the news about my sister, Ansley Brookshire?"

The former sheriff nodded sagely. "You still looking for that woman seen arguing with your father that night? Suppose you think that's the birth mother. Just like I told you before, I got an anonymous phone call. Didn't see it myself. Can't tell you—"

"The caller? Man or woman?"

Otis sucked at something in his teeth for a moment. "Woman."

"She disguised her voice, because you know everyone in this county?"

The old former sheriff smiled at that remark, exposing several missing teeth. "She tried."

"Who called, Otis?"

"No one reliable, so I had no reason to—"

"Who?"

"Cora Brooks."

Willie swore under his breath.

"See why I paid it little mind? So your father had an argument with some woman on the street in front of a bar. All that proved was that he was in no shape when he started across that railroad track."

Turning, Willie walked away. "Next time you come out here," Otis called after him, "at least bring a six-pack, or better yet, a bottle of whiskey. Your father would have."

Willie called James. He needed to get back to the office. Mostly, he wasn't up to interviewing Cora Brooks. Not today.

Cora Brooks had a reputation in the county for butting into other people's business. Usually it involved a pair of binoculars and a prying disposition. Putting her nose in places it didn't involve had gotten her house burned down some time ago. Since then she'd moved one of those tiny houses that had gained popularity onto her property.

As he drove into her yard, he saw that this house had a balcony on its third floor, making the place resemble a shoe. The old woman who lived in the shoe opened the door before he could even get out of his SUV. She had a shotgun in the crook of her arm but smiled when she saw him.

"Jimmy D," she called out in a voice both irritatingly harsh and high.

"I go by James now."

She laughed at that, a sound like fingernails down a blackboard. "You're still a Colt. Can't hide from that." She appeared older, frailer and maybe a little more hunched over, but he knew she was still as sharp as that tongue of hers.

"I would imagine you know why I'm here," he said. "What's it going to cost me to find out what you saw the night my father died?"

"Sure took you long enough to come to me," she said and eyed him, as if calculating in her mind what she could get out of him.

Cora set down the end of the stock and leaned on the shotgun. "That woman who hired you, the one staying at the motel, she's one of yourn, isn't she?"

He didn't bother to answer, figuring if Cora knew, then the whole county did by now. "Was the woman that night in front of the bar the woman she's looking for?"

"You mean the woman who born her?"

James waited, thinking about all the times he and his brothers had caught Cora spying on them. She owned a small strip of land next to their ranch. They used to steal apples off her trees. When they were really little, she'd shoo them away with a broom. After that it was rock salt from her shotgun.

"You know Penny Graves?" Cora asked.

He nodded. The mayor's assistant's name just kept coming up. He felt his heart beat a little faster. Penny's grandmother had been a midwife years ago. Penny had borrowed the pickup from Mark's lot to do some business, allegedly for the mayor.

"You should talk to her," Cora said.

James considered the older woman. "You've known this all along?" He was surprised she hadn't come to him asking for money for the information. That was her usual MO. "Why now?"

She shrugged her narrow shoulders. "A girl should know her mother."

"Even if the mother doesn't want to be found?"

Cora met his gaze. "Who says she doesn't want to be found?"

"Then why hasn't *she* come forward?" he demanded. "She has to have heard that her daughter is looking for her."

"Guess you'll have to ask her that yourself," Cora said. "Now get off my property. I'd hate to have to call the law like in the old days." She smiled when she said it, though. "Never thought I'd see a Colt as a PI, let alone a sheriff. Guess I've lived too long." With that, she turned and went back inside her tiny house.

As he left, he glanced back to see her on the top balcony watching him drive away.

It was late afternoon when James called. Buck and Ansley had been for a swim in the creek after the Colt wives had left. He'd told himself that he was just trying to keep her mind off everything. At least that was partly true.

James broke the news about Maribelle and Harrison having allegedly gone on vacation. "But I just got a call from Willie. They've both been picked up for questioning. They were trying to leave the country from a small airport back in New York. Also, we might be making progress on finding Ansley's mother. I talked to Cora. You know Penny Graves, right?"

Know probably wasn't the right word, but he said, "Yes?" He listened as his friend told him that he'd sent Davy up to check out her cabin. "It's secluded—great place to hide out. Might have even been a great place to have a baby. Davy looked through the windows and saw something interesting—a basket with yarn and knitting needles."

"Let me guess. Pink and blue yarn." Buck let out a low whistle and listened as James told him about his visit to Cora Brooks. "Sounds like we need to talk to Penny."

"If she's the birth mother, she might open up to you—if Ansley was with you. She'll be at work tomorrow, but after that she's going on vacation."

Buck swore under his breath. "That sounds like an ambush."

"It might not be Penny. You know Cora. She could just be yanking our chains. Knitting needles and even pink and blue yarn don't necessarily prove anything." But all trails seemed to have led to Penny. Of course, the trails had also once led to Judy Ramsey. As far as he knew, Penny and Judy traveled in very different circles. But then again, he'd have never expected Judy Ramsey's and Maribelle Brookshire's paths to ever cross, either.

"What is it?" Ansley asked as Buck disconnected.

He turned slowly to look at her. She'd been standing by the window looking out at the pine-covered mountains to the east but now waited expectantly. Her hair was still damp from their swim, her cheeks flushed from the sun. She couldn't have looked more beautiful.

Buck told her everything James had told him, including about Maribelle and Harrison being found and detained. "James thinks we should talk to Penny Graves."

"Who's Penny?" she asked.

He found it hard to describe her. Never married, Penny Graves was a slight woman who walked with a limp from a horseback accident. Buck remembered her coming to the rodeos out at the ranch. She was a woman who loved horseflesh. She was also a woman who could hide in the crowd—she blended in, had a way of going unnoticed. Had Del seen something in her that others didn't? Was that what had possibly attracted him to her?

"She's the mayor's assistant," he said. "Her grandmother was a midwife."

He knew James, Tommy and Davy were still working to find Ansley's birth mother, while Willie had put a BOLO out on the Brookshires. And still no sign of Lanny. Yet. Had Buck not been here with Ansley, he would have felt more anxious for answers. Even Ansley seemed at peace here on the ranch.

He liked this feeling of limbo, knowing that once she found her birth mother, she would be gone. As for Maribelle and Harrison, they'd been found. Whether Maribelle would be arrested and stand trial for Judy Ramsey's murder, that was another story.

In the meantime… "James said we could catch Penny in her office tomorrow—before she leaves on vacation."

Ansley nodded. "Then that's what we'll do."

He smiled. "What do you say to a horseback ride? We can watch the sunset from my favorite place on the ranch."

"Let me get dressed. I'll meet you in the stables."

Ansley stepped into the shower. Her face felt flushed from the sun, from the kiss, from the sunset and Buck. She still couldn't believe everything that had happened. There were moments when she regretted going looking for her birth mother, because as Buck said, she'd kicked over an anthill. But she'd also met Buck. Had released a part of her that she hadn't known existed.

They'd ridden the horses up the mountain to a spot

on the edge of a cliff where the pines opened up. He'd spread a blanket on the ground, and they'd watched the sunset far off to the west—then made love before riding back to the ranch house in the twilight.

Her whole body had tingled. She'd never made love outside in the aura of the setting sun. She'd never felt such passion, such emotion. This cowboy…how was she ever going to give him up? Their lives were miles apart. They'd both gone into this encounter knowing it was only temporary, hadn't they?

She stood under the hot spray, hating the thought of it being over. Buck had opened up a whole world to her that she'd never known, and her brothers were here and their wives, whom she adored.

As she stepped out of the shower and began to dry off, she heard her cell phone ringing and hurried to answer it. "Hello?" She was half-afraid of who it would be, but saw Gage's number on the caller ID. She hadn't heard from him since the day he'd set her up to be abducted and taken to the institution. If she hadn't been strapped down, she would have gone for his throat.

"Don't hang up. It's about your mother."

"I was just thinking about you," she said. "Have you now decided to help me find my mother?"

Silence, then a sheepish, "Maribelle's been released from custody. She needs to see you." He rushed on. "She says she will tell you everything. She's flying back to Bozeman tomorrow. She feels terrible about everything," Gage rushed on. "She just wants to tell you herself what happened all those years ago. Ansley?"

She'd been looking out the window at the rolling foothills, the pine-covered mountain she'd ridden a horse up only hours ago. Gage had broken the spell.

She wished she hadn't answered the call. But now that she had...

"I'll think about it and let her know."

As she disconnected, she debated telling Buck. He would try to talk her out of going or insist on going with her. She told herself she'd sleep on it and decide what to do in the morning. From the beginning, she'd wanted the truth from Maribelle, to hear it from her own lips. She needed the whole story before she could put that part behind her.

Buck woke to the distant sound of a dog barking. His dad had taken his dog with him. He lay perfectly still in the darkness, his arm around Ansley, as he listened. He recognized the bark. A neighboring rancher's dog often wandered over into their yard after chasing a rabbit or a fox or even a deer.

He carefully removed his arm from around Ansley. She sighed in her sleep and rolled over. He waited to make sure she was still asleep before he slipped out of bed, pulled on his jeans and padded out into the living room.

The night was dark, clouds low, no stars. He thought he could smell rain on the air as he picked up the loaded shotgun and opened the front door. The worn wood of the porch felt cold on his bare feet as he eased out, then stopped to listen.

He could no longer hear the dog. Closer, the wind sighed in the pine boughs. Nothing moved. Until it did.

Lanny Jackson sprang out of the darkness from the right side of the porch. Buck swung the shotgun, but not quick enough. He felt something cold and hard strike his temple. The blow staggered him, but he didn't go down. Fighting blacking out from the blow, he heard the tire iron fall to the porch floor as Lanny grappled for the shotgun.

"I'm going to kill you, you cocky cowboy bastard," the bodyguard growled, so close Buck could smell the man's rancid breath. Lanny was strong and filled with fury for the other times they'd crossed paths.

Buck had let his guard down the past few days, having expected Lanny to make his move right away, since he didn't seem like the patient kind. Because of that miscalculation, Buck had thought with the cops after Maribelle, Lanny had taken off for the hills.

He'd been wrong, and it was about to cost him his life. Yet all he could think about was Ansley.

Ansley woke, sitting straight up in bed. At first she didn't know what had awakened her, until she realized it had been the sound of a gunshot. She looked to the other side of the bed as fear stole her breath. No Buck.

Hurrying, she sprang from the bed, throwing on clothes as she frantically tried to think of what to do. The bedroom door stood open. She saw no lights on in the house as she padded out. "Buck?"

She heard a commotion toward the front of the house. Through the sheer curtains, she could see the shapes of two men struggling for what appeared to be a shotgun. Buck and Lanny?

Her cell phone was back by the bed, but it wouldn't do any good to call for help. No one could get out here in time. What she needed was a weapon. She rushed into the kitchen. Even in the dark she could make out the hanging pots and skillets. But it was the block of knives that she raced for, picking the largest one and rushing toward the front door.

She'd barely reached the door when she heard the second shotgun blast. Throwing open the door, she lunged out. Shotgun in hand, Lanny was standing over Buck, who was bleeding on the porch floorboards. Her heart a thunder, she saw him put the barrel to Buck's head.

After that, everything happened so fast. With no thought but to stop Lanny, she rushed across the floor, knife raised. The bodyguard must have heard the door being thrown open. He started to turn, but by then she was already bringing the knife down, catching him in the side as he turned toward her. He let out a howl, swinging the shotgun in her direction with one hand as he pulled out the knife with the other. She heard the knife clatter to the porch floor.

She didn't see the barrel of the shotgun swinging toward her until it clipped the side of her head, dropping her to her knees. She thought Lanny would shoot her, too, but her heart was so filled with regret over what he'd done to Buck that she felt no fear as he towered over her.

"I should have killed you a long time ago," Lanny said. "Harrison told me that if institutionalizing you didn't work, I was to take care of you. That's right—your own father."

"He's not my father," she spat at him as she saw Buck push himself awkwardly to his feet behind Lanny. He had the fallen knife in his hand, and then he was driving the blade into the bodyguard's back.

Lanny let out another howl of pain as the shotgun fell from his hands. He staggered a step and fell to the side, knocking over a porch chair as he went down.

Ansley scrambled to her feet and rushed to Buck in time to catch him in her arms before he collapsed to the floor.

Chapter 18

Willie left his brothers at the hospital. Buck had come out of surgery. The doctor said if he regained consciousness, he would survive. Ansley had been by his bedside and refused to leave since they'd been brought in.

"Let her stay," he'd told the doctor. "What can it hurt?"

As he climbed into his patrol SUV, he slammed his fist into the steering wheel. He couldn't remember ever being this angry. Maribelle and Harrison had been picked up at a private airport attempting to leave the country, but both had already been released.

The Gallatin County sheriff said that they didn't have enough to hold them without more evidence. The Brookshires were both going to get away with murder and so much more unless Willie could find more proof.

He sat for a moment, trying to calm down. He

couldn't let this go. Judy Ramsey had been murdered on his watch. If nothing else, he would put the fear of God into Maribelle Brookshire. He started his patrol SUV and raced by the sheriff's office to pick up what he needed before he headed for the Brookshire Estate.

When the housekeeper answered the door, he pushed his way in. Maribelle didn't seem surprised to see him. She was sitting in a large leather chair in front of a crackling fire having a drink. She didn't move as he stormed in.

Pulling out the copy of Judy Ramsey's letter, he thrust it into her face.

"I know you killed her," he said. "She left a letter saying that if anything happened to her, you were the one who killed her. This proves you did it."

"What kind of foolishness is this?" she demanded after barely glancing at the paper before balling it up and throwing it into the fire.

"You do realize that isn't the original, right?"

The woman picked up her drink. "If you had proof, I would have been arrested instead of just being questioned. You should leave. If I call my husband..."

"I think you should call your husband, Mrs. Brookshire, because this isn't over. A woman was murdered, and she named you her murderer. I'll be back, only next time, you'll be doing a perp walk to my patrol car. If it's the last thing I do, I'll see you behind bars." He tipped his Stetson and walked out. Behind him, he heard swearing and things breaking.

He'd upset her but had accomplished little else. He had no evidence. He didn't even have proof that the two women had ever met. No way would this case get near a courtroom without a hell of a lot more.

Willie called home. After he told Ellie what he'd done, she chuckled and said, "Feel better?"

"A little." He smiled at just the sound of his wife's voice. How he loved this woman. She kept him centered. "I'm on my way home."

"Drive careful."

"Any word on Buck?"

"The same. We're all praying for him," Ellie said. "He's strong like the lot of you Colts. He'll pull through."

Willie sure hoped so. He felt as if he and his brothers had gotten Buck into this mess. His cell phone rang. He saw it was Ansley and quickly picked up. "Tell me Buck is awake."

"Sorry," she said. "The doctor says there is nothing any of us can do but let his body heal and pray. But there is something I can do until he wakes up. I need your help."

"I wasn't sure you would come," Maribelle said when she opened the door to Ansley the next afternoon.

"Where's Ingrid?" she asked as she stepped inside, feeling goose bumps rise on her arms. The house felt too empty, too quiet. Ansley couldn't help questioning if this had been a mistake. All she'd been able to think about since last night was Buck. But as the doctor who'd performed the surgery had said, there was nothing she could do for him. He'd promised to notify her the moment Buck regained consciousness.

"Gage said you were finally going to tell me the truth," she said as Maribelle closed the door, locking them both alone inside this huge house.

"I'm so glad you and Gage are talking," the woman

she'd believed was her mother said as she motioned toward the living room. "He's a fine young man. I hope you give him another chance. Would you like a drink? I could really use one."

"I'm fine," she said as she watched Maribelle go to the bar and pour herself a stiff drink. Was it possible she hadn't heard about Lanny's death after he'd tried to kill her and Buck? Or about Buck being in a coma in the hospital? No, more than likely, she was merely ignoring it, determined that Ansley would marry Gage and everything would go back to Brookshire normal.

"I know I handled things badly," Maribelle was saying. "I should have told you the truth from the beginning and saved us all a lot of trouble." She sounded too cheerful. It put Ansley's nerves on edge as she moved to the couch but didn't sit until she heard Maribelle behind her.

"When I called, you said you would tell me the truth if I came to see you," she said. "I'm waiting."

Maribelle made a disappointed face. "At least sit down. Please."

Ansley waited until the woman sat before she moved to sit closer to her. "I've waited my whole life to hear this," she said in answer to Maribelle's raised-brow questioning look. "But the moment you start lying to me again, I'm walking out of here, and I won't be back."

"Fine."

"You bought me from Judy Ramsey. Why don't you start there. How did you even meet the woman? You didn't live in the same town, let alone travel in the same circles."

Maribelle took a slug of her drink. "She was working for the caterer at a party I attended. I just happened to hear her throwing up in the ladies' room. I asked if she was pregnant. She said she was. I wanted a daughter so badly, so I asked if she was having a girl. She said she was. And that was that. We agreed on a price. It was impulsive. I knew nothing about the woman. Harrison would have had a fit if he'd known where I got you from, which is why I didn't want you finding your birth mother." She took another healthy drink of her cocktail.

"So you bought me from Judy Ramsey for fifty thousand dollars," Ansley said.

"I would have paid any price. I ached for a daughter." Her face fell. "Turns out I probably wasn't mother material. But I guess I don't have to tell you that."

She couldn't help but wonder why Maribelle was being so open, so candid. "I appreciate you telling me the truth. So you were worried that I'd find out that Judy Ramsey was my mother? Were you worried she would ask for more money? Or that she'd tell me everything?"

"Well, she'd kept our secret for more than twenty-eight years," Maribelle said. "But when you were so determined to find her, I feared she would weaken. Harrison couldn't know about any of it. I'm sure you can understand. He makes allowances for me, but if something like this came out..."

Ansley stared at her. Maribelle still thought the baby had been Judy's. "I get it. That's why you had to kill her."

Maribelle looked up, and their gazes met before she finished her drink and rose to pour herself another one.

"You killed the wrong woman."

Swinging around too quickly, Maribelle sloshed booze onto the carpet. "What are you talking about?"

"Judy Ramsey wasn't my birth mother."

"You're mistaken." She sounded confused, thrown

off balance. One hand held the newly poured drink; the other grabbed the edge of the bar to steady herself. "If anyone should know, I should."

"Judy Ramsey tricked you. She must have lost whatever baby she thought she was carrying or had never been pregnant at all, because the coroner said she'd never given birth. Nor did her DNA match mine."

Maribelle's eyes widened, fear suddenly in her eyes. "That's not possible. If you're not Judy's, then... Where did Judy get you?"

"She played you right to the end, letting you believe that only the two of you knew your secret. There's someone else out there who can expose you and what you did, and you don't even know who it is. Probably won't until she shows up at your trial to testify."

Ansley tried not to take satisfaction in seeing Maribelle stumble to her chair and sit down heavily, clearly shaken. She reminded herself that the woman was probably at least partially responsible for Buck being in the hospital.

"You're lying," Maribelle said, but with little conviction.

"You should have gotten the truth out of Judy before you killed her. Too late now."

"She was mumbling something about insurance, but I thought..."

Ansley nodded. "She wrote it all down, everything about the arrangement you made with her and that if she died, you killed her."

"That ridiculous letter the sheriff tried to show me?" She scoffed.

"You thought she was just trying to stop you from pulling the trigger, right? Well, she did have insurance. But the real evidence against you will be my birth mother when she comes forward with what she knows."

Maribelle was shaking her head. "Judy swore that she didn't tell anyone."

"Was that before or after you shot her?"

"Stop saying that," the woman snapped, finally acting more like the mother Ansley had grown up with. "I did what I had to do. I did it for you as well as our family. If you had just listened to me and not gone looking for the woman, none of this would have happened. I wouldn't have been forced to shoot that bitch."

"Or have me institutionalized?"

"That was your own fault. You wouldn't listen to reason. If it wasn't for that cowboy, you'd still be locked up. I would have left you there until you came to your senses or until you rotted. You've always been a disappointment to me." She took a gulp of her drink.

"So you did tell Lanny to kill not just Buck but me as well."

Maribelle glared over at her. "I told Harrison that Lanny was worthless. I should have known he'd mess it up. Gage is right. You don't deserve being a Brookshire. When you find whoever gave you birth, change your name since you're dead to me. If Lanny wasn't such a screwup I would be at your funeral right now." She downed the rest of her drink. "Where do you think you're going?" she demanded as Ansley rose from her chair. "I wanted to see you because I need to make sure you're not going to keep turning over rocks looking for whoever did pop you out."

"I've heard enough," she said as she started for the door.

"You might as well sit back down. You aren't going

anywhere. I knew I couldn't trust you. I knew I'd have to deal with you myself."

At the door, Ansley unlocked it before turning to face Maribelle—and the gun she was holding. "Do you really think you can get away with shooting me, too?"

"You underestimate me just like Judy Ramsey did," Maribelle said. "Harrison's new bodyguard will clean up the mess, just like Lanny cleaned up Judy Ramsey after I told him where to find what was left of her."

"You're that sure you can get away with murder again?"

Maribelle laughed. "I'll never go to prison. I'm too rich and Harrison is too powerful in this state. I can get away with murder. I already have."

"Probably not this time," Ansley said as the law enforcement officers rushed in, guns drawn, and quickly disarmed Maribelle. As they put on the handcuffs, she screamed that she'd only been trying to defend herself against Ansley, who'd come here to kill her.

"I hope you heard all of that," she said to Willie and the Gallatin County sheriff.

"Loud and clear," Willie said. "Are you all right?"

"I will be," she said as a female officer removed the wire. All she could think about was getting back to Lonesome. Buck was still unconscious. After a stop by the hospital, she was going to finish what she'd started.

Chapter 19

The city offices were about to close when Ansley walked into the mayor's outer office. The name on the desk read Penny Graves. The woman behind the desk was just as Buck had described her. Penny instantly seemed flustered, making Ansley feel as if she'd come to the right place.

"I'm Ansley Brookshire," she said. "I'd like to talk to you about Del Colt."

Penny started to rise but then lowered herself back into her chair. "I don't have anything to say to you." She started to reach for her phone. "You need to leave."

"What I need is the truth. A lot of people have suffered because of this lie. Buck Crawford is in the hospital. The doctor doesn't know if he is going to make it because of me. Because I wanted so badly to find the woman who gave birth to me. Why is it such a secret that Judy Ramsey is now dead and Buck…" She heard a door open and turned to find a dark-haired woman standing in the doorway.

"Mayor Conrad, I was just about to call security," Penny said as she got to her feet. "I can handle this."

"That won't be necessary." The mayor stepped forward even as Penny tried to argue against it. She was tall, her hair chin length, her eyes blue. She held out her hand. "I'm Beth. You're right. We should have met a long time ago. Let's step into my office."

Ansley looked from the mayor to her assistant, who began to sob as she dropped back into her chair. She kept mumbling, "I'm sorry. I'm so sorry."

"It's all right, Penny," Beth Conrad said, putting a hand on her assistant's shoulder. "Everything is all right." Penny sobbed harder.

Chapter 20

"I don't know where to begin," the mayor said once she and Ansley were seated in her office, the door closed. Still, Ansley could hear the woman on the other side of the door crying. "Please excuse Penny. She was only trying to protect me."

"Protect you from me or the truth?"

Their gazes met and held. Tears filled Beth's eyes. "Both. When I heard that some young woman was in town looking for her birth mother, I never dreamed you were looking for me. I was told that you died at birth. That's what I've believed for the past almost thirty years until…" She glanced toward the door and the sound of the distressed woman on the other side.

Ansley shook her head. "I don't understand."

"Penny has been my best friend since we were kids. We're like sisters. She's always been there for me, running interference, watching my back, fighting my battles. She was there when I realized I was pregnant. I was twenty-three, on a break from law school, unmarried and in love with a man who I thought wasn't available."

"Del Colt."

She nodded. "I'd always loved him as far back as I can remember. He married young after falling for Mary Jo. It's understandable. There was something about her that was so appealing—at least for a while. They had Willie right away. I don't know how much you know about his marriage. He kept it from most people. Mary Jo wasn't well. The night I got pregnant, Del broke down and told me what he'd been going through for years. Mary Jo was bipolar. She was also an alcoholic. She would be fine, and then she would take off on a runner. Often he didn't know where she was for days. By the time he found her, she'd be in such bad shape that he'd have to hospitalize her until the next time."

Beth took a breath and seemed to steady herself. "Del loved her, but she was slowly killing him. We'd always been friends. I knew he cared about me. The night he called, he told me that he loved me and had for some time. Mary Jo had finally agreed to a divorce. As much as it broke his heart, he wanted a fresh start with me. He'd been raising the three boys pretty much alone. Mary Jo had no interest in them, but she didn't want to let Del go." She shook her head.

"What neither of us knew was that Mary Jo had purposely gone off the pill. After agreeing to the divorce, she'd begged for one last night together. She got pregnant with Davy even though her doctors had warned her she couldn't have another child without risking her life."

Ansley knew that she had died shortly after Davy was born.

"I saw what Del was going through after he found out about Mary Jo's pregnancy. We'd used protection that night, but I'd still gotten pregnant. I couldn't tell him for so many reasons. I confided in my best friend. Penny's grandmother was a midwife. She agreed to bring my baby into the world. I dropped out of law school when I started showing, and I went to Penny's family cabin up in the mountains. That's where you were born."

"How did Judy Ramsey get involved?"

"She followed Penny up at the cabin. She'd been in the drugstore when Penny picked up some prenatal vitamins for me. She just assumed Penny was the one who was pregnant. Judy and Penny had some kind of rivalry since grade school. Judy was planning to expose her."

Ansley groaned inwardly. "Or Judy had lost her baby or was never really pregnant but had already made a fifty-thousand dollar deal with my—with Maribelle Brookshire. Did she cut you in?"

The mayor flushed. "I had no idea that money was involved. The way Judy had explained it to Penny was that Maribelle couldn't have a child of her own and was desperate to adopt. By then, I knew I couldn't keep you and stay in Lonesome. I was deep in debt from college and what law school I'd managed to attend. I agreed to give you up because I wanted the best for you. I thought I was doing the right thing. But I have to tell you," she added quickly, "I wouldn't have done it had I known you lived. I would have kept you. I'm sure that's why Penny lied to me."

"You thought I died?"

"That's why when I heard you were in town looking for your birth mother, I knew you couldn't be looking for me.

"Apparently I barely survived a difficult delivery," the mayor continued. "Thank heavens Penny's grandmother was there and knew what she was doing. I lost a lot of blood, and for a while, I guess she feared they were going to lose me. When I came to, Penny told me the news."

"I'm sorry but how could you ever forgive Penny for lying to you like that?"

Beth's smile was rueful. "I asked for her help. She did what she thought was best. I think she knew that I never could have given up you or your brother had I known you both had survived."

"My brother?" Ansley asked, heart lodged in her throat.

"I'm sorry. I thought you knew. I was pregnant with twins."

Chapter 21

Buck opened his eyes to the very sight he'd hoped to see—Ansley. She smiled and moved quickly to his bedside.

"I am so glad to see those blue eyes," she said, her smile widening as tears filled her own eyes. She took his hand and squeezed it. "Welcome back. I've missed you."

"I was having a dream about you," he said, his voice rough. "I was worried I might never see you again."

"No chance of that," she said as she poured him a cup of water and helped him sit up a little to drink.

He took a sip, cleared his throat. "Lanny?"

She shook her head.

"I was hoping he'd live long enough to rat out Maribelle." Ansley smiled a smile he was becoming very familiar with. "What did you do?"

She told him about her visit to Brookshire Estate and how Willie had helped her along with the Gallatin County sheriff. "I was wearing a wire. I got her to admit to killing Judy Ramsey and much more."

Buck lay back, smiling at her. He'd thought he would never trust another woman. He hadn't met Ansley Brookshire, aka DelRae Colt, yet. "You are really something."

"I'm glad you think so."

"I feel like I've missed so much. Gage?"

"Holding Maribelle's hand, the ever-loyal almost son-in-law.

"But that's not the big news," Ansley said as she pulled up a chair. "I went to see Penny Graves." His eyes widened in alarm. "She isn't my biological mother."

"I'm sorry." He squeezed her hand. "Once I'm up and out of here—"

"Mayor Beth Conrad is."

"What?"

She nodded and told him about her visit to city hall. He had the feeling that she'd been leaving the best for last. She had that impish smile going again. "I'm going to need your help—and my brothers' as well. Beth was pregnant with twins."

Buck thought he'd misheard her. "*Twins.* Are you telling me there is another one of you out there?"

"Not quite. I have a brother. I haven't told anyone but you. I was hoping you'd get out of here and we could tell my other brothers together."

Lying back, Buck shook his head. "I don't know how to react to this news."

"It's great news. Penny swears my brother lived. The bad news is that Judy Ramsey told her she had someone who desperately wanted to raise him—a different buyer. Unfortunately, Judy took that information to her grave with her.

"Once you're out of here, I thought we'd tell the Colts," Ansley said. "Not sure how they are going to take it."

"Yes, you are. Look how they welcomed you into the family."

"Beth wants to be there, as soon as you are well enough to leave the hospital."

"Beth and Del. That's makes so much more sense," Buck said.

"They were in love," Ansley said and smiled that smile he loved.

"Just like us," the cowboy said and pulled her down for a kiss.

Ansley hadn't been taking calls from Maribelle from jail. She'd been denied bail because she was a flight risk. Harrison had also been arrested as coconspirator. Both were awaiting trial for the killing of Judy Ramsey and for the attempted murder of Ansley and Buck Crawford. So Ansley wasn't surprised when it was Gage who called on Maribelle's behalf again.

"Your mother needs to see you," Gage said. "She's desperate."

"I'm sure she is. She's facing prison for her crimes."

"She's begging to see you," her former fiancé said. "Your father wants to see you as well."

Ansley thought of all the times that neither had wanted much to do with her. Now they both wanted to see her? "I'll see them," she said. She'd already been warned that her adoptive mother was behaving in a delusional manner, as if she didn't understand the gravity of the charges against her. Ansley hadn't known what to expect when she was led back into a room where her mother, wrists cuffed and attached to the table, was waiting.

"I'm so glad you stopped by," Maribelle said, brightening when she saw her, as if Ansley had stopped by the house for a visit—not the county jail, where she was awaiting trial. "I'm going to need something decent to wear to my upcoming hearing. I'm thinking the coral dress. It's always been lucky for me." She smiled. "Your father says I look good in it. You don't think it's too bright, do you? Definitely not the navy one. It's too drab for a courtroom. Makes me look like I have something to hide. Don't forget the shoes that go with the coral dress, and I'll need the handbag I always wear with it."

Ansley nodded as she took a chair across the table. She doubted her adoptive mother needed a handbag for her arraignment but didn't mention it. "Fine, but I need something from you."

Maribelle straightened regally. "Well, under the circumstances, I'm not sure how much help I can offer. Couldn't it wait until I get out of here?"

"What did you do with the other baby?"

"What other baby?" She looked genuinely perplexed.

"My mother gave birth to twins. A boy and a girl. You took the girl, me. What happened to my brother?"

Maribelle frowned. "How should I know? I paid for only one child, a daughter. I didn't even know there was another baby."

Ansley stared at her for a moment, then rose. "I assumed you wanted to see me because you would need clothes for your hearing. I brought the navy dress with some navy heels, because you do have something to hide."

Maribelle gave her an appalled look. "You're joking. I can't possibly wear that."

"I can get the coral one, with the matching shoes and handbag, but I'm not going to go get them until you tell me. What happened to my twin brother?" Her adoptive mother started to argue, but Ansley stopped her. "Otherwise you can wear the navy dress."

"Those aren't even the right shoes," Maribelle cried. "You're doing this to torment me."

"The truth. If I walk out that door, it won't be to get you the other dress. I'll put all your clothes in a dumpster."

She let out a horrified gasp. "Do you have any idea how much my wardrobe costs?" Ansley started to turn to leave. "Wait. My lawyer said there are going to be cameras in the courtroom. You don't want to do this to me. I'm embarrassed enough being locked up here."

"What happened to my twin?"

Chapter 22

Once Buck was released from the hospital and back on his feet, they all gathered in the Colt Brothers main office. James had arranged chairs around his father's big desk, saying it felt appropriate to meet here. He'd had to borrow seats from the sandwich shop next door that Lori used to own so they could all sit.

Ansley had spearheaded the meeting. Beth had agreed to come and bring her best friend and assistant, Penny, with her. Buck had picked Ansley up. They'd arrived early, joining the brothers and their wives.

There was expectation in the air. Ansley couldn't help but think about her father, since he was why they were all crowded in his office tonight.

"Ansley wanted me to be the one to tell you everything," Beth began and told everyone the events that had changed so many people's lives. "I loved Del and, in turn, you boys. I don't know if you remember me babysitting when you were growing up. I tried to help Del when Mary Jo was…wasn't able. I would have done anything for your father. That's why after he told me that Mary Jo was pregnant, I kept my pregnancy from him. I knew he wouldn't leave her now. Then when she died, and your father was so filled with guilt… There was no reason to tell him and make things worse."

"But he must have found out," Willie said. "What about the necklace with DelRae's name on it?"

"Even though I'd decided to give up the babies, I wanted them to have something," Beth said. "I took up knitting. I was terrible at it, but I made each baby a blanket."

"The pink and blue yarn," Ansley said, her voice breaking. She looked at Penny. "So you sent the blue blanket with my twin brother?"

Penny nodded. "I'd also picked up a few clothes for each of them—you—down at the yarn shop. Beth wanted you to have clothes in case your adoptive parents weren't prepared, since you came early."

"That doesn't explain the necklace," Willie said.

"It's all my fault," Penny said. "I did something so stupid."

"No," Beth told her. "You did everything to help me." She looked at Willie. "I had the necklace made with the name DelRae on it and a bracelet with Del Junior, DJ, on it. It was silly and sentimental, but if I was going to give up the babies, I wanted them have something from me and their father. I had Penny order them at the closest jewelry shop. I had no idea that your father had ordered things from the same shop for Mary Jo over the years or that there would be a mix-up years later.

"If anyone is to blame, it's me," Beth said and swallowed. "After I lost the babies, I went back to law school, staying away from Lonesome out of shame. I'd heard that Del had quit the rodeo and started his own PI business. Davy had graduated from high school. All of you boys were rodeoing. I knew Del had to be so proud. I knew it was too late for us, but I needed to come home. I left the firm I'd been working for and moved my law practice to Lonesome. I had so many regrets and was terrified of seeing your father for fear he would see the truth, see my guilt, see my heartbreak and never forgive me for what I'd done. He was busy with his first big case, finding out who'd killed little Billy Sherman."

Beth took a breath before continuing. "I went up to the cabin where I'd spent some of the happiest and saddest time of my life. I found the necklace I'd had Penny make for my baby girl. But couldn't find the bracelet for my son. When I asked Penny—"

"I told her it was buried with him," Penny said. "Then she wanted to see their graves. I told her that they had grown over. I wasn't even sure where they were and that I'd gotten rid of the bracelet. It was supposed to have gone in the bag with the clothes and baby blanket that I gave Judy to give to the adoptive mother. I either missed it or it fell out. I put DJ's in his bag."

"How did my father get the necklace?" Willie asked.

"I stupidly took it back to the store where I'd bought it. I couldn't throw it away. It was gold. So silly. The clerk at the store called him, thinking he'd ordered it and just hadn't picked it up," Penny said. "Once Del found out I was the one who'd ordered it, he put two and two together…" She began to cry. "He confronted me outside the bar. He had the necklace and was demanding to know the truth."

"In front of the bar, the night he died," Willie said.

Penny dropped her head. "He handed me the necklace with DelRae engraved on it and demanded an explanation. I lied, told him yes, Beth had been pregnant, yes, I did order the necklace, but the baby died. He was heartbroken, desperate to find Beth. He kept saying, 'She was pregnant with my baby, with my daughter? How could she keep that from me? Where is she? I need to see Beth. This is all my fault.'"

Penny broke down for a moment. "I didn't know what to do. He was so upset. I'd promised Beth I would never tell. I had to tell him that she'd been pregnant. My heart was breaking, but the babies were gone." She shook her head, tears running down her face.

Beth put an arm around her and handed her a tissue. "Penny was only doing what I asked her to. What I thought was best for everyone at the time. If I could do it over…" She made a swipe at her own eyes. "But I can't."

"I've always believed that my father's death wasn't an accident," Willie said. "We've all wanted to believe that. We couldn't understand why he didn't see or hear the train or why he was on that road that night. The same road that led to Penny's cabin in the mountains."

"He was looking for me," Beth said, her voice breaking. "He was coming to find me. If he'd been in his right mind. If he'd seen the train…"

The room grew quiet for a few minutes.

"I tried to get Ansley to quit looking for Beth," Penny said. "I put that note under your motel room door, and I followed you in Mark's old pickup. I was just trying to protect Beth—and myself." She cried harder. "I never thought that Beth would ever find out that I went ahead with the adoptions. I thought it would be easier if she thought the babies had both died." She turned to Beth. "I'm so sorry."

"I know," Beth said drawing her friend close. "We all did what we thought was best at the time. No one wishes we'd done it differently more than me."

Ansley felt her heart break as the Colt women rose and went to comfort Beth and Penny. She joined them, thinking of how different all their lives could have been, but this was the way life had played out.

Beth drew Ansley close, both of them crying in both happiness at finding each other and regret for what could have been. Ansley would never know her father, but she'd found her mother—and her family.

She could feel the forgiveness filling Del Colt's PI office. His sons now knew the truth. Del had been trying to reach the woman he loved, filled with regret for all that they'd lost. Filled maybe, too, with what could have been. They would never know. Del would never know that he had a daughter who'd come looking for her family and found four brothers and their families, along with the woman who'd given her life. He would also never know that he had another son—a son Ansley would find—with the help of her family. They would all heal, because they would pull together, she thought as felt her brothers' arms come around her and Beth. Their love for Del and each other would always keep them together.

Chapter 23

After everyone but the brothers had left, James pulled out the blackberry brandy. "We have to talk about this," he said. "Brandy before? Or after?"

Tommy grabbed the bottle from him and began to fill the small paper cups. "I, for one, am still in shock. I don't want to believe any of it."

But they all did believe it, James thought as he glanced at his older brother. "Did you know about our mother's...problems?"

Willie looked at his boots for a moment before taking a cup of brandy from his brother, but he didn't drink. "I was just a kid. But I knew something was wrong. Dad always seemed to be protective of me when she... wasn't herself, and then she'd be gone again. I never knew when she'd be back. But when she returned, they were happy. I was happy. She seemed best when she was pregnant, first with you, James. But after you were born, she was weird again and Dad didn't seem to trust her with a baby or a toddler, so she was gone again. Every time he had to take her away, he came back so sad." Willie took a drink of the brandy.

"That had to be hard for you," James said, but Willie only shrugged.

"The only thing that made Dad happy was the rodeo circuit," Willie continued. "I do remember Beth taking care of us sometimes when we were in Lonesome. Dad could have left us behind, but he wanted us with him on the road. There were always women around to take care of us. Probably buckle bunnies with a crush on our father. No wonder, though, that we all grew up loving the sights, sounds and smells of a rodeo. It was in us from the time we were born."

"Dad knew something was wrong with our mother, and yet they just kept having kids," Tommy said.

Willie took a drink before he said, "I think Dad hoped each time she returned that this would be the time she would make it. Also, she was happiest pregnant. But the last time she came back, when you were six, Tommy, I remembered them arguing. Then they seemed to make up, and I realized that she was pregnant again."

"That's when she'd agreed to the divorce, according to Beth," Davy said. "Don't you think Dad might have married Beth if our mother hadn't gotten pregnant with me?"

"None of that matters now," Willie said. "We got you, and we're okay with that."

Davy chuckled. "Why aren't we all more screwed up than we are?"

"Because we had Dad and we had each other," James said. "I remember Willie taking care of us, too. I know I could change diapers when I was three. Tommy was like a little mother to you, Davy. We were all protective of you."

"She died right after I was born?" he asked.

"Shortly afterward," Willie said and looked around the room. "It was an overdose. She got hold of some pills. I'm sure Dad blamed himself for that, too."

"How could we grow up with what had seemed like a normal childhood with all of this going on?" Tommy asked.

"Because, like I said, we had Dad and he loved us," James said.

"He let us run wild," Willie said.

Tommy laughed. "And somehow we all turned out okay."

"He must have really loved her." Davy finished his brandy and looked at his brothers. "But it sounds like he loved Beth, too, and now we have a sister by another mother."

"But Ansley's all Colt," Willie said, admiration in his voice. "She's the one who suggested wearing a wire to get evidence from a woman we knew was a killer…" He shook his head. "She's the reason Maribelle and Harrison Brookshire are facing prison."

"DelRae," Davy said. "DelRae Colt. Think she'll change her name? It will be like we're twins."

"Darned close," James said and room grew quiet.

"Might as well address the elephant in the room." Willie cleared his throat and reached for the brandy bottle. He began to refill each of their cups. "Not that I ever doubted it, but with the DNA results all back, we know that Beth Conrad and Dad conceived a daughter and another son. Penny swears that the son was born alive and that Judy Ramsey promised she'd found him a good home."

James saw the skeptical looks around the room. "Let's say she told the truth. Our half brother could be like Ansley and not even realize he was adopted, since we're all betting the adoption was done illegally. How would we even begin to find him?"

"I don't know," Willie said. "I just know that we have to. Ansley won't rest until we do, and neither will I." He glanced at his brothers and raised his cup. "To your next big case." They all drank and put the bottle away.

Buck found his father in the corral working with a green-broke yearling.

Climbing up onto the railing, he sat and watched his father doing what he loved most. It had always seemed strange to him that his father raised rough stock for rodeos but spent his free time breaking horses to ride. His father, like his grandfather, had made a good living providing stock for cowboys to try to ride, the rougher the better. Neither man had rodeoed. Buck himself had for a while, but he got tired of picking himself up from the dirt.

"How'd your meeting go in town?" his father asked without turning around. He wondered how long the man had known he'd been there.

"Fine."

Wendell Crawford turned from the horse to look at him and frowned. "Fine?"

Buck shrugged. "Got a minute?"

This made his father smile before he turned the horse

back out to pasture and headed for the house. Margarita, a new addition to the Crawford household, met them as they reached the house. "Have a seat out here on the porch. I have peach coffee cake, fresh from the oven. I'll bring you both some if you're interested," she said as she wiped her hands on her apron and smiled at Wendell as he said they would be interested. "Coffee for you both?"

"I'd love some," Buck said and grinned at his father as he pulled up a chair on the porch.

"Don't say it." Wendell took a chair. Buck could see a slight flush to his father's face. He'd met Margarita at the post office, run into her at the grocery store and crossed paths yet again at the steak house one night. She was new to town, widowed and had been raised on a ranch. She loved horses.

His father had asked her out to the ranch, and over the weeks that followed, she'd given up the place she'd bought in town and moved onto the ranch. Buck had never seen his father happier.

"I like it," he said now to his father.

"You would. You're a damned romantic," Wendell said.

Buck laughed. "I guess I am. You know I'm going to marry Ansley."

His father nodded. "She's a beautiful woman. I like her. Think she'll be happy in Lonesome?"

"If you're trying to point out the obvious, I've got it. I have nothing to offer a woman like her."

"That's not true, Buck. And not what I'm saying at all." He shook his head. "You going to stay working with the Colt brothers?"

"Don't know. Maybe. Probably."

"What I know, son, is that you've never been interested in the rough stock business. Fortunately, your brother is. He wants to buy me out of the business. Got it into his head that I might want to spend more time traveling. I have no intention of going anywhere farther than town and back. My point is that this ranch is still yours, too. But if you want a house on it, you're going to have to build one."

Buck laughed. "I can do that. There's a spot by the river I'm partial to."

His father smiled. "I just want you to be happy— and not leave the land you love, even for the woman you love."

"Ansley knows me, Dad. That's why she's moving the design part of her jewelry business to Lonesome and opening a small gift shop."

Wendell nodded. "I've always figured it would take a special woman for you to ever trust again. I'm glad it's Ansley. She seems to have a head on her shoulders. That she's fallen for you tells me that she's one smart woman."

Margarita brought out the coffee and peach coffee cake and then excused herself.

Buck smiled at his father, amused. "What about you? A wedding in your future?"

"Eat your cake," Wendell said. "Your brother and I could lend a hand on that house you're going to build."

"Thanks," he said and took a bite of the cake. "Delicious cake, Margarita," he called back into the house as a white SUV came up the drive.

As Ansley parked and got out, Margarita said from the doorway, "Another coffee and more cake."

"Bring a piece out for yourself," his father said. "Buck and I have had our talk. Join us."

He heard a chuckle from inside the house as Ansley climbed the porch steps.

"Am I interrupting anything?" she asked, glancing at them suspiciously.

"Not a thing," his father said. "Not a thing."

"How's your mother?" Buck asked Ansley.

"Good. I can't believe that we now have time to get to know each other," she said. "We're so much alike." She laughed. "I used to dream of finding her, and now I have. But I never expected to find my family, let alone you."

"If you two are going to get mushy," Wendell said, pretending to rise from his chair. They shooed him back down. "Seriously, I'm happy for you both."

Later after the four of them had enjoyed cake and coffee on the porch, Margarita and his father went inside. Buck and Ansley helped clear up the dishes and came back out on the porch. They sat and talked as the sun set, taking the last of twilight with it. Buck took her hand. "Come on, I've got something I want to show you." Over their heads, stars had begun to pop out.

He walked her down by the river. "Have you ever seen a sky like that?"

She shook her head as she stared up at the stars filling the dark night from horizon to horizon. "It's beautiful."

"*You're* beautiful," he said, drawing her close. He looked into her blue eyes in the starlight, remembering the first time. Fate had brought them together. Fate had delivered the woman he wanted to spend the rest of his life with. "I love you, Ansley Brookshire Del-Rae Colt Conrad."

She laughed, the happiest sound he thought he'd ever heard. "I love you, Buck Crawford."

"I know Beth wants to give you her name," he said, taking both of her hands in his. "So do I. I want to marry you, make babies with you, raise them here on this ranch. Does that sound like something you might be interested in?"

"Oh, Buck, I've never wanted anything more."

He grinned. "So you'll marry me?"

"Can we invite all of my family?"

"We are talking about the ones not behind bars, right?" She nodded. "Then I wouldn't have it any other way."

"There's just one thing," she said. "I want my twin there."

Buck nodded. "I had a feeling you'd say that." He pulled her to him. "We're going to have to find him, and quickly, because I can't wait to make you my bride and start working on those babies. I hear twins run in your family."

"Oh, Buck." She kissed him, promising a lifetime of love.

* * * * *

WEDDING AT
CARDWELL RANCH

This is dedicated to my readers and my Facebook friends who shared their "gaslighting" ideas and proved that they think as creepy me.

If you haven't already, come say hello on my author Facebook page.

Thanks for stopping by Cardwell Ranch!

Chapter 1

Allison Taylor brushed back a lock of her hair and willed herself not to scream.

"Is something wrong?" her brother-in-law asked from the kitchen doorway, startling her and making her jump.

She dropped the heavy covered pot she'd taken from the pantry a little too hard onto the counter. The lid shifted, but not enough that she could see inside.

"Didn't mean to scare you," Drew Taylor said with a laugh as he lounged against the kitchen door frame. "I was cravin' some of your famous chili, but I think maybe we should go out."

"I just need a minute. If you could see to Natalie…"

"She's still asleep. I just checked." Drew studied her for a long moment. Like his brother, he had russet-brown hair and dark brown eyes and classic good looks.

His mother had assured both of her sons that they were wonderful. Fortunately Drew had taken it with a grain of salt—unlike his brother Nick.

"Are you okay, Allie? I've been so worried about you since Nick…"

"I'm fine." She didn't want to talk about her presumed-dead husband. She really just wanted her brother-in-law to go into the other room and leave her alone for a moment.

Drew had been a godsend. She didn't know what she would have done without him, she thought as she pulled a band from her jeans pocket and secured her long, blond hair in a single tail at the back of her head.

When she'd mentioned how nice his brother was to Nick shortly after they married, he'd scoffed.

"Just be glad he likes you. He's about the only one in my family," he had added with a laugh.

"Why don't you let me help you with that," Drew said now as he took a step toward her. He frowned as his gaze went to the pot and the pile of ingredients she'd already stacked up on the counter. The chili pot was the last thing she'd brought into the kitchen from the porch of the small cabin. "You kept the pot?"

So his mother had told him about the incident.

He must think I'm losing my mind just like his mother and sister do.

The worst part was she feared they were right.

Allie looked down at the heavy cast-iron pot with its equally heavy cast-iron lid. Her hand trembled as she reached for the handle. The memory of the last time she'd lifted that lid—and what she'd found inside—sent a shudder through her.

The covered cast-iron casserole pot, enameled white

inside and the color of fresh blood on the outside, had been a wedding present from her in-laws.

"She does know how to cook, doesn't she?" her mother-in-law, Mildred, had asked all those years ago as if Allie hadn't been standing there. Mildred was a twig-thin woman who took pride in these things: her petite, slim, fifty-eight-year-old body, her sons and her standing in the community. Her daughter, Sarah, was just the opposite of her mother, overweight and dumpy by comparison. And Mildred was always making that comparison to anyone who would listen, including Sarah.

Mildred was on her fourth husband and lived in one of the more modest mansions at Big Sky. Of her two sons, Nick had been the baby—and clearly her favorite.

Nick had laughed that day when his mother had asked if his new wife could cook. "She makes pretty good chili, I'll give her that," he told Mildred. "But that's not why I married her." He'd given Allie a side hug, grinning like a fool and making her blush to the roots of her hair.

Nick had liked to say he had the prettiest wife in town. "Just make sure you stay that way," he'd always add. "You start looking like my sister and you can pack your bags."

The red, cast-iron, covered pot she was now reaching for had become her chili pot.

"Allie, I thought you'd thrown that pot away!" Drew reached to stop her, knocking the lid off in the effort. It clattered to the counter.

Allie lunged back, her arm going up protectively to shield her face. But this time the pot was empty. No half-dead squirrel inside it.

"I'm throwing this pot in the trash," Drew announced. "If just the sight of it upsets you—"

"No, your mother will have a fit."

"Let her." He swept pot and lid off the counter and carried it out to the garbage can.

When he came back into the room, he looked at her and shook his head. "Allie, you've got to pull it together. Maybe you should go back to the doctor and see if there is something else he can give you. You're strung like a piano wire."

She shook her head. "I don't need a doctor." She just needed for whatever was happening to her to stop.

His gaze moved past her, his expression going from a concerned frown to a smile. "Hey, girl," he said as his five-year-old niece came into the kitchen. He stepped past Allie to swing Nat into his arms. "I came over to check on the two of you. Mama was going to cook us some dinner but I think we should go out to eat. What do you say?"

Allie started to argue that she couldn't let Drew do any more for them and she sure couldn't afford to go out to eat, but stopped as her daughter said, "Are you sick, Mama?" Her precious daughter looked to her with concern. Allie saw the worry in Nat's angelic face. She'd seen it too much lately. It was bad enough that Natalie had recently lost her father. Now more than ever she needed her mother to be sane.

"I'm fine, sweetie. It's too hot for chili, anyway. So let's go out, why not?" Allie said, relieved and thankful for Drew. Not just for coming by to check on them, but for throwing out the pot. She hadn't because her mother-in-law was upset enough and the Taylors were the only family she had, especially now.

"Just let me freshen up and change," she said as Drew took Nat to look for her shoes.

In the bathroom, Allie locked the door, turned on the shower and stripped off her clothes. She was still sweating from fear, her heart beating hard against her chest.

"You found a what in the chili pot?" her mother-in-law had asked in disbelief when Allie had called her—a huge mistake in retrospect. But at the time, she'd hoped her mother-in-law would understand why she couldn't keep the pot. Why she didn't want it in her house.

"I found a squirrel in that cast-iron pot you gave me. When I picked up the lid—"

"No way would a squirrel get into your cabin, let alone climb under a heavy lid like that. Why would it? You must have imagined it. Are you still on those drugs the doctor gave you after my Nicky died?"

Allie's husband had always been "my Nicky" to his mother while Mildred had insisted Allie call *her* "Mother Taylor."

"No, Mother Taylor, I told you." Allie's own mother had died when she was nineteen. Her father had moved, remarried and started a new family. They'd lost touch. "I quit taking the pills a long time ago."

"I think it's those pills," Mildred had said as if Allie hadn't spoken. "You said they had you seeing things that weren't there."

"The squirrel *was* there. I had to take it out back and—"

"If I were you, I'd talk to your doctor. Why do you need the pills, anyway? It isn't like you're still grieving over my Nicky. Charlotte Reynolds told me she saw you having lunch the other day, you and Natalie, and you were *laughing*."

Allie had closed her eyes, remembering the lunch in question. "I am trying to make things more normal for Nat."

"Well, it looks bad, you having a good time while your poor husband is barely cold in his grave."

She wanted to mention that Nick wasn't in his grave, but knew better than to bring that up. "It's been eight months."

"Like you have to tell me that!" Mildred sniffed and blew her nose. She'd cried constantly over the death of her favorite son and couldn't understand why Allie wasn't still doing the same.

"We all grieve in our own way and I have a young daughter to raise," Allie had said more times than she wanted to recall.

The phone call had ended with Mildred crying and talking about what a wonderful man her Nicky had been. A lie at best. He'd been a lousy husband and an even worse father, but now that he was dead, he would always be the wonderful man Mildred remembered.

After that, she'd learned her lesson. She kept the other crazy things that had been happening to herself. If Mildred knew, she would have her in a straitjacket. And little Nat...? She couldn't bear to think about Mildred having anything to do with raising her daughter.

"So," Drew said as she and Nat sat across from him in a booth at a local café later that evening. "Did I hear you've gone back to work?"

It was impossible to keep anything a secret in this canyon, Allie thought. She had hoped to keep it from the Taylor family as long as possible.

"Dana Savage called me about doing a Western wedding up at her ranch for her cousin Tag and his soon-to-be wife, Lily." She didn't mention that she'd accepted the job several months ago. Or how badly she needed the money. With the investigation into Nick's presumed death still unresolved, the insurance company was holding off paying her. Not that it would last long if she didn't get back to work.

Her mother-in-law kept mentioning "that big insurance check my Nicky left you," but the insurance money would barely cover a couple years of Natalie's college, if that. And Allie hoped to invest it for that very use.

"I've been doing some work at Cardwell Ranch. Nice people to work for. But are you sure you're up to it?" Drew asked quietly, real concern in his tone. "Mother mentioned that she was worried about you. She said you were still taking the pills and they were making you see things?"

Of course Mildred told Drew and his sister, Sarah, everything. Allie tried not to show her irritation. She had no appetite, but she attempted to eat what she could. She didn't want Drew mentioning to his mother, even accidentally, that she wasn't eating much. Mildred would make it into her not taking care of herself.

"I'm fine. I'm *not* taking the pills. I told your mother—"

He held up his hand. "You don't have to tell me about my mother. She hears only what she wants to hear. I'm on your side. I think going back to work might be the best thing for you. So what do you plan to do with Natalie? I don't have to tell you what Mother is going to say."

"Nat's going with me," Allie said emphatically. "Dana has children she can play with. As a matter of fact, Dana is going to teach Nat to ride a horse."

Natalie grinned and clapped her small hands excitedly. She was the spitting image of Allie at that age: straight, pale blond hair cut in a bob, green eyes with a pert little nose and deep dimples. Allie got the blond hair from her Scandinavian mother and the green eyes from her Irish father.

There was no sign of the Taylor family in her daughter, something that had caused a lot of speculation from not only Nick, but his mother.

Nat quickly told her uncle that it would be a very gentle horse and Dana's kids Hank and Mary were riding before they were even her age. "The twins are too young to ride yet," she announced.

"Dana wouldn't let Nat do it if she thought it wasn't all right," Allie added.

"I'm sure it will be fine," Drew said, but she could tell that he already knew what her mother-in-law was going to have to say about it. "Cardwell Ranch is where the wedding is going to be, I take it?"

"The wedding will be in a meadow on the ranch with the reception and a lot of other events in the large, old barn."

"You know that we've been invited," Drew said almost in warning.

The canyon was its own little community, with many of the older families—like Dana's—that dated back to the eighteen hundreds before there was even a paved road through it. Mildred Taylor must be delighted to be invited to a wedding of a family that was like old canyon royalty. Mother Taylor might resent the Cardwell clan, say things behind their back, but she would never outright defy them since everyone loved Dana Cardwell Savage and had held great respect for her mother, Mary Justice.

"How are things with you?" Allie asked.

"Everything's fine." He smiled but she'd seen the lines around his eyes and had heard that his construction company was struggling without Nick.

He'd been so generous with her and Natalie that she feared he was giving away money he didn't have.

She was just thankful when the meal was over and Drew dropped her and Nat off at the small cabin in the Gallatin Canyon where she'd lived with Nick until his disappearance. *The canyon* as it was known, ran from the mouth just south of Gallatin Gateway almost to West Yellowstone, fifty miles of winding road that trailed the river in a deep cut through the mountains.

The drive along the Gallatin River was breathtaking, a winding strip of highway that followed the blue-ribbon trout stream up over the Continental Divide. In the summer as it was now, the Gallatin ran crystal clear over tinted green boulders. Pine trees grew dark and thick along its edge and against the steep mountains. Aspens, their leaves bright green, grew among the pines.

Sheer rock cliffs overlooked the highway and river, with small areas of open land. The canyon had been mostly cattle and dude ranches, a few summer cabins and homes—that was until Big Sky resort and the small town that followed developed at the foot of Lone Mountain.

Luxury houses had sprouted up all around the resort, with Mother Taylor's being one of them. Fortunately, some of the original cabins still remained and the majority of the canyon was National Forest so it would always remain undeveloped.

Allie's was one of the older cabins. Because it was small and not in great shape, Nick had gotten a good deal on it. Being in construction, he'd promised to enlarge it and fix all the things wrong with it. That hadn't happened.

After Drew left, Allie didn't hurry inside the cabin. It was a nice summer night, the stars overhead glittering brightly and a cool breeze coming up from the river.

She had begun to hate the cabin—and her fear of what might be waiting for her inside it. Nick had been such a force of nature to deal with that his presence seemed to have soaked into the walls. Sometimes she swore she could hear his voice. Often she found items of his clothing lying around the house as if he was still there—even though she'd boxed up his things and taken them to the local charity shop months ago.

Just the thought of what might be waiting for her inside the cabin this time made her shudder as she opened the door and stepped in, Nat at her side.

She hadn't heard Nick's voice since she'd quit taking the drugs. Until last night. When she'd come into the living room, half-asleep, she'd found his favorite shirt lying on the floor by the couch. She'd actually thought she smelled his aftershave even though she'd thrown the bottle away.

The cabin looked just as she'd left it. Letting out a sigh of relief, she put Nat to bed and tried to convince herself she hadn't heard Nick's voice last night. Even the shirt that she'd remembered picking up and thinking it felt warm and smelled of Nick before she'd dropped it over the back of the couch was gone this morning, proving the whole incident had been nothing but a bad dream.

"Good night, sweetheart," she said and kissed her daughter's forehead.

"Night," Nat said sleepily and closed her eyes.

Allie felt as if her heart was going to burst when she looked at her precious daughter. She couldn't let Mildred get her hands on Nat. But if the woman thought for a moment that Allie was incapable of raising her daughter…

She quickly turned out the light and tiptoed out of the room. For a moment, she stood in the small living area. Nick's shirt wasn't over the back of the couch so that was a relief.

So many times she had stood here and wished her life could be different. Nick had been so sweet while they were dating. She'd really thought she'd met her Prince Charming—until after the wedding and she met the real Nick Taylor.

She sighed, remembering her decision soon after the wedding to leave him and have the marriage annulled, but then she'd realized she was pregnant. Had she really been so naive as to think a baby would change Nick into the man she'd thought she'd married?

Shaking her head now, she looked around the cabin, remembering all the ideas she had to fix the place up and make it a home. Nick had hated them all and they had ended up doing nothing to the cabin.

Well, she could do what she wanted now, couldn't she? But she knew, even if she had the money, she didn't have the heart for it. She would never be able to exorcize Nick's ghost from this house. What she really wanted was to sell the cabin and move. She promised herself she would—once everything with Nick's death was settled.

Stepping into her bedroom, she was startled to see a pile of her clothes on her bed. Had she taken them out of the closet earlier when she'd changed to go to dinner? Her heart began to pound. She'd been upset earlier but she wouldn't have just thrown her clothes on the bed like that.

Then how had they gotten there? She'd locked the cabin when she'd left.

Panicked, she raced through the house to see if anything was missing or if any of the doors or windows had been broken into. Everything was just as she'd left it—except for the clothes on her bed.

Reluctantly, she walked back into her bedroom half-afraid the clothes wouldn't still be on the bed. Another hallucination?

The clothes were there. Unfortunately, that didn't come as a complete relief. Tonight at dinner, she'd worn capris, a blouse and sandals since it was June in Montana. Why would she have pulled out what appeared to be almost everything she owned from the closet? No, she realized, not *everything*. These were only the clothes that Nick had bought her.

Tears blurred her eyes as she started to pick up one of the dresses. Like the others, she hated this dress because it reminded her of the times he'd made her wear it and how the night had ended. It was very low cut in the front. She'd felt cheap in it and told him so but he'd only laughed.

"When you've got it, flaunt it," he'd said. "That's what I say."

Why hadn't she gotten rid of these clothes? For the same reason she hadn't thrown out the chili pot after the squirrel incident. She hadn't wanted to upset her mother-in-law. Placating Mother Taylor had begun right after Allie had married her son. It was just so much easier than arguing with the woman.

"Nick said you don't like the dresses he buys you," Mildred had said disapprovingly one day when she'd stopped by the cabin and asked Allie why she wasn't wearing the new dress. "There is nothing wrong with looking nice for your husband."

"The dresses he buys me are just more revealing than I feel comfortable with."

Her mother-in-law had mugged a face. "You'd better loosen up and give my son what he wants or he'll find someone who will."

Now as she reached for the dress on the top of the pile, she told herself she would throw them out, Mother Taylor be damned.

But the moment she touched the dress, she let out a cry of surprise and panic. The fabric had jagged cuts down the front. She stared in horror as she saw other deep, angry-looking slices in the fabric. *Who had done this?*

Her heart in her throat, she picked up another of the dresses Nick had made her wear. Her sewing scissors clattered to the bedroom floor. She stared down at the scissors in horror, then at the pile of destroyed clothing. All of the dresses Nick had bought her had been ruined.

Allie shook her head as she dropped the dress in her hand and took a step back from the bed. Banging into the closed closet doors, she fought to breathe, her heart hammering in her chest. *Who did this?* Who *would* do this? She remembered her brother-in-law calling from out in the hall earlier, asking what was taking her so long before they'd gone to dinner. But that was because she'd taken a shower to get the smell of her own fear off her. It wasn't because she was in here cutting up the clothes her dead husband had made her wear.

Tears welled in her eyes, making the room blur. She shoved that bitter thought away and wiped at her tears. She wouldn't have done this. She *couldn't* have.

Suddenly, she turned and stared at the closed closet door with mounting fear. Slowly, she reached for the knob, her hand trembling. As the closet door came open, she froze. Her eyes widened in new alarm.

A half dozen new outfits hung in the otherwise nearly empty closet, the price tags still on them. As if sleepwalking, Allie reached for one of the tags and stared in shock at the price. Hurriedly, she checked the others. She couldn't afford any of them. So where had they come from?

Not only that, the clothes were what she would call "classic," the type of clothes she'd worn when she'd met Nick. The kind of clothes she'd pleaded with him to let her wear.

"I want other men to look at you and wish they were me," Nick had said, getting angry.

But when she and Nick went out and she wore the clothes and other men did look, Nick had blamed her.

"You must have given him the eye," Nick would say as they argued on the way home. "Probably flipped your hair like an invitation. Who knows what you do while I'm at work all day."

"I take care of your daughter and your house."

Nick hadn't let her work after they'd gotten married, even though he knew how much she loved her wedding planning business. "Women who work get too uppity. They think they don't need a man. No wife of mine is going to work."

Allie had only the clothes he bought her. She'd purchased little since his death because the money had been so tight. Nick had wanted to know about every cent she'd spent, so she hadn't been able to save any money, either. Nick paid the bills and gave her a grocery allowance. He said he'd buy her whatever she needed.

Now she stared at the beautiful clothes hanging in her closet. Beautiful blouses and tops. Amazing skirts and pants and dresses. Clothes Nick would have taken out in the yard and burned. But Nick was gone.

Or was he? He still hadn't been declared legally dead. That thought scared her more than she wanted to admit. What if he suddenly turned up at her door one night?

Was that what was making her crazy? Maybe she *had* done this. She had yearned for clothing like this and hated the clothes Nick had bought her, so had she subconsciously…

Allie stumbled away from the closet, bumped into the corner of the bed and sat down hard on the floor next to it. Her hand shook as she covered her mouth to keep from screaming. Had she shoplifted these clothes? She couldn't have purchased them. Just as she couldn't have cut up the dresses and not remembered. There had to be another explanation. Someone was playing a horrible trick on her.

But even as she pondered it, more rational thoughts came on its heels. Did she really believe that someone had come into the cabin and done this? Who in their right mind would believe that?

Pushing herself up, she crawled over to where she'd dropped her purse as she tried to remember even the last time she'd written a check. Her checkbook wasn't in her purse. She frowned and realized she must have left it in the desk when she'd paid bills.

Getting up she walked on wobbly legs to the desk in

the corner, opened the drawer and took out her check-book. Her fingers shook with such a tremor that she could barely read what was written in it.

But there it was. A check for more than eight hundred dollars! The handwriting was scrawled, but she knew it had to be hers. She saw the date of the check. *Yesterday?*

She had dropped Nat off for a playdate and then gone into Bozeman… Could she account for the entire afternoon? Her heart pounded as she tried to remember everything she'd done and when she might have bought these clothes. She'd been wandering around in a daze since Nick's death. She couldn't account for every minute of yesterday, but what did that matter? The proof was staring her in the face.

Allie shoved the checkbook into the drawer and tried to pull herself together. She had to think about her daughter.

"You're fine," she whispered to herself. "Once you get back to work…" She couldn't have been more thankful that she had the Cardwell Ranch wedding. More than the money, she needed to do what she loved—planning weddings—and get her mind off everything else.

Once she was out of this house she'd shared with Nick… Yes, then she would be fine. She wouldn't be so…forgetful. What woman wouldn't feel she was losing her mind, considering what she'd been going through?

Chapter 2

"Who's that singing?" five-year-old Ford Cardwell asked as he and his father followed the sound.

Jackson Cardwell had parked the rental SUV down by his cousin Dana's ranch house when they'd arrived, but finding no one at home, they'd headed up the hill toward the barn and the van parked in front of it.

"I have no idea, son," Jackson said, but couldn't help smiling. The voice was young and sweet, the song beautiful. "It sounds like an angel."

"It *is* an angel," Ford cried and pointed past the barn to the corrals.

The girl was about his son's age, but while Ford had taken after the Cardwell side of the family with his dark hair and eyes, this child had pale blond hair and huge green eyes.

When she saw them, she smiled, exposing two deep

dimples. Both children were adorable, but this little girl was hands down more angelic-looking and—Jackson would bet—*acting* than Ford.

She wore cowboy boots with a pale green-and-white-polka-dotted, one-piece, short jumpsuit that brought out the emerald-green of her eyes. Jackson saw that the girl was singing to several horses that had come up to the edge of the corral fence.

The girl finished the last of the lyrics before she seemed to notice them and came running over. "If you're looking for my mother, she's in the barn working."

Next to him, Jackson saw that his son had apparently been struck dumb.

"I'm Nat," the girl announced. "My name is really Natalie, though." She shifted her gaze to the mute Ford. "Everyone calls me Nat, so you can if you want to."

"This is my son, Ford."

Nat eyed Ford for a moment before she stepped forward and took his hand. "Come on, Ford. You'll probably want to see the rest of the animals. There are chickens and rabbits and several mules along with all the horses. Don't worry," she added before Jackson could voice his concern. "We won't get too close. We'll just pet them through the corral fence and feed the horses apples. It's okay. Mrs. Savage showed me how."

"Don't go far," Jackson said as the precocious Nat led his son toward several low-slung buildings. The girl was busy talking as they left. Ford, as far as Jackson could tell, hadn't uttered a word yet.

As he turned back toward the barn, he saw the logo on the side of the van: Weddings by Allie Knight. The logo looked old as did the van.

The girl had said her mother was working in the barn. That must be where the wedding was going to be held. His brother Tag had mentioned something about his wedding to Lily McCabe being very *Western*.

"You mean like Texas meets Montana?" Jackson had joked.

"Something like that. Don't worry. You'll feel right at home."

His brother's wedding wasn't what had him worried. After talking to Tag for a few moments on the phone, he'd known his brother had fallen head over heels for Lily. He was happy for him.

No, what worried Jackson was nailing down the last of the plans before the wedding for the opening of a Texas Boys Barbecue joint in Big Sky, Montana. He had hoped that all of the brothers would be here by now. Laramie and Austin hadn't even flown up to see the space Tag had found, let alone signed off on the deal.

From the time the five brothers had opened their first restaurant in an old house in Houston, they'd sworn they would never venture outside of Texas with their barbecue. Even as their business had grown and they'd opened more restaurants and finally started their own franchise, they had stayed in the state where they'd been raised.

Jackson understood why Tag wanted to open one here. But he feared it had nothing to do with business and everything to do with love and not wanting to leave Montana, where they had all been born.

Before the wedding had seemed the perfect time for all of them to get together and finalize the deal. Hayes had come here last month to see if the restaurant was even feasible. Unfortunately, Hayes had gotten sidetracked, so now it was up to the rest of them to make sure Tag was doing the best thing for the business—and before the wedding, which was only four days away.

He hoped all his brothers arrived soon so they could get this over with. They led such busy lives in Texas that they hardly ever saw each other. Tag had said on the phone he was anxious to show him the building he'd found for the new restaurant. Tag and Hayes had already made arrangements to buy the building without the final okay from the other brothers, something else that made Jackson nervous.

Jackson didn't want this move to cause problems among the five of them. So his mind was miles away as he started to step into the dim darkness inside the barn.

The cool air inside was suddenly filled with a terrified scream. An instant later, a black cat streaked past him and out the barn door.

Jackson raced into the barn not sure what he was going to find. What he found was a blond-haired woman who shared a striking resemblance to the little girl who'd been singing outside by the corrals.

While Nat had been angelic, this woman was as beautiful as any he'd ever seen. Her long, straight, blond hair was the color of sunshine. It rippled down her slim back. Her eyes, a tantalizing emerald-green, were huge with fear in a face that could stop traffic.

She stood against the barn wall, a box of wedding decorations open at her feet. Her eyes widened in even more alarm when she saw him. She threw a hand over her mouth, cutting off the scream.

"Are you all right?" he asked. She didn't appear to be hurt, just scared. No, not scared, *terrified*. Had she seen a mouse? Or maybe something larger? In Texas it might have been an armadillo. He wasn't sure what kind of critters they had this far north, but something had definitely set her off.

"It was nothing," she said, removing her hand from her mouth. Some of the color slowly returned to her face but he could see that she was still trembling.

"It was *something,*" he assured her.

She shook her head and ventured a look at the large box of decorations at her feet. The lid had been thrown to the side, some of the decorations spilling onto the floor.

He laughed. "Let me guess. That black cat I just saw hightailing it out of here… I'm betting he came out of that box."

Her eyes widened further. *"You saw it?"*

"Raced right past me." He laughed. "You didn't think you imagined it, did you?"

"It happened so fast. I couldn't be sure."

"Must have given you quite a fright."

She let out a nervous laugh and tried to smile, exposing deep dimples. He understood now why his son had gone mute. He felt the same way looking at Natalie's mother. There was an innocence about her, a vulnerability that would make a man feel protective.

Just the thought made him balk. He'd fallen once and wasn't about to get lured into that trap again. Not that there was any chance of that happening. In a few days he would be on a plane back to Texas with his son.

"You know cats," he said, just being polite. "They'll climb into just about anything. They're attracted by pretty things." Just like some cowboys. Not him, though.

"Yes," she said, but didn't sound convinced as she

stepped away from the box. She didn't look all that steady on her feet. He started to reach out to her, but stopped himself as she found her footing.

He couldn't help noticing that her eyes were a darker shade of green than her daughter's. "Just a cat. A black one at that," he said, wondering why he felt the need to fill the silence. "You aren't superstitious, are you?"

She shook her head and those emerald eyes brightened. That with the color returning to her cheeks made her even more striking.

This was how he'd fallen for Ford's mother—a pretty face and what had seemed like a sweet disposition in a woman who'd needed him—and look how that had turned out. No, it took more than a pretty face to turn his head after the beating he'd taken from the last one.

"You must be one of Tag's brothers," she said as she wiped her palms on her jeans before extending a hand. Along with jeans, she wore a checked navy shirt, the sleeves rolled up, and cowboy boots. "I'm Allie Taylor, the wedding planner."

Jackson quickly removed his hat, wondering where he'd left his manners. His mother had raised him better than this. But even as he started to shake her hand, he felt himself hesitate as if he were afraid to touch her.

Ridiculous, he thought as he grasped her small, ice-cold hand in his larger, much warmer one. "Jackson Cardwell. I saw your van outside. But I thought the name on the side—"

"Taylor is my married name." When his gaze went to her empty ring finger, she quickly added, "I'm a widow." She pulled back her hand to rub the spot where her wedding band had resided not that long ago. There was a thin, white line indicating that she hadn't been widowed long. Or she hadn't taken the band off until recently.

"I believe I met your daughter as my son and I were coming in. Natalie?"

"Yes, my baby girl." Her dimpled smile told him everything he needed to know about her relationship with her daughter. He knew that smile and suspected he had one much like it when he talked about Ford.

He felt himself relax a little. There was nothing dangerous about this woman. She was a single parent, just like him. Only she'd lost her husband and he wished he could get rid of his ex indefinitely.

"Your daughter took my son to see the horses. I should probably check on him."

"Don't worry. Nat has a healthy respect for the horses and knows the rules. Also Warren Fitzpatrick, their hired man, is never far away. He's Dana's semi-retired ranch manager. She says he's a fixture around here and loves the kids. That seems to be his job now, to make sure the kids are safe. Not that there aren't others on the ranch watching out for them, as well. Sorry, I talk too much when I'm...nervous." She took a deep breath and let it out slowly. "I want this wedding to be perfect."

He could tell she was still shaken by the black cat episode. "My brother Tag mentioned that Dana and the kids had almost been killed by some crazy woman. It's good she has someone she trusts keeping an eye on the children, even with everyone else on the ranch watching out for them. Don't worry," he said, looking around the barn. "I'm sure the wedding will be perfect."

The barn was huge and yet this felt almost too intimate standing here talking to her. "I was just about to get Ford and go down to the house. Dana told me she was baking a huge batch of chocolate chip cookies and to help ourselves. I believe she said there would also be homemade lemonade when we got here."

Allie smiled and he realized she'd thought it was an invitation. "I really need to get these decorations—"

"Sorry. I'm keeping you from your work." He took a step back. "Those decorations aren't going to put themselves up."

She looked as if she wasn't so sure of that. The cat had definitely put a scare into her, he thought. She didn't seem sure of anything right now. Allie looked again at the box of decorations, no doubt imagining the cat flying out of it at her.

Glancing at her watch, she said, "Oh, I didn't realize it was so late. Nat and I are meeting a friend for lunch. We need to get going."

Jackson was suddenly aware that he'd been holding his hat since shaking Allie's hand. He quickly put it back on as they walked out of the barn door into the bright sunshine. "My son is quite taken with your daughter," he said, again feeling an unusual need to fill the silence.

"How old is he?"

"Ford's five."

"Same age as Nat."

As they emerged into the beautiful late-June day, Jackson saw the two children and waved. As they came running, Nat was chattering away and Ford was hanging on her every word.

"They do seem to have hit it off." Allie sounded surprised and pleased. "Nat's had a hard time lately. I'm glad to see her making a new friend."

Jackson could see that Allie Taylor had been having

a hard time, as well. He realized she must have loved her husband very much. He knew he should say something, but for the life of him he couldn't think of what. He couldn't even imagine a happy marriage. As a vehicle came roaring up the road, they both turned, the moment lost.

"Hey, bro," Tanner "Tag" Cardwell called from the rolled down window of his pickup as he swung into the ranch yard. "I see you made it," he said, getting out to come over and shake his brother's hand before he pulled Jackson into a hug. Tag glanced over at Ford and Natalie and added with a laugh, "Like father like son. If there's a pretty female around, you two will find them."

Jackson shook his head. That had been true when he'd met Ford's mother. But since the divorce and the custody battle, he'd been too busy single-handedly raising his son to even think about women. That's why red flags had gone up when he'd met Allie. There was something about her that had pulled at him, something more than her obvious beauty.

"Dana's right behind me with the kids," Tag said. "Why don't I show you and Ford to your cabin, then you can meet everyone." He pointed up in the pines that covered the mountainside. "Let's grab your bags. It's just a short walk."

Jackson turned to say goodbye to Allie, but she and her daughter had already headed for the old van.

"Come on, Nat, we're meeting Belinda for lunch," Allie said as the Cardwell men headed for the cabins on the mountain behind the barn. Working here had been a godsend. Nat was having a wonderful time. She loved Dana's children. Hank was a year older than Nat, with

Mary being the same age. Dana's twin boys, Angus and Brick, were just over a year and her sister Stacy's daughter, Ella, was a year and a half. Dana had her hands full but Stacy helped out with the younger ones. All of them loved the animals, especially the horses.

True to her word, Dana had made sure Nat had begun her horseback riding lessons. Nat was a natural, Dana had said, and Allie could see it was true.

Their few days here so far had been perfect.

Until the cat, there hadn't been any other incidents.

Her friend Belinda Andrews was waiting for them at a little Mexican food place near Meadow Village at Big Sky. While other friends had gone by the wayside since she'd married Nick six years ago, Belinda hadn't let Nick run her off. Allie suspected that, like her, she didn't have a lot of friends and Nick, while he'd made it clear he didn't like Belinda, had grudgingly put up with her the times they'd crossed paths.

"I hope we didn't keep you waiting," Allie said as she and Nat met Belinda on the patio. "You didn't have any trouble getting off work for the wedding shoot?" Belinda worked for a local photographer, but freelanced weddings. It was how they'd met back when Allie had her own wedding planning business.

Belinda grinned. "All set for the Tag Cardwell and Lily McCabe wedding. I took Dana up on her offer. I'm moving into one of the guest cabins later today!"

Allie wasn't all that surprised. Dana had offered her a cabin, as well, while she was preparing everything for the wedding. But since she lived just down the highway a few miles, Allie thought it best to remain at home for Nat's sake. Her daughter had had enough changes in her life recently.

"You really are excited about this," Allie said, noticing how nice Belinda looked. Her friend was dressed in a crop top and cut-off jeans, her skin tanned. Her dark hair was piled haphazardly up on her head, silver dangly earrings tinkled from her earlobes and, while she looked makeup free, Allie could tell she wasn't.

Belinda looked enchanting, a trick Allie wished she could pull off, she thought. On the way here, she'd pulled her hair up in a ponytail and even though she'd showered this morning, she'd forgone makeup. Nick was always suspicious when she wore it when he wasn't around so she'd gotten out of the habit.

Inside the café, Nat asked if she could play in the nearby area for kids and Allie said she could as long as she didn't argue about coming back to eat when her meal came.

"You look…pale," Belinda said, studying her after they were seated outside on the patio under an umbrella so they could see Nat. "You haven't had anymore of those…incidents, have you?"

Allie almost laughed at that. "I just need to get more sun," she said and picked up her menu to hide behind.

"I know you too well," Belinda said, dragging down the menu so she could look into her eyes. "What's happened *now?*"

"A black cat jumped out of one of my decoration boxes and scared me just before I came over here. And guess what? Someone else saw it." *So there,* she wanted to say, *I don't need my head examined.*

Belinda nodded, studying her. "A *black* cat?"

"Yes, a *black* cat and I didn't imagine it. One of the Cardwell brothers saw it, as well." She couldn't even voice how much of a relief that had been.

"That's all that's happened?"

"That's it." She had to look down at the menu to pull off the lie and was just glad when Belinda didn't question her further. She hadn't told *anyone* about the shredded dresses from her closet or the new clothes she'd taken back. The sales associate hadn't remembered her, but said the afternoon when the clothing was purchased had been a busy one. None of the other sales associates remembered her, but agreed they'd been too busy to say for sure. She'd ended up keeping two of the outfits to wear while working the rehearsal dinner and the wedding.

"I already moved some of my things into the cabin," Belinda said.

Allie couldn't help being surprised. "Already? Why didn't you stop by the barn and say hello?" Allie had suggested Belinda as the wedding photographer and felt responsible and anxious since this was her first wedding in five years.

"You were busy," her friend said. "We can't keep each other from our jobs, right?"

"Right." She loved that Belinda understood that. In truth, Allie had been hesitant to suggest her friend. She didn't want to have to worry about Belinda, not with everything else that she had going on in her life right now. While her friend was a great photographer, sometimes she got sidetracked if a handsome man was around. But when she'd broached the subject with the bride-to-be, Lily had been delighted that it was one other thing she didn't have to worry about.

Dana had been kind enough to offer Belinda a cabin on the ranch for the five-day affair. "It will make it easier for you to get great shots if you're staying up here and experiencing all the wedding festivities," Dana had said. "And any friend of Allie's is a friend of ours."

She and Belinda had been friends since grade school. Lately they hadn't been as close, probably Allie's fault. Belinda was in between men right now, and much wilder, freer and more outspoken than Allie had ever been. But Belinda didn't have a five-year-old daughter, either.

"You have no idea what this means to me," Belinda said now. "I've been dying to photograph a Western wedding for my portfolio."

"Your portfolio?"

Belinda looked embarrassed as if she'd let the cat out of the bag, so to speak. "I'm thinking about opening my own studio."

"That's great." Allie was happy for her friend, although she'd wondered if Belinda had come into some money because it wouldn't be cheap and as far as she knew Belinda lived from paycheck to paycheck like everyone else she knew.

The waitress came and took their orders. A light breeze stirred the new leaves on the nearby trees. The smell of summer mixed with that of corn tortillas, the most wonderful smell of all, Allie thought. They sipped Mexican Cokes, munched on chips and salsa to the sound of Latin music playing in the background and Allie felt herself begin to relax.

"I wasn't going to bring this up," Belinda said, "but you know that psychic that I've seen off and on?"

Allie fought not to roll her eyes.

"I know you say you don't believe in this stuff, but she said something interesting when I mentioned you."

"You told her about *me?*" Allie hadn't meant for her

voice to rise so high. Her daughter looked over. She smiled at Nat and quickly changed her tone. "I really don't want you talking to anyone about me, let alone a…" She tried to come up with a word other than *charlatan*.

Belinda leaned forward, unfazed. "She thinks what's happening to you is because of guilt. Simply put, you feel guilty and it is manifesting itself into these…*incidents*."

Allie stared at her. Leave it to Belinda to get right to the heart of it.

Her friend lowered her voice as if afraid Nat might be listening. "It makes sense, if you think about it. Nick didn't know you were—" she glanced at Nat "—leaving him and going to file for custody of you-know-who, but *you* did know your plan. Then he goes and gets himself…" She grimaced in place of the word *killed*. "Something like that has to mess with your mind."

"Yes, losing your husband does mess with your mind no matter what kind of marriage you had." Fortunately, the waitress brought their food. Allie called Nat up to the table and, for a few moments, they ate in silence.

"The thing is…" Belinda said between bites.

"Can't we just enjoy our meal?" Allie pleaded.

Her friend waved that suggestion away, but didn't say more until they had finished and Nat had gone back to the play area.

"The psychic thinks there is more to it," Belinda said. "What if Nick *knew* about your…plan?"

"What are you saying?"

"Come on. You've been over Nick for a long time. His death wouldn't make you crazy—"

"I'm not crazy," she protested weakly.

"But what if he *did* know or at least suspected? Come on, Allie. We both know it was so not like Nick to go hunting up into the mountains alone, knowing that the grizzlies were eating everything they could get their paws on before hibernation." She didn't seem to notice Allie wince. "Didn't the ranger say Nick had food in his backpack?"

"He didn't take food to attract a bear, if that's what you're saying. He planned to stay a few days so of course he had food in his backpack."

"I'm not trying to upset you. But if he went up there to end it all, that was his choice. You can't go crazy because you feel guilty."

Her stomach turned at the thought of the backpack she'd been asked to identify. It had been shredded by the grizzly's claws. She'd been horrified to think of what the bear had done to Nick. She would never forget the officer who'd brought her the news.

"From what we've been able to assess at the scene, your husband was attacked by a grizzly and given the tracks and other signs—"

"Signs?"

"Blood, ma'am."

She'd had to sit down. "You're telling me he's... dead?"

"It certainly looks that way," the ranger had said. Four days later, the search for Nick Taylor was called off because a winter storm had come in and it was believed that there was little chance he could have survived such an attack without immediate medical attention.

"Nick wouldn't," she managed to say now. In her heart of hearts, the man she knew so well, the man she'd been married to for more than six years, wouldn't purposely go into the woods with a plan to be killed by a grizzly.

But Nick had always been unpredictable. Moody and often depressed, too. The construction business hadn't been doing well even before Nick's death. What would he have done if he'd known she was leaving him and taking his daughter? Hadn't she been suspicious when Nick told her of his plan to go hunting alone? She'd actually thought he might be having an affair and wanted to spend a few days with his mistress. She'd actually hoped that was the case.

"You're going by yourself?" she'd asked. Nick couldn't even watch football by himself.

"I know things haven't been great with us lately," he'd said. That alone had surprised her. She really thought Nick hadn't noticed or cared. "I think a few days apart is just what we both need. I can tell you aren't happy. I promise you there will be changes when I get back and maybe I'll even come home with a nice buck." He'd cupped her face in his hands. "I don't think you know what you mean to me, but I promise to show you when I get back." He'd kissed her then, softly, sweetly, and for a moment, she'd wondered if Nick could change.

"You're wrong about Nick," she said now to Belinda. "If he was going to end it, he would have chosen the least painful way to do it. Not one—" she looked at Nat, who was swinging nearby, humming to herself and seemingly oblivious to their conversation "—that chose him. He had a gun with him he could have used."

"Maybe he didn't get the chance, but you're probably right," Belinda said and grabbed the check. "Let me get this. I didn't mean to upset you. It's just that you need to get a handle on whatever's been going on with you for you-know-who's sake." She cut her eyes to Nat, who headed toward them as they stood to leave.

"You're right about the guilt, though," Allie said, giving her friend that. She'd known as she'd watched Nick leave that day to go up into the mountains that nothing could change him enough to make her stay. She was going to ask him for a divorce when he came back.

Belinda changed the subject. "I saw your brother-in-law, Drew, earlier on the ranch."

Allie nodded. "He mentioned he was working up there. His construction company built the guest cabins."

"I'd forgotten that." Belinda frowned. "I was talking to Lily about photos at the rehearsal dinner. Did you know that Sarah is one of her bridesmaids?"

"My sister-in-law worked with Lily one season at her brother James's Canyon Bar." Allie had the impression that Lily didn't have a lot of female friends. Most of the math professors she knew were male, apparently. "I think James feels sorry for Sarah and you know Lily, she is so sweet."

"I have to hand it to Sarah, putting up with her mother day in and day out," Belinda said.

Allie didn't want to think about it. Along with fewer incidents the past few days, she'd also been blessed with no visits from her mother-in-law and Sarah.

"Sarah's a saint, especially—" Belinda lowered her voice "—the way Mildred treats her. She is constantly bugging her about her weight and how she is never going to get a husband… It's awful."

Allie agreed.

"I don't understand why she doesn't leave."

"Where would she go and what would she do?" Allie said. "Sarah was in college when Mildred broke her leg.

She quit to come home and take care of her mother. Mildred has milked it ever since. It used to annoy Nick, Sarah living in the guesthouse. He thought Sarah was taking advantage of his mother."

"Ha, it's the other way around. Sarah is on twenty-four-hour call. She told me that her mother got her out of bed at 2:00 a.m. one time to heat her some milk because she couldn't sleep. I would have put a pillow over the old nag's face."

Allie laughed and changed the subject. "You look especially nice today," she commented, realizing that her friend had seemed happier lately. It dawned on her why. "There's someone new in your life."

Belinda shrugged. She didn't like to talk about the men she dated because she thought it would jinx things for her. Not talking about them didn't seem to work, either, though. Belinda was so superstitious. Why else would she see a psychic to find out her future?

"This is going to be so much fun, the two of us working together again. Don't worry. I won't get in your way." Belinda took her hand. "I'm sorry I upset you. Sometimes I don't have the brains God gave a rock."

She didn't think that was the way the expression went, but said nothing. Belinda could be so…annoying and yet so sweet. Allie didn't know what she would have done without her the past few years. Belinda had been the only person she would talk freely to about Nick and the trouble between them.

"I'm just worried about you, honey," Belinda said, squeezing her hand. "I really think you should see someone—"

"I don't need a shrink."

"Not a shrink. Someone more…spiritual who can

help you make sense of the things that you say keep happening."

"Things *do* keep happening," she snapped. "I'm not making them up."

"So talk to this woman," Belinda said just as adamantly. She pressed a business card into Allie's hand.

She glanced at it and groaned. "Your psychic friend?"

"She might be the *only* person who can help you," Belinda said cryptically. She gripped Allie's hand tighter. "She says she can get you in touch with Nick so you can get past this."

Allie stared at her for a moment before laughing out loud. "You have got to be kidding. What does she use? A Ouija board?"

"Don't laugh. This woman can tell you things that will make the hair on your head stand straight up."

That's all I need, she thought, reminded of Jackson Cardwell asking her if she was superstitious.

"Call her," Belinda said, closing Allie's fingers around the woman's business card. "You need closure, Allie. This woman can give it to you. She's expecting your call."

"I've been expecting your call, as well," said a sharp, older voice.

They both turned to see Mildred and her daughter. From the looks on their faces, they'd been standing there for some time.

Chapter 3

"Want to see the building for Montana's first Texas Boys Barbecue?" Tag asked after they'd dropped Jackson and Ford's luggage off at the small cabin on the side of the mountain and gone down to meet cousin Dana and her brood.

Dana Cardwell Savage was just as Tag had described her. Adorable and sweet and delighted that everyone was coming for the wedding.

"How is your cabin?" she asked after introducing him to her children with husband, Marshal Hud Savage. Hank was the spitting image of his father, Dana said, and six now. Mary was five and looked just like her mom. Then there were the twins, Angus and Brick, just a year and a half old with the same dark hair and eyes as all the Cardwells.

"The cabin is great," Jackson said as Ford instantly

bonded with his second cousins. "Thank you so much for letting me stay there."

"Family is why we had them built," Dana said. "My Texas cousins will always have a place to stay when you visit. Or until you find a place to live in Montana when you realize you want to live up here," she added with a wink. "Isn't that right, Tag?"

"I would love to visit, but I'm never leaving Texas," Jackson said.

"Never say never," Tag commented under his breath. "I was just about to take him down to see the restaurant location."

Ford took off with the other kids into a room full of toys and didn't even look back as his father left. Jackson almost felt as if he were losing his son to Montana and the Cardwell clan.

"Are you sure you don't want to wait until everyone gets here?" he asked as they left.

"Hayes and Laramie are flying in tomorrow. I was hoping you would pick them up at the airport. Austin is apparently on a case tying up some loose ends." He shrugged. Of the five of them, Austin was the loner. He was dedicated to his job and being tied up on a case was nothing new. "Anyway, it's your opinion I want. You're better at this than all three of them put together."

"So you haven't heard from Austin on the deal," Jackson guessed.

Tag shook his head. "You know how he is. He'll go along with whatever everyone else says. Come on," he said with a laugh when Jackson groaned. "I really do want your opinion."

"*Honest* opinion?" Jackson asked.

"Of course."

Jackson glanced around as they drove out of the ranch and down the highway to the turnoff to Big Sky. Being the youngest, he didn't remember anything about Montana. He'd been a baby when his mother had packed up her five sons and taken them to Texas.

Big Sky looked more like a wide spot in the road rather than a town. There were clusters of buildings broken only by sagebrush or golf greens.

"This is the lower Meadow Village," Tag told him. "There is also the Mountain Village higher up the mountain where the ski resort is. You really have to see this place in the winter. It's crazy busy around the holidays. There are a lot of second homes here so the residents fly in and spend a few weeks generally in the summer and the holidays. More and more people, though, are starting to live here year-round. There is opportunity here, Jackson."

Jackson wanted to tell his brother that he didn't need to sell him. He'd go along with whatever the others decided. In fact, he'd already spoken to Hayes about it. Once Hayes got on board, it was clear to Jackson that this was probably a done deal. The holdout, if there was one, would be Austin and only because he wouldn't be available to sign off on the deal. Even Laramie sounded as if he thought the restaurant was a good idea.

"Where does Harlan live?" Jackson asked as they drove past mansions, condos and some tiny old cabins that must have been there before anyone even dreamed of a Big Sky. He had only a vague recollection of his father from those few times Harlan had visited Texas when he was growing up.

"He lives in one of those cabins back there, the older ones. We can stop by his place if you like. More than likely he and Uncle Angus are down at the Corral Bar. It's their favorite watering hole. Maybe we could have a beer with them later."

"I'm sure I'll see him soon enough." Harlan was a stranger who hadn't even made Jackson's wedding, not that the marriage had lasted long, anyway. But he felt no tie to the man who'd fathered him and doubted he ever would. It was only when he thought about Ford that he had regrets. It would have been nice for Ford to have a grandfather. His ex-wife's family had no interest in Ford. So the only family his son had in Texas was Jackson's mother, Rosalee Cardwell and his brother Laramie. Tag had already moved to Montana and Hayes would be moving here soon.

"I'm getting to know Dad," Tag said. "He's pretty remarkable."

"Tell me about your wedding planner," Jackson said, changing the subject then regretting the topic he'd picked when his brother grinned over at him. "I'm just curious about her." He hadn't told anyone about the cat or the terrified woman he'd found in the barn earlier. Her reaction seemed over the top given it had only been a cat. Though it *had* been a black one. Maybe she *was* superstitious.

"Allie's great. Dana suggested her. That's our Dana, always trying to help those in need. Allie lost her husband eight months ago. Terrible thing. He was hunting in the mountains and apparently killed by a grizzly bear."

"Apparently?"

"They never found his body. They think the bear dragged the body off somewhere. Won't be the first time remains have turned up years later in the mountains—if they turn up at all. They found his backpack and enough blood that he can be declared legally dead but I guess the insurance company has been dragging its feet."

Jackson thought of Allie and her little girl, Nat. "How horrible for them."

"Yeah, she's been having a hard time both emotionally and financially according to Dana, who suggested her for our wedding planner because of it. But Lily loves Allie and, of course, Natalie. That little girl is so darned bright."

"Yeah, Ford is definitely taken with her." But his thoughts were on Allie and her reaction to the cat flying out of that box of wedding decorations. It must have scared her half out of her wits in the emotional state she was in. "That was nice of Dana to hire her."

"Allie worked as a wedding planner before she married Nick Taylor. Dana offered Allie and Nat one of the new guest ranch cabins where we're staying. But I guess she thinks it would be better for Natalie to stay in their own home."

"Where do Allie and her daughter live now?"

"An old cabin down by the river. I'll show you on the way back." Tag swung into a small complex and turned off the engine. "Welcome to the site of the next Texas Boys Barbecue joint."

"I thought you had a job," Mildred said to Allie over the sound of brass horns playing cantina music at the Mexican café.

"They allow lunch breaks," she said. "But I really need to get back." She excused herself to go to the ladies' room.

Mildred turned to Natalie, leaned down and pinched her cheek. "How is my sweetie today? Grandma misses you. When are you coming to my house?"

In the restroom, Allie splashed cold water on her face and tried to calm down. How much had they heard?

Enough that they had been looking at her strangely. Or was that all in her mind, as well? But if they heard Belinda trying to get her to see a psychic so she could reach Nick on the other side... Allie could well imagine what they would think.

She hurried, not wanting to leave Natalie with her grandmother for long. She hated it, but Mildred seemed to nag the child all the time about not spending enough time with her.

Leaving the restroom, she saw that Sarah and her mother hadn't taken a seat. Instead, they were standing at the takeout counter. There was no avoiding talking to them again.

"I couldn't help but overhear your...friend suggesting you see a...psychic?" Mother Taylor said, leaving no doubt that they had been listening. "Surely she meant a psychiatrist, which indicates that you are still having those hallucinations." She quirked an eyebrow, waiting for an answer.

"Belinda was only joking. I'm feeling much better, thank you."

Mildred's expression said she wasn't buying a minute of it. "Sarah, I left my sweater in the car."

"I'll get it, Mother." Sarah turned and headed for their vehicle parked out front.

"How is this...job of yours going?" Mildred asked. "I've never understood what wedding planners do."

Allie had actually told her once, listing about fifty things she did, but Mildred clearly hadn't been listening.

"I'll have to tell you sometime," she said now. "But I need to get back to it. Come on, Natalie."

"You should let me have her for the rest of the day," Mildred said. "In fact, she can spend the night at my house."

"I'm sorry, but Natalie is getting horseback riding lessons this afternoon," Allie lied. "She's having a wonderful time with Dana's children."

"Well, she can still—"

"Not only that, I also prefer to have Nat with me right now. It's hard enough without Nick." Another lie followed by the biggest truth of all, "I need my daughter right now."

Mildred looked surprised. "That's the first time I've heard you mention my Nicky in months." She seemed about to cry. Sarah returned with her sweater, slipping it around her shoulders without even a thank-you from Mildred.

Nearby, Belinda was finishing up their bill.

"I really should get back to work." Allie tried to step past her mother-in-law, but the older woman grabbed her arm. "I worry that you are ill-equipped to take care of yourself, let alone a child. I need Natalie more than you do. I—"

Allie jerked her arm free. "Natalie would be heartbroken if she was late to her horseback riding lesson." She hurried to her daughter, picked up her purse off the table and, taking Nat's hand, left the restaurant, trying hard not to run.

She told herself to calm down. Any sign of her being upset and her in-laws would view it as her being unable to take care of Nat. But all she wanted was to get away and as quickly as possible.

But as she and Nat reached her van and she dug in her purse for her keys, she realized they weren't there. Her heart began to pound. Since Nick's death, she was constantly losing her keys, her purse, her sunglasses… her mind.

"Forgetfulness is very common after a traumatic event," the doctor had told her when she'd gotten an appointment at her in-laws' insistence.

"It scares me. I try to remind myself where I put things so this doesn't happen, but when I go back to get whatever it was… I'm always so positive that's where I left it. Instead, I find it in some…strange place I could never imagine."

The doctor had chuckled and pulled out his prescription pad. "How are you sleeping?" He didn't even wait for her to answer. "I think once you start sleeping through the night, you're going to find that these instances of forgetfulness will go away."

The pills had only made it worse, though, she thought now as she frantically searched for her van keys. She could feel Nat watching her, looking worried. Sometimes it felt as if her five-year-old was taking care of her instead of the other way around.

"It's okay, sweetheart. Mama just misplaced her keys. I'm sure they're in here…."

"Looking for these?" The young waitress from the café came out the door, holding up her keys.

"Where did you find them?" Allie asked, thinking they must have fallen out of her purse at the table and ended up on the floor. That could happen to anyone.

"In the bathroom sink."

Allie stared at her.

"You must have dropped them while you were washing your hands," the young woman said with a shrug as she handed them over.

As if that was likely. She hadn't even taken her purse to the restroom, had she? But she had it now and she couldn't remember. She'd been so upset to see Sarah and Mildred.

"Nat, what was Grandmother saying to you in the restaurant?"

"She wanted me to go to her house but I told her I couldn't. I'm going horseback riding when we get to the ranch," Nat announced. "Dana is taking me and the other kids." Her lower lip came out for a moment. "Grandma said she was really sad I wasn't going with her."

"Yes," Allie said as, with trembling fingers, she opened the van door. Tears stung her eyes. "But today is a happy day so *we* aren't going to be sad, right? There are lots of other days that you can spend with your grandmother." Nat brightened as she strapped her into her seat.

Just a few more minutes and she and Nat would be out of here. But as she started the van, she looked up to find Mother Taylor watching her from beside Sarah's pearl-white SUV. It was clear from her expression that she'd witnessed the lost-key episode.

From the front steps of the restaurant, Belinda waved then made the universal sign to telephone.

Allie knew Belinda didn't mean call her. Reaching in her pocket, she half expected the psychic's business card to be missing. But it was still there, she realized with sagging relief. As crazy as the idea of reaching Nick beyond the grave was, she'd do *anything* to make this stop.

* * *

When Allie and her daughter returned, Jackson was watching her from inside his cousin's two-story ranch house.

"She lost her husband some months back," Dana said, joining him at the window.

"I wasn't—"

"He went up into the mountains during hunting season," she continued, ignoring his attempt to deny he'd been wondering about Allie. "They found his backpack and his rifle and grizzly tracks."

"Tag mentioned it." Tag had pointed out Allie's small, old cabin by the river on their way back to the ranch. It looked as if it needed work. Hadn't Tag mentioned that her husband was in construction? "Tag said they never found her husband's body."

Dana shook her head. "But Nick's backpack was shredded and his rifle was half-buried in the dirt with grizzly tracks all around it. When he didn't show up after a few days and they had no luck finding him…"

"His remains will probably turn up someday," Hud said as he came in from the kitchen. Dana's husband, Hud, was the marshal in the canyon—just as his father had been before him. "About thirty years ago now, a hiker found a human skeleton of a man. He still hasn't been identified so who knows how long he'd been out there in the mountains."

"That must make it even harder for her," Jackson said.

"It was one reason I was so glad when she decided to take the job as wedding planner."

He watched Allie reappear to get a box out of the van. She seemed nervous, even upset. He wondered if something had happened at lunch. Now at least he understood why she had overreacted with the black cat.

Hud kissed his wife, saying he had to get back to work, leaving Dana and Jackson alone.

"Our fathers are setting up their equipment on the bandstand in the barn," Dana said. "Have you seen Harlan yet?"

"No," Jackson admitted. "Guess there is no time like the present, huh?"

Jackson hadn't seen his father in several years, and even then Harlan hadn't seemed to know how to act around him—or his other sons, for that matter. As they entered the barn, Tag joining them, he saw his father and uncle standing on the makeshift stage, guitars in their hands, and was surprised when he remembered a song his father had once sung to him.

He didn't know how old he'd been at the time, but he recalled Harlan coming into his bedroom one night in Texas and playing a song on his guitar for him. He remembered being touched by the music and his father's voice.

On stage, the two brothers began playing their guitars in earnest. His father began singing. It was the voice Jackson remembered and it was like being transported back to his childhood. It rattled him more than he wanted to admit. He'd thought he and his father had no connection. But just hearing Harlan sing made him realize that he'd been lying to himself about not only the lack of connection, but also his need for it.

Harlan suddenly broke off at the sight of his sons. He stared through the dim barn for a moment, then put down his guitar to bound off the stage and come toward Jackson. He seemed young and very handsome, belying his age, Jackson thought. A man in his prime.

"Jackson," he said, holding out his hand. His father's hand was large and strong, the skin dry, callused and warm. "Glad you made it. So where are the rest of your brothers?"

"They're supposed to fly in tomorrow. At least Laramie and Hayes are," Tag said. "Austin... Well, he said he would do his best to make it. He's tied up on a case, but I'm sure you know how that goes." At Christmas, Tag had found out what their father did besides drink beer and play guitar—and shared that amazing news with them. Both Harlan and his brother Angus had worked undercover as government agents and still might, even though they were reportedly retired.

"Duty calls sometimes," Harlan agreed. "I'm glad I'm retired."

"Until the next time someone gets into trouble and needs help," Tag said.

Harlan merely smiled in answer.

Jackson was glad to see that his brother and their father could joke. Tag, being the oldest, remembered the years living in Montana and their father more than his brothers.

"The old man isn't so bad," Tag had told them after his visit at Christmas. "He's starting to grow on me."

Jackson had laughed, but he'd been a little jealous. He would love for his son to have a grandfather. He couldn't imagine, though, how Harlan could be a part of his only grandson's life, even if he wanted to. Texas and Montana were just too far apart. And Harlan probably had no interest, anyway.

"Where's that bride-to-be?" Uncle Angus asked Tag as he hopped off the stage and came toward them.

"Last minute preparations for the wedding," Tag said. "You can't believe the lists she's made. It's the mathematician in her. She's so much more organized than I am. Which reminds me, Jackson and I have to drive down to Bozeman to pick up the rings."

"It took a wedding to get you Cardwell boys to Montana, I see." Uncle Angus threw an arm around Jackson. "So how are you liking it up here? I saw that boy of yours. Dana's got him riding horses already. You're going to have one devil of a time getting him to go back to Texas after this."

Didn't Jackson know it. He'd hardly seen his son all day. Even now Ford had been too busy to give Jackson more than a quick wave from the corral where he'd been with the kids and the hired man, Walker.

"Ford is going to sleep like a baby tonight after all this fresh air, sunshine and high altitude," Jackson said. "He's not the only one," he added with a laugh.

"It's good for him," Harlan said. "I was talking to him earlier. He's taken with that little girl."

"Like father like son," Tag said under his breath as Allie came in from the back of the barn.

Jackson saw her expression. "I think I'd better go check on my son," he said as he walked toward Allie. He didn't have time to think about what he was about to do. He moved to her, taking her arm and leading her back out of the barn. "What's wrong?"

For a moment she looked as if she were going to deny anything was. But then tears filled her eyes. He walked her around the far side of the barn. He could hear Dana out by the corral instructing the kids in horseback riding lessons. Inside the barn, his father and uncle struck up another tune.

"It's nothing, really," she said and brushed at her tears. "I've been so forgetful lately. I didn't remember that the band would be setting up this afternoon."

He saw that she held a date book in her trembling hand.

"It wasn't written down in your date book?"

She glanced at her book. "It was but for some reason I marked it out."

"No big deal, right?"

"It's just that I don't remember doing it."

He could see that she was still upset and wondered if there wasn't something more going on. He reminded himself that Allie had lost her husband only months ago. Who knew what kind of emotional roller coaster that had left her on.

"You need to cut yourself more slack," he said. "We all forget things."

She nodded, but he could see she was still worried. No, not worried, scared. He thought of the black cat and had a feeling it hadn't been her first scare like that.

"I feel like such a fool," she said.

Instinctively, he put his arm around her. "Give yourself time. It's going to be all right."

She looked so forlorn that taking her in his arms seemed not only the natural thing to do at that moment, but the only thing to do under the circumstances. At first she felt board-stiff in his arms, then after a moment she seemed to melt into him. She buried her face into his chest as if he were an anchor in a fierce storm.

Suddenly, she broke the embrace and stepped back.

He followed her gaze to one of the cabins on the mountainside behind him and the man standing there.

"Who is that?" he asked, instantly put off by the scowling man.

"My brother-in-law, Drew. He's doing some repairs on the ranch. He and Nick owned a construction company together. They built the guest cabins."

The man's scowl had turned into a cold stare. Jackson saw Allie's reaction. "We weren't doing anything wrong."

She shook her head as the man headed down the mountainside to his pickup parked in the pines. "He's just very protective." Allie looked as if she had the weight of the world on her shoulders again.

Jackson watched her brother-in-law slowly drive out of the ranch. Allie wasn't the only one the man was glaring at.

"I need to get back inside," she said and turned away.

He wanted to go after her. He also wanted to put his fist into her brother-in-law's face. *Protective my butt,* he thought. He wanted to tell Allie to ignore all of it. Wanted... Hell, that was just it. He didn't know what he wanted at the moment. Even if he did, he couldn't have it. He warned himself to stay away from Allie Taylor. Far away. He was only here for the wedding. While he felt for the woman, he couldn't help her.

"There you are," Tag said as he came up behind them. "Ready to go with me to Bozeman to get the rings?"

Jackson glanced toward the barn door Allie was stepping through. "Ready."

Chapter 4

As Jackson started to leave with his brother, he turned to look back at the barn. Just inside the door he saw Allie. All his survival instincts told him to keep going, but his mother had raised a Texas cowboy with a code of honor. Or at least she'd tried. Something was wrong and he couldn't walk away.

"Give me just a minute," he said and ran back. As he entered the barn, he saw Allie frantically searching for something in the corner of the barn. His father and brother were still playing at the far end, completely unaware of them.

"What are you looking for?"

She seemed embarrassed that he'd caught her. He noticed that she'd gone pale and looked upset. "I know I put my purse right there with my keys in it."

He glanced at the empty table. "Maybe it fell under

it." He bent down to look under the red-and-white-checked tablecloth. "The barn is looking great, by the way. You've done a beautiful job."

She didn't seem to hear him. She was moving from table to table, searching for her purse. He could see that she was getting more anxious by the moment. "I know I put it right there so I wouldn't forget it when I left."

"Here it is," Jackson said as he spied what he assumed had to be her purse not on a table, but in one of the empty boxes that had held the decorations.

She rushed to him and took the purse and hurriedly looked inside, pulling out her keys with obvious relief.

"You would have found it the moment you started loading the boxes into your van," he said, seeing that she was still shaken.

She nodded. "Thank you. I'm not usually like this."

"No need to apologize. I hate losing things. It drives me crazy."

She let out a humorless laugh. "Crazy, yes." She took a deep breath and let it out slowly. Tears welled in her eyes.

"Hey, it's okay."

He wanted to comfort her, but kept his distance after what had happened earlier. "It really is okay."

She shook her head as the music stopped and quickly wiped her eyes, apologizing again. She looked embarrassed and he wished there was something he could say to put her at ease.

"Earlier, I was just trying to comfort you. It was just a hug," he said.

She met his gaze. "One I definitely needed. You have been so kind...."

"I'm not kind."

She laughed and shook her head. "Are you always so self-deprecating?"

"No, just truthful."

"Well, thank you." She clutched the keys in her hand as if afraid she would lose them if she let them out of her sight.

At the sound of people approaching, she stepped away from him.

"Let me load those boxes in your van. I insist," he said before she could protest.

As Dana, Lily and the kids came through the barn door they stopped to admire what Allie had accomplished. There were lots of oohs and ahhs. But it was Lily whose face lit up as she took in the way the barn was being transformed.

Jackson shifted his gaze to Allie's face as she humbly accepted their praise. Dana introduced Jackson to Lily. He could see right away why his brother had fallen for the woman.

"Please come stay at one of the guest cabins for the rest of the wedding festivities," Dana was saying to Allie.

"It is so generous of you to offer the cabin," Allie said, looking shocked at the offer.

"Not at all. It will make it easier for you so you don't have to drive back and forth. Also I'm being selfish. The kids adore Natalie. It will make the wedding a lot more fun for them."

Allie, clearly fighting tears of gratitude, said she would think about it. Jackson felt his heartstrings pulled just watching. "I'll work hard to make this wedding as perfect as it can be. I won't let you down."

Lily gave her a hug. "Allie, it's already perfect!"

Jackson was surprised that Lily McCabe had agreed to a Western wedding. According to the lowdown he'd heard, Lily taught mathematics at Montana State University. She'd spent her younger years at expensive boarding schools after having been born into money.

Jackson wondered if the woman had ever even been on a horse—before she met the Cardwells. Apparently, Allie was worried that a Western wedding was the last thing a woman like Lily McCabe would want.

"Are you sure this is what *you* want?" Allie asked Lily. "After all, it is *your* wedding."

Lily laughed. "Just to see the look on my parents' faces will make it all worthwhile." At Allie's horrified look, she quickly added, "I'm kidding. Though that is part of it. But when you marry into the Cardwell family, you marry into ranching and all that it comes with. I want this wedding to be a celebration of that.

"This is going to be the best wedding ever," Lily said as she looked around the barn. "Look at me," she said, holding out her hands. "I'm actually shaking I'm so excited." She stepped to Allie and gave her another hug. "Thank you so much."

Allie appeared taken aback for a moment by Lily's sudden show of affection. The woman really was becoming more like the Cardwells every day. Or at least Dana Cardwell. That wasn't a bad thing, he thought.

"We should probably talk about the other arrangements. When is your final dress fitting?"

"Tomorrow. The dress is absolutely perfect, and the boots!" Lily laughed. "I'm so glad Dana suggested red boots. I love them!"

This was going to be like no wedding Allie had ever

planned, Jackson thought. The Cardwells went all out, that was for sure.

He looked around the barn, seeing through the eyes of the guests who would be arriving for the wedding. Allie had found a wonderful wedding cake topper of a cowboy and his bride dancing that was engraved with the words: *For the rest of my life.* Tag had said that Lily had cried when she'd seen it.

The cake was a little harder to nail, according to Tag. Jackson mentally shook his head at even the memory of his brother discussing wedding cakes with him. Apparently, there were cake designs resembling hats and boots, covered wagons and cowhide, lassoes and lariats, spurs and belt buckles and horses and saddles. Some cakes had a version of all of them, which he could just imagine would have thrown his brother for a loop, he thought now, grinning to himself.

"I like simple better," Lily had said when faced with all the options. "It's the mathematician in me."

Allie had apparently kept looking until she found what she thought might be the perfect one. It was an elegant white, frosted, tiered cake with white roses and ribbons in a similar design as Lily's Western wedding dress.

"I love it," Lily had gushed. "It's perfect."

They decided on white roses and daisies for her bouquet. Bouquets of daisies would be on each of the tables, the vases old boots, with the tables covered with red-checked cloths and matching napkins.

Jackson's gaze returned to Allie. She seemed to glow under the compliments, giving him a glimpse of the self-assured woman he suspected she'd been before the tragedy.

"Jackson?"

He turned to find Tag standing next to him, grinning.

"I guess you didn't hear me. Must have had your mind somewhere else." Tag glanced in Allie's direction and then wisely jumped back as Jackson took a playful swing at him as they left the barn.

"You sure waited until the last minute," Jackson said to his brother as they headed for Tag's vehicle. "Putting off the rings…" He shook his head. "You sure you want to go through with this?"

His brother laughed. "More sure than I have been about anything in my life. Come on, let's go."

"I'll see if Ford wants to come along," Jackson said. "I think that's enough cowboying for one day."

But when he reached the corral, he found his son wearing a straw Western hat and atop a huge horse. Jackson felt his pulse jump at the sight and his first instinct was to insist Ford get down from there right away.

But when he got a good look at his son's face, his words died on a breath. He'd never seen Ford this happy. His cheeks were flushed, his eyes bright. He looked… proud.

"Look at me," he called to his father.

All Jackson could do was nod as his son rode past him. He was incapable of words at that moment.

"Don't worry about your son," his father said as he joined him at the corral fence. "I'll look after him until you get back."

Allie listened to Jackson and Tag joking with each other as they left the barn. Jackson Cardwell must think her the most foolish woman ever, screaming over noth-

ing more than a cat, messing up her date book and panicking because she'd misplaced her purse.

But what had her still upset was the hug. It had felt
so good to be in Jackson's arms. It had been so long
since anyone had held her like that. She'd felt such an
overwhelming need...

And then Drew had seen them. She'd been surprised
by the look on his face. He'd seemed...angry and upset
as if she was cheating on Nick. Once this investigation was over, maybe they could all put Nick to rest.
In the meantime, she just hoped Drew didn't go to his
mother with this.

Instinctively, she knew that Jackson wouldn't say
anything. Not about her incidents or about the hug.

Dana announced she was taking the kids down to the
house for naptime. Allie could tell that Nat had wanted
to go down to the house—but for lemonade and cookies.
Nat probably needed a nap, as well, but Allie couldn't
take her up to the cabin right now. She had work to do
if she hoped to have the barn ready for the rehearsal
dinner tomorrow night.

"I really need your help," she told her daughter. Nat
was always ready to give a helping hand. Well, she was
before the Cardwell Ranch and all the animals, not to
mention other kids to play with.

"Okay, Mama." She glanced back at the barn door
wistfully, though. Nat had always wanted brothers and
sisters, but they hadn't been in Allie's plans. She knew
she could take care of one child without any help from
Nick. He'd wanted a boy and insisted they try for another child soon after Nat was born.

Allie almost laughed. Guilt? She had so much of it
where Nick and his family were concerned. She had

wanted to enjoy her baby girl so she'd gone on the pill behind Nick's back. It had been more than dishonest. He would have killed her if he had found out. The more time that went by, the less she wanted another child with her husband so she'd stayed on the pill. Even Nick's tantrums about her not getting pregnant were easier to take than having another child with him.

She hadn't even told Belinda, which was good since her friend was shocked when she told her she was leaving Nick and moving far away.

"Divorcing him is one thing," Belinda had said. "But I don't see how you can keep his kid from him or keep Nat from his family."

"Nick wanted a son. He barely takes notice of Nat. The only time he notices her is when other people are around and then he plays too rough with her. When she cries, he tells her to toughen up."

"So you're going to ask for sole custody? Isn't Nick going to fight you?"

Allie knew it would be just like Nick to fight for Nat out of meanness and his family would back him up. "I'm going to move to Florida. I've already lined up a couple of jobs down there. They pay a lot more than here. I really doubt Nick will bother flying that far to see Nat—at least than a few times."

"You really are going to leave him," Belinda had said. "When?"

"Soon." That had been late summer. She'd desperately wanted a new start. Nick would be occupied with hunting season in the fall so maybe he wouldn't put up much of a fight.

Had Belinda said something to Nick? Or had he just seen something in Allie that told him he had lost her?

"How can I help you, Mama?" Nat asked, dragging her from her thoughts.

Allie handed her daughter one end of a rope garland adorned with tiny lights in the shape of boots. "Let's string this up," she suggested. "And see how pretty it looks along the wall."

Nat's eyes lit up. "It's going to be beautiful," she said. *Beautiful* was her latest favorite word. To her, most everything was beautiful.

Allie yearned for that kind of innocence again—if she'd ever had it. But maybe she could find it for her daughter. She had options. She could find work anywhere as a wedding planner, but did she want to uproot her daughter from what little family she had? Nat loved her uncle Drew and Sarah could be very sweet. Mildred, even as ungrandmotherly as she was, was Nat's only grandmother.

Allie tried to concentrate on her work. The barn was taking shape. She'd found tiny cowboy boot lights to put over the bar area. Saddles on milk cans had been pulled up to the bar for extra seating.

Beverages would be chilling in a metal trough filled with ice. Drinks would be served in Mason jars and lanterns would hang from the rafters for light. A few bales of hay would be brought in around the bandstand.

When they'd finished, Allie plugged in the last of the lights and Nat squealed with delight.

She checked her watch. "Come on," she told her daughter. "We've done enough today. We need to go into town for a few things. Tomorrow your aunt Megan will be coming to help." Nat clapped in response. She loved her auntie Megan, Allie's half sister.

After Allie's mother died, her father had moved

away, remarried and had other children. Allie had lost touch with her father, as well as his new family. But about a year ago, her stepsister Megan had found her. Ten years younger, Megan was now twenty-three and a recent graduate in design. When she'd shown an interest in working on the Cardwell Ranch wedding, Allie had jumped at it.

"I really could use the help, but when can you come down?" Megan lived in Missoula and had just given her two weeks' notice at her job.

"Go ahead and start without me. I'll be there within a few days of the wedding. That should be enough time, shouldn't it?"

"Perfect," Allie had told her. "Natalie and I will start. I'll save the fun stuff for you." Natalie loved Megan, who was cute and young and always up for doing something fun with her niece.

The thought of Megan's arrival tomorrow had brightened Natalie for a moment, but Allie now saw her looking longingly at the Savage house.

"How about we have something to eat while we're in Bozeman?" Allie suggested.

Nat's eyes widened with new interest as she asked if they could go to her favorite fast-food burger place. The Taylors had introduced her daughter to fast food, something Allie had tried to keep at a minimum.

But this evening, she decided to make an exception. She loved seeing how happy her daughter was. Nat's cheeks were pink from the fresh air and sunshine.

All the way into town, she talked excitedly about the horses and the other kids. This wedding planner job at Cardwell Ranch was turning out to be a good thing for both of them, Allie thought as they drove home.

By the time they reached the cabin Nat had fallen asleep in her car seat and didn't even wake up when Allie parked out front. Deciding to take in the items she'd purchased first, then bring in her daughter, Allie stepped into the cabin and stopped dead.

At the end of the hall, light flickered. A candle. She hadn't lit a candle. Not since Nick. He liked her in candlelight. The smell of the candle and the light reminded her of the last time they'd had sex. Not made love. They hadn't made love since before Natalie was born.

As she started down the hallway, she told herself that she'd thrown all the candles away. Even if she'd missed one, she wouldn't have left a candle burning.

She stopped in the bedroom doorway. Nick's shirt was back, spread on the bed as if he were in it, lying there waiting for her. The smell of the sweet-scented candle made her nauseous. She fought the panicked need to run.

"Mama?" Nat's sleepy voice wavered with concern. "Did Daddy come back?" Not just concern. Anxiety. Nick scared her with his moodiness and surly behavior. Nat was smart. She had picked up on the tension between her parents.

Allie turned to wrap her arms around her daughter. The warmth of her five-year-old, Nat's breath on her neck, the solid feel of the ground under her feet, those were the things she concentrated on as she carried Natalie down the hallway to her room.

Her daughter's room had always been her haven. It was the only room in the house that Nick hadn't cared what she did with. So she'd painted it sky-blue, adding white floating clouds, then trees and finally a river as green and sunlit as the one out Nat's window.

Nick had stuck his head in the door while she was painting it. She'd seen his expression. He'd been impressed—and he hadn't wanted to be—before he snapped, "You going to cook dinner or what?" He seemed to avoid the room after that, which was fine with her.

Now, she lay down on the bed with Nat. It had been her daughter's idea to put stars on the ceiling, the kind that shone only at night with the lights out.

"I like horses," Nat said with a sigh. "Ms. Savage says a horse can tell your mood and that if you aren't in a good one, you'll get bucked off." She looked at her mother. "Do you think that's true?"

"I think if Ms. Savage says it is, then it is."

Nat smiled as if she liked the answer.

Allie could tell she was dog-tired, but fighting sleep.

"I'm going to ride Rocket tomorrow," Natalie said.

"Rocket? That sounds like an awfully fast horse." She saw that Nat's eyelids had closed. She watched her daughter sleep for a few moments, then eased out of bed.

After covering her, she opened the window a few inches to let the cool summer night air into the stuffy room. Spending time with her daughter made her feel better, but also reminded her how important it was that she not let anyone know about the things that had been happening to her.

She thought of Jackson Cardwell and the black cat that had somehow gotten into her box of decorations. She hadn't imagined that. She smiled to herself. Such a small thing and yet...

This time, she went straight to her bedroom, snuffed out the candle and opened the window, thankful for the breeze that quickly replaced the sweet, cloying scent with the fresh night air.

On the way out of the room, she grabbed Nick's shirt and took both the shirt and the candle to the trash, but changed her mind. Dropping only the candle in the trash, she took the shirt over to the fireplace. Would burning Nick's favorite shirt mean she was crazy?

Too bad, she thought as she dropped the shirt on the grate and added several pieces of kindling and some newspaper. Allie hesitated for only a moment before lighting the paper with a match. It caught fire, crackling to life and forcing her to step back. She watched the blaze destroy the shirt and reached for the poker, determined that not a scrap of it would be left.

She had to get control of her life. She thought of Jackson Cardwell and his kindness. He had no idea how much it meant to her.

As she watched the flames take the last of Nick's shirt, she told herself at least this would be the last she'd see of that blamed shirt.

Chapter 5

Jackson met Hayes and Laramie at the airport, but while it was good to see them, he was distracted.

They talked about the barbecue restaurant and Harlan and the wedding before McKenzie showed up while they were waiting for their luggage to pick up Hayes. Hayes had been in Texas tying up things with the sale of his business.

Jackson had heard their relationship was serious, but seeing McKenzie and Hayes together, he saw just how serious. Another brother falling in love in Montana, he thought with a shake of his head. Hayes and McKenzie would be joining them later tonight at the ranch for dinner.

He and Laramie ended up making the drive to Cardwell Ranch alone. Laramie talked about the financial benefits of the new barbecue restaurant and

Jackson tuned him out. He couldn't get his mind off Allie Taylor.

Maybe it was because he'd been through so much with his ex, but he felt like a kindred spirit. The woman was going through her own private hell. He wished there was something he could do.

"Are you listening?" Laramie asked.

"Sure."

"I forget how little interest my brothers have in the actual running of this corporation."

"Don't let it hurt your feelings. I just have something else on my mind."

"A woman."

"Why would you say that, knowing me?"

Laramie looked over at him. "I was joking. You swore off women after Juliet, right? At least that's what you… Wait a minute, has something changed?"

"Nothing." He said it too sharply, making his brother's eyebrow shoot up.

Laramie fell silent for a moment, but Jackson could feel him watching him out of the corner of his eye.

"Is this your first wedding since…you and Juliet split?" Laramie asked carefully.

Jackson shook his head at his brother's attempt at diplomacy. "It's not the wedding. There's this…person I met who I'm worried about."

"Ah. Is this person—"

"It's a woman, all right? But it isn't like that."

"Hey," Laramie said, holding up his hands. "I just walked in. If you don't want to tell me—"

"She lost her husband some months ago and she has a little girl the same age as Ford and she's struggling."

Laramie nodded. "Okay."

"She's the wedding planner."

His brother's eyebrow shot up again.

"I'll just be glad when this wedding is over," Jackson said and thought he meant it. "By the way, when is Mom flying in?" At his brother's hesitation, he demanded, "What's going on with Mom?"

Allie had unpacked more boxes of decorations by the time she heard a vehicle pull up the next morning. Natalie, who had been coloring quietly while her mother worked, went running when she spotted her aunt Megan. Allie smiled as Megan picked Nat up and swung her around, both of them laughing. It was a wonderful sound. Megan had a way with Natalie. Clearly, she loved kids.

"Sorry I'm so late, but I'm here and ready to go to work." Megan was dressed in a T-shirt, jeans and athletic shoes. She had taken after their father and had the Irish green eyes with the dark hair and complexion. She was nothing short of adorable, sweet and cute. "Wow, the barn is already looking great," she exclaimed as she walked around, Natalie holding her hand and beaming up at her.

"I helped Mama with the lights," Nat said.

"I knew it," Megan said. "I can see your handiwork." She grinned down at her niece. "Did I hear you can now ride a horse?"

Natalie quickly told her all about the horses, naming each as she explained how to ride a horse. "You have to hang on to the reins."

"I would imagine you do," Megan agreed.

"Maybe you can ride with us," Nat suggested.

"Maybe I can. But right now I need to help your mom."

Just then Dana stuck her head in the barn doorway and called to Natalie. Allie introduced Dana to her stepsister, then watched as her daughter scurried off for an afternoon ride with her friends. She gave a thankful smile to Dana as they left.

"Just tell me what to do," Megan said and Allie did, even more thankful for the help. They went to work on the small details Allie knew Megan would enjoy.

Belinda stopped by to say hello to Megan and give Allie an update on the photos. She'd met with Lily that morning, had made out a list of photo ideas and sounded excited.

Allie was surprised when she overheard Belinda and Megan discussing a recent lunch. While the three of them had spent some time together since Megan had come back into Allie's life, she hadn't known that Belinda and Megan had become friends.

She felt jealous. She knew it was silly. They were both single and probably had more in common than with Allie, who felt as if she'd been married forever.

"How are you doing?" Megan asked after Belinda left.

"Fine."

"No, really."

Allie studied her stepsister for a moment. They'd become close, but she hadn't wanted to share what was going on. It was embarrassing and the fewer people who knew she was losing her mind the better, right?

"It's been rough." Megan didn't know that she had been planning to leave Nick. As far as her sister had known, Allie had been happily married. Now Allie regretted that she hadn't been more honest with Megan.

"But I'm doing okay now," she said as she handed Megan another gift bag to fill. "It's good to be working again. I love doing this." She glanced around the barn feeling a sense of satisfaction.

"Well, I'm glad I'm here now," Megan said. "This is good for Natalie, too."

Good for all of us, Allie thought.

Jackson looked at his brother aghast. "Mom's dating?" He should have known that if their mom confided in anyone it would be Laramie. The sensible one, was what she called him, and swore that out of all her sons, Laramie was the only one who she could depend on to be honest with her.

Laramie cleared his throat. "It's a little more than dating. She's on her honeymoon."

"Her *what?*"

"She wanted it to be a surprise."

"Well, it sure as hell is that. Who did she marry?"

"His name is Franklin Wellington the Fourth. He's wealthy, handsome, very nice guy, actually."

"*You've* met him?"

"He and Mom are flying in just before the wedding on his private jet. It's bigger than ours."

"Laramie, I can't believe you would keep this from the rest of us, let alone that Mom would."

"She didn't want to take away from Tag's wedding but they had already scheduled theirs before Tag announced his." Laramie shrugged. "Hey, she's deliriously happy and hoping we will all be happy for her."

Jackson couldn't believe this. Rosalee Cardwell hadn't just started dating after all these years, she'd gotten married?

"I wonder how Dad will take it?" Laramie said. "We all thought Mom had been pining away for him all these years..."

"Maybe she was."

"Well, not anymore."

* * *

"But you *have* to go on the horseback ride," Natalie cried.

As he stepped into the cool shade, Jackson saw Allie look around the barn for help, finding none. Hayes was off somewhere with his girlfriend, McKenzie, Tag was down by the river writing his vows, Lily was picking her parents up at the airport, Laramie had restaurant business and Hud was at the marshal's office, working. There had still been no word from Austin. Or their mother.

Wanting to spend some time with his son, Jackson had agreed to go on the short horseback ride with Dana and the kids that would include lunch on the mountain.

"Dana promised she would find you a very gentle horse, in other words, a really *old* one," Megan joked.

Natalie was doing her "please-Mama-please" face.

"Even my dad is going to ride," Ford said, making everyone laugh.

Allie looked at the boy. "Your dad is a cowboy."

Ford shook his head. "He can't even rope a cow. He tried once at our neighbor's place and he was really bad at it. So it's okay if you're really bad at riding a horse."

Jackson smiled and ruffled his son's hair. "You really should come along, Allie."

"I have too much work to—"

"I will stay here and get things organized for tomorrow," Megan said. "No more arguments. Go on the ride with your daughter. Go." She shooed her toward the barn door.

"I guess I'm going on the horseback ride," Allie said. The kids cheered. She met Jackson's gaze as they walked toward the corral where Dana and her ranch hand, Walker, were saddling horses. "I've never been on a horse," she whispered confidentially to Jackson.

"Neither had your daughter and look at her now," he said as he watched Ford and Natalie saddle up. They both had to climb up the fence to get on their horses, but they now sat eagerly waiting in their saddles.

"I'll help you," Jackson said as he took Allie's horse's reins from Dana. He demonstrated how to get into the saddle then gave her a boost.

"It's so high up here," she said as she put her boot toes into the stirrups.

"Enjoy the view," Jackson said and swung up onto his horse.

They rode up the mountain, the kids chattering away, Dana giving instructions to them as they went.

After a short while, Jackson noticed that Allie seemed to have relaxed a little. She was looking around as if enjoying the ride and when they stopped in a wide meadow, he saw her patting her horse's neck and talking softly to it.

"I'm afraid to ask what you just said to your horse," he joked as he moved closer. Her horse had wandered over to some tall grass away from the others.

"Just thanking him for not bucking me off," she admitted shyly.

"Probably a good idea, but your horse is a she. A mare."

"Oh, hopefully, she wasn't insulted." Allie actually smiled. The afternoon sun lit her face along with the smile.

He felt his heart do a loop-de-loop. He tried to rein it back in as he looked into her eyes. That tantalizing green was deep and dark, inviting, and yet he knew a man could drown in those eyes.

Suddenly, Allie's horse shied. In the next second it

took off as if it had been shot from a cannon. To her credit, she hadn't let go of her reins, but she grabbed the saddlehorn and let out a cry as the mare raced out of the meadow headed for the road.

Jackson spurred his horse and raced after her. He could hear the startled cries of the others behind him. He'd been riding since he was a boy, so he knew how to handle his horse. But Allie, he could see, was having trouble staying in the saddle with her horse at a full gallop.

He pushed his harder and managed to catch her, riding alongside until he could reach over and grab her reins. The horses lunged along for a moment. Next to him Allie started to fall. He grabbed for her, pulling her from her saddle and into his arms as he released her reins and brought his own horse up short.

Allie slid down his horse to the ground. He dismounted and dropped beside her. "Are you all right?"

"I think so. What happened?"

He didn't know. One minute her horse was munching on grass, the next it had taken off like a shot.

Jackson could see that she was shaken. She sat down on the ground as if her legs would no longer hold her. He could hear the others riding toward them. When Allie heard her daughter calling to her, she hurriedly got to her feet, clearly wanting to reassure Natalie.

"Wow, that was some ride," Allie said as her daughter came up.

"Are you all right?" Dana asked, dismounting and joining her.

"I'm fine, really," she assured her and moved to her daughter, still in the saddle, to smile up at her.

"What happened?" Dana asked Jackson.

"I don't know."

"This is a good spot to have lunch," Dana announced more cheerfully than Jackson knew she felt.

"I'll go catch the horse." He swung back up into the saddle and took off after the mare. "I'll be right back for lunch. Don't let Ford eat all the sandwiches."

Allie had no idea why the horse had reacted like that. She hated that she was the one who'd upset everyone.

"Are you sure you didn't spur your horse?" Natalie asked, still upset.

"She isn't wearing spurs," Ford pointed out.

"Maybe a bee stung your horse," Natalie suggested.

Dana felt bad. "I wanted your first horseback riding experience to be a pleasant one," she lamented.

"It was. It is," Allie reassured her although in truth, she wasn't looking forward to getting back on the horse. But she knew she had to for Natalie's sake. The kids had been scared enough as it was.

Dana had spread out the lunch on a large blanket with the kids all helping when Jackson rode up, trailing her horse. The mare looked calm now, but Allie wasn't sure she would ever trust it again.

Jackson met her gaze as he dismounted. Dana was already on her feet, heading for him. Allie left the kids to join them.

"What is it?" Dana asked, keeping her voice down.

Jackson looked to Allie as if he didn't want to say in front of her.

"Did I do something to the horse to make her do that?" she asked, fearing that she had.

His expression softened as he shook his head. "You didn't do *anything*." He looked at Dana. "Someone shot the mare." He moved so Dana could see the bloody spot on the horse. "Looks like a small caliber. Probably a .22. Fortunately, the shooter must have been some distance away or it could have been worse. The bullet barely broke the horse's hide. Just enough to spook the mare."

"We've had teenagers on four-wheelers using the old logging roads on the ranch," Dana said. "I heard shots a few days ago." Suddenly, all the color drained from Dana's face. "Allie could have been killed," she whispered. "Or one of the kids. When we get back, I'll call Hud."

Jackson insisted on riding right beside Allie on the way back down the mountain. He could tell that Allie had been happy to get off the horse once they reached the corral.

"Thank you for saving me," she said. "It seems like you keep doing that, doesn't it?" He must have looked panicked by the thought because she quickly added, "I'm fine now. I will try not to need saving again." She flashed him a smile and disappeared into the barn.

"Ready?" Tag said soon after Jackson had finished helping unsaddle the horses and put the tack away.

Dana had taken the kids down to the house to play, saying they all needed some downtime. He could tell that she was still upset and anxious to call Hud. "Don't forget the barbecue and dance tonight," she reminded him. "Then tomorrow is the bachelor party, right?"

Jackson groaned. He'd forgotten that Tag had been waiting for them all to arrive so they could have the party. The last thing he needed was a party. Allie's horse taking off like that... It had left him shaken, as well. Dana was convinced it had been teenagers who'd shot the horse. He hoped that was all it had been.

"Glad you're back," Tag said. "We're all going down to the Corral for a beer. Come on. At least four of us are here. We'll be back in time for dinner."

Ford was busy with the kids and Dana. "Are you sure he isn't too much?" Jackson asked his cousin. "I feel like I've been dumping him on you since we got here."

She laughed. "Are you kidding? My children adore having their cousin around. They've actually all been getting along better than usual. Go have a drink with your brothers. Enjoy yourself, Jackson. I suspect you get little time without Ford."

It was true. And yet he missed his son. He told himself again that he would be glad when they got back to Texas. But seeing how much fun Ford was having on the ranch, he doubted his son would feel the same.

Allie stared at her date book, heart racing. She'd been feeling off balance since her near-death experience on the horse. When she'd told Megan and Belinda about it on her return to the barn, they'd been aghast.

She'd recounted her tale right up to where Jackson had returned with the mare and the news that it had been shot.

"That's horrible," Megan said. "I'm so glad you didn't get bucked off. Was the mare all right?"

Belinda's response was, "So Jackson saved you? Wow, how romantic is that?"

Needing to work, Allie had shooed Belinda out of the barn and she and Megan had worked quietly for several hours before she'd glanced at her watch and realized something was wrong.

"The caterer," Allie said. "Did she happen to call?"

Megan shook her head. "No, why?"

"Her crew should have been here by now. I had no idea it was so late." Allie could feel the panic growing. "And when I checked my date book…"

"What?" Megan asked.

"I wouldn't have canceled." But even as she was saying it, she was dialing the caterer's number.

A woman answered and Allie quickly asked about the dinner that was to be served at Cardwell Ranch tonight.

"We have you down for the reception in a few days, but… Wait a minute. It looks as if you did book it."

Allie felt relief wash through her, though it did nothing to relieve the panic. She had a ranch full of people to be fed and no caterer for the barbecue.

"I'm sorry. It says here that you called to cancel it yesterday."

"That's not possible. It couldn't have been me."

"Is your name Allie Taylor?"

She felt her heart drop. "Yes."

"It says here that you personally called."

Allie dropped into one of the chairs. She wanted to argue with the woman, but what good would it do? The damage was done. And anyway, she couldn't be sure she hadn't called. She couldn't be sure of anything.

"Just make sure that the caterers will be here on the Fourth of July for the wedding reception and that no one, and I mean not even me, can cancel it. Can you do that for me?" Her voice broke and she saw Megan looking at her with concern.

As she disconnected, she fought tears. "What am I going to do?"

"What's wrong?"

Her head snapped up at the sound of Jackson's voice. "I thought you were having beers with your brothers?"

"A couple beers is all I can handle. So come on, what's going on?"

She wiped at her eyes, standing to turn her back to him until she could gain control. What the man must think of her.

"The caterer accidentally got canceled. Looks like we might have to try to find a restaurant tonight," Megan said, reaching for her phone.

"Don't be ridiculous," Jackson said, turning Allie to look at him. "You have some of the best barbecue experts in the country right here on the ranch. I'll run down to the market and get some ribs while my brothers get the fire going. It's going to be fine."

This last statement Allie could tell was directed at her. She met his gaze, all her gratitude in that one look.

Jackson tipped his hat and gave her a smile. "It's going to be better than fine. You'll see."

"I hope you don't mind," Allie heard Jackson tell Dana and Lily. "I changed Allie's plans. I thought it would be fun if the Cardwell boys barbecued."

Dana was delighted and so was Lily. They insisted she, Natalie, Megan and Belinda stay and Allie soon found herself getting caught up in the revelry.

The Texas Boys Barbecue brothers went to work making dinner. Allie felt awful that they had to cook, but soon saw how much fun they were having.

They joked and played around while their father and Dana's provided the music. All the ranch hands and neighbors ended up being invited and pretty soon it had turned into a party. She noticed that even Drew, who'd been working at one of the cabins, had been invited to join them.

The barbecue was amazing and a lot more fun than the one Allie had originally planned. Everyone complimented the food and the new restaurant was toasted as a welcome addition to Big Sky.

Allie did her best to stay in the background. The day had left her feeling beaten up from her wild horseback ride to the foul-up with the caterer, along with her other misadventures. She was just happy to sit on the sidelines. Megan and Belinda were having a ball dancing with some of the ranch hands. All the kids were dancing, as well. At one point, she saw Jackson showing Ford how to do the swing with Natalie.

Someone stepped in front of her, blocking her view of the dance floor. She looked up to see Drew.

"I don't believe you've danced all night," he said.

"I'm really not—"

"What? You won't dance with your own brother-in-law? I guess you don't need me anymore now that you have the Cardwells. Or is it just one Cardwell?"

She realized he'd had too much to drink. "Drew, that isn't—"

"Excuse me," Jackson said, suddenly appearing beside her. "I believe this dance is mine." He reached for Allie's hand.

Drew started to argue, but Jackson didn't give him a chance before he pulled Allie out onto the dance floor. The song was a slow one. He took her in his arms and pulled her close.

"You really have to quit saving me," she said only half joking.

"Sorry, but I could see you needed help," Jackson

said. "Your brother-in-law is more than a little protective, Allie."

She didn't want to talk about Drew. She closed her eyes for a moment. It felt good in the cowboy's arms. She couldn't remember the last time she'd danced, but that felt good, too, moving to the slow country song. "You saved my life earlier and then saved my bacon tonight. Natalie thinks you're a cowboy superhero. I'm beginning to wonder myself."

He gave her a grin and a shrug. "It weren't nothin', ma'am," he said, heavy on the Texas drawl. "Actually, I don't know why my brothers and I hadn't thought of it before. You did me a favor. I'd missed cooking with them. It was fun."

"Did I hear there is a bachelor party tomorrow night?"

Jackson groaned. "Hayes is in charge. I hate to think." He laughed softly. "Then the rehearsal and dinner the next night and finally the wedding." He shook his head as if he couldn't wait for it to be over.

Allie had felt the same way—before she'd met Jackson Cardwell.

Drew appeared just then. "Cuttin' in," he said, slurring his words as he pried himself between the two of them.

Jackson seemed to hesitate, but Allie didn't want trouble. She stepped into Drew's arms and let him dance her away from the Texas cowboy.

"What the hell do you think you're doing?" Drew demanded as he pulled her closer. "My brother is barely cold in his grave and here you are actin' like—"

"The wedding planner?" She broke away from him as the song ended. "Sorry, but I'm calling it a night. I have a lot of work to do tomorrow." With that she went to get Natalie. It was time to go home.

Chapter 6

Allie was getting ready to go to the ranch the next morning when she heard a vehicle pull up. She glanced out groaning when she saw it was Drew. Even more disturbing, he had his mother with him. As she watched them climb out, she braced herself for the worst. Drew had been acting strangely since he'd seen her with Jackson that first time.

"Hi," she said opening the door before either of them could knock. "You just caught me heading out."

"We *hoped* to catch you," Mildred said. "We're taking Natalie for the day so you can get some work done."

Not may we, but *we're taking*. "I'm sorry but Natalie already has plans."

Mildred's eyebrow shot up. "Natalie is five. Her plans can change."

"Natalie is going with the Cardwells—"

"The Cardwells aren't family," Mildred spat.

No, Allie thought, *but I wish they were.* "If you had just called—"

"I'm sure Nat would rather spend the day with her grandmother than whatever you have planned for—" Mildred broke off at the sound of a vehicle coming up the road toward them.

Who now? Allie wondered, fearing she was about to lose this battle with her in-laws—and break her daughter's heart. Her pulse did a little leap as she recognized the SUV as the one Jackson Cardwell had been driving yesterday. But what was he doing here? Allie had said she would bring Nat to the ranch.

Jackson parked and got out, Ford right behind him. He seemed to take in the scene before he asked, "Is there a problem?"

"Nothing to do with you," Drew said.

"Jackson Cardwell," he said and held out his hand. "I don't believe we've been formally introduced."

Drew was slow to take it. "Drew Taylor." Allie could see her brother-in-law sizing up Jackson. While they were both a few inches over six feet and both strong-looking, Jackson had the broader shoulders and looked as if he could take Drew in a fair fight.

Mildred crossed her arms over her chest and said, "We're here to pick up my granddaughter."

"That's why *I'm* here," Jackson said. Just then Natalie came to the door. She was dressed for the rodeo in her Western shirt, jeans and new red cowboy boots. Allie had braided her hair into two plaits that trailed down her back. A straw cowboy hat was perched on her head, her smile huge.

"I'm going to the rodeo with Ford and Hank and Mary," Nat announced excitedly. Oblivious to what was going on, she added, "I've never been to a rodeo before."

"Hop into the rig with Ford. I borrowed a carseat from Dana," Jackson said before either Drew or Mildred could argue otherwise.

With a wave, Nat hurried past her grandmother and uncle and, taking Ford's hand, the two ran toward the SUV.

Allie held her breath as she saw Drew ball his hands into fists. She'd never seen him like this and realized Jackson was right. This was more than him being protective.

Jackson looked as if he expected Drew to take a swing—and was almost daring him to. The tension between the two men was thick as fresh-churned butter. Surely it wouldn't come to blows.

"Are you ready?" Jackson said to her, making her blink in surprise. "Dana gave me your ticket for the rodeo."

He *knew* she wasn't planning to go. This wedding had to be perfect and let's face it, she hadn't been herself for some time now.

"Going to a rodeo is part of this so-called wedding planning?" Mildred demanded. She lifted a brow. "I heard it also entails dancing with the guests."

"All in a day's work," Jackson said and met Allie's gaze. "We should get going. Don't want to be late." He looked to Drew. "Nice to meet you." Then turned to Mildred. "You must be Allie's mother-in-law."

"Mildred." Her lips were pursed so tightly that the word barely came out.

"I just need to grab my purse," Allie said, taking advantage of Jackson's rescue, even though she knew it would cost her.

When she came back out, Jackson was waiting for her. He tipped his hat to Drew and Mildred as Allie locked the cabin door behind her. She noticed that

Mother Taylor and Drew were still standing where she'd left them, both looking infuriated.

She hated antagonizing them for fear what could happen if they ever decided to try to take Natalie from her. If they knew about just a few of the so-called incidents...

Like Nat, Allie slipped past them out to the SUV and didn't let out the breath she'd been holding until she was seated in the passenger seat.

"That looked like an ambush back there," Jackson said as they drove away.

She glanced back knowing she might have escaped this time, but there would be retribution. "They mean well."

Jackson glanced over at her. "Do they?"

She looked away. "With Nick gone... Well, we're all adjusting to it. I'm sure they feel all they have left of him is Nat. They just want to see more of her."

He could see that she felt guilty. His ex and her family had used guilt on him like a club. He remembered that beat-up, rotten feeling and hated to see her going through it.

In the backseat, Natalie was telling Ford about something her horse had done yesterday during her ride. They both started laughing the way only kids can do. He loved the sound.

"Thank you for the rescue, but I really can't go to the rodeo. You can drop me at the ranch," Allie said, clearly nervous. "I need to check on things."

"You've done a great job. A few hours away at the rodeo is your reward. Dana's orders. She's the one who sent me to get you, knowing you wouldn't come unless I did."

"I really should be working."

"When was the last time you were at a rodeo?" he asked.

She chewed at her lower lip for a moment. "I think I went with some friends when I was in the fifth grade."

He smiled over at her. "Well, then it is high time you went again."

"I want an elephant ear!" Ford cried from the backseat.

"An elephant ear?" Nat repeated and began to giggle.

"So Nat's never been to a rodeo, either?" Jackson asked.

"No, I guess she hasn't."

"Well, she is going today and she and her mother are going to have elephant ears!" he announced. The kids laughed happily. He was glad to hear Ford explaining that an elephant ear really was just fried bread with sugar and cinnamon on it, but that it was really good.

Allie seemed to relax, but he saw her checking her side mirror. Did she think her in-laws would chase her down? He wouldn't have been surprised. They'd been more than overbearing. He had seen how they dominated Allie. It made him wonder what her husband had been like.

When they reached the rodeo grounds, Dana and Hud were waiting along with the kids and Tag and Lily and Hayes and McKenzie and Laramie.

"Oh, I'm so glad you decided to come along," Dana said when she saw Allie. "Jackson said he wasn't sure he could convince you, but he was darned sure going to try." She glanced at her cousin. "He must be pretty persuasive."

"Yes, he is," Allie said and smiled.

Jackson felt a little piece of his heart float up at that smile.

Easy, Texas cowboy, he warned himself.

But even as he thought it, he had to admit that he was getting into the habit of rescuing this woman—and enjoying it. Allie needed protecting. How badly she needed it, he didn't yet know.

It was the least he could do—until the wedding. And then he and Ford were headed back to Texas. Allie Taylor would be on her own.

Just the thought made him scared for her.

Allie couldn't remember the last time she'd had so much fun. The rodeo was thrilling, the elephant ear delicious and the Cardwells a very fun family. She'd ended up sitting next to Jackson, their children in front of them.

"I want to be a barrel racer," Natalie announced.

"We'll have to set up some barrels at the ranch," Dana said. "Natalie's a natural in the saddle. She'd make a great barrel racer."

"Well, I'm not riding the bulls," Ford said and everyone laughed.

"Glad you came along?" Jackson asked Allie as he offered some of his popcorn.

She'd already eaten a huge elephant ear and loved every bite, but she still took a handful of popcorn and smiled. "I am. This is fun."

"You deserve some fun."

Allie wasn't so sure about that. She wasn't sure what she deserved, wasn't that the problem? She leaned back against the bleachers, breathing in the summer day and wishing this would never end.

But it did end and the crowd began to make their

way to the parking lot in a swell of people. That's when she saw him.

Nick. He was moving through the crowd. She'd seen him because he was going in the wrong direction—in their direction. He wore a dark-colored baseball cap, his features lost in the shadow of the cap's bill. She got only a glimpse— Suddenly, he turned as if headed for the parking lot, as well. She sat up, telling herself her eyes were deceiving her. Nick was dead and yet—

"Allie, what it is?" Jackson asked.

In the past when she'd caught glimpses of him, she'd frozen, too shocked to move. She sprang to her feet and pushed her way down the grandstand steps until she reached the ground. Forcing her way through the crowd, she kept Nick in sight ahead of her. He was moving fast as if he wanted to get away.

Not this time, she thought, as she felt herself gaining on him. She could see the back of his head. He was wearing his MSU Bobcat navy ball cap, just like the one he'd been wearing the day he left to go up into the mountains—and his favorite shirt, the one she'd burned.

Her heart pounded harder against her ribs. She told herself she wasn't losing her mind. She couldn't explain any of this, but she knew what she was seeing. Nick. She was within yards of him, only a few people between them. She could almost reach out and grab his sleeve—

Suddenly, someone grabbed her arm, spinning her around. She stumbled over backward, falling against the person in front of her, tripping on her own feet before hitting the ground. The fall knocked the air from her lungs and skinned her elbow, worse, her pride. The crowd opened a little around her as several people stopped to see if she was all right.

But it was Jackson who rushed to help her up. "Allie, are you all right?"

All she could do was shake her head as the man she thought was Nick disappeared into the crowd.

"What's going on?" Jackson asked, seeing how upset she was. Had he said or done something that would make her take off like that?

She shook her head again as if unable to speak. He could tell *something* had happened. Drawing her aside, he asked her again. The kids had gone on ahead with Dana and her children.

"Allie, talk to me."

She looked up at him, those green eyes filling with tears. "I saw my husband, Nick. At least I think I saw him." She looked shocked as she darted a glance at the crowd, clearly expecting to see her dead husband again.

"You must think I'm crazy. *I* think I'm crazy. But I saw Nick. I know it couldn't be him, but it looked so much like him…." She shivered, even though the July day was hot. "He was wearing his new ball cap and his favorite shirt, the one I burned…" She began to cry.

"Hey," he said, taking her shoulders in his hands to turn her toward him. "I don't think you're crazy. I think you've had a horrible loss that—"

"I didn't *love* him. I was *leaving* him." The words tumbled out in a rush. "I… I…*hated* him. I *wanted* him gone, not dead!"

Jackson started to pull her into his arms, but she bolted and was quickly swept up in the exiting crowd. He stood for a moment, letting her words sink in. Now, more than ever, he thought he understood why she was letting little things upset her. Guilt was a powerful thing. It explained a lot, especially with her relationship with her in-laws that he'd glimpsed that morning. How long had they been browbeating her? he wondered. Maybe her whole marriage.

He found himself more curious about her husband, Nick Taylor. And even more about Allie. Common sense told him to keep his distance. The wedding was only days away, then he and Ford would be flying back to Houston.

Maybe it was because he'd gone through a bad marriage, but he felt for her even more now. Like her, he was raising his child alone. Like her, he was disillusioned and he'd certainly gone through a time with his ex when he thought he was losing his mind. He'd also wished his ex dead more than once.

Allie caught up to Dana as she was loading all the kids into her Suburban. Hud had brought his own rig since he had to stop by the marshal's office.

"Mind if I catch a ride with you?" Allie asked. "Jackson had some errands to run in town." The truth was that after her outburst, she was embarrassed and knew Dana had room for her and Nat in the Suburban.

"Of course not."

Allie had stopped long enough to go into the ladies' room and wash her face and calm down. She knew everyone had seen her take off like a crazy woman. She felt embarrassed and sick at heart, but mostly she was bone-deep scared.

When she'd seen Jackson heading for the parking lot, she'd motioned that she and Nat were going with Dana. He'd merely nodded, probably glad.

Dana didn't comment on Allie's red eyes or her impromptu exit earlier, though as she joined them at the

Suburban. Instead, Dana made small talk about the rodeo, the weather, the upcoming wedding.

They were almost back to the ranch before Dana asked, "How are things going?" over the chatter of the kids in the back of the SUV.

Allie could tell that she wasn't just making conversation anymore. She really wanted to know. "It's been hard. I guess it's no secret that I've been struggling."

Dana reached over and squeezed her hand. "I know. I feel so bad about yesterday. I'm just so glad you weren't hurt." She smiled. "You did a great job of staying on that horse, though. I told Natalie how proud I was of you."

Allie thought of Jackson. He'd saved her life yesterday. She remembered the feel of his arms as he'd pulled her from the horse—and again on the dance floor last night. Shoving away the memory, she reminded herself that once the wedding was over, he and Ford would be leaving. She was going to have to start saving herself.

"Did Hud find out anything about who might have shot the horse?" she asked, remembering Hud talking to the vet when he'd stopped by to make sure the mare was all right.

"Nothing yet, but he is going to start gating the roads on the ranch. We can't keep people from the forest service property that borders the ranch, but we can keep them at a distance by closing off the ranch property. In the meantime, if there is anything I can do to help you…"

"Dana, you've already done so much. Letting Natalie come to the ranch and teaching her to ride…" Allie felt overwhelmed at Dana's generosity.

"Let's see if you thank me when she's constantly bugging you about buying her a horse," Dana joked. "Seriously, she can always come up to the ranch and ride. And if someday you do want a horse for her…"

"Thank you. For everything."

"I love what you've done to the barn," Dana said, changing the subject. "It is beyond my expectations and Lily can't say enough about it. I'm getting so excited, but then I'm a sucker for weddings."

"Me, too," Allie admitted. "They are so beautiful. There is so much hope and love in the air. It's all like a wonderful dream."

"Or fantasy," Dana joked. "Nothing about the wedding day is like marriage, especially four children later."

No, Allie thought, but then she'd had a small wedding in Mother Taylor's backyard. She should have known then how the marriage was going to go.

"Have you given any more thought to moving up to a guest cabin?" Dana asked.

"I have. Like I said, I'm touched by the offer. But Natalie has been through so many changes with Nick's death, I think staying at the cabin in her own bed might be best. We'll see, though. She is having such a great time at the ranch and as the wedding gets closer…"

"Just know that I saved a cabin for you and Natalie," Dana said. "And don't worry about your daughter. We have already adopted her into the family. The kids love her and Ford…." She laughed and lowered her voice, even though the kids weren't paying any attention behind them. "Have you noticed how tongue-tied he gets around her?"

They both laughed, Allie feeling blessed because she felt as if she, too, had been adopted into the family. The Cardwells were so different from the Taylors. She pushed that thought away. Just as she did the memory of that instant when she would have sworn she saw Nick at the rodeo.

Every time she thought she was getting better, stronger, something would happen to make her afraid she really was losing her mind.

"Hey," Belinda said, seeming surprised when Allie and Nat walked into the barn that afternoon. "Where have you been? I thought you'd be here working."

"We went to the rodeo!" Natalie said. "And now I'm going to go ride a horse!" With that she ran out of the barn to join the other kids and Dana.

"You went to the rodeo?"

"You sound like my in-laws," Allie said. "Yes, I was invited, I went and now I will do the last-minute arrangements for the rehearsal dinner tomorrow and it will all be fine."

Belinda lifted a brow. "Wow, what a change from the woman who was panicking because she couldn't find her keys the other day. Have you been drinking?"

"I'm taking my life back." She told her friend about the candle, Nick's shirt and what she did with it. Also about chasing the man she thought was Nick at the rodeo. "I almost caught him. If someone hadn't grabbed my arm…"

Belinda's eyes widened in alarm. "Sorry, but doesn't that sound a little…"

"Crazy? Believe me, I know. But I was sick of just taking it and doing nothing."

"I can see you thinking you saw someone who looked like Nick at the rodeo…."

"He was wearing his favorite shirt and his new ball cap."

Belinda stared at her. "The shirt you'd burned a few nights ago, right?"

Allie regretted telling her friend. "I know it doesn't make any sense. But all these things that have been happening? I'm not imagining them." From her friend's expression, she was glad she hadn't told her about the dresses or the new clothes she'd found in her closet.

"Sweetie," Belinda asked tentatively. "Did you give any more thought to making that call I suggested?"

"No and right now I have work to do."

"Don't we all. Some of us didn't spend the day at the rodeo."

Her friend actually sounded jealous. Allie put it out of her mind. She had to concentrate on the wedding. The barn looked beautiful. After the rehearsal dinner tomorrow night, she would get ready for the wedding. All she had to do was hold it together until then.

Megan came in with her list of last-minute things that needed to be tended to before the wedding rehearsal.

"I'll meet you down in the meadow in a few minutes." Left alone, Allie looked around the barn. She was a little sad it would be over. Jackson and Ford would be returning to Texas. Nat was really going to miss them.

And so are you.

Allie wasn't sure what awakened her. Dana had insisted she take the rest of the day off and spend it with Natalie.

"You have accomplished so much," Dana had argued. "Tomorrow is another day. The men are all going with Tag for his bachelor party tonight. I plan to turn in early with the kids. Trust me. We all need some downtime before the wedding."

Emotionally exhausted, Allie had agreed. She and Nat had come back to the cabin and gone down to the river until dinner. Nat loved building rock dams and playing in the water.

After dinner even Natalie was exhausted from the full day. After Allie had put her down to sleep, she'd turned in herself with a book. But only a few pages in, she had turned out the light and gone to sleep.

Now, startled awake, she lay listening to the wind that had come up during the night. It was groaning in the boughs of the pine trees next to the cabin. Through the window, she could see the pines swaying and smell the nearby river. She caught only glimpses of the moon in a sky filled with stars as she lay listening.

Since Nick's death she didn't sleep well. The cabin often woke her with its creaks and groans. Sometimes she would hear a thump as if something had fallen and yet when she'd gone to investigate, she would find nothing.

One time, she'd found the front door standing open. She had stared at it in shock, chilled by the cold air rushing in—and the knowledge that she distinctly remembered locking it before going to bed. Only a crazy woman would leave the front door wide open.

Now, though, all she heard was the wind in the pines, a pleasant sound, a safe sound. She tried to reassure herself that everything was fine. She thought of her day with the Cardwell family and remembered how Jackson had saved her by having the Cardwell brothers make their famous Texas barbecue for supper. She smiled at the memory of the brothers in their Texas Boys Barbecue aprons joking around as they cooked.

She'd overheard one of the brothers say he was glad to see Jackson loosening up a little. Allie found herself watching him earlier at the rodeo, wondering how he was doing as a single father. She didn't feel as if she'd done very well so far as a single mother.

Ford was having a sleepover at the main house at the ranch again tonight. Allie knew if Nat had known about it, she would have wanted to stay, as well. But she suspected that Dana had realized that she needed her daughter with her tonight. What a day! First a run-in earlier with Mildred and Drew... Allie felt a chill at the memory. They had both been so furious and no doubt hurt, as well. Then thinking she saw Nick. She shook her head and, closing her eyes, tried to will herself to go back to sleep. If she got to thinking about any of that—

A small thump made her freeze. She heard it again and quickly swung her legs over the side of the bed. The sound had come from down the hall toward the bedroom where Natalie was sleeping.

Allie didn't bother with her slippers or her robe; she was too anxious as she heard another thump. She snapped on the hall light as she rushed down the short, narrow hallway to her daughter's room. The door she'd left open was now closed. She stopped in front of it, her heart pounding. The wind. It must have blown it shut. But surely she hadn't left Nat's window open that much.

She grabbed the knob and turned, shoving the door open with a force that sent her stumbling into the small room. The moon and starlight poured in through the gaping open window to paint the bedroom in silver as the wind slammed a loose shutter against the side of the cabin with a thump.

Allie felt her eyes widen as a scream climbed her throat. Nat's bed was empty.

Chapter 7

Jackson felt at loose ends after the bachelor party. Part of the reason, he told himself, was because he'd spent so little time with his son. Back in Texas on their small ranch, he and Ford were inseparable. It was good to see his son having so much fun with other children, but he missed him.

Tonight Ford was having a sleepover at the main house with Dana's brood. He'd wanted to say no when Dana had asked, but he had seen that Ford had his heart set and Jackson had no choice but to attend Tag's bachelor party.

Fortunately, it had been a mild one, bar-hopping from the Corral to Lily's brother's bar at Big Sky, The Canyon Bar. They'd laughed and joked about their childhoods growing up in Texas and talked about Tag's upcoming wedding and bugged Hayes about his plans with McKenzie. Hayes only grinned in answer.

Hud, as designated driver, got them all home just after midnight, where they parted company and headed to their respective cabins. That was hours ago. Jackson had slept for a while before the wind had awakened him.

Now, alone with only his thoughts, he kept circling back to Allie. She'd had fun at the rodeo—until she'd thought she'd seen her dead husband. He blamed her in-laws. He figured they'd been laying a guilt trip on her ever since Nick Taylor had been presumed dead. Her run-in with them that morning must have made her think she saw Nick. He wanted to throttle them for the way they treated Allie and shuddered at the thought of them having anything to do with raising Natalie.

Allie was too nice. Did she really believe they meant well? Like hell, he thought now. They'd been in the wrong and yet they'd made her feel badly. It reminded him too much of the way his ex had done him.

It had been fun cooking with his brothers again—just as they had when they'd started their first barbecue restaurant. Allie'd had fun at the barbecue, too. He'd seen her laughing and smiling with the family. He'd enjoyed himself, as well. Of course Austin still hadn't arrived. But it was nice being with the others.

As much as he'd enjoyed the day, he felt too antsy to sleep and admitted it wasn't just Ford who was the problem. He tried to go back to sleep, but knew it was impossible. He had too much on his mind. Except for the wind in the pines, the ranch was quiet as he decided to go for a walk.

Overhead the Montana sky was a dazzling glitter of starlight with the moon peeking in and out of the clouds.

The mountains rose on each side of the canyon, blacker than midnight. A breeze stirred the dark pines, sending a whisper through the night.

As he neared his rental SUV, he decided to go for a ride. He hadn't had that much to drink earlier and, after sleeping for a few hours, felt fine to drive.

But not far down the road, he found himself slowing as he neared Allie's cabin. The cabin was small and sat back from the highway on the river.

He would have driven on past, if a light hadn't come on inside the cabin.

Something about that light coming on in the wee hours of the morning sent a shiver through him. He would have said he had a premonition, if he believed in them. Instead, he didn't question what made him turn down her road.

Just as he pulled up to the cabin, Allie came running out.

At first he thought she'd seen him turn into her yard and that was why she'd come running out with a flashlight. But one look at her wild expression, her bare feet and her clothed in nothing but her nightgown, and he knew why he'd turned into her cabin.

"Allie?" he called to her as he jumped out. "Allie, what's wrong?"

She didn't seem to hear him. She ran toward the side of the cabin as if searching furiously as her flashlight beam darted into the darkness. He had to run after her as she headed around the back of the cabin. He grabbed her arm, thinking she might be having a nightmare and was walking in her sleep.

"Allie, what's wrong?"

"Nat! She's gone!"

He instantly thought of the fast-moving river not many yards out the back door. His gaze went to Allie's feet. "Get some shoes on. I'll check behind the house."

Taking her flashlight, he pushed her toward the front door before running around to the back of the cabin. He could hear and smell the river on the other side of a stand of pines. The July night was cool, almost cold this close to the river. Through the dark boughs, he caught glimpses of the Gallatin River. It shone in the moon and starlight, a ribbon of silver that had spent eons carving its way through the granite canyon walls.

As he reached the dense pines, his mind was racing. Had Natalie gotten up in the night and come outside? Maybe half-asleep, would she head for the river?

"Natalie!" he called. The only answer was the rush of the river and moan of the wind in the pine boughs overhead.

At the edge of the river, he shone the flashlight beam along the edge of the bank. No tracks in the soft earth. He flicked the light up and down the area between the pines, then out over the water. Exposed boulders shone in the light as the fast water rushed over and around them.

If Natalie had come down here and gone into the swift current...

At the sound of a vehicle engine starting up, he swung his flashlight beam in time to see a dark-colored pickup take off out of the pines. Had someone kidnapped Natalie? His first thought was the Taylors.

As he ran back toward the cabin, he tried to tell himself it had probably been teenagers parked down by the river making out. Once inside, he found Allie. She'd pulled on sandals and a robe and had just been heading out again. She looked panicked, her cheeks wet with tears.

"You're sure she isn't somewhere in the house," he said, thinking about a time that he'd fallen asleep under his bed while his mother had turned the house upside down looking for him.

The cabin was small. It took only a moment to search everywhere except Nat's room. As he neared the door to the child's bedroom, he felt the cool air and knew before he pushed open the door that her window was wide open, the wind billowing the curtains.

He could see the river and pines through the open window next to the bed. No screen. What looked like fresh soil and several dried pine needles were on the floor next to the bed. As he started to step into the room, a sound came from under the covers on the bed.

Jackson was at the bed in two long strides, pulling back the covers to find a sleeping Natalie Taylor curled there.

Had she been there the whole time and Allie had somehow missed her?

Allie stumbled into the room and fell to her knees next to her daughter's bed. She pulled Nat to her, snuggling her face into the sleeping child.

Jackson stepped out of the room to leave them alone for a moment. His heart was still racing, his fear now for Allie rather than Nat.

A few minutes later, Allie came out of her daughter's room. He could see that she'd been crying again.

"She's such a sound sleeper. I called for her. I swear she wasn't in her bed."

"I believe you."

"I checked her room. I looked under her bed…."

The tears began to fall again. "I looked in her closet. I called her name. *She wasn't there.* She wasn't anywhere in the cabin."

"It's all right," Jackson said as he stepped to her and put his arms around her.

Her voice broke as she tried to speak again. "What if she was there the whole time?" she whispered against his chest. He could feel her trembling and crying with both relief and this new fear. "She can sleep through anything. Maybe—"

"Did you leave the window open?"

"I cracked it just a little so she could get fresh air...."

"Natalie isn't strong enough to open that old window all the way like that."

Allie pulled back to look up at him, tears welling in her green eyes. "I *must* have opened it. I *must* have—"

He thought of the pickup he'd seen leaving. "There's something I need to check," he said, picking up the flashlight from where he'd laid it down just moments before. "Stay here with Natalie."

Outside he moved along the side of the house to the back, shining the flashlight ahead of him. He suspected what he would find so he wasn't all that surprised to discover the boot prints in the soft dirt outside Nat's window.

Jackson knelt down next to the prints. A man-size boot. He shone the light a few feet away. The tracks had come up to the window, the print a partial as if the man had sneaked up on the toes of his boots. But when the prints retreated from the child's window, the prints were full boot tracks, deep in the dirt as if he'd been carrying something. The tracks disappeared into the dried needles of the pines, then reappeared, this time headed back to the house. When the man had returned Natalie to her bed—and left dried pine needles and dirt on the bedroom floor.

Allie sat on the edge of her daughter's bed. She'd always loved watching Natalie sleep. There was something so incredibly sweet about her that was heightened when she slept. The sleep of angels, she thought as she watched the rise and fall of her daughter's chest.

Outside the now closed window, Jackson's shadow appeared and disappeared. A few minutes later, she heard him come back into the cabin. He came directly down the hall, stopping in Nat's bedroom doorway as if he knew she would be sitting on the side of the bed, watching her daughter sleep. That was where he would have been if it had been his son who'd gone missing, he thought.

She was still so shaken and scared. Not for Natalie, who was safe in her bed, but for herself. How could she have thought her daughter was missing? She really was losing her mind. Tucking Nat in, she checked to make sure the window was locked and left the room, propping the door open.

Jackson followed her into the small living room. She held her breath as she met his gaze. He was the one person who had made her feel as if she was going to be all right. He'd seen the black cat. He'd sympathized with her when she'd told him about misplacing her car keys and messing up her date book.

But earlier he'd looked at her as if she were a hysterical woman half out of her mind. She *had* been. Maybe she *was* unstable. When she'd found Nat's bed empty— Just the thought made her blood run cold again.

"I swear to you she wasn't in her bed." She could hear how close she was to breaking down again.

He must have, too, because he reached over and gripped her arm. "You didn't imagine it any more than you did the black cat."

She stared at him. "How can you say that?"

"Someone was outside Natalie's window tonight. There were fresh tracks where he'd stood. He took Natalie."

Her heart began to thunder in her ears. "Someone tried to…" She couldn't bring herself to say the words as she imagined a shadowed man taking her baby girl out through the window. "But why…?"

"He must have heard me coming and changed his mind," Jackson said.

"Changed his mind?" This all felt too surreal. First Nick's death then all the insane incidents, now someone had tried to take her child?

"Why don't you sit down," Jackson suggested.

She nodded and sank into the closest chair. He took one and pulled it next to hers.

"Is there someone who would want to take your daughter?" he asked.

Again she stared at him, unable to speak for a moment. "Why would anyone want to kidnap Natalie? I don't have any money."

He seemed to hesitate. "What about your husband's family?"

Jackson saw that he'd voiced her fear. He'd seen the way her in-laws had been just that morning. It wasn't much of a stretch that they would try to take Natalie. But through an open window in the middle of the night?

"They've made no secret that they want to see her more, but to steal her from her bed and scare me like this?"

Scare her. He saw her eyes widen in alarm and he took a guess. "There have been other instances when something happened that scared you?"

Her wide, green eyes filled with tears. "It was nothing. Probably just my imagination. I haven't been myself since…"

"Tell me about the incidents."

She swallowed and seemed to brace herself. "I found a squirrel in my cast-iron pot that has a lid."

"A live squirrel?"

"Half dead. I know it sounds crazy. How could a squirrel get under a heavy lid like that?"

"It couldn't. What else?"

She blinked as if stunned that he believed her, but it seemed to free her voice. "My husband used to buy me clothes I didn't like. I found them all cut up but I don't remember doing it. My brother-in-law took Nat and me out for dinner and when I got back they were lying on the bed and there were new clothes in the closet, eight hundred dollars' worth, like I would have bought if…"

"If you had bought them. Did you?"

She hesitated. "I don't think so but there was a check missing from my checkbook and when I took them back to the store, the clerks didn't remember who'd purchased them."

"No one was ever around when any of these things happened?"

She shook her head. "When I told my mother-in-law about the squirrel in the pot…she thought I was still taking the drugs the doctor gave me right after Nick's death. The drugs did make me see things that weren't there...." Her words fell away as if she'd just then realized something. "Unless the things *had* been there."

Allie looked up at him, tears shimmering in her eyes. "Like the black cat.... I wasn't sure I'd even seen it until you..."

It broke his heart. For months after her husband's death, she'd been going through this with no one who believed her.

"I don't think you imagined any of these things that have been happening to you," he said, reaching for her hand. "I think someone wants you to *believe* you are losing your mind. What would happen if you were?"

She didn't hesitate an instant. "I would lose Natalie."

As relieved as she was, Allie had trouble believing what he was saying. She got up and started to make a fire.

"Let me do that," Jackson said, taking a handful of kindling from her.

Allie moved restlessly around the room as he got the blaze going. "You think it's someone in Nick's family?"

"That would be my guess. It's clear they want Natalie, especially your mother-in-law. Would her son, Drew, help her?"

She shook her head. "Nick would do whatever his mother wanted. But Drew..." She didn't want to believe it, but he seemed to have turned against her lately. She felt sick at the thought that she might have been wrong about him all this time.

"You must think I'm such a fool."

"My mother said be careful what family you're marrying into. I didn't listen. I didn't even *know* the woman

I was really marrying. But then she hid it well—until we were married."

"I know exactly what you're saying."

His chuckle held no humor. "I learned the hard way."

"So did I. I would have left Nick, if he hadn't disappeared.... I suppose you heard that he went hiking up in the mountains late last fall and was believed killed by a grizzly."

He nodded. "I'm sorry. You must have all kinds of conflicting emotions under the circumstances."

Allie let out a sigh. "You have no idea. Or maybe you do. My friend Belinda says my so-called incidents are brought on by my guilt. She's even suggested that I see a psychic to try to contact Nick on the other side to make the guilt go away."

He shook his head. "I think there is a very sane explanation that has nothing to do with guilt, and the last thing you need is some charlatan who'll only take your money."

She laughed. "That was exactly what I thought." She couldn't believe how much better she felt. She hadn't felt strong for so long. Fear had weakened her, but Jackson's words brought out some of the old Allie, that strong young woman who'd foolishly married Nick Taylor.

He hadn't broken her at first. It had taken a few years before she'd realized what he'd done to her. She no longer had her own ideas—if they didn't agree with his. He dressed her, told her what friends he liked and which ones he didn't.

He'd basically taken over her life, but always making it seem as if he were doing her a favor since he knew best. And she had loved him. At least at first so she'd gone along because she hadn't wanted to upset him.

Nick could be scary when he was mad. She'd learned not to set him off.

When Nick had been nice, he'd been so sweet that she had been lulled into thinking that if she was just a little more accommodating he would be sweet all the time.

"Belinda thinks Nick knew that I was leaving him and went up in the mountains to…"

"Kill himself? What do you think?" Jackson asked.

"Nick did say he wanted to change and that he was sorry about the way he'd acted, but…"

"You didn't believe it?"

She shook her head. "The Nick I knew couldn't change even if he'd wanted to."

So why had Nick Taylor gone up into the mountains last fall and never come back? Jackson wondered.

The fact that his body hadn't been found made Jackson more than a little suspicious. If the man had purposely gone to the mountains intending to die and leave his wife and child alone, then he was a coward. If he set the whole thing up and was now trying to have his wife committed…

The timing bothered him. His stomach roiled with anger at the thought. "Is there any chance he knew of your plans?"

"I didn't think so. For months I'd been picking up any change he left lying around. I also had been skimping on groceries so I could save a little. He might have noticed." She looked away guiltily. "I also took money out of his wallet if he'd been drinking. I figured he wouldn't know how much he spent. He never said anything."

Jackson hoped this bastard was alive because he

planned to punch him before the man went to prison for what he was doing to this woman. Not letting her have her own money was a sin in any marriage, no matter what some head-of-the household types said.

"I hate to even ask this, but is there any chance—"

"Nick is still alive?" She stood and paced around the room. "That would explain it, wouldn't it? Why I think I see him or why I smell his aftershave in the house, even though I threw out the bottle months ago. Why when I start feeling better, he shows up."

"Like at the rodeo?" Jackson asked, feeling his skin crawl at the thought of the bastard. "This only happens when there is no one else around who sees him, right?"

She nodded. "It all happens in a split second so I can't be sure. At the rodeo, though, I almost caught him. Just a few more yards..." Allie's eyes suddenly widened. "I remember now. Someone grabbed my arm and spun me around. That's why I fell."

"You think it was someone who didn't want you to catch him."

"Did you see anyone you recognized in the crowd before you found me?"

He thought for a moment. "I wasn't looking for anyone but you, I'm sorry. Allie, all of this is classic gaslighting. Someone wants to unnerve you, to make you think you're imagining things, to make you doubt your own reality and ultimately make you doubt your own sanity."

She met his gaze. Her eyes filled with tears. "You think it's Nick?"

"I think it's a possibility. If he suspected you were going to leave him and take Natalie...he might have staged his death. He had the most to lose if you left him and with his body never being found..."

* * *

Nick alive? Allie felt a chill move through her. Her husband had been a ghost, haunting her from his mountain grave for months. Now he had taken on an even more malevolent spirit.

She got up and threw another log on the fire. But not even the hot flames could chase away the icy cold that had filled her at the thought of Nick still alive. Not just alive but stalking her, trying to make her think she was crazy. Still, why—

"You think he's after Natalie," she said and frowned. "He's never cared that much about her. He wanted a son and when he didn't get one…"

"Believe me. I know what it's like to have a vindictive spouse who would do anything to hurt me—including taking a child she didn't really want."

"Oh, Jackson, I'm so sorry."

"If your husband is alive, you can bet he is behind all of this."

If Nick really was alive, then Drew would know. It would also explain why Drew was being so protective and acting jealous over Jackson.

Jackson stepped to her. "There is one thing you can count on. It's going to get worse. Nick will have to escalate his plan. He probably has a story already planned for when he comes stumbling out of the mountains after being attacked and having no memory for months. But that story won't hold up if it goes on much longer. I don't want to scare you, but if whoever is behind this can't drive you crazy, they might get desperate and decide the best way to get Natalie is to get rid of her mother for good."

She shuddered.

"Sorry," he said. "I know it seems like a leap…"

Jackson looked to the dark window before returning his gaze to her. "But if your husband is alive, then you have to assume he is watching your every move."

If Nick wasn't, then Drew was doing it for him, she realized. "You really think it's possible?" she asked in a whisper as if not only was he watching but he was listening, as well.

"Given what has been happening to you and the fact that his body was never found?" Jackson nodded. "But if he is alive, we can't let him know that we're on to him."

We. That had such a wonderful sound. She had felt so alone in all this. Suddenly, she wasn't. Jackson believed her. He didn't think she was crazy. Far from it. He thought all of this was happening because someone wanted her to *believe* she was crazy. Maybe not just *someone,* but the man she'd married.

She swallowed back the bile that rose in her throat at the thought of how far her husband had gone and to what end? "He must have known I was leaving him and taking Natalie."

"That would be my guess. With you in the nuthouse, he could reappear and take your daughter."

The thought of Natalie with a man who would do something like that turned her blood to ice.

"But if he is alive, then—" Jackson seemed to hesitate "—then I really can't see how he could have pulled this off without help."

Allie knew what he was saying. Not just Drew but Mildred and Sarah might be in on this. "His brother, Drew, has been around a lot since Nick…disappeared and has helped out financially until the investigation is over. His mother's never liked me and didn't believe me when I've told her about only some of the things that have been happening. Or at least she pretended not to."

Jackson nodded. "What about Drew's sister, Sarah?"

"She's afraid of Mother Taylor, not that I can blame her."

He looked away for a moment. "What about the two women working with you on the wedding?"

"*Belinda and Megan?* Belinda's the only friend who stuck with me after I married Nick. He tried to run her off but she wasn't having any of it." Allie didn't want to believe it. Refused to. She shook her head. "She's been on my side against them. And Megan? She's my *stepsister* I never knew until…"

"Until?" he prompted.

"I guess it was right before Nick died. Megan contacted me. She was just finishing up her college degree at the University of Montana in Missoula. After my mother died, my father remarried several times and had more children. He moved away and I lost track of him and my step-siblings. Megan was like a gift coming into our lives when she did. Nat adores her. I adore her. You can't think she is somehow involved in any of this."

Jackson didn't say anything. He didn't have to. His skepticism was written all over his face. "It's the timing that bothers me."

She nodded. He thought she was naive. She'd always been too trusting. Isn't that what Nick had told her time and time again?

Allie quickly turned away as she felt hot tears scald her eyes. All of this was just too much. She thought of her daughter and hurriedly wiped at her tears. Straightening her back, she felt a surge of anger and turned back to face Jackson.

"Whoever is doing this, they aren't going to win. What do we do?" she asked.

"We catch them. Do you have a photograph of Nick?"

As she left the room, she noticed that the sun had come up. She came back with a snapshot. "This is the only one I could find. It's one of Nick and his brother, Drew. Nick is the one on the right."

Jackson looked down at the photo. "They look alike."

"Do they?" she said, looking at the snapshot he was holding. "I guess they do a little," she said, surprised that she hadn't noticed it because their personalities were so different. "Drew was always the quiet one. Nick was his mother's favorite. I'm sure that had something to do with why he was so cocky and smart-mouthed. Drew was the one always standing back watching."

"Did Drew resent that?" Jackson asked.

Allie frowned. "I don't know. He didn't seem to. Just the other day he was telling me how hard it was to keep the business going without Nick."

Jackson turned thoughtful for a moment. "You mentioned something about Belinda wanting you to see some psychic so you could reach Nick on the other side? I think you should do it."

Allie blinked in surprise. "Seriously? You don't think I'm messed up enough?"

"It's Belinda's idea, right? If she is involved, then this séance with the psychic is a trap. But since we are on to them now, it would help to know what they have planned for you. I suspect it won't be pleasant, though. I'm sure it is supposed to push you over the edge, if you aren't already dangling there. Do you think you can handle it?"

She raised her chin, her eyes dry, resolve burning in

her like a blazing fire. She thought of the people who had been tricking her for months. Anger boiled up inside her along with a steely determination. She hadn't felt this strong in years. "I can handle it."

Jackson smiled at her. "Good." He checked his watch. "Give the psychic a call. Calling this early she will think you are desperate to see her, exactly what we want her to think."

Allie dug the card out, glad now that she'd saved it. She took a breath, let it out and dialed the number. Jackson stepped closer so he could hear.

She was surprised when a young-sounding woman answered after three rings.

"I'm sorry to call so early but I need your help. My friend Belinda suggested I call you." Jackson gave her a thumbs-up.

"You must be Allie. I was hoping you'd call. You're in danger—and so is your daughter. I need to see you as soon as possible."

"Is today too soon, then?" Allie asked.

"Why don't you come this evening, say about eight? Will that work for you?"

Allie met Jackson's gaze. He nodded. "That would be fine. I hope you can help me."

"I will do my best but ultimately it will be up to the spirits."

Jackson swore softly as Allie disconnected. "Spirits my ass. Between now and then, I will try to find out everything I can about the people with access to you." He reached over and took her hand. "Don't worry. We're going to catch these bastards."

Chapter 8

When Jackson returned to the ranch, he found his brothers, told them what he thought was going on and asked for their help. He no longer kidded himself that he wasn't involved.

"I can talk to the cops about what they found in the mountains," Hayes said. "You say Nick Taylor's body still hasn't been found? Isn't that odd? He died late last fall and even with hikers in the area, no remains have turned up?"

"No, that's what makes me suspicious," Jackson said. "His claw-shredded backpack and rifle were discovered at the scene with grizzly prints in the dirt and enough blood to make them believe he was killed there. But still no remains of any kind."

Hayes nodded. "I'll get right on it."

"What can I do?" Laramie asked.

"Financials on everyone involved including Allie's friend Belinda Andrews and her stepsister, Megan

Knight, as well as all of the Taylor family. Nick and his brother, Drew, were partners in a construction company called Gallatin Canyon Specialty Construction."

"You got it," Laramie said. "What about Allie herself?"

"Sure, and Nick, just in case he had something going on that she didn't know about," Jackson said.

"Wait a minute," Tag said. "What about me?"

"You, brother dear, are getting married. You just concentrate on your lovely bride-to-be," Jackson told him. Tag started to object. "If you're going to be hanging around the ranch here, then do me a favor. Keep an eye on Drew Taylor. He's apparently doing some repairs here."

Jackson stopped by the barn to find Allie and Megan hard at work putting together centerpieces for the tables. Allie pretended she needed something from her van and got up to go outside with him.

"No more trouble last night?" he asked, seeing worry in her gaze.

"None. I'm just having a hard time believing any of that happened last night." She glanced around as if she expected Nick to materialize before her gaze came back to him. Or maybe she was worried about her brother-in-law, Drew, seeing them together again. "I can't believe Belinda or Megan—"

"Have you seen Belinda?"

"She had to go into Bozeman. She left about twenty minutes ago, why?"

He shook his head. "You better get back inside. Try not to let on that you're suspicious."

She sighed. "You don't know how hard that is."

"I can imagine." He gave her an encouraging smile. "Just be your usual sweet self." He loved it when she returned his smile and those gorgeous dimples of hers showed.

As she went back into the barn and rejoined Megan, he headed up the hillside. Belinda was staying in the last guesthouse to the east. Each cabin was set away from the others in the dense pines for the most privacy.

A cool pine-scented breeze restlessly moved the boughs over his head as he walked on the bed of dried needles toward Belinda's cabin. He could hear the roar of the river and occasionally the sound of a semi shifting down on the highway far below. A squirrel chattered at him as he passed, breaking the tranquility.

He was almost to her cabin when he heard the crack of a twig behind him and spun around in surprise.

His brother Hayes grinned. "I would imagine the cabin will be locked," he said as he stepped on past to climb the steps to the small porch and try the door. "Yep, I know your lock-picking skills are rusty at best." He pulled out his tool set.

Jackson climbed the steps and elbowed his brother out of the way. "I told Dana I was locked out. She gave me the master key." He laughed and opened the door.

"You know I do this for a living, right?" his brother asked.

"I'd heard that. But are you any good?"

Hayes shot him a grin and headed for the log dresser in the room with the unmade bed.

Jackson glanced around the main room of the cabin and spotted Belinda's camera bag. He could hear his brother searching the bedroom as he carefully unzipped the bag. There were the usual items found in a professional photographer's large bag. He carefully took out the camera, lens and plastic filter containers and was about to put everything back, thinking there was nothing to find when he saw the corner of a photo protruding from one of the lower pockets.

"What did you find?" Hayes asked as he returned after searching both bedrooms.

Jackson drew out the photos and thumbed through them. They were shots taken with apparent friends. Each photo had Belinda smiling at the camera with her arm around different friends, all women. He was thinking how there wasn't one of her and Allie, when he came to the last photo and caught his breath.

"Who is that?" Hayes asked.

"Allie's husband, Nick, and her best friend Belinda Andrews. Allie said that Nick never liked Belinda." The snapshot had been taken in the woods along a trail. There was a sign in the distance that said Grouse Creek Trail. Nick had his arm possessively around Belinda. Both were smiling at each other rather than the camera the way lovers do.

"Apparently, they liked each other a lot more than Allie knew," Hayes said. "But you know what is really interesting about that photo? That trailhead sign behind them."

"Let me guess. Up that trail is where Nick Taylor was believed to have been killed."

When they'd finished the centerpieces, Allie sent Megan into Bozeman for an order of wedding items that had been delayed. It had been difficult working with her and suspecting her of horrible things. Allie was relieved when she was finally alone in the barn.

Everything was coming along on schedule. It had been Dana's idea to start days early. "I don't want you to feel any pressure and if you need extra help, you just let me know," Dana had said.

"No, I'm sure that will be fine."

"I want you to have some free time to go for a horseback ride or just spend it on the ranch with your daughter."

"You are so thoughtful," Allie had said.

"Not at all. I just know what it's like with a little one, even though Natalie isn't so little anymore," she said with a laugh. "I promise I will keep your daughter busy so you can work and not have to worry about her having a good time."

Dana had been good to her word. Allie stepped outside the barn now to check on Natalie only to find her on the back of a horse about to take a short ride up the road for another picnic with Dana and the other children.

"Come along," Dana encouraged. "Warren would be happy to saddle you a horse. You know what they say about almost falling off a horse, don't you?" she asked with a smile. "You have to get back on."

Allie laughed, thinking that was exactly what she was doing with her life, thanks to Jackson. She was tempted to go on the ride until she saw him headed her way. "Next time."

"We're going to hold you to it," Dana said. "In fact, we're all going on a ride tomorrow before the rehearsal dinner. Plan on coming along." With that they rode off, the kids waving and cheering as they disappeared into the pines.

Jackson waved to his son, making the same promise before he continued on down the mountainside toward her.

When she saw his expression, her heart fell. He'd discovered something and whatever it was, it wasn't good.

"Let's go up to my cabin," Jackson said as he glanced around. "We can talk there."

They made the short hike up the mountainside. His cabin faced the river, sheltered in the pines and was several dozen yards from the closest cabin where his brothers were staying together.

"What is it?" Allie asked the moment they were inside.

Jackson handed her a snapshot in answer.

She looked down at her smiling husband and her best friend. There was no doubt what she was looking at but still she was shocked and found it hard to believe. For more than six years Belinda and Nick had acted as if they couldn't stand each other. Had it been a lie the entire time?

"When was this taken?" she asked.

Jackson shook his head. "There isn't a date. I found it in her camera bag with a lot of other photos of her with friends."

Allie raised an eyebrow. "You aren't going to try to convince me that they are just friends."

He shook his head. "You weren't at all suspicious?"

She laughed as she made her way to the couch and sat down. The ground under her feet no longer felt stable. "Nick always said I was too trusting. Belinda was the only friend who could put up with Nick. So I guess a part of me suspected that Nick liked her more than he let on."

"I'm sorry."

"Don't be. I stopped loving Nick Taylor the year we got married. If I hadn't gotten pregnant with Nat..." She tossed the photo on the coffee table in front of her.

"She was the only one you told about your plans to leave Nick?" he asked as he took a seat across from her.

Allie let out a laugh. "So of course she told him."

"More than likely," he agreed. "There's more." He took a breath and let it out as he studied her. "You sure you want to hear all of this?"

She sat up straighter. "Let me have it."

"I got my brothers to help me. They have the expertise in their chosen fields that we needed. Hayes talked to the cops, who had a copy of Nick's file with reports from the hiker who found the backpack and rifle to the warden who investigated the initial scene. He reported that there was sufficient evidence to assume that Nick was dead based on the shredded backpack and the amount of blood soaked into the pine needles."

"So…he's dead?"

"Or he made it look that way," Jackson said. "No DNA was tested at the scene because there didn't appear to be a need to do so. But there are still a lot of questions. No shots were fired from the rifle, leading the investigators to believe he didn't have time to get off a shot before he was attacked by the bear. Or he could have staged the whole thing. But the incidents you've been having with things disappearing and reappearing, those can't be Nick. If he's alive, he has to keep his head down."

"So we're back to my in-laws and Belinda and Megan."

"I'm afraid so. Belinda, if involved with Nick, would be the obvious one. Was she around before any of the incidents happened?"

Allie thought back to when her keys had ended up in the bathroom sink at the Mexican restaurant. She'd left her purse at the table, but then Sarah and her mother had been there, too. She sighed, still refusing to believe it, even after seeing the photo. "Yes, but Belinda wouldn't—"

"Wouldn't have an affair with your husband behind your back?"

"She's been so *worried* about me."

Jackson raised a brow.

Allie hugged herself against the thought of what he was saying. Belinda *had* apparently betrayed her with Nick. Maybe Jackson was right. Then she remembered something. "Belinda has a new man in her life. I know the signs. She starts dressing up and, I don't know, acting different. The man can't be Nick. That photo doesn't look recent of her and Nick. Why would she be acting as if there was someone new if it was Nick all these months?"

"Maybe he's been hiding out and has only now returned to the canyon."

That thought turned her stomach. "If he's come back…"

"Then whoever has been gaslighting you must be planning on stepping up their plan," Jackson said.

She turned to look at him as a shiver raced through her. "The psychic. Maybe this is their grand finale, so to speak, and they have something big planned tonight to finally send me to the loony bin."

"Maybe you shouldn't go—"

"No. Whatever they have planned, it won't work. They've done their best to drive me crazy. I know now what they're up to. I'll be fine."

"I sure hope so," Jackson said.

"What is the lowdown on the Taylor family?" Jackson asked Hud after dinner that evening at the ranch. They'd had beef steaks cooked on a pitchfork in the fire and eaten on the wide porch at the front of the house. The night had been beautiful, but Jackson was too antsy to appreciate it. He was worried about Allie.

She'd dropped Natalie by before she and Belinda had left. He hadn't had a chance to speak with her without raising suspicion. All he could do was try his best to find out who was behind the things that had been happening to her.

"Old canyon family," Hud said. "Questionable how they made their money. It was rumored that the patriarch killed someone and stole his gold." Hud shrugged. "Mildred? She married into it just months before Bud Taylor died in a car accident. She's kept the name even though she's been through several more husbands. I believe she is on number four now. Didn't take his name, though. He's fifteen, twenty years older and spends most of his time with his grown children back in Chicago."

"And the daughter?"

"Sarah?" Hud frowned. "Never been married that I know of. Lives in the guesthouse behind her mother's. No visible means of support."

"The brothers had a construction company together?"

"They did. Nick was the driving force. With him gone, I don't think Drew is working all that much."

"Just between you and me, Allie was planning to leave Nick Taylor before he went up in the mountain and disappeared," Jackson said, taking the marshal into his confidence.

Hud looked over at him. "What are you getting at?"

"Is there any chance Nick Taylor is alive?"

Hud frowned. "You must have some reason to believe he is."

"Someone has been gaslighting Allie."

"For what purpose?"

"I think someone, probably in the Taylor family, wants to take Natalie away from her."

"You seem better," Belinda noted on the drive out of the canyon. She'd insisted on driving Allie to the psychic's house, saying she didn't trust Allie to drive herself if the psychic said anything that upset her.

Allie had been quiet most of the drive. "*Do* I seem better?" Did her friend seem disappointed in that?

"Maybe this isn't necessary."

That surprised her. "I thought you were the one who said I had to talk to this psychic?"

"I thought it would help."

"And now?" Allie asked.

"I don't want her to upset you when you seem to be doing so well."

"That's sweet, but I'm committed…so to speak."

Belinda nodded and kept driving. "Seriously, you seem so different and the only thing that has changed that I can tell is Jackson Cardwell showing up."

Allie laughed. "Just like you to think it has to be a man. Maybe I'm just getting control of my life."

Her friend looked skeptical. "Only a few days ago you were burning Nick's favorite shirt so it didn't turn up again."

"Didn't I tell you? The shirt *did* turn up again. I found it hanging in the shower this morning. Now I ask you, how is that possible?"

"You're sure you burned it? Maybe you just—"

"Dreamed it?" Allie smiled. That was what they wanted her to think. She looked over at Belinda, worried her old friend was up to her neck in this, whatever it was.

Allie fought the urge to confront her and demand to know who else was behind it. But Belinda turned down a narrow road, slowing to a stop in front of a small house with a faint porch light on.

Showtime, Allie thought as she tried to swallow the lump in her throat.

Chapter 9

Belinda's apartment house was an old, five-story brick one a few blocks off Main Street in Bozeman.

Laramie waited in the car as lookout while Jackson and Hayes went inside. There was no password entry required. They simply walked in through the front door and took the elevator up to the third floor to room 3B. It was just as Allie had described it, an apartment at the back, the door recessed so even if someone had been home on the floor of four apartments, they wouldn't have seen Hayes pick the lock.

"You're fast," Jackson said, impressed.

Hayes merely smiled and handed him a pair of latex gloves. "I'm also smart. If you're right and Nick Taylor is alive and this becomes a criminal case… You get the idea. It was different up on the ranch. This, my brother, is breaking and entering."

Jackson pulled on the gloves and opened the door. As he started to draw his flashlight out of his pocket, Hayes snapped on an overhead light.

"What the—"

"Jackson," his brother said and motioned toward the window. The curtains were open, the apartment looking out onto another apartment building. While most of the curtains were drawn in those facing this way, several were open.

Hayes stepped to the window and closed the curtains. "Nothing more suspicious than two dudes sneaking around in a woman's apartment with flashlights."

He had a point. "Let's make this quick."

"I'm with you," Hayes said and suggested the best place to start.

"If I didn't know better, I'd think you'd done this before," Jackson joked.

Hayes didn't answer.

In the bedroom in the bottom drawer of the bureau under a bunch of sweaters, Jackson found more photos of Belinda and Nick, but left them where he'd found them.

"So you think I'm right and Nick is alive," Jackson said.

Hayes shrugged.

Jackson finished the search of the bedroom, following his brother's instructions to try to leave everything as he had found it.

"Find anything?" he asked Hayes when he'd finished.

"She recently came into thirty-eight thousand dollars," Hayes said, thumbing through a stack of bank statements he'd taken from a drawer.

"Maybe it's a trust fund or an inheritance."

"Maybe. Or blackmail money or money Nick had hidden from Allie," Hayes said as he put everything back. "Laramie would probably be able to find out what it was if we had more time. Did you put the photos back?"

"All except one. I want to show it to Allie. It looks more recent to me."

Hayes looked as if he thought that was a bad idea. "You're messing with evidence," he reminded him.

"I'll take that chance," Jackson said.

His brother shook his head as he turned out the light and moved to the window to open the curtains like he'd found them.

"Does anyone else know how involved you are with the wedding planner?" Silence. "I didn't think so. Better not let cousin Dana find out or there will be hell to pay. She is very protective of people she cares about. She cares about that woman and her child. If you—"

"I'm not going to hurt her." He couldn't see his brother's expression in the dark. He didn't have to.

Allie braced herself. She hadn't shared her fears about the visit with the psychic with Jackson before she'd left. She hadn't had to. She'd seen the expression on his face as he watched her leave. He was terrified for her.

For months someone had been trying to push her over the edge of sanity. She had a bad feeling that the psychic was part of the master plan, a shocker that was aimed at driving her insane. By now, they probably thought she was hanging on by a thread. While she was stronger, thanks to Jackson and his determination that she was perfectly sane and those around her were the problem, there was a part of her that wasn't so sure about that.

Just this morning, she'd stepped into the bathroom, opened the shower curtain and let out a cry of shock and disbelief. Nick's favorite shirt was hanging there, the same shirt she'd burned in the fireplace a few nights ago. Or at least one exactly like it. Worse, she smelled his aftershave and when she opened the medicine cabinet, there it was in the spot where he always kept it—right next to his razor, both of which she had thrown out months ago.

Had he hoped she would cut her wrists? Because it had crossed her mind. If it hadn't been for Natalie... and now Jackson...

"Remember, you're that strong woman you were before you met Nick Taylor," Jackson had said earlier.

She'd smiled because she could only vaguely remember that woman. But she wanted desperately to reacquaint herself with her. Now all she could do was be strong for her daughter. She couldn't let these people get their hands on Natalie.

Belinda parked in front of a small house and looked over at her. "Ready?"

Allie could hear reluctance in her friend's voice. If Jackson was right and Nick was behind this, then Allie suspected he was forcing Belinda to go through with the plan no matter what.

But that's what she had to find out. If Nick was alive. She opened her car door and climbed out. The night air was cool and scented with fresh-cut hay from a nearby field. It struck her how remote this house was. The closest other residence had been up the road a good half mile.

If a person was to scream, no one would hear, Allie thought, then warned herself not to bother screaming. Belinda and the psychic were probably hoping for just such a reaction.

"I was surprised when you agreed to do this," Belinda said now, studying her as she joined Allie on the path to the house.

"I told you. I would do anything to make whatever is happening to me stop." Allie took a deep breath and let it out. "Let's get this over with."

They walked up the short sidewalk and Belinda knocked. Allie noticed that there weren't any other vehicles around except for an old station wagon parked in the open, equally old garage. If Nick was here he'd either been dropped off or he'd parked in the trees at the back of the property.

The door was opened by a small, unintimidating woman wearing a tie-dyed T-shirt and worn jeans. Her feet were bare. Allie had been expecting a woman in a bright caftan wearing some sort of headdress. She was a little disappointed.

"Please come in," the woman said in what sounded like a European accent. "I am Katrina," she said with a slight nod. "It is so nice to meet you, Allie. Please follow me. Your friend can stay here."

Belinda moved to a couch in what Allie assumed was the sparsely furnished living area.

Allie followed the woman down a dim hallway and through a door into a small room dominated by a table and two chairs. The table was bare.

Katrina closed the door, making the room feel even smaller. She took a seat behind the desk and motioned Allie into the chair on the opposite side.

This felt silly and it was all Allie could do not to laugh. She and a friend in the fifth grade had stopped at the fortune teller's booth at the fair one time—her friend Willow's idea, not hers.

"I want to know if I am going to marry Curt," her friend had said.

Allie could have told her that there was a good chance she wasn't going to marry some boy in her fifth grade class.

The fortune teller had told them they would have long, happy lives and marry their true loves. Five dollars each later they were standing outside the woman's booth. Willow had been so excited, believing what the fortune teller had said was that she would marry Curt. She'd clearly read what she wanted into the woman's words.

Willow didn't marry Curt but maybe she had found her true love since she'd moved away in sixth grade when her father was transferred. Allie hadn't had a happy life nor had she apparently married her true love and now here she was again sitting across from some woman who she feared really might know her future because she was about to control it.

"I understand you want me to try to reach your husband who has passed over," Katrina said. "I have to warn you that I am not always able to reach the other side, but I will try since your friend seems to think if I can reach…"

"Nick," Allie supplied.

"Yes, that it will give you some peace." The woman hesitated. "I hope that will be the case. It isn't always, I must warn you. Do you want to continue?"

Allie swallowed and nodded.

"Give me your hands. I need you to think of your

husband." Katrina dimmed the lights and reached across the table to take Allie's hands in hers. "It helps if you will close your eyes and try to envision your husband."

That was about the last thing Allie wanted to do, but as Katrina closed hers, Allie did the same. She couldn't help but think of Nick and wonder if he was watching her at this very moment.

"While we're breaking the law, there is one other place I'd like to have a look before we head back," Jackson said to his brothers.

Hayes looked disapproving. "What part of breaking and entering don't you understand?"

"You can wait in the car."

Gallatin Canyon Specialty Construction was located on the outskirts of town next to a gravel pit. The industrial area was dark this time of the night as Jackson pulled in with his lights out and parked.

"Allie said the company hasn't been doing very well without Nick and wasn't doing that well even before Nick allegedly died," Jackson said. "I just want to take a look at the books."

"Good thing you brought me along," Laramie said. "You did mean, you want me to take a look, right?"

Jackson laughed. "Yeah, if you don't mind."

Hayes sighed and they all got out and walked toward the trailer that served as the office. Hayes unlocked the door then said, "I'll stand guard. Make it quick," before disappearing into the darkness.

"You do realize you might be jeopardizing everything by doing this," Laramie said. "Is this woman worth it?"

Jackson didn't answer as he pulled on the latex

gloves Hayes had shoved at him in the car and handed his brother a pair before turning on a light and pointing at the file cabinets.

It wasn't until they were all three back in the car and headed south toward Cardwell Ranch that Jackson asked his brother what he'd found, if anything.

After Laramie tried to explain it in fiduciary terms, Hayes snapped, "The bottom line, please."

Laramie sighed. "It is clear why you all leave the business part of Texas Boys Barbecue up to me. All right, here it is. Drew Taylor is broke and has been siphoning off the money from the business before the sale."

"Sale?" Jackson said.

"While not of general knowledge, Drew has been trying to sell the business through a company in other states."

"That's suspicious," Hayes said.

"Is his mother involved in the construction business?" Jackson asked.

Laramie chuckled. "Excellent question. I believe she might have been a silent partner, which I take to mean she provided some of the money. Until recently, Drew was writing her a check each month."

"Think she knows what her son is up to?" Hayes asked.

"Doubtful. According to Allie, Mother Taylor rules the roost. Everyone is afraid of her."

"Sounds like our boy Drew is planning to escape in the dark of night," Hayes commented and Jackson agreed.

"As for the rest of the people you asked me to look at the finances of, Mildred Taylor is fine as long as her old, absentee husband sends her a check each month. She and her daughter live off the old man. Nick wasn't much of a breadwinner. Montana winters slow down construction, apparently. But he did okay. After his death, there wasn't much in his personal account."

"So the thirty-eight thousand Belinda just received wasn't from Nick, then," Hayes said.

Laramie continued, "Nick did, however, leave a hundred-thousand-dollar insurance policy, which is supposed to pay out any day once Nick has finally been ruled legally deceased."

"A hundred thousand?" Jackson exclaimed. "That doesn't seem like enough money to put Allie into the nuthouse for."

Laramie and Hayes agreed. "There could be other insurance policies I'm not aware of."

"What about Megan Knight?" Jackson asked.

"Just finished college, has thousands of dollars in student loans," Laramie said. "Majored in psychology so unless she goes to grad school…"

"What do you all make of this?" Jackson asked.

"Well," his brother Laramie said. "I've always said follow the money. That will usually take you to the source of the problem."

"So we have Drew siphoning money from the business and Belinda coming into some money and Megan needing money to pay off her student loans," Jackson said. "So which of them has motive to want Allie in the nuthouse?"

"Your guess is as good as mine," Hayes said. "That photo you took from Belinda's apartment of her and Nick? The lovebirds didn't look like they were getting along."

"Wait a minute," Laramie said from the backseat. "Are you thinking with Nick gone, Drew and Belinda hooked up?"

"Good question," Jackson said.

"I've heard of stranger things happening," Hayes said.

"Or maybe it's blackmail money," Jackson said. "Maybe Belinda has something on Drew and he's the source of the thirty-eight thousand."

"Or Drew is simply taking money from the business and giving it to Belinda to give to Nick," Hayes threw in.

"Which would mean that Drew knows Nick is alive," Jackson said.

"Or at least he has been led to believe his brother is alive according to Belinda," Hayes said.

"You two are making my head spin," Laramie cried and both brothers laughed. "No wonder I prefer facts and figures. They are so much less confusing."

"He's right," Hayes said. "It could be simple. Nick's dead, Belinda got her money from another source entirely and Drew is blowing his on beer."

As they reached Cardwell Ranch, Jackson glanced at the time. "Let's hope Allie gets some answers tonight," he said, unable to keep the worry out of his voice. "Who knows what horrors they have planned for her."

"Allie."

Nick's voice made Allie jump, but Katrina held tight to her hands. Goose bumps skittered over her skin as Nick spoke again.

"Allie?" His voice seemed to be coming from far away.

"We're here, Nick," Katrina said after she'd spent

a good five minutes with her eyes closed, calling up Nick's spirit. "Is there something you want to say to Allie?"

She heard him groan. The sound sent her heart pounding even harder. Somehow it was more chilling than his saying her name.

"Please, Nick, do you have a message for Allie?"

Another groan, this one sounding farther away. Katrina seemed anxious as if she feared she was going to lose Nick before he said whatever it was he wanted to say.

Allie doubted that was going to happen, but maybe the woman would try to drag this out, get more money from her by making her come back again.

She tried to pull away, but Katrina tightened her hold, pulling her forward so her elbows rested on the table.

"Nick, please, give your wife the peace she desperately needs."

Another groan. "Allie, *why?*" The last word was so ghostly that Allie felt her skin crawl. At that moment, she believed it was Nick calling to her from the grave.

"What are you asking?" Katrina called out to him.

Silence. It was so heavy that it pressed against Allie's chest until she thought she couldn't breathe.

Then a groan as forlorn as any she'd ever heard filled the small room. She shivered. "Allie," Nick said in a voice that broke. "Why did you kill me?"

Chapter 10

Allie jerked her hands free and stumbled to her feet. She didn't realize she'd made a sound until she realized she was whimpering.

As the lights came up, she saw that Katrina was staring at her in shock as if whoever was behind this hadn't taken her into their confidence. Either that, or she was a good actress.

Allie rushed out of the room and down the hallway. Belinda wasn't in the living room, where she'd been told to wait. Opening the door, Allie ran outside, stopping only when she reached Belinda's car.

None of that was real. But it had been Nick's voice; there was no doubt about that. He was either alive... or they'd somehow gotten a recording of Nick's voice. *That wasn't Nick speaking from his grave.* Intellectually, she knew that. But just hearing Nick's voice and those horrible groans…

Belinda came bursting out of the house. Allie turned to see Katrina standing at the doorway looking stunned. Or was that, too, an act?

"Allie?" Belinda ran to her looking scared. "What happened in there?"

She ignored the question. "Where were you?"

Belinda seemed taken aback by her tone, if not her question. "I had to go to the bathroom. I was just down the hall. Are you all right?"

"I want to go." Katrina was still standing in the doorway. Allie reached for the door handle but the car was locked. "Belinda, I want to *go*."

"Okay, just a sec." She groped in her purse for her keys.

"Can't find them?" Allie taunted with a sneer. "Maybe you left them in the bathroom sink."

Belinda glanced up in surprise, frowning as if confused. "No, I have them. Honey, are you sure you're all right?"

Allie laughed. "How can you seriously ask that?"

Belinda stared at her for a moment before she opened the car doors and went around and slid behind the wheel.

They rode in silence for a few minutes before Belinda said, "I'm sorry. Clearly, you're upset. I thought—"

"What did you think?" Allie demanded.

Belinda shot her a glance before returning to her driving. "I seriously thought this might help."

"Really? Was it your idea or Nick's?"

"Nick's?" She shot her another quick look.

"I *know,* Belinda." Silence. "I know about you and Nick." Belinda started to deny it, but Allie cut her off.

"You two had me going for a while, I'll give you that. I really did think I was losing my mind. But not anymore. How long have you and Nick been having an affair?"

"Allie—"

"I don't have to ask whose plan this was. It has Nick written all over it."

"Honey, I honestly don't know what you're talking about."

"No?" Allie reached into her pocket and pulled out the photo of Belinda and Nick standing next to the trailhead sign at Grouse Creek. "As you've often said, a picture is worth a thousand words."

Belinda groaned, not unlike Nick had back at the alleged psychic's. "It isn't what you think."

Allie laughed again as she put the photo back in her pocket. "It never is."

"I'm sorry." She sounded as if she were crying, but Allie could feel no compassion for her.

"What was the point of all that back there?" Allie demanded as they left the Gallatin Valley behind and entered the dark, narrow canyon.

"I swear I don't know what you're talking about. What happened in there that has you so angry and upset?"

"Don't play dumb, Belinda. It doesn't become you. But tell me, what's next?" Allie demanded. "You failed to make me crazy enough that you could take Natalie. Is it the insurance money? Is that what you're planning to use to open your own studio? But in order to get it, you're going to have to kill me. Is that the next part of your plot, Belinda?"

The woman gasped and shot her a wide-eyed look. "You sure you aren't crazy, because you are certainly talking that way. That photo of me and Nick? That was before he met and married you. I broke up with him. Why do you think he didn't like me? Why do you think he put up with me? Because I threatened to tell you about the two of us." She took a breath and let it out. "As for me trying to make you think you were crazy..." Belinda waved a hand through the air. "That's ridiculous. I'm the one who has been trying to help you. I should have told you about me and Nick, but it was water under the bridge. And Nick's insurance money? I don't need it. Remember I told you about my eccentric aunt Ethel? Well, it seems she'd been socking money away in her underwear drawer for years. Thirty-eight thousand of it was left to me, tax free. That's what I plan to use to start my own photo studio. Allie, no matter what you think, I'm your *friend*."

She had thought so, but now she didn't know what to believe. "How did you come up with the idea of me going to see Katrina?" she challenged.

Belinda drove in silence, the canyon highway a dark ribbon along the edge of the river. "I told you. I'd seen Katrina a few times. But the idea for you to go see her so you could try to reach Nick and get closure? That was your sister *Megan*'s idea."

Jackson found himself walking the floor of his cabin until he couldn't take it anymore. Finally, he heard the sound of a vehicle, saw the headlights coming up the road and hurried down to the barn where Allie had left her van.

He waited in the shadows as both women got out of Belinda's car, neither speaking as they parted ways.

"Are you all right?" Jackson asked Allie as he

stepped from the shadows. She jumped, surprised, and he mentally kicked himself for scaring her. "I'm sorry. I've been pacing the floor. I was so worried about you."

Her features softened. "I'm okay." She looked drained.

"If you don't want to talk about it tonight..."

Allie gave him a wane smile. "Natalie is staying with your family and I'm not going to be able to sleep, anyway."

"Do you mind coming up to my cabin?"

She shook her head and let him lead her up the mountainside through the pines. It was only a little after ten, but most everyone had turned in for the night so there was little light or sound on the ranch. Under the thick pine boughs, it was cool and dark and smelled of summer.

Jackson realized he was going to miss that smell when he returned to Texas. He didn't want to think about what else he might miss.

Once inside the cabin, they took a seat on the couch, turning to face each other. It was warm in the cabin away from the chill of the Montana summer night. Without prompting, Allie began to relate what had happened slowly as if she was exhausted. He didn't doubt she was.

He hated putting her through this. She told him about the ride to the psychic's and Belinda's apparent hesitancy to let her go through with it. Then she told him about Katrina and the small remote house.

"It all felt silly and like a waste of time, until I heard Nick's voice."

He looked at her and felt his heart drop. Hearing her

husband's voice had clearly upset her. It surprised him that whoever was behind this had gone that far.

"You're sure it was Nick's voice."

She nodded. "It sounded as if it was far away and yet close."

"Could it have been a recording?"

"Possibly. His words were halting as if hard for him to speak and he...groaned." She shuddered. "It was an awful sound, unearthly."

"I'm so sorry. After you left, I regretted telling you to go." He sighed. "I was afraid it would just upset you and accomplish nothing."

"It gets worse. Nick...accused me of...killing him."

"*What?* That's ridiculous. I thought a grizzly killed him."

She shrugged. "The psychic believed it. You should have seen her face."

"Allie, the woman was in on it. This was just another ploy. You knew that going in."

"But I didn't know I would hear his voice. I didn't know he would ask me why I'd killed him. I didn't..." The tears came in a rush, dissolving the rest of whatever she was going to say.

Jackson pulled her to him. She buried her face into his chest. "None of this is real, Allie. Are you listening to me? None of it. They just want you to believe it is."

After a few moments, the sobs stopped. He handed her a tissue from the box by the couch and she got up and moved to the window. His cabin view was the rock cliff across the valley and a ribbon of Gallatin River below it.

As he got up, he moved to stand behind her. He could

see starlight on that stretch of visible river. It shone like silver.

"If Nick is alive and I believe he is, then he has tried to do everything he can to make you think you're losing your mind. It hasn't worked. This isn't going to work, either. You're stronger than that."

"Am I?" she asked with a laugh. "I am when I'm with you, but…"

He turned her to face him. "You just needed someone to believe in you. I believe in you, Allie."

She looked up at him, her green eyes full of hope and trust and—

His gaze went to her mouth. Lowering his head, he kissed her.

A low moan escaped her lips. As he drew her closer, Allie closed her eyes, relishing in the feel of her body against his. It had been so long since a man had kissed her let alone held her. She couldn't remember the last time she'd made love. Nick had seemed to lose interest in her toward the end, which had been more than fine with her.

She banished all thoughts of Nick as she lost herself in Jackson's kiss. Her arms looped around his neck. She could feel her heart pounding next to his. Her breasts felt heavy, her nipples hard and aching as he deepened the kiss. A bolt of desire like none she'd ever known shot through her veins as he broke off the kiss to plant a trail of kisses down the column of her neck to the top of her breasts.

At her cry of arousal, Jackson pulled back to look into her eyes. "I've told myself all the reasons we shouldn't do this, but I want to make love to you."

"Yes," she said breathlessly, throwing caution to the wind. She wanted him, wanted to feel his bare skin against her own, to taste his mouth on hers again, to look up at him as he lowered himself onto her. She ached for his gentle touch, needed desperately to know the tenderness of lovemaking she'd never experienced with Nick but sensed in Jackson.

He swept her up in his arms and carried her to the bedroom, kicking the door closed before he carefully lowered her to the bed. She looked into his dark eyes as he lay down next to her. He touched her face with his fingertips, then slipped his hand around to the nape of her neck and drew her to him.

His kiss was slow and sensual. She could feel him fighting his own need as if determined to take it slow as he undid one button of her blouse, then another. She wanted to scream, unable to stand the barrier of their clothing between them. Grabbing his shirt, she pulled each side apart. The snaps sung as the Western shirt fell open exposing his tanned skin and the hard muscles under it.

She pressed her hands to his warm flesh as he undid the last button on her blouse. She heard his intake of breath an instant before she felt his fingertips skim across the tops of her breasts. Pushing her onto her back, he dropped his mouth to the hard points of her nipples, sucking gently through the thin, sheer fabric of her bra.

She arched against his mouth, felt him suck harder as his hand moved to the buttons of her jeans. With agonizing deliberate movements, he slowly undid the buttons of her jeans and slipped his hand beneath her panties. She cried out and fumbled at the zipper of his jeans.

"Please," she begged. "I need you."

"Not yet." His voice broke with the sound of his own need. "Not yet."

His hand dipped deeper into her panties. She arched against it, feeling the wet slickness of his fingers. He'd barely touched her when she felt the release.

"Oh, Allie," he said as if he, too, hadn't made love for a very long time. He shifted to the side to pull off her jeans and panties. She heard him shed the rest of his own clothing and then he was back, his body melding with hers in a rhythm as old as life itself.

They made love twice more before the dawn. Jackson dozed off at some point, but woke to find Allie sleeping in his arms.

She looked more peaceful than she had since he'd met her. Like him, he suspected she hadn't made love with anyone for a very long time—much longer than her husband had allegedly been dead.

He cursed Nick Taylor. How could the fool not want this woman? How could the man mistreat someone so wonderful, not to mention ignore a child like Natalie? When he found the bastard…

When is it that you plan to find him?

The thought stopped him cold. There were only two more days until the wedding. He and Ford had tickets to fly out the following day.

He couldn't leave Allie now when she needed him the most. But how could he stay? He had Ford to think about. His son would be starting kindergarten next month. Jackson wasn't ready. He'd received a list from the school of the supplies his son would need, but he hadn't seen any reason to get them yet, thinking there was plenty of time. Same with the boy's new clothes.

He thought of his small ranch in Texas. Most of the land was leased, but he still had a house down there in the summer heat. He couldn't stay away indefinitely. What if he couldn't find Nick Taylor before Ford's school started?

His thoughts whirling, he looked down at Allie curled up next him and felt a pull so strong that it made him ache. What was he going to do?

Whatever it was, he couldn't think straight lying next to this beautiful, naked woman. As he tried to pull free, she rolled away some, but didn't wake.

Slipping out of bed, he quickly dressed and stepped outside. The fresh Montana morning air helped a little. Earlier he'd heard voices down by the main house. He hoped to catch his brothers as he headed down the mountain. He needed desperately to talk to one of them, even though he had had a bad feeling what they were going to say to him. He'd been saying the same thing to himself since waking up next to Allie this morning.

Allie woke to an empty bed. For a moment, she didn't know where she was. As last night came back to her with Jackson, she hugged herself. The lovemaking had been…amazing. This was what she'd been missing out on with Nick. Jackson had been so tender and yet so… passionate.

She lay back listening, thinking he must be in the bathroom or maybe the small kitchen. After a few minutes, she sat up. The cabin was too quiet. Surely Jackson hadn't left.

Slipping her feet over the side of the bed, she tiptoed

out of the bedroom. The bathroom was empty. So was the living room and kitchen. Moving to the front window, she glanced out on the porch. No Jackson.

For a moment, she stood staring out at the view, trying to understand what this meant. Had he finally come to his senses? That was definitely one explanation.

Had he realized they had no future? That was another.

Hurrying into the bathroom, she showered, and, forced to put on the clothes she'd worn the night before, dressed. Fortunately, she'd been wearing jeans, a tank top and a blouse. She tucked the blouse into her large shoulder bag, pulled her wet hair up into a ponytail and looked at herself in the mirror.

Her cheeks were flushed from the lovemaking and the hot shower. Her skin still tingled at even the thought of Jackson's touch. She swallowed. Hadn't she warned herself last night of all the reasons they shouldn't make love?

At a knock on the cabin door, she jumped. Her heart leaped to her throat as she saw a dark, large shadow move on the porch beyond the curtains. Jackson wouldn't knock. Maybe it was one of his brothers.

She held her breath, hoping he would go away. She didn't want to be caught here, even though she knew his brothers wouldn't tell anyone.

Another knock.

"Jackson?" Drew Taylor's voice made her cringe. She put her hand over her mouth to keep from crying out in surprise. "I need to check something in your cabin." She heard him try the door and felt her heart drop. What if Jackson had left the door open?

She was already backing up, frantically trying to

decide where she could hide, when she heard Drew try the knob. Locked.

He swore, thumped around on the porch for a moment then retreated down the steps.

Allie finally had to let out the breath she'd been holding. If Drew had caught her here… What would he have done? Tell Nick. But what would a man who had faked his death do to stop his plan from working? She thought of Jackson and felt her heart drop. She'd put Jackson's life in danger, as well.

She waited until she was sure Drew had gone before she cautiously moved to the door, opened it and peered out. She could see nothing but pines as she slipped out and hurried across the mountainside, planning to slip into the barn as if she'd come to work early.

With luck, no one would be the wiser.

Allie didn't see Drew. But he saw her.

Chapter 11

Dana was sitting on the porch as Jackson approached the house. She motioned for him to join her.

"Where is everyone?" he asked, taking the rocker next to her.

"Early morning ride. Hud took everyone including the kids. Quiet, isn't it?" She glanced over at him. "How are you this morning?"

"Fine." He would have said great, but he had a bad feeling where Dana was headed with the conversation.

"I'm worried about Allie," she said, looking past him to the mountainside.

He glanced back toward the cabins in time to see Allie hurrying toward the barn from the direction of his cabin.

"Is she all right?"

In truth, he didn't know how she was. He regretted

leaving before she'd awakened, but he'd needed to get out of there. "I—"

"She's been through so much. I would hate to see her get hurt. Wouldn't you?"

He felt as if she'd slapped him. He closed his eyes for a moment before he turned to look at her. "I told myself not to get involved, but…"

"So now you are involved?" Dana frowned. "She's in trouble, isn't she?"

Jackson nodded. "I have to help her." Even if it meant staying in Montana longer, he couldn't abandon her. Isn't that what had scared the hell out of him when he'd awakened this morning? He was in deep, how deep, he didn't want to admit. "She's going through some things right now but she's working so hard on the wedding, it will be fine."

Dana studied him openly. "You care about her."

"I'm not going to hurt her."

"I hope not." She gave him a pat on the shoulder as she rose and went inside the house.

Jackson sat looking after his cousin, mentally kicking himself. *"What the hell are you doing?"*

"I was going to ask you the same thing." Laramie came walking up.

As he climbed the porch, Jackson said, "I thought you went riding with the others."

"I've been working," his brother said as he took a seat next to him. He shook his head. "I hope you know what you're doing, Jackson." He sighed and pulled out a sheet of paper. "Allie's mother spent the last seven years of her life in a mental institution. Paranoid schizophrenia."

As Allie slipped into the barn, she was surprised to see Belinda setting up her gear for a shoot. She'd half expected Belinda to be gone after their argument last night. In fact, Allie had almost called several photographers she knew to see if they could possibly fill in at the last minute.

"So you're still here," she said as she approached Belinda.

"Where did you think I would be?"

"I wasn't sure. I thought you might have quit."

Belinda shook her head. "You really do have so little faith in me. I'm amazed. I'm the one who has stuck by you all these years. I'm sorry about…everything. But I'm here to do a job I love. Surely you understand that."

Allie did and said as much. "If I've underestimated you—"

Her friend laughed. "Or overestimated me given that you think I'm capable of some diabolical plot to destroy you. And what? Steal your cabin on the river? Steal Nick's insurance money?" Her eyes widened. "Or was it steal Natalie?" Belinda looked aghast. "Oh, Allie, no wonder you're so upset. I get it now."

She felt tears rush her eyes as Belinda pulled her into a stiff, awkward hug.

"No matter what you believe, I'm still your friend," Belinda said as she broke the embrace and left the barn, passing Megan, who looked bewildered as she came in.

Allie waited until she and Megan were alone before she spoke to her stepsister about what Belinda had told her. She didn't want to believe Megan had anything to do with the psychic or what had happened last night. Either Belinda was lying or there had to be another explanation.

"I need to ask you something."

"You sound so serious," Megan said. "What is it?"

"Was it your idea for me to see the psychic?"

Megan frowned. "I guess I was the one who suggested it. When Belinda told me about some of the things you'd been going through, I thought— Allie, why are you so upset?"

Allie had turned away, unable to look at her sister. Now she turned back, just as unable to hide her disappointment. "Why would you do that?"

"I just told you. I thought it would help."

"Trying to reach Nick on...the other side?" she demanded. "You can't be serious."

"A girl I knew at college lost her mother before the two of them could work some things out. She went to a psychic and was able to put some of the issues to rest. I thought..." Her gaze locked with her sister's. "I wanted to help you. I couldn't bear the things Belinda was telling me. It sounded as if you'd been going through hell. If I was wrong, I'm sorry."

Allie studied her for a moment. "You would never betray me, would you, Megan?"

"What a strange question to ask me."

"This past year since you came into my life and Natalie's... It's meant so much to both of us. Tell me you wouldn't betray that trust."

Megan frowned. "Does this have something to do with Jackson Cardwell? Is he the one putting these ideas in your head?"

"He has a theory about the so-called incidents I've been having," Allie confided. "He thinks someone is trying to make me think I'm crazy in order to take Natalie from me."

"That sounds...crazy in itself. Allie, I hate to say this, but you are starting to sound like your—"

"Don't say it," Allie cried. Wasn't that her real un-

derlying fear, the one that had haunted her her whole
life? That she was becoming sick like her mother? She
rubbed a hand over the back of her neck. What was she
sure of right now? She'd thought Jackson, but after this
morning… "I know it sounds crazy, but if it's true, I
have to find out who is behind it."

"And Jackson is *helping* you?" Megan said and
frowned. "Or is he complicating things even more?
You aren't…falling for him, are you?"

Jackson wasn't sure what he was going to say to
Allie. He felt like a heel for leaving her alone this morning. She must be furious with him. No, he thought, not
Allie. She would be hurt, and that made him feel worse
than if she was angry.

He headed for the barn to apologize to her. Once inside, though, he didn't see Allie.

"She said she had to run an errand," Megan told him
with a shrug.

Glancing outside, he saw her van still parked where
it had been last night. "Did she go on foot?"

"Her brother-in-law offered her a ride."

"Drew?" Jackson felt his heart race at the thought
of Allie alone with that man. "Do you know where
they went?"

Megan shook her head and kept working.

"You don't like me," he said, stepping farther into
the barn. "Why is that?"

"I don't think you're good for my sister."

"Based on what?" he had to ask. "We have barely
met."

"She told me about this crazy idea you have that
someone is causing these incidents she's been having."

"You disagree?"

Megan gave him an impatient look. "I know the Taylors. The last thing they want is a five-year-old to raise."

"So you think what's been happening to Allie is all in her head?"

She put down what she'd been working on and gave him her full attention for the first time. "You just met her. You don't know anything about her. I love my stepsister, but I don't think she has been completely honest with you. Did you know that her mother spent her last years in a mental hospital? Or that she killed herself?"

"You aren't trying to tell me it runs in the family."

Megan raised a brow. "Allie's been through a lot. She has some issues she hasn't gotten past, including the fact that she wanted her husband gone. So she already told you about that, huh?" He nodded. "Did she also tell you that she bought a gun just before Nick went up into the mountains? That's right. I wonder what happened to it." She shrugged. "Like I said, I love Allie and Nat, but I also know that Allie hated her husband and would have done anything to escape him."

Allie had been on her way to her van when Drew had suddenly appeared next to her.

"Where you off to?" he'd asked.

"I just have to pick up some ribbon at the store," she'd said, trying to act normal. What a joke. She hadn't felt *normal* in so long, she'd forgotten what it felt like. Worse, she feared that Drew would find out about last night. The Taylors wouldn't hesitate to use it against her, claiming it proved what a terrible mother she was.

Allie felt guilty enough. Her husband had been dead only months and here she was making love with another man. Did it matter that she hadn't loved Nick for years? She had a child to think about and Jackson Cardwell would be leaving in two days' time. Then what?

It would be just her and Nat and the Taylors.

"I'll give you a ride," Drew said. She started to argue but he stopped her. "It would be stupid to take your van when I'm going that way, anyway. You pick up your ribbon. I'll pick up the chalk I need next door at the hardware store. We'll be back here before you know it."

All her instincts warned her not to get into the pickup with him, but she couldn't think of a reason not to accept the ride without acting paranoid. Did she really think he would take her somewhere other than the store and what? Attack her?

She climbed into the passenger side of the pickup and remembered something Nick had said not long before he'd left to go hunting that day.

"You're so damned trusting, Allie. I worry about you. Don't you get tired of being so nice?" He'd laughed and pretended he was joking as he pulled her close and kissed the top of her head. "Don't change. It's refreshing."

It also had made it easier for him to control her.

"You want to know something crazy?" Drew said as he started the engine and drove down the road toward Big Sky. "When I got here this morning, your van was where you'd left it last night. There was dew on the window. I checked the motor. It hadn't been moved and even more interesting, you were nowhere to be found."

She didn't look at him as he roared down the road. Ahead she could see the bridge that spanned the Gallatin River. Why hadn't she listened to her instincts and not gotten into the vehicle with Drew?

"It was like a mystery. I love mysteries. Did I ever tell you that?"

A recent rainstorm had washed out some of the road just before the bridge, leaving deep ruts that were to be filled this afternoon. Couldn't have the wedding guests being jarred by the ruts.

"I saw you come out of Jackson Cardwell's cabin this morning." Drew swore as he braked for the ruts. "You slut." He started to backhand her, but had to brake harder as he hit the first rut so his hand went back to the wheel before it reached its mark. "How could you screw—"

Allie unsnapped her seat belt and grabbed the door handle.

As the door swung open, Drew hit the brakes even harder, slamming her into the door as she jumped. She hit the soft earth at the side of the road, lost her footing and fell into the ditch.

Drew stopped the truck. She heard his door open and the shocks groan as he climbed out. By then she was on her feet and headed into the pines next to the road, running, even though her right ankle ached.

"Allie!" Drew yelled from the roadbed. "You could have killed yourself. You're crazy, you know that?"

She kept running through the pines. Her brother-in-law was right. She had been stupid. Stupid to get into the truck with him when all her instincts had been telling her not to, and crazy to jump out.

Behind her, she heard the truck engine rev, then the pickup rumble over the bridge. She slowed to catch her breath then limped the rest of the way back to the barn, telling herself she was through being naive and trusting.

* * *

Jackson didn't see Allie until that evening at the wedding rehearsal so he had no chance to get her alone. "We need to talk," he whispered in those few seconds he managed to get her somewhat alone.

She met his gaze. "Look, I think I already know what you're going to say."

"I doubt that." She wore a multicolored skirt and top that accentuated her lush body. "You look beautiful. That top brings out the green in your eyes."

"Thank you." Something glinted in those eyes for a moment. "Jackson—"

"I know. This isn't the place. But can we please talk later? It's important."

She nodded, though reluctantly.

He mentally kicked himself for running out on her this morning as he stood there, wanting to say more, but not able to find the right words.

Allie excused herself. He watched her head for the preacher as the rehearsal was about to begin. Was she limping?

All day he'd stewed over what Megan had told him. She was wrong about Allie, but he could understand why she felt the way she did. Maybe she really did love her sister. Or maybe not.

Belinda was busy behind her camera, shooting as they all went to their places. As one of the best men, Jackson was in a position to watch the others. He hadn't seen much of Sarah Taylor. But Sarah, her mother and brother would be at the rehearsal dinner tonight. He watched Sarah enter the barn and start up the aisle toward the steps to where the preacher was standing along with the best men and the groom.

An overweight woman with dull, brown hair pulled severely back from her face, Sarah seemed somewhere else, oblivious to what was happening. Either that or bored. Four more bridesmaids entered and took their places.

Harlan and Angus broke into "Here Comes the Bride" on their guitars and Lily came out of a small-framed building next to the meadow with her father and mother. Jackson hadn't met either of them yet but he wanted to laugh when he saw them looking as if in horror. Lily was smiling from ear to ear. So was her brother Ace from the sidelines. But clearly her parents hadn't expected this kind of wedding for their only daughter.

Jackson looked over at Allie. She really was beautiful. She glanced to the parking lot and quickly looked away as if she'd seen something that frightened her.

He followed her gaze. Drew Taylor stood lounging against his pickup, a malicious smirk on his face as if he was up to something.

The rehearsal went off without a hitch. Allie tried to breathe a sigh of relief. Dana had booked an Italian restaurant in Bozeman for the night of the rehearsal dinner. "I know it's not the way things are normally done," she'd said with a laugh. "But Lily and I discussed it."

Dana had insisted anyone involved in the wedding had to be there so that meant Allie and Natalie as well as Megan and Belinda.

They'd just gotten to the restaurant when Allie heard a strident voice behind her say, "There you are."

She bristled but didn't turn, putting off facing her mother-in-law as long as possible.

"Sarah thinks you're avoiding us," Mildred said. "But why would you do that?"

Allie turned, planting a smile on her face. "I wouldn't."

"Hmmm," her mother-in-law said. She gave Allie the once-over. "You look different."

Allie remembered that she was wearing one of two outfits that she hadn't taken back to the store. This one was a multicolored top and skirt that Jackson had said brought out the green in her eyes. She loved it and while it was more expensive than she could really afford, she'd needed something to wear tonight.

"Where did you get that outfit?" Mildred asked, eyeing her with suspicion.

"I found it in my closet," Allie said honestly.

"Really?"

Allie felt a hand take hers and looked up to see Jackson.

"I saved you a spot down here," he said and led her to the other end of the table, away from the Taylors.

Dana had insisted that there be no prearranged seating. "Let everyone sit where they want. I like people to be comfortable." Lily had seemed relieved that she could sit by Tag, away from her parents.

Allie was grateful to Jackson for saving her. Dinner was served and the conversation around the table was light with lots of laughter and joking. She was glad Jackson didn't try to talk to her about last night.

It had been a mistake in so many ways. But tomorrow after the wedding, they would say goodbye and he and Ford would fly out the next day. She told herself that once the wedding was over, everything would be all right.

A part of her knew she was only kidding herself. There hadn't been any more incidents, no misplaced keys, no Nick sightings, no "black cat" scares and that almost worried her. What had changed? Or was Nick and whomever he had helping him just waiting to ambush her?

She had a feeling that the séance with the psychic hadn't produced the results they'd wanted. Now she, too, was waiting. Waiting for the other shoe to drop.

Just let it drop after the wedding, she prayed. Jackson and Ford would be back in Texas. Whatever was planned for her, she felt she could handle it once this job was over. The one thing Jackson had done was made her feel stronger, more sure of herself. He'd also reminded her that she was a woman with needs that had long gone unmet until last night.

"Stop telling stories on me," Tag pleaded at the dinner table across from her. "Lily is going to change her mind about marrying me."

"Not a chance, cowboy," Lily said next to him before she'd kissed him to hoots and hollers.

Even Sarah seemed to be enjoying herself with the other bridesmaids since they had all worked together at Lily's brother's bar.

Allie avoided looking down the table to see how the Taylors were doing. She was so thankful to be sitting as far away from them as possible, especially Drew. To think that she'd trusted him and thought he'd really had her and Nat's best interests at heart. She'd felt his eyes on her all night. The few times she'd met his gaze, he'd scowled at her.

She glanced over at the children's table to see her daughter also enjoying herself. Dana's sister Stacy had the children at a separate table. Allie saw that her daughter was being on her best behavior. So ladylike, she was even using the manners Allie had taught her. She felt a swell of pride and told herself that she and Natalie were going to be all right no matter what happened after the wedding.

To her surprise, her eyes welled with tears and she quickly excused herself to go to the ladies' room. The bathroom was past an empty section of the restaurant, then down a long hallway. She was glad that no one had followed her. She needed a few minutes alone.

Inside the bathroom, she pulled herself together. Last night with Jackson had meant more to her than she'd admitted. It had hurt this morning when he hadn't been there, but she could understand why he'd panicked. Neither of them took that kind of intimacy lightly.

Feeling better, she left the bathroom. As she reached the empty section of the restaurant, Drew stepped in front of her, startling her. She could smell the alcohol on him. The way he was standing... She recognized that stance after five years of being married to his brother.

Drew was looking for a fight. How had she thought the brothers were different? Because she hadn't seen this side of Drew. Until now.

"You *jumped* out of my truck. What the hell was that? Do I scare you, Allie?" he asked, slurring his words and blocking her way.

"Please, Drew, don't make a scene."

He laughed. "Oh, you don't want Dana to know that you slept with her cousin?"

"Drew—"

"Don't bother to lie to me," he said as he stepped

toward her, shoving her back. "I *saw* you." His voice broke. "How can you do this to my brother?"

"Nick's…gone."

"And forgotten. Is that it?" He forced her back against the wall, caging her with one hand on each side of her.

"Please, Drew—"

"If Nick really was out of the picture…" He belched. "You have to know I've always wanted you," he said drunkenly. Before she could stop him, he bent down and tried to kiss her.

She turned her head to the side. He kissed her hair, then angrily grabbed her jaw in one hand. His fingers squeezed painfully as he turned her to face him.

"What? Am I not good enough for you?"

"Drew—"

Suddenly he was jerked away. Allie blinked as Jackson hauled back and swung. His fist connected with Drew's jaw and he went down hard, crashing into a table.

"Are you all right?" Jackson asked, stepping to her.

She nodded and glanced at her brother-in-law. He was trying to get up, but he seemed to take one look at Jackson and decided to stay down.

"You'll pay for that!" he threatened as she and Jackson headed back toward their table. Allie knew he wasn't talking to Jackson. She would pay.

"If he bothers you again—" Jackson said as if reading her mind.

"Don't worry about me."

"How can I not?" he demanded. "That was about me, wasn't it?"

"Drew was just looking for a reason."

"And I provided it."

"He saw me leaving your cabin this morning," she said. "I don't think he's told anyone, but he will. I just wanted to warn you. I'm afraid what Nick might do to you."

"Allie, I don't give a damn about any of that. What I'm sorry about was leaving you this morning," he said, bringing her up short as he stopped and turned her to face him. "There is so much I want to say to you—"

"Oh, there you are," Mildred Taylor said as she approached. "I was just looking for Drew. I thought you might have seen him. Allie, you look terrible. I knew this job was going to be too much for you."

Natalie and Ford came running toward them. Mildred began to say something about giving Allie and Nat a ride home, but then Drew appeared, rubbing his jaw.

"Drew, whatever happened to you?" Mildred cried.

"I still need to talk to you," Jackson whispered to Allie, who was bending down to catch her daughter up into her arms.

"After the wedding," she said as she lifted Natalie, hugging her tightly. "Tonight I just need to take my daughter home."

Jackson wanted to stop her. But she was right. The wedding was the important thing right now. After that…

Chapter 12

Wedding day. Allie woke at the crack of dawn. She couldn't help being nervous and excited. The wedding was to be held in a beautiful meadow near the house. Those attending had been told to wear Western attire as the seating at the wedding would be hay bales.

Drew had constructed an arch for the bride and groom to stand under with the preacher. Allie had walked through everything with the bride and groom, the caterer and the musicians. The barn was ready for the reception that would follow. But she still wanted to get to the ranch early to make sure she hadn't forgotten anything.

The last few days had felt like a roller-coaster ride. Today, she needed calm. Jackson hadn't tried to contact her after she and Natalie left the restaurant with Dana and family last night and she was glad. She needed time with her daughter.

Natalie hadn't slept in her own bed for several nights now. Allie made sure her daughter's window was locked as she put her to bed. She checked the other windows and the door. Then, realizing that any of the Taylors could have a key to her cabin, she pushed a straight-back chair under the doorknob.

She and Natalie hadn't been disturbed all night. At least not by intruders. In bed last night, Allie couldn't help but think about Jackson. And Nick.

"Please, just let me get through this wedding," she'd prayed and had finally fallen asleep.

Now as she drove into the ranch, she saw that Dana and the kids were waiting for Natalie.

"We have a fun morning planned," Dana said with a wink. "You don't have to worry about anything today."

Allie wished that was true. She looked down at the meadow to see that Megan was up early. She was sitting on a hay bale looking as if she were staring at the arch. Imagining her own wedding? Allie wondered as she approached.

"Good morning," she said and joined her sister on the bale.

"It's perfect. Drew really did do a good job," Megan said.

The arch had been made out of natural wood that blended in beautifully with its surroundings. Allie had asked Lily if she wanted it decorated with flowers.

"There will be enough wildflowers in the meadow and I will be carrying a bouquet. I think that is more than enough."

She had agreed and was happy that Lily preferred the more minimalist look.

"Have you been up to the barn?" Allie asked.

"Not yet." Megan finally looked over at her. "How are you?"

"Fine."

Her sister eyed her. "You can lean on me. I'm here for you and Natalie."

Allie hugged her, closing her eyes and praying it was true. She couldn't bear the thought of Megan betraying not only her but Natalie, as well.

Together they walked up to the barn. Allie turned on the lights and gasped.

Jackson had tossed and turned all night—after he'd finally dropped off to sleep. He felt as if he'd let Allie down. Or maybe worse, gotten involved with her in the first place, knowing he would be leaving soon.

She wasn't out of the woods yet. She had to know that whoever was messing with her mind wasn't through. He still believed it had to be Nick. He had the most to gain. It scared Jackson to think that whoever was behind this might try to use Tag's wedding to put the last nail in Allie's coffin, so to speak.

His fear, since realizing what was going on, was that if they couldn't drive her crazy, they might actually try to kill her.

He was just getting dressed when he heard the knock at his cabin door. His mood instantly lifted as he thought it might be Allie. She'd said she would talk to him *after* the wedding. Maybe she had changed her mind. He sure hoped so.

Jackson couldn't hide his disappointment when he opened the door and saw his brothers standing there.

"I found something that I think might interest you," Laramie said and he stepped back to let them enter.

"Shouldn't you be getting ready for your wedding?" he asked Tag, who laughed and said, "I have been getting ready for months now. I just want this damned wedding over."

They took a seat while he remained standing. From the expressions on their faces, they hadn't brought good news.

"Nick and his brother, Drew, took out life insurance policies on each other through their construction business," Laramie said.

"That isn't unusual, right?" he asked.

"They purchased million-dollar policies and made each other the beneficiary, but Nick purchased another half million and made Allie the beneficiary."

Jackson let out a low whistle. "All Allie knew about was the hundred-thousand-dollar policy." He saw Hayes lift a brow. "She didn't kill her husband."

"Whether she knew or not about the policies, I believe it supports your theory that Nick is alive and trying to get that money," Laramie said.

"It hasn't paid out yet, right?"

"She should be getting the checks next week."

Jackson raked a hand through his hair. Allie was bound to have been notified. Maybe it had slipped her mind. "You're sure she is the beneficiary?"

Laramie nodded.

"Who gets the money if Allie is declared incompetent?"

"Her daughter, Natalie."

Jackson groaned. "Then this is why Nick is trying to have Allie committed. He, and whoever he is working with, would get the money and Natalie."

"Only if Nick is alive and *stays* dead," Hayes pointed out.

"If Nick stays dead the money would be used at the discretion of Natalie's *guardian*."

Jackson looked at his brother, an ache starting at heart level. "Who is her guardian?"

"Megan Knight. The policy was changed eight months ago—just before Nick Taylor went up into the mountains hunting and a guardian was added."

Allie couldn't even scream. Her voice had caught in her throat at the sight in the barn. Last night when she'd left, the barn had been ready for the reception except for putting out the fresh vases of flowers at each setting. The tables had been covered with the checked tablecloths and all the overhead lanterns had been in place along with the decorations on the walls and in the rafters.

"Oh, my word," Megan said next to her.

Allie still couldn't speak. Someone had ripped the tablecloths from the tables and piled them in the middle of the dance floor. The old boots that served as centerpieces that would hold the fresh flowers were arranged on the floor in a circle as if the invisible people in them were dancing.

Megan was the first one to move. She rushed to the tablecloths and, bending down, picked up the top one. "They've all been shredded." She turned to look at Allie, concern in her gaze.

"You can't think I did this."

Her sister looked at the tablecloth in her hand before returning her gaze to Allie. "This looks like a cry for help."

Allie shook her head. "It's someone who hates me."

"Hates you? Oh, Allie."

"What's happened?"

She swung around to see Jackson standing in the doorway. Tears filled her eyes. She wanted to run out the barn door and keep running, but he stepped to her and took one of her hands.

"I was afraid they weren't done with you," he said. "How bad is it?" he asked Megan.

"The tablecloths are ruined. Fortunately, whoever did this didn't do anything to the lanterns or the other decorations in the rafters. Probably couldn't reach them since the ladders have all been packed away." This last was directed at Allie, her meaning clear.

"Tag already ordered tablecloths for the restaurant," Jackson said, pulling out his cell phone. "I'll see if they've come in. We can have this fixed quickly if they have." He spoke into the phone for a moment. When he disconnected, he smiled at Allie and said, "Tag will bring up the red-checked cloths right away. With their help, we'll have it fixed before anyone else hears about it."

Allie went weak with relief as he quickly got rid of the ruined tablecloths and Tag showed up with new ones from the restaurant. With the Cardwell brothers' help, the problem was solved within minutes.

"I want at least two people here watching this barn until the wedding is over," Jackson said.

"I'll talk to Dana and see if there are a couple of ranch hands who can help," Laramie said.

"That really isn't necessary," Megan said. "I will stay here to make sure nothing else happens."

Jackson shook his head. "I'm not taking any chances.

I'll feel better if you aren't left alone here. Whoever is doing this… Well, I think it might get dangerous before it's over."

"Why don't you just admit that you think I'm involved in this," Megan said and looked sadly at her sister. "Apparently, you aren't the only one who's paranoid." She sighed. "Whatever you need me to do. I don't want anything to spoil this wedding."

Jackson had planned to talk to Allie about the insurance policies, but he realized it could wait until after the wedding. Allie's spirit seemed buoyed once the barn was ready again and a ranch hand stayed behind with Megan to make sure nothing else went wrong.

He was having a hard time making sense of the insurance policy news. Why would Nick Taylor change the guardian from his brother to Allie's stepsister, Megan? The obvious answer would be if the two were in cahoots.

That would break Allie's heart, but a part of her had to know that her sister thought all of this was in her head. Megan had given him the impression that she was ready to step in as more than Natalie's guardian.

Jackson reminded himself that it was his brother's wedding day. As much as he didn't like weddings and hadn't attended one since his marriage had ended, he tried to concentrate on being there for Tag. He couldn't help being in awe as Allie went into wedding-planner mode. He admired the way she handled herself, even with all the stress she was under in her personal life. The day took on a feeling of celebration; after all it was the Fourth of July.

At the house, Allie made sure they were all ready,

the men dressed in Western attire and boots, before she went to help the bride. Jackson had seen his father and uncle with their guitars heading for the meadow. They would be playing the "Wedding March" as well as accompanying several singers who would be performing. He just hoped everything went smoothly for Tag and Lily's sake, as well as Allie's.

"Look who's here," Laramie said, sounding too cheerful.

Jackson turned to see his mother on the arm of a nice-looking gray-haired Texas oilman. Franklin Wellington IV had oil written all over him. Jackson tried not to hold it against the man as he and his brothers took turns hugging their mother and wishing her well before shaking hands with Franklin.

His mother *did* look deliriously happy, Jackson had to admit, and Franklin was downright friendly and nice.

"Time to go," Allie said, sticking her head into the room where he and his brothers had been waiting.

Jackson introduced her to his mother and Franklin. He saw his mother lift a brow in the direction of Laramie and groaned inwardly. She would trust Laramie to tell her why she was being introduced to the wedding planner.

Allie didn't notice the interplay as she smiled at Tag. "Your bride looks absolutely beautiful and you don't look so bad yourself."

She was quite pretty, as well, in her navy dress with the white piping. She'd pulled her hair up. Silver earrings dangled at her lobes. She looked professional and yet as sexy as any woman he'd ever known. He felt a sense of pride in her, admiring her strength as well as her beauty. She'd been through so much.

Hell, he thought as he took his place, I *am* falling for her. That realization shook him to the soles of his boots.

In the meadow, his father and uncle began to play the "Wedding March" at Allie's nod. Compared to most, the wedding was small since Tag and Lily knew few people in Big Sky. But old canyon friends had come who had known the Cardwells, Savages and Justices for years.

As Lily appeared, Jackson agreed with Allie. She looked beautiful. He heard his brother's intake of breath and felt his heart soar at the look on Tag's face when he saw his bride-to-be. For a man who had sworn off weddings, Jackson had to admit, he was touched by this one.

The ceremony was wonderfully short, the music perfect and when Tag kissed the bride, Jackson felt his gaze searching for Allie. She was standing by a tree at the edge of the meadow. She was smiling, her expression one of happy contentment. She'd gotten them married.

Now if they could just get through the reception without any more trouble, he thought.

At the reception, Jackson watched the Taylor family sitting at a table away from the others. Mildred had a smile plastered on her face, but behind it he could see that she was sizing up everyone in the room. Her insecurities were showing as she leaned over and said something to her daughter.

Whatever her mother said to her, Sarah merely nodded. She didn't seem to have any interest in the guests, unlike her mother. Instead, she was watching Allie. What was it that Jackson caught in her gaze? Jealousy? Everyone at the wedding had been complimenting Allie on the job she'd done. Sarah couldn't have missed that.

Nor, according to Hud, had Sarah ever been married.

She had to be in her late thirties. Was she thinking that it might never happen for her? Or was she content with living next to her mother and basically becoming her mother's caregiver?

Sarah reached for one of the boot-shaped cookies with Tag and Lily's wedding date on them. Her mother slapped her hand, making Sarah scowl at her before she took two cookies.

He wondered what grudges bubbled just below the surface in any family situation, let alone a wedding. Weddings, he thought, probably brought out the best and worst of people, depending how happy or unhappy you were in your own life.

As happy as he was for Tag, it still reminded him of his own sorry marriage. What did this wedding do to the Taylor clan? he wondered as he studied them. It certainly didn't seem to be bringing out any joy, that was for sure.

But his side of the family were having a wonderful time. He watched his brother Tag dancing with his bride. Their mother was dancing with her new husband, both women looking radiant. It really was a joyous day. Dana and Hud had all the kids out on the floor dancing.

Jackson thought the only thing that could make this day better would be if he could get the wedding planner to dance with him.

Allie tried to breathe a little easier. The wedding had gone off without a hitch. Lily had been exquisite and Tag as handsome as any Cardwell, which was saying a lot. Allie had teared up like a lot of the guests when the two had exchanged their vows. She'd always loved weddings. This one would remain her favorite for years to come.

When the bride and groom kissed, she'd seen Jackson looking for her. Their eyes had locked for a long moment. She'd pulled away first, a lump in her throat, an ache in her heart. The wedding was over. There was nothing keeping Jackson and Ford in Montana.

Whoever had been trying to gaslight her, as Jackson had called it, hadn't succeeded. Maybe now they would give up trying. She certainly hoped so. If Nick was alive, then she should find out soon. The insurance check for the hundred thousand would be deposited into her account next week. She'd already made plans for most of it to go into an interest-bearing account for Natalie's college.

Allie wondered what would happen then. If Nick was alive, would he just show up at her door? Or would the media be involved with reporters and photographers snapping photos of him outside the cabin as he returned from his ordeal?

All she knew was that the only way Nick could get his hands on the insurance money would be if he killed her. That thought unnerved her as she surveyed the reception. Belinda was busy shooting each event along with some candid shots of guests. Allie had to hand it to her, she appeared to be doing a great job.

Everything looked beautiful. Megan had taken care of the flowers in the boot vases, put the attendees' gifts on the tables and made sure the bar was open and serving. Appetizers were out. Allie checked to make sure the caterer was ready then looked around for her daughter. Nat was with the other kids and Dana. Allie had bought her a special dress for the wedding. Natalie looked beautiful and she knew it because she seemed to glow.

Her tomboy daughter loved getting dressed up. She smiled at the thought. She was thinking that they should dress up more when Mildred Taylor let out a scream at a table near the dance floor and stumbled to her feet.

Allie saw that she was clutching her cell phone, her other hand over her mouth.

"What is it?" Dana demanded, moving quickly to the Taylors' table.

"It's *my Nicky,*" Mildred cried, her gaze going to Allie, who froze thinking it was already happening. She was so sure she knew what her mother-in-law was about to say, that she thought she'd misunderstood.

"His body has been found," Mildred managed to say between sobs. She cried harder. "They say he was *murdered.*"

Chapter 13

Pandemonium broke out with Mildred Taylor shrieking uncontrollably and everyone trying to calm her down.

Jackson looked over at Allie. All the color had bled from her face. He moved quickly to her. "Let's get you out of here," he said, taking her hand. "You look like you could use some fresh air."

"I'll see to Natalie," Dana said nearby as she motioned for Jackson and Allie to go.

Allie looked as if she were in shock. "It just won't end," she said in a breathless rush as he ushered her outside. "It just won't end."

"I'm so sorry," Jackson said, his mind reeling, as well.

"I was so sure he was *alive*." She met his gaze. "I thought…"

"We both thought he was alive. I'm as floored as you

are." He realized that wasn't possible. Nick Taylor had been her husband, even if he had been a bad one, she would still be shocked and upset by this news. He was the father of her child.

"Nick was *murdered?* How is that possible? They found his backpack and his gun and the grizzly tracks."

"We need to wait until we have all the details," he said as his brothers Hayes and Laramie joined them.

"We're headed down to the police station now," Hayes said. "I'll let you know as soon as I have any information."

"Thank you." Jackson swallowed the lump in his throat. His brothers had been so great through his divorce and custody battle, and now this. He couldn't have been more grateful for them.

"The police will be looking for me," Allie said, her eyes widening.

He saw the fear in her eyes and at first had misunderstood it then he remembered what had happened at the psychic's. "No one believes you killed your husband."

"*Someone* already does."

"That's crazy. How could whoever was behind the séance know that Nick was even murdered unless they did the killing?"

She shook her head. "Mildred has blamed me for his death all along. Belinda thought I drove him to kill himself. Don't you see? They didn't have to know it was true. They just wanted me to feel responsible. Now that it *is* true… Even dead, he's going to ruin my life."

The last of the sun's rays slipped behind the mountains to the west, pitching the canyon in cool twilight. Inside the barn, the reception was continuing thanks to Megan and Dana, who had taken over.

"I need to go back in."

"No." Jackson stopped her with a hand on her arm. "You did a great job. No one expects you to do any more. You don't have to worry about any of that."

She met his gaze. "I don't understand what's going on."

"My brothers will find out. Allie, I'm sorry I left you the other morning. I...panicked. But I'm not leaving you now."

Allie shook her head and took a step back from him. "This isn't your problem. You should never have gotten involved because it's only going to get worse."

He remembered what Laramie had told him about the insurance policy and realized she was right. The money would definitely interest the police. He looked toward the barn. Some guests had come out into the evening air to admire the sunset.

"Please, come up to my cabin with me so we have some privacy. There's something important I need to tell you." He saw her expression and realized that she'd misunderstood.

She looked toward the barn, then up the mountain in the direction of his cabin.

"I just need to talk to you," he assured her.

"That wasn't what I..." She met his gaze. "Jackson, I've caused you enough grief as it is. If the Taylors come looking for me—"

"Let me worry about your in-laws. As for Drew, he won't be bothering you as long as I'm around."

She smiled at that. They both knew that once he left she would again be at the mercy of not just Drew but also the rest of the Taylor family.

He wanted to tell her he wouldn't leave her. But he couldn't make that promise, could he?

She was on her own and she knew it.

"Come on," he said and reached for her hand.

Darkness came on quickly in the narrow canyon because of the steep mountains on each side. Allie could hear the fireworks vendors getting ready for the wedding grand finale and glanced at her watch. They were right on time. Maybe she wasn't as necessary as she'd thought since everything seemed to be going on schedule without her.

Overhead the pines swayed in the summer night's breeze. Jackson was so close she could smell his woodsy aftershave and remember his mouth on hers. The perfect summer night. Wasn't that what she'd been thinking earlier before her mother-in-law had started screaming?

Nick was dead. Murdered.

For days now she'd believed he was alive and behind all the weird things that had been happening to her. Now how did she explain it?

Jackson stopped on the porch. "We can talk privately here, if you would be more comfortable not going inside." He must have seen the answer in her expression because he let go of her hand and moved to the edge of the porch.

Inside the cabin she would remember the two of them making love in his big, log-framed bed. Her skin ached at the memory of his touch.

"Allie, I hate to bring this up now, but the police will ask you…" He leaned against the porch railing, Allie just feet away. "Were you aware that your husband and brother-in-law took out life insurance policies on each other when they started their construction business?"

"No, but what does that have to do with me?"

"They purchased million-dollar policies and made the other brother the beneficiary, but Nick purchased another half million and made you beneficiary. He never mentioned it to you?"

She shook her head, shocked by the news and even more shocked by how it would look. "You think a million and a half dollars in insurance money gives me a motive for killing him."

"I don't, but I think the police might, given that just before your husband went up into the mountains on his hunting trip, he changed the beneficiary of his million-dollar insurance policy from Drew to you."

Allie didn't think anything else could surprise her. "Why would he do that?" Her eyes filled with tears as a reason came to her. She moved to the opposite railing and looked out across the darkening canyon. "Maybe he did go up there to kill himself," she said, her back to Jackson.

"Hayes will find out why they think he was murdered. In the meantime—"

All the ramifications of this news hit her like a battering ram. "What happens if I'm dead?" She had been looking out into the darkness, but now swung her gaze on him. "Who inherits the money?"

"Natalie. The money would be used for her care until she was twenty-one, at which time her guardian—"

"Her *guardian?*"

"Nick named a guardian in case of your…death or incarceration."

Allie's voice broke. *"Who?"*

"Originally Drew was listed as guardian on the policies, but Nick changed that, too, right before he headed for the mountains." He met her gaze. "Megan, as your next closest kin, even though she isn't a blood relative."

She staggered under the weight of it. She couldn't deal with this now. She had the wedding. "The fireworks show is about to start," she said. "I have to finish—"

"I'm sure Dana will see that the rest of the wedding goes off like it is supposed to," Jackson said, blocking her escape. "No one expects you to continue, given what's happened."

"I took the job. I want to finish it," Allie said, hugging herself against the evening chill. "I thought you would understand that."

"I do. But—" His cell phone rang. "It's Hayes." He took the call.

She had no choice but to wait. She had to know what he'd found out at the police station. As she waited, she watched the lights of Big Sky glitter in the growing darkness that fell over the canyon. A breeze seemed to grow in the shadowed pines. The boughs began to move as if with the music still playing down in the barn.

After a moment, Jackson thanked his brother and disconnected. She remained looking off into the distance, her back to him, as he said, "Nick Taylor's remains were found in a shallow grave. There was a .45 bullet lodged in his skull. The trajectory of the bullet based on where it entered and exited, along with the fact that it appears someone tried to hide the body... It's being investigated as a homicide."

She felt a jolt when he mentioned that the bullet was

a .45 caliber and knew Jackson would have seen it. Still, she didn't turn.

"Megan told me you bought a gun and that it disappeared from the cabin," he said. She could feel his gaze on her, burning into her back. He thought he knew her. She could imagine what was going through his mind. He would desperately want to believe she had nothing to do with her husband's murder. "Was the gun you purchased a—"

"Forty-five?" She nodded as she turned to look at him. "Everyone will believe I killed him. You're not even sure anymore, are you?"

"Allie—" He took a step toward her, but she held up her hand to ward him off. It had grown dark enough that she couldn't make out his expression unless he came closer, which was a godsend. She couldn't bear to see the disappointment in his face.

Below them on the mountain everyone was coming out of the barn to gather in the meadow for the fireworks. She suddenly ached to see her daughter. Natalie had been all that had kept her sane for so long. Right now, she desperately needed to hold her.

What would happen to Natalie now? She was trembling with fear at the thought that came to her and would no doubt have already come to the police—and eventually Jackson. She didn't want to be around when that happened.

"With my husband dead, that is three insurance policies for more than a million and a half," she said. "Mother Taylor is convinced I've made up all the stories about someone gaslighting me, as you call it. She thinks I have some plot to make myself rich at her poor

Nicky's expense. I'm sure she's shared all of that with the police by now. Maybe I did do it."

He stepped to her and took her shoulders in his hands. "Don't. You didn't kill your husband and you *know* damned well that I believe you."

"Your ex-wife, she was a liar and con woman, right? Isn't that why you were so afraid to get involved with me? What makes you so sure I'm not just like her?"

"You can't push me away." He lifted her chin with his fingers so she couldn't avoid his gaze. Their faces were only a few inches apart. "You aren't like her."

"What if I'm crazy?" Her voice broke. "Crazy like a fox?" The first of the fireworks exploded, showering down a glittering red, white and blue light on the meadow below them. The boom echoed in her chest as another exploded to the oos and ahs of the wedding party. She felt scalding tears burn her throat. "What if Mother Taylor is right and all of this is some subconscious plot I have to not only free myself of Nick, but walk away with a million and a half dollars, as well?"

Jackson couldn't bear to see Allie like this. He pulled her to him and, dropping his mouth to hers, kissed her. She leaned into him, letting him draw her even closer as the kiss deepened. Fireworks lit the night, booming in a blaze of glittering light before going dark again.

Desire ignited his blood. He wanted Allie like he'd never wanted anyone or anything before. She melted into him, warm and lush in his arms, a moan escaping her lips.

Then suddenly he felt her stiffen. She broke away. "I can't keep doing this," she cried and, tearing herself from his arms, took off down the steps and through the trees toward the barn.

He started after her, but a voice from the darkness stopped him.

"Let her go."

He turned to find his brother Laramie standing in the nearby trees. More fireworks exploded below them. "What are you doing, little brother?"

"I'm in love with her." The words were out, more honest than he'd been with even himself—let alone Allie.

"Is that right?" Laramie moved to him in a burst of booming light from the meadow below. "So what are you going to do about it?"

Jackson shook his head. "I... I haven't gotten that far yet."

"Oh, I think you've gotten quite far already." Laramie sighed. "I don't want to see you jump into anything. Not again."

"She is nothing like Juliet."

His brother raised a brow. "I knew one day you would fall in love again. It was bound to happen, but Jackson, this is too fast. This woman has too many problems. Hayes and I just came from the police station. They are going to be questioning her about her husband's murder. It doesn't look good."

"She had nothing to do with his death."

"She owns a .45 pistol, the one they suspect is the murder weapon."

Jackson sighed and looked toward the meadow below. It was cast in darkness. Had the fireworks show already ended? "She did but whoever is trying to have her committed, took it to set her up. You know as well as I do that someone has been gaslighting her."

Laramie shook his head. "We only know what Allie has been telling you."

His first instinct was to get angry with his brother, but he understood what Laramie was saying. There was no proof. Instead, the evidence against her was stacking up.

"I believe her and I'm going to help her," he said as he stepped past his brother.

"I just hope you aren't making a mistake," Laramie said behind him as Jackson started down the mountainside.

He'd only taken a few steps when he saw people running all over and heard Allie screaming Natalie's name. He took off running toward her.

"What's wrong?" he demanded when he reached her.

"Nat's gone!" Allie cried.

Chapter 14

"She *can't* be gone," Jackson said. "She was with Dana, right?"

"Dana said the kids were all together, but after one of the fireworks went off, she looked over and Nat wasn't with them. She asked Hank and he said she spilled her lemonade on her dress and went to the bathroom to try to wash it off. Dana ran up to the house and the barn, but she wasn't there." Allie began to cry. "She found this, though." She held up the tie that had been on Nat's dress. "Natalie might have gone looking for me. Or someone took her—"

"Allie," he said, taking her shoulders in his hands. "Even if she left the meadow to go to the house, she couldn't have gotten far. We'll find her."

The search of the ranch area began quickly with everyone from the wedding party out looking for the child.

"I turned my back for just a moment," Dana said, sounding as distraught as Allie when Jackson caught up with her.

"It's not your fault. If anyone is to blame, it's me. I've been trying to help Allie and have only made things worse. I need to know something," he said as he watched the searchers coming off the mountain from the cabins. No Natalie. "Did you see anyone go toward the house about the time you realized she was gone?"

She shook her head. "You mean Drew or his mother? They both left earlier to go talk to the police."

"What about his sister, Sarah? Have you seen her?"

Dana frowned. "She didn't leave with them, now that I think about it, and I haven't seen her since Nat went missing."

Jackson spotted Belinda trying to comfort Allie down by the main house. "How about Megan?"

She shook her head. "I haven't seen either of them." Dana looked worried. "You don't think—"

He did think. He ran down the slope toward the house and Allie. "Did either of you see Sarah or Megan?"

They looked at him in surprise.

"They left together not long after the fireworks started," Belinda said. "Sarah said she had a headache and asked Megan to give her a ride."

Jackson looked at Allie. "You know where Sarah lives, right?"

"You think they took Nat?" Allie looked even more frightened.

"Belinda, stay here and keep us informed if the searchers find Nat. Come on. Let's see if they have Natalie or might have seen her since they left about the time she went missing."

* * *

Each breath was a labor as Allie stared out the windshield into the darkness ahead. She fought not to break down but it took all of her strength. She'd never been so frightened or felt so helpless. All she could do was pray that Natalie was safe.

"If they took her, then I'm sure they wouldn't hurt her," she said, needing desperately to believe that. "Sarah might have thought it was getting too late for Natalie to be out. Or maybe Nat's dress was so wet—"

"We're going to find her." Jackson sounded convinced of that.

She glanced over at him. His strong hands gripped the wheel as he drove too fast. He was as scared as she was, she realized. Like her, he must be blaming himself. If the two of them hadn't left the wedding…

"Tell me where to turn. I don't know where they live."

"Take a left at the Big Sky resort turnoff. Mother Taylor… Mildred lives up the mountain."

"They don't have that much of a head start," he said, sounding as if he was trying to reassure himself as much as her.

"This is all my fault." She didn't realize she'd said the words aloud until he spoke.

"No, if anyone is to blame it's me," he said as he reached over and squeezed her hand. "You have been going through so much and all I did was complicate things for you."

She let out a nervous laugh. "Are you kidding? I would have been in a straitjacket by now if it wasn't for you. I still might end up there, but at least I had this time when there was someone who believed me."

"I *still* believe you. You're not crazy. Nor did you have anything to do with your husband's death. You're being set up and, if it is the last thing I do, I'm going to prove it."

Allie couldn't help but smile over at him. "Thank you but I can't ask you to keep—"

"You're not asking. There's something else I need to say." He glanced over at her before making the turn at Big Sky then turned back to his driving. "I hadn't been with another woman since my ex. I didn't *want* anyone. The mere thought of getting involved again... Then I met you," he said shooting her a quick look as they raced up the mountain toward Big Sky Resort.

"Turn at the next left when we reach the top of the mountain," she said, not sure she wanted to hear what he had to say.

"I hadn't felt anything like that in so long and then we made love and..."

She really didn't need him to let her down easy. Not right now. All she wanted to think about was Natalie. If he was just doing this to keep her from worrying... "You don't have to explain."

"I do. I panicked because making love with you was so amazing and meant so much and..." He shook his head. "I... I just needed time to digest it all. And, truthfully, I was scared. Ford's mom did a number on me. Admittedly, we were both young, too young to get married, let alone have a child together. I had this crazy idea that we wanted the same things. Turned out she wanted money, a big house, a good time. When she got pregnant with Ford..." He slowed to make the turn.

"It's up this road about a mile. Turn left when you see the sign for Elk Ridge."

He nodded. "Juliet didn't want the baby. I talked her into having Ford. She hated me for it, said it was going to ruin her figure." He shook his head at the memory. "I thought that after he was born, her mothering instincts would kick in. My mistake. She resented him even more than she did me. She basically handed him to me and went out with her friends."

"I can't imagine."

He glanced over at her. "No, *you* can't." He sighed. "After that, she started staying out all night, wouldn't come home for days. Fortunately, the barbecue businesses took off like crazy so I could stay home with Ford. I asked for a divorce only to find out that my wife liked being a Cardwell and didn't want to give up what she had, which was basically no responsibilities, but lots of money and freedom to do whatever she wanted."

"Keep going up this road," she told him. Then after a moment, said, "She didn't want a divorce."

"No. She said that if I pushed it, she would take Ford."

"How horrible," Allie cried. Hadn't that been her fear with Nick? Hadn't she worried that he would be a bastard and try to hurt them both when she told him she was leaving him?

"After the battle I fought to keep my son, I was… broken."

"I understand. The last thing you wanted was to get involved with a woman who only reminded you of what you'd been through."

He glanced over at her. "That was part of it." He didn't say more as he reached the turnoff for Mildred Taylor's house and the guesthouse where her daughter, Sarah, lived. He turned down it and Mildred's house came into view.

* * *

Jackson had almost told Allie how he felt about her. That he loved her. But as he'd turned and seen Mildred Taylor's big house, he'd realized the timing was all wrong. First they had to find Natalie.

He prayed she would be here, safe. But if so, did the Taylors seriously think they could get away with this? Had they told someone they were taking Natalie and the person just forgot or couldn't find Allie and left? Was there a logical explanation for this?

He hoped it was just a misunderstanding. But in his heart, he didn't believe for a minute that Allie had imagined the things that had been happening to her. Someone was behind this and they weren't finished with Allie yet. What scared him was that one of them could have murdered Nick.

His heart began to pound harder as he pulled in front of the large stone-and-log house set back against the mountainside. There were two vehicles parked in front and the lights were on inside the massive house. He parked and opened his door, anxious to put Nat in her mother's arms. Allie was out her door the moment he stopped.

"Who all lives here?" Jackson asked as he caught up to her.

"Just Mildred in the main house. Sarah stays in the guesthouse behind it. Drew lives down in Gateway but he stays with his mother a lot up here. That's his pickup parked next to Mildred's SUV so he must be here."

As Jackson passed Mildred's SUV, he touched the hood. Still warm. They at least hadn't been here long.

"What does Sarah drive?" he asked, glancing toward the dark guesthouse.

"A pearl-white SUV. I don't see it."

At Allie's knock, he heard movement inside the house. If they were trying to hide Natalie, it wouldn't do them any good. He looked back down the mountainside telling himself that if Natalie was in this house, he'd find her.

Drew opened the door and looked surprised to see them standing there.

"Where is Natalie?" Allie cried as she pushed past him.

"Natalie?" Drew barely got the word out before Jackson pushed past him, as well. The two of them stormed into the main part of the house.

Mildred was seated on one of the large leather couches facing the window in the living room, a glass of wine in her hand. She looked up in surprise.

"Where is she?" Allie demanded. "I know you have my daughter."

"Natalie?" Mildred asked, frowning. "You can't *find* her?"

"They seem to think we have her," Drew said, closing the front door and joining them. "We've been at the police station. Why would you think we had Natalie?"

"Allie, stay here. I'll search the house," Jackson said.

"You most certainly will not," Mildred cried. "I'll call the cops."

"Call the cops, but I suspect the marshal is already on his way here," he told her and wasn't surprised when Drew stepped in front of him as if to block his way.

"You really want to do this now? Your niece is missing. If you don't have her, then we need to be out looking for her, not seeing who is tougher between you and me."

"We don't have her," Drew said, "and you're not—"

Jackson hit him and didn't wait around to see if he got up.

He stormed through the house, calling Nat's name. There were a lot of rooms, a lot of closets, a lot of places to look. But it didn't take him long to realize she wasn't here. Whatever they might have done with her, she wasn't in this house.

"I'm going to have you arrested for trespassing and barging into our house and attacking my son," Mildred threatened but hadn't made the call when he returned. Drew had a package of frozen peas he was holding to his eye as he came out of the kitchen.

"Mildred swears she hasn't seen Sarah," Allie told him.

"Well, Natalie isn't here. I think we should still check the guesthouse."

"You planning to break in?" Drew asked. "Or would you like me to get the key?"

Mildred pushed to her feet. "Drew, you are most certainly not going to—"

"Shut up, Mother," he snapped. "Aren't you listening? Natalie is missing. If I can help find her, I will. What I'd like to know is why you aren't upset about it. If you know where Nat is, Mother, you'd better tell me right now."

Jackson felt his cell phone vibrate, checked it and said, "I just got a text that the marshal is on his way. Mrs. Taylor, you could be looking at felony kidnapping," he warned.

Allie stared at her mother-in-law, seeing a pathetic, lonely woman who now looked trapped.

"She's not in the guesthouse," Mildred said. "She's *fine*. She's with Sarah and Megan."

"Where?" Allie demanded, her heart breaking at the thought of Megan being involved in this. "Why would they take her?"

Mildred met her gaze. "Because you're an unfit mother. Megan told me all about your mother and her family. Crazy, all of them. And you? You see things and do things that prove you can't raise my Nicky's baby girl. She needs *family*. Natalie needs her *grandmother*," she said before bursting into tears.

"Call them and tell them to bring Natalie back," Jackson ordered.

"He's right, Mother. Natalie belongs with her mother."

"How can you say that?" Mildred cried, turning on her son. "I told you about all the crazy things she's been doing. Did you know she cut up all those lovely dresses my Nicky had bought her? She never liked them and with him gone—" Mildred stopped as if she felt Allie staring at her in shock. "She's *crazy*. Just look at her!"

"The dresses. I never told anyone other than Jackson about finding them cut up on my bed," Allie said, surprised by how normal her voice sounded. Even more surprised by the relief she felt. "It was the night Drew took Natalie and me to dinner. *You?* You bought the clothes in the closet that I found. No wonder you asked me about what I was wearing at the rehearsal dinner. You knew where I kept my checkbook in the desk drawer. Nick would have told you about the kind of clothes I liked. Forging my signature on a check wouldn't have been hard, not for a woman who has been forging her husband's signature on checks for years."

Mildred gasped. "Where would you get an idea like that?"

"*Your Nicky* told me. You've been stealing from the elderly man you married to keep up the lifestyle you believe you deserve. But you don't deserve my daughter."

"Is that true, Mother?" Drew asked with a groan.

"Never mind that cheap bastard. Men never stay so yes, I took advantage while it lasted and now he's divorcing me. Happy?" Mildred thrust her finger at Allie. "But you, you killed my Nicky!"

"How can you say that?" Allie demanded. "You can't really believe I followed him up into the mountains."

"You *paid* someone to kill him. I know you did," the older woman argued. "When I came over that weekend, you were packing up some of Nicky's belongings. You knew he was dead before we even heard."

"That was just some things he left out before he went hunting."

"She's lying," Mildred cried as she looked from Jackson to Drew. "She knew Nicky wasn't coming back. She was packing. I saw that she'd cleaned out the closet before she closed the bedroom door."

"I was packing my own things and Natalie's," Allie said. "I was planning to leave Nick. Ask Belinda. She'll tell you. I wanted a divorce."

Mildred looked shocked. "Why would you want to leave my Nicky? You must have found another man."

"No," Allie said, shaking her head. "I know how much you loved him but I didn't see the same man you did. Nick wasn't any happier than I was in the marriage."

"Oh, I have to sit down," Mildred cried. "Can't you

see? She had every reason to want Nicky dead. She's admitted it."

"Make the call to your daughter, Mrs. Taylor," Jackson said, handing her his phone.

At the sound of a siren headed toward the house, Mildred took his phone.

"You'll get your daughter back, but only temporarily," her mother-in-law spat after making the call. "Once you go to prison for my Nicky's murder, you will get what you deserve and I will get my Nicky's baby."

"And all Nick's insurance money," Jackson said. "Isn't that what this is really about?"

Mildred didn't answer as Marshal Hud Savage pulled up out front.

Chapter 15

Emotionally exhausted, all Allie could think about was holding her daughter. They'd all waited, the marshal included, until Megan and Sarah brought Natalie to the Taylor house.

Allie swept her daughter up into her arms, hugging her so tightly that Natalie cried, "Mama, you're squishing me!"

Hud took Mildred, Drew, Megan and Sarah down to the marshal's office to question them.

"Why don't you come stay at the ranch," Jackson suggested, but all Allie wanted to do was take her daughter home. "Okay, I'll drop you off there. I can give you a ride to the ranch in the morning to pick up your van."

She looked into his dark eyes and touched his arm. "Thank you."

They didn't talk on the drive to her cabin. Natalie fell asleep after complaining that she'd missed most of the fireworks. Apparently, Sarah and Megan had told her they were taking her to see her mama and that it was important.

As they drove, pockets of fireworks were going off around them. Allie had forgotten it was the Fourth of July. Even the wedding seemed like it had been a long time ago.

"If you need anything…" Jackson said after he'd insisted on carrying Natalie into her bed. He moved to the cabin door. "I'm here for you, Allie."

She could only nod, her emotions long spent.

"I'll see you tomorrow."

Allie doubted that. Jackson and Ford would be flying out. She told herself that she and Natalie were safe as she locked the front door, leaned against it and listened to Jackson drive away.

But in her heart she knew they wouldn't be safe until Nick's killer was caught.

"I ruined Tag and Lily's wedding," Jackson said with a groan the next morning at breakfast.

"You did not," Dana said, patting his hand as she finished serving a huge ranch breakfast of elk steaks, biscuits and gravy, fried potatoes and eggs. She had invited them all down, saying that she knew it had been a rough night. Hud had left for his office first thing this morning.

The wedding couple had stayed at Big Sky Resort last night and flown out this morning to an undisclosed location for their two-week-long honeymoon.

"They loved everything about the wedding," Dana

said. "They were just worried about Allie after Mildred's announcement and then concerned for Natalie. I'm just so thankful that she was found and is fine. I can't imagine what Sarah and Megan were thinking."

Jackson had filled everyone in on what had happened at the Taylors' and how apparently Mildred, Sarah and Megan had been gaslighting Allie.

"Oh, Allie must be heartbroken to find out her stepsister was in on it," Dana said.

"I'm sure Hud will sort it out," Jackson said as he watched his son eating breakfast with the Savage clan at the kid table. Ford, he noticed, had come out of his shell. Jackson couldn't believe the change in the boy from when they had arrived at the ranch. Montana had been good for his son.

"Natalie is safe and so is Allie, at least for the moment," he said. "The problem is Nick's murder," he said, dropping his voice, even though he doubted the kids could hear, given the amount of noise they were making at their table.

"They still don't know who killed him?" Dana asked.

Jackson shook his head. "Mildred is convinced Allie paid someone to do it. The police want to talk to her."

"You sound worried," Dana noted. "And your brothers haven't said a word," she said, looking from Hayes to Laramie and finally Jackson. "Why is that?"

"They've been helping me do some investigating," he admitted.

Dana rolled her eyes. "I should have known that was what was going on." She glanced at Hayes and Laramie. "You found something that makes her look guilty?"

"Someone is setting her up," Jackson said.

"The same people who tried to drive her crazy?" she asked.

"Maybe not. There could be more going on here than even we know." Jackson couldn't help sounding worried as he got to his feet. "Hayes and I are going to take her van to her. She called this morning. A homicide detective from Bozeman wants to see her."

Allie had awakened in Natalie's bed to the sound of the phone. She'd expected it to be Jackson. That sent her heart lifting like helium. But as she reminded herself he was leaving today, her moment of euphoria evaporated.

Reaching for the receiver, she had a bad feeling it wasn't going to be good news. "We would like to ask you a few questions," the homicide detective told her. "When would be a good time?"

After she'd hung up, she'd called Jackson and told him the news.

"You knew this was coming. It's nothing to worry about," he'd told her, but she'd heard concern in his voice. "Do you want me to go with you?"

"No. This is something I have to do alone. Anyway, aren't you flying out today?"

Silence, then, "I canceled our flight."

"You shouldn't have done that," she said after a moment.

"Allie, I can't leave yet. I saw that the key is in the van. Hayes and I will bring it over."

"There is no hurry. I don't see the homicide detective until later."

Their conversation had felt awkward and ended just as badly. Allie told herself she couldn't keep leaning on Jackson. She knew now what Mildred and her daughter and Megan had done to her. She could understand Sarah going along with whatever her mother said, but Megan?

She'd felt like family. But then so had Drew.

Allie made Natalie her favorite pancakes when she woke up, then they went for a walk down by the river. Nat did love to throw rocks into the water. Allie watched the ripples they made, thinking about Jackson and the ripples he'd made in her life.

After a while, they walked back to the cabin. Dana had called saying she would love to take Natalie while Allie went to talk to the detective.

"If you trust me with her. I wouldn't blame you if you didn't. Just let me know."

Allie called Dana right back. "I would always trust you with Natalie and she would love to see the kids, not to mention Sugar, the horse."

Dana laughed and Allie could hear tears in her voice. "I was afraid you would never forgive me."

"There is nothing to forgive. Megan and Sarah took advantage of the fireworks show and the wedding."

"What were they thinking? Did they really believe they could get away with keeping her?"

"I suppose they thought I would come unglued, which I did, proving that I was unbalanced. If it hadn't been for Jackson..." She really hadn't meant to go there.

"Is Natalie all right?"

"She didn't even realize anything was amiss. Apparently, they told her they were taking her to me, but when they reached Megan's motel room, they told her I was going to meet them there. Nat ended up falling asleep. So she had no idea what was going on."

"Thank goodness."

"I'll drop Nat off on my way, if that's okay."

"That's wonderful. We can't wait to see her. Tell her to wear her boots. We'll go for a ride."

"You need to take the hint," Hayes said as he and Jackson drove away from Allie's cabin. They'd dropped off the van, Allie had thanked them and that was that, so Jackson knew what his brother was getting at. "Allie is handling all of this fine. I'm not sure there is anything you can do from here on out."

"You think she had him killed?" Jackson demanded.

Hayes shrugged. "I don't know her as well as you think you do. I don't think she paid anyone to do it. But if she gave Drew any kind of opening with her, I think he would have killed his brother for her—and the insurance money."

"She wasn't in cahoots with Drew. And stop doing that," he snapped as his brother shrugged again. "Do you realize how cynical you've become? Worse, does McKenzie?"

Hayes smiled. "Speaking of McKenzie... I'm opening a private investigator business here."

"You think that's a newsflash?" Jackson laughed. "We've all seen that coming for a mile. So when is the wedding?"

"I'm thinking we might elope. I'm not sure the family can live through another Cardwell Ranch wedding."

"Which reminds me, still no word from Austin?"

"You know our brother when he's on a case. But I am a little worried about him. I really thought he'd make Tag's wedding."

"Yeah, me too. Maybe I'll give a call down there. Knowing him, he probably didn't list any of us as emergency contacts."

* * *

Allie tried to get comfortable in the chair the homicide detectives offered her. The room was like any office, no bare lightbulb shining into her eyes, no cops threatening her. But she still shifted in her chair.

On the drive here, she'd tried to concentrate on who might have killed Nick. Belinda had been up that trail with Nick when the two of them had been dating. Drew usually went hunting with his brother. Had Drew gone this time, as well, gotten in an argument with Nick and killed him?

She shuddered at the path her thoughts had taken. Did she really think someone in Nick's own family had killed him?

Better that than to think that her stepsister, Megan, had. Allie felt sick at the thought. Her sister had called this morning but Allie hadn't picked up.

"I need to explain," Megan had said on voice mail. "I did what I did for Natalie's sake. I love you and my niece. I really believed I was protecting you both. I had no idea Mildred and Sarah were doing those things to you, making you behave the way they told me you were. Please call me so we can talk about this."

The larger of the two homicide detectives cleared his voice. His name tag read Benson. "We need to know where you were the weekend your husband went up into the mountains."

"I was home that whole weekend."

"Did you talk to anyone? Anyone stop by?"

Allie tried to remember. Her mind was spinning. They thought she'd had something to do with Nick's death? Of course they did, given the insurance policies and her mother-in-law's rantings and ravings.

Just yesterday, she'd been sure that Nick was alive. Jackson had been convinced, as well. She'd been even more convinced when she'd heard his voice at the séance. Nick's voice accusing her of killing him. She shivered at the memory.

"Mrs. Taylor?" the smaller of the two, whose name tag read Evans, asked.

She blinked. No one called her Mrs. Taylor. Mrs. Taylor was Nick's mother. "Please, call me Allie. I just need a moment to think." Had anyone stopped by that weekend?

Fighting all her conflicting thoughts, she tried to remember. Nick had left early, having packed the night before. He'd seemed excited about the prospect of going alone on this hunt. Why hadn't she noticed that something was wrong right there? It was the first red flag.

Had anyone stopped by? No. She frowned. She'd tried to call Belinda but hadn't been able to reach her, she recalled now. She'd wanted to tell her what Nick had said about making some changes when he returned from his hunting trip. She'd had misgivings about the trip even then and she'd needed to talk to someone. Had she worried that he might be thinking of killing himself?

"I don't remember anyone stopping by," she said, trying to keep her thoughts on the question. She ticked off everyone on her fingers. "I couldn't reach my friend Belinda." Had she tried Megan? "Or my stepsister, Megan. And my in-laws. I think that was the weekend that Mildred and Sarah went on a shopping trip to Billings. Drew… I don't know where he was. I didn't talk to him."

She looked up to see that both detectives were studying her. They were making her even more nervous.

"I was alone with my daughter that whole weekend." She had no alibi. But they didn't really think she'd followed Nick up in the mountains and killed him, did they?

"Was it unusual for your husband to go hunting alone?"

"Very. I didn't think he had. I thought he was having an affair. I was surprised when I learned that he really had gone into the mountains."

The detectives shared a look before the lead one asked, "Did you have any reason to believe your husband was having an affair?"

"No. I guess it was wishful thinking. It would have made it easier for me."

The two shared another look. "Easier?"

She met the smaller detective's gaze. "I was going to leave Nick." Why not admit it? They probably already knew this after talking to her in-laws and Belinda and Megan. "But I didn't want him dead. You asked what I was doing that weekend? I didn't leave the house. I had my five-year-old daughter to take care of that weekend and I was busy packing."

"When were you planning to tell him?" Benson asked.

"As soon as he returned."

Evans picked up a sheet of paper from the desk. "Mrs. Tay— Excuse me, Allie, you own a .45 pistol?"

Chapter 16

The gun. What had she been thinking when she'd bought it? Had she really thought that pulling it on Nick would be a good idea? She'd wanted something to protect herself for when she told him she was leaving.

Now she saw how ridiculous that was. Nick would have taken it away from her, knowing she couldn't shoot him and then he would have been so furious....

"Yes, I bought the gun for protection."

Benson raised a brow. "Protection? Against whom?"

"I was planning to leave my husband. My daughter and I would be alone—"

"But you hadn't left him yet," Evans pointed out. "So why buy a .45 pistol only days before your husband was to go on his hunting trip?"

"I... I...was afraid of how Nick was going to take

it when he returned and I told him I was leaving him. Sometimes he scares me."

The two detectives exchanged another look.

"But it was impulsive and silly because Nick would have known I couldn't use it on him. He would have taken it away from me and..." She swallowed.

"You were afraid of your husband," Benson said.

"Sometimes."

"Where is the gun now?" Evans asked.

"I don't know. When I heard that Nick had been killed with a .45, I looked for it, but it was gone." Allie could see the disbelief written all over their faces. Hadn't she known when she looked that it would be gone?

"I think someone is trying to set me up for his murder," she blurted out and instantly regretted it when she saw their expressions. Apparently, they'd heard this type of defense before.

"You're saying someone took the gun to frame you?" Benson asked. "Who knew you'd bought it?"

Allie met his gaze. "I didn't tell anyone, if that is what you're asking."

"Who had access to your house?" Evans asked.

"It's an old cabin. I don't know how many people might have a key. Nick was always going to change the locks..."

"Your in-laws? Did they have keys?" Benson asked.

"Yes."

"Friends?"

"Belinda and my stepsister, Megan, know where there's a key to get in."

"Where did you keep the gun that someone could

have found it? You have a five-year-old. I assume you didn't just leave the gun lying around," Benson asked.

"Of course not. I put it on the top shelf of the closet. It wasn't loaded."

"But there were cartridges for it with the gun?"

She nodded.

"When was the last time you saw it?" Evans asked.

"The day I bought it. I put it on the shelf behind some shoe boxes... I'd forgotten all about it with Nick's... death...and all."

"So you were just going to leave him," Evans said. "This man who you said scared you sometimes, you were going to allow him to have joint custody of your child?"

"It hadn't gotten that far. I guess it would have been up to the court—"

"Oh, so you'd already seen a lawyer about a divorce?" Benson asked.

"Not yet. I couldn't afford to see one until I got a job and Nick wouldn't allow me to work."

The detectives exchanged looks.

"Was your husband abusive?" Benson asked not unkindly.

Allie hesitated. "He was...controlling."

"And he scared you," Evans said.

"Yes, sometimes. What is it you want me to say? He wasn't a good husband or father to our daughter. And yes, sometimes he scared me."

"Mrs. Taylor, did you kill your husband?" Evans asked.

"No. I told you. I could never—"

"Did you get your brother-in-law, Drew, or someone else close to you to do the killing for you?" Benson asked.

"*No!* I didn't want to be married to Nick anymore but I didn't want him dead."

Evans leaned forward. "But look how it turned out. Nick is no longer around to scare you, even sometimes. Your daughter is safe from him. And you are a wealthy woman thanks to his insurance money. Better than a divorce and a lengthy battle over your daughter, wouldn't you say?"

Allie felt as if the detectives had beaten her as she stumbled out of the police station. For a moment she forgot where she'd parked the van. Panic sent her blood pressure soaring before she spotted it. There it was, right where she'd left it. And there was...

"Jackson?"

He pushed off the van and moved quickly to her. "I had to see you before I left."

She frowned, still feeling off balance. "I thought you weren't flying out yet?"

"It's my brother Austin. He's a sheriff's deputy in Texas. He's been shot. He's critical. I have to fly out now. Franklin and Mom already left. Hayes, Laramie and I are taking the corporate jet as soon as I get to the airport."

"I'm so sorry, Jackson. Does Tag know?"

"We weren't able to reach him. He and Lily wanted their honeymoon to be a secret... Ford is staying with Dana until I get back. But I couldn't leave without seeing you. Are you all right?"

She started to say she was fine, but she couldn't get the lie past her lips. Her eyes filled with tears. "They think I killed Nick. Everyone does."

"Not me," he said and pulled her into his arms. "When I get back, we'll sort this out. I'm sorry I have to go."

She pulled back, brushed at her tears. "I'll say a prayer for your brother." As he ran to his rented SUV, she turned in time to see Detective Evans watching her from the front of the building. He looked like a man who'd just received a gift he hadn't expected. Jackson Cardwell. Another motive as to why she'd want her husband gone for good.

The jet owned by the corporation was waiting on the tarmac when Jackson arrived at the airport. He ran to climb aboard and Laramie alerted the captain that they were ready.

"Have you heard any more from Mom or the hospital?" Jackson asked as he buckled up.

"I just got off the phone with Mom," Hayes said. "Austin's still in surgery." His tone was sufficient for Jackson to know it didn't look good.

"Do we know what happened?" he asked as the plane began to taxi out to the runway.

"You know how hard it is to get anything out of the sheriff's department down there," Hayes said. "But I got the impression he was on one of the dangerous cases he seems to like so well." He raked a hand through his hair. "There was a woman involved. He'd apparently gone into a drug cartel to get her out."

"That sounds just like Austin," Jackson said with a sigh as the jet engine roared and the plane began to race down the runway. "Did he get her out?"

"Don't know. Doubtful, though, since some illegal immigrants found him after he'd been shot and got him to a gas station near the border."

Hayes shook his head. "Some of the same illegal immigrants his department is trying to catch and send back over the border. What a mess down there. I'm glad I'm done with it."

His brothers looked at him in surprise as the plane lifted off the ground.

"McKenzie and I signed the papers on a ranch in the canyon not far from Cardwell Ranch. When I get back, we're eloping. She's already looking for some office space for me at Big Sky to open a private investigation office up here."

"Congratulations," Laramie said.

"Have you told Mom?" Jackson asked. "I'm wondering how she is going to feel losing another son to Montana?" The plane fell silent as he realized she might be losing another son at this very moment, one that not even Montana got a chance to claim.

Speaking of Montana, he thought as he looked out the window at the mountains below them. He'd hated leaving Allie, especially as upset as she'd been. He promised himself he would return to the canyon just as soon as he knew his brother was going to be all right.

He said a prayer for Austin and one for Allie, as well.

Dana had called to say she was taking the kids on a horseback ride and that Allie could pick Natalie up later, if that was all right. Ford apparently was very upset and worried about his uncle Austin, so Dana was trying to take their minds off everything for a while.

Not wanting to go back to an empty cabin, Allie had busied herself with errands she'd put off since the wedding preparation. It was late afternoon by the time she got home. She'd called the ranch only to find out that Dana and the kids had gone to get ice cream and would be back soon.

Allie was carrying in groceries and her other purchases when she heard the vehicle pull up. She'd hoped to get everything put away before she went to pick up Natalie. She carried the bags into the cabin, dumping them on the kitchen counter, before she glanced out the window to see her mother-and sister-in-law pull up. She groaned as the two got out and came to the door.

For just an instant, she thought about not answering their knock, but they must have seen her carrying in her groceries. Mildred wasn't one to take the hint and go away.

"I just got back from the police station," she said as she opened the door. "I'm really not in the mood for visitors." She couldn't believe either of them would have the gall to show their faces around here after what they'd done. Well, they weren't coming in. Whatever they had to say, they could say it on the front step.

Allie had already talked to Hud this morning. He'd questioned all of them last night, but had had to let them all go. Maybe they had come by to apologize, but Allie doubted it.

"I just got a call from the police," Mildred said indignantly. "Why would you tell them that Sarah and I went to Billings the weekend my Nicky was killed?"

"I thought you had." She knew she shouldn't have been surprised. No apology for what they had tried to do to her.

"We'd planned to go, but Sarah was sick that whole weekend." She sniffed. "I was alone when I got the call about my Nicky." She glared at her daughter for a moment. "Sarah had taken my car down to the drugstore to get more medicine since her car was in the shop. I couldn't even leave the house to go to Drew." Mildred sighed.

"I'm sorry you were alone, Mother. I came right back. I couldn't have been gone more than five minutes after you got the call," Sarah said.

"That was the longest five minutes of my life," Mildred said with another sniff.

"I guess I had forgotten the two of you hadn't gone to Billings, but I'm sure you straightened it out with the police," Allie said. "And Sarah couldn't have known that would be the time you would get the call about Nick," Allie pointed out.

Sarah gave her a grateful smile, then added, "I hate to ask, but do you happen to have a cola in your fridge?"

"Oh, for crying out loud, Sarah, how many times have I told you that stuff is horrible for you?" her mother demanded.

"Help yourself," Allie said, moving to the side of the doorway to let her pass. She saw that the sun had disappeared behind Lone Mountain, casting the canyon in a cool darkness. Where had this day gone? "I hate to run you off, but I have to go pick up Natalie."

"Once this foolishness is over, I hope you'll forgive me and let me spend some time with my granddaughter," Mildred said.

As Sarah came out with a can of cola, Allie moved aside again to let her pass, hoping they would now leave.

Mildred looked in the yard at Nick's pickup, where it had been parked since someone from the forest service had found it at the trailhead and had it dropped off. "Why are you driving that awful van of yours?

You should either drive Nicky's pickup or sell it. Terrible waste to just let it sit."

Allie planned to sell the pickup but she'd been waiting, hoping in time Mildred wouldn't get so upset about it.

"I'd like to buy it," Sarah said, making them both turn to look at her in surprise.

"What in the world do you need with Nicky's pickup?" Mildred demanded. "I'm not giving you the money for it and I couldn't bear looking at it every day."

"It was just a thought," Sarah said as she started toward her SUV. The young woman took so much grief from her mother.

Her gaze went to Nick's pickup. The keys were probably still in it, she realized. As Sarah climbed behind the wheel and waited for her mother to get into the passenger side of the SUV, Allie walked out to the pickup, opened the door and reached inside to pull the keys.

The pickup smelled like Nick's aftershave and made her a little sick to her stomach. She pocketed the keys as she hurriedly closed the door. The truck was Nick's baby. He loved it more than he did either her or Natalie. That's why she was surprised as she started to step away to see that the right rear panel near the back was dented. She moved to the dent and ran her fingers over it. That would have to be fixed before she could sell it since the rest of the truck was in mint condition.

Just something else to take care of, she thought as she dusted what looked like chalky white flakes off her fingers. She looked up and saw that her in-laws hadn't left. Mildred was going on about something. Sarah was bent toward the passenger seat apparently helping her mother buckle up. Mildred was probably giving her hell, Allie thought.

When Sarah straightened, she looked up from behind the wheel and seemed surprised to see Allie standing by Nick's truck. Her surprise gave way to sadness as she looked past Allie to her brother's pickup.

Was it possible Sarah really did want Nick's pickup for sentimental reasons? Maybe she should have it. Allie had never thought Sarah and her brother were that close. Well, at least Nick hadn't been that crazy about his sister. He'd been even more disparaging than his mother toward Sarah.

Allie met her sister-in-law's dark gaze for a moment, feeling again sorry for her. Maybe she would just give her the pickup. She waved as Sarah began to pull away, relieved they were finally leaving.

Her cell phone rang. She hoped it was Jackson with news of his brother. She said a silent prayer for Austin before she saw that it was Dana.

"Is everything all right?" Allie asked, instantly afraid.

"Ford is still upset about his uncle. Natalie told him that you were picking her up soon…"

Allie knew what was coming. She couldn't bear the thought. She wanted Natalie home with her. The way things were going, she feared she might soon be under arrest for Nick's murder. She didn't know how much time she and Nat had together.

"Natalie wishes to speak with you," Dana said before Allie could say no.

"Mama?" Just the sound of her daughter's voice made her smile. "Please say I can stay. Ford is very sad about his uncle. Please let me stay."

"Maybe Ford could come stay with you—"

"We're all going to sleep in the living room in front of the fire. Mrs. Savage said we could. She is going to make popcorn. It is Mary and Hank's favorite."

Allie closed her eyes, picturing how perfect it would be in front of Dana's fireplace in that big living room with the smell of popcorn and the sound of children's laughter. She wanted to sleep right in the middle of all of them.

"Of course you need to stay for your new friend," she heard herself say as tears burned her eyes. "Tell Mrs. Savage that I will pick you up first thing in the morning. I love you."

"I love you, too, Mama." And Natalie was gone, the phone passed to Dana, who said, "I'm sorry. This was the kids' idea."

"It's fine."

"What about you? How did it go with the police?"

"As expected. They think I killed Nick. Or at least got someone to do it for me."

"That's ridiculous. Allie, listen, you shouldn't be alone. Why don't you come stay here tonight? I think you need your daughter. Do you like butter on your popcorn? Come whenever you want. Or take a little time for yourself. If you're like me, when was the last time you got a nice leisurely bath without being interrupted? Whatever you need, but bring your pjs. We're having a pajama party. Right now the kids all want to go help feed the animals. See you later."

As the jet touched down just outside of Houston, Hayes got the call from their mother. Jackson watched his expression, waiting for the news. Relief flooded his brother's face. He gave thumbs up and disconnected.

"Mom says Austin is out of surgery. The doctor says he should make it."

Jackson let out the breath he'd been holding. As the plane taxied toward the private plan terminal, he put in a call to Allie. It went straight to voice mail.

He left a message, telling her the good news, then asking her to call when she got the message. "I'm worried about you." As he disconnected, he realized he'd been worried the entire flight about both his brother and Allie.

"I can't reach Allie."

His brothers looked at him in concern as the plane neared the small brightly lit terminal. It was already dark here, but it would still be light in Montana.

"Call Dana," Hayes said. "She's probably over there."

He called. "No answer."

"They probably went for a horseback ride," Laramie said. "Wasn't that what Ford told you they were going to do the last time you talked to him?"

Jackson nodded, telling himself his brother was probably right. He glanced at Hayes. He understood what Laramie couldn't really grasp. Laramie was a businessman. Hayes was a former sheriff's deputy, a private investigation. He understood Jackson's concern. There was a killer still loose in Montana.

The plane came to a stop. Jackson tried Allie again. The call again went straight to voice mail. He got Mildred Taylor's number and called her.

"Have you seen Allie?" he asked. He couldn't explain his fear, just a feeling in the pit of his stomach that was growing with each passing minute.

"Earlier. She wouldn't even let me in her house." She sniffed. "She was on her way to Cardwell Ranch to pick up Natalie the last I saw of her. Driving that old van. Why she doesn't drive Nickie's pickup I will never—"

He disconnected and tried Dana. Still no answer. He tried Allie again. Then he called the marshal's office in Big Sky.

"Marshal Savage is unavailable," the dispatcher told him.

"Is there anyone there who can do a welfare check?"

"Not at the moment. Do you want me to have the marshal call you when he comes in?"

Jackson started to give the dispatcher his number but Hayes stopped him.

"Take the plane," Hayes said. "Mother said it would be hours before we could even see Austin. I'll keep you informed of his progress."

"Are you kidding?" Laramie demanded. "What is it with you and this woman? Have you forgotten that she's the number one suspect in her husband's murder?"

"She didn't kill him," Jackson and Hayes said in unison.

"Let us know as soon as you hear something," Hayes said.

Jackson hugged his brother, relieved that he understood. He moved to cockpit and asked the pilot how long before they could get the plane back in the air. As Hayes and Laramie disembarked, he sat down again and buckled his seatbelt, trying to remain calm.

He had no reason to believe anything had happened. And yet…that bad feeling he'd gotten when her phone had gone to voice mail had only increased with each passing second. His every instinct told him that Allie was in real trouble.

Chapter 17

Allie had taken a hot bath, but had kept it short. She was too anxious to see her daughter. She changed her clothes, relieved she was going to Dana's. She really didn't want to be alone tonight. She'd heard Natalie's happy chatter in the background and couldn't wait to reach the ranch.

In fact, she had started out the door when she realized she didn't have her purse or her van keys. Leaving the door open, she turned back remembering that she'd left them on the small table between the living room and kitchen when she brought in her groceries earlier.

She was sure she'd left her purse on the table, but it wasn't there. As she started to search for it, she began to have that awful feeling again. Her mind reeled. Mildred wasn't still fooling with her, was she? No, Mildred hadn't come into the cabin. But Sarah had. Why would Sarah hide her purse? It made no sense.

Racking her brain, she moved through the small cabin. The purse wasn't anywhere. On her way back through, she realized she must have left it in the van. She was so used to leaving her purse on that small table, she'd thought she remembered doing it again.

She started toward the open door when a dark figure suddenly filled the doorway. The scream that rose in her throat came out a sharp cry before she could stop it.

"Drew, you scared me. I didn't hear you drive up."

"My truck's down the river a ways. I was fishing...."

The lie was so obvious that he didn't bother finishing it. He wasn't dressed for fishing nor was he carrying a rod.

"The truth is, I wanted to talk to you and after everything that's happened, I thought you'd chase me off before I could have my say."

"Drew, this isn't a good time. I was just leaving."

He laughed. "That's exactly why I didn't drive up in your yard. I figured you'd say something just like that."

"Well, in this case, it's true. Natalie is waiting for me. I'm staying at Cardwell Ranch tonight. Dana is going to be wondering where I am if I don't—"

"This won't take long." He took a breath. "I'm so sorry for everything."

Allie felt her blood heat to boiling. No one in this family ever listened to her. How dare he insist she hear him out when she just told him she was leaving? "You and your mother tried to drive me insane."

"I didn't know anything about that, I swear," Drew cried. "Mother told me that you had already forgotten about Nick. It was breaking her heart. She said you needed to be reminded and if you saw someone who looked like Nick..."

"You expect me to believe that?"

He shrugged. "It's true. I did it just to shut her up. You know how Mother is."

She did. She also knew arguing about this now was a waste of time and breath. She glanced at the clock on the mantel. "I really need to go."

"Just give me another minute, please. Also I wanted to apologize for the other night. I had too much to drink." He shook his head. "I don't know what I was thinking. But you have to know, I've always liked you." He looked at her shyly. "I would have done anything for you and now the cops think I killed Nick for you."

Her pulse jumped, her heart a thunder in her chest. "That's ridiculous."

"That's what I told them. I could never hurt my brother. I loved Nick. But I have to tell you, I was jealous of him when he married you."

"Drew, I really don't have time to get into this right—"

"Don't get me wrong," he said as if she hadn't spoken. "If I thought there was chance with you…"

A ripple of panic ran up her spine. "There isn't, Drew."

"Right. Jackson Cardwell."

"That isn't the reason."

"Right," he said sarcastically. His jaw tightened, his expression going dark. She'd been married to his brother long enough to know the signs. Nick could go from charming to furious and frightening in seconds. Apparently so could his brother.

"Drew—"

"What if I did kill him for you, Allie?" He stepped toward her. "What if I knew where he would be up that trail? What if I wanted to save you from him? You think I don't know how he was with you?" He let out a laugh. "Jackson Cardwell isn't the only knight in shining armor who wants to come to your rescue."

She didn't want to hear his confession and feared that was exactly what she was hearing. "Drew, I would never want you to hurt your brother for any reason, especially for me."

"Oh yea? But what if I did, Allie? Wouldn't you owe me something?"

He took another a step toward her.

She tried to hold her ground but Drew was much stronger, much larger, much scarier. With Nick, she'd learned that standing up to him only made things worse. But she was determined that this man wasn't going to touch her. She'd backed down too many times with Nick.

"This isn't happening, Drew." She stepped to the side and picked up the poker from the fireplace. "It's time for you to go."

She could almost read his mind. He was pretty sure he could get the poker away from her before she did much bodily harm to him. She lifted it, ready to swing, when she heard a vehicle come into the yard.

Drew heard it to. "Jackson Cardwell to the rescue again?"

But it couldn't be Jackson. He was in Texas by now.

Allie was relieved to see his sister Sarah stick her head in the door. "I hope I'm not interrupting anything," she said into the tense silence.

"Not at all," Allie assured her sister-in-law. Her voice sounded more normal than she'd thought it would. Had Drew just confessed to killing Nick? "Drew was just leaving."

"We're not through talking about this," he said as he started for the door.

"Oh, I think we already covered the subject. Good-bye, Drew."

"Is everything all right?" Sarah asked as Allie returned the poker to its spot next to the fireplace. She stepped in and closed the door behind her.

"Fine. You didn't happen to see my purse when you were here earlier, did you? Dana is expecting me and I can't seem to find it."

"No. You still haven't picked up Natalie?"

"No, Dana invited me for a sleepover with the kids. I was just heading there when Drew arrived."

"I didn't see his truck," Sarah said, glancing toward the window.

"He said he parked it down river where he was fishing." She glanced around the living room one more time. "I need to find my purse and get going."

"Your purse? Oh, that explains why you didn't answer your cell phone. I tried to call you," Sarah said. "Do you want me to help you look?"

"No, maybe I'll just take Nick's truck." The idea repulsed her, but she was anxious to get to the ranch. "I'm sure my purse will turn up. Oh, that's right, I was going out to check the van and see if I left it there when Drew showed up."

"So you're off to a kids sleepover?"

Allie knew she should be more upset with Sarah for taking Natalie last night, but Sarah had always done her mother's bidding. Allie couldn't help but feel sorry for the woman.

"Nat wanted to spend the night over there for Ford. He's upset about his uncle Austin, who was shot down in Texas. His brothers should be at the hospital by now. No wonder I haven't heard anything with my cell phone missing."

"Natalie and Ford sure hit it off, didn't they? It's too bad Nat doesn't have a sibling. I always thought you and Nick would have another child."

Allie found Nick's truck keys in her jacket pocket and held them up. "If you still want Nick's truck, you can have it. I was planning to sell it. But the back side panel is dented." She frowned. "It's odd that Nick didn't mention it. You know how he was about truck…"

Her thoughts tumbled over each other in a matter of an instant as her gaze went to her fingers and she remembered the white flakes she'd brushed off the dent. It hadn't registered at the time. The dent. The white paint from the vehicle that had hit it. Pearl white on Nick's black pickup.

Nick would have been out of his mind if someone had hit his pickup. So it couldn't have happened before his hunting trip, which meant it happened where? At the trailhead?

Another vehicle must have hit the pickup. Allie's thoughts fell into a straight, heart-stopping line. A pearl-white vehicle like the one Sarah was having repaired the day the call came about Nick's death.

Allie felt the hair rise on the back of her neck as she looked up and saw Sarah's expression.

"I knew you would figure it out the minute I saw you standing next to the dent in Nick's pickup. Nick was so particular about his truck. One little scratch and he would have been losing his mind. Isn't that what you were realizing?"

"Oh Sarah," she said, her heart breaking.

"That's all you have to say to the woman who killed your husband?" she asked as she pulled Allie's .45 out of her pocket and pointed the barrel at Allie's heart.

* * *

Jackson had left his rental car at the Bozeman airport. The moment the jet landed he ran to it and headed up the canyon. He tried Allie again. Still no answer. He left a message just in case there was a good reason she wasn't taking calls.

The only reason he could come up with was that she was at Dana's with the kids and didn't want to be disturbed. But she would have taken his calls. She would have wanted to know how Austin was doing.

He tried Dana and was relieved when at least she answered. "I'm looking for Allie. Have you seen her?"

"Not yet. I talked to her earlier. I told her to take a nice hot, long bath and relax, then come over for a sleepover." He could hear Dana let out a surprised sound. "I didn't realize it was so late. She should have been here by now."

"Her calls are going straight to voice mail."

"I'm sure she's just running late…" Dana sounded worried. "How is Austin?"

"He's out of surgery. The doctor said he should make it. I left Hayes and Laramie in Houston."

"Where are you now?"

"On my way to Allie's cabin. If you hear from her, will you please call me?"

He disconnected and drove as fast as he could through the winding narrow canyon. Something was wrong. Dana felt it, too. He prayed that Allie was all right. But feared she wasn't.

Realizing his greatest fear, he called Drew's number. When he'd heard the part Allie's brother-in-law had played in gaslighting her, he'd wanted to punch Drew again. He didn't trust the man, sensed he was a lot like Nick had been; another reason to hate the bastard.

But Jackson also worried that Drew might have killed Nick. The problem was motive. He wouldn't benefit from his brother's death since Nick had changed his beneficiaries on his insurance policy. Or was there something else Drew wanted more than money?

It came to him in a flash. Allie. If he had her, he would also have Nick's money and Nick's life.

Drew answered on the third ring. "What?" He sounded drunk.

Jackson's pulse jumped. "Have you seen Allie?"

"Who the hell is this?"

"Jackson Cardwell." He heard Drew's sneer even on the phone.

"What do *you* want? Just call to rub it in? Well, you haven't got Allie yet so I wouldn't go counting your chickens—"

His heart was pounding like a war drum. "Is she with you?"

Drew laughed. "She's having a sleepover but not with me. Not yet."

"She isn't at the sleepover. When did you see her?"

Finally picking up on Jackson's concern, he said, "She was with my sister at the cabin."

Jackson frowned. "Your sister?"

"They both think I killed Nick. But Sarah had more of a motive than I do. She hated Nick, especially since he'd been trying to get Mother to kick her out. Sarah might look sweet, but I have a scar from when we were kids. She hit me with a tire iron. A tire iron! Can you believe that?"

Jackson saw the turnoff ahead. As he took it, his headlights flashed on the cabin down the road. There were three vehicles parked out front. Nick's black pickup. Allie's van. Sarah's pearl-white SUV.

Chapter 18

"I don't understand," Allie said. "Why would you kill your brother?"

Sarah smiled. "Sweet, lovable *Nickie?* You of all people know what he was like. You had to know the way he talked about me."

Allie couldn't deny it. "He was cruel and insensitive, but—"

"He was trying to get Mother to kick me out without a cent!" Her face reddened with anger. "I gave up my life to take care of her and Nickie is in her ear telling her I am nothing but a parasite and that if she ever wants to see me get married, she has to kick me out and force me to make it on my own. Can you believe that?"

She could. Nick was often worried about any money that would be coming to him via his mother. He was afraid Sarah would get the lion's share because his mother felt sorry for her.

"He was jealous," Allie said. "He was afraid you were becoming her favorite just because she depends on you so much."

Sarah laughed. "Her *favorite?* She can't stand the sight of me. She'd marry me off in a heartbeat if she could find someone to take me off her hands."

"That isn't true. You know she would be lost without you." With a start, Allie realized that Mildred was going to get a chance to see what life was like without Sarah once Sarah went to prison. That is, unless she got away with murdering Nick. With Allie out of the way, Sarah just might.

"I still can't believe you killed him," Allie said as she searched her mind for anything within reach of where she was standing that she could use to defend herself. Something dawned on her. "How did you get my gun?"

"Mother had sent me to your cabin to see if you still had that pink sweater she gave you for Christmas. You never wore it and it was driving her crazy. I told her pink didn't look good on you, but she got it on sale… You know how she is."

Oh yes, she knew. That ugly pink sweater. Allie had put the gun under it behind the shoe boxes.

"When I found the gun, I took it. I was thinking I would try to scare Nick. After all, we have the same genes. He should have known I could be as heartless as him. But Nick had always underestimated me. I tried to talk to him, but he went off on women, you in particular."

Allie blinked in surprise. *"Me?"*

"He said some women needed to be kept in their

place and that you thought you were going to leave him and take his child. He had news for you. He laughed, saying how you'd been stealing small amounts of his money thinking he wouldn't notice but he was on to you. He'd given you a few days to think about what you were doing, but when he came back there were going to be big changes. He was going to take you in hand. He said, 'I'll kill her before I'll let her leave me.' Then he told me to get out of his way and took off up the trail."

So Nick hadn't been promising to change, she thought. He was going to change her when he got back. Allie felt sick to her stomach, imagining what Nick would have been like if he had ever returned home to find her packing to leave him.

"His parting shot was to yell back at me. 'You big fat ugly pig. Go home to your mommy because when I get back your butt is out of that guesthouse.' Then he laughed and disappeared into the trees."

"Oh, Sarah, I'm so sorry. Nick was horrible. If you tell the police all of this—and I will back you up—I'm sure they will—"

"Will what? Let me go? You can't be that naive. I'll go to prison."

Allie had a crazy thought that prison would be preferable to living with Mildred Taylor.

"No, Allie, there is another way. You are the only one who knows what I did."

"If you kill me, they'll eventually catch you and since this will be cold-blooded murder, you will never get out of prison. Don't throw your life away because of Nick."

"I'm going to make you a deal," Sarah said. "I will spare your daughter if you do what I say."

"What? You would hurt Natalie?" Allie's terror

ramped up as she realized this was a woman who felt no remorse for killing her own brother. Nor would she feel any for killing her sister-in-law now. That she could even think of hurting Natalie...

"Do you know why I look like I do?" Sarah asked. "I made myself fat after my mother's first divorce when I was just a little older than Natalie." She stepped closer, making Allie take a step back. "My stepfather thought I was adorable and couldn't keep his hands off me. My other stepfathers were just as bad until I gained enough weight that, like my mother, they only had contempt for me."

Allie couldn't hold back the tears. "I'm so sorry. I had no idea."

"No one did. My mother knew, though." Her eyebrow shot up. "That surprises you?" She laughed. "You really have no idea what *Mother Taylor* is capable of doing or why she dotes on her granddaughter. This latest husband is divorcing her, but there will be another husband, one who will think your little Natalie is adorable. Think about that. You do what I say and I will make sure what happened to me doesn't happen to Nat."

Allie was too stunned almost to breathe. What was Sarah saying?

"That's right, Mother Taylor *needs* Natalie," her sister-in-law said. "Now you can either take this gun and shoot yourself or I will shoot you. But if I have to do it, I will probably get caught as you say and go to prison. Imagine what will happen to Natalie without me here to protect her. Oh, and don't even think about turning the gun on me because trust me I will take you with me and Natalie will have a new grandpa, one who will adore her."

Allie couldn't bear the choice Sarah was demanding she make. "Natalie needs me," she pleaded as she looked at the .45 her sister-in-law held out to her.

"She needs me more. Just imagine the danger Natalie would have been in if I hadn't warned you."

"Don't you think I suspected something was wrong at that house? I didn't like Natalie going there. I didn't trust your family."

"With good reason as it turns out. You have good mothering instincts. I wonder what my life would have been like if I'd had a good mother?"

Allie's heart went out to her even though the woman was determined she would die tonight. "I'm so sorry. Sarah, but we don't have to do this. I won't tell the police about the dent in the pickup."

"You're too honest. Every time you saw me, we would both know." She shook her head. "One day you would have to clear your conscience. You know what would happen to me if I went to prison. No, this is the best way. Think of your daughter."

How could she think of anything else? That's when she heard the vehicle approaching.

Sarah got a strange look on her face as she cocked her head at the sound of the motor roaring up into the yard. "This has to end now," she said.

Allie couldn't imagine who had just driven up. Dana and the kids? She couldn't take the chance that someone else would walk into this.

She grabbed for the gun.

Jackson hit the door running. He told himself he was going to look like a damned fool barging in like this. But all his instincts told him something was very wrong.

As he burst through the door, he saw Allie and Sarah. Then he saw the gun they were struggling over.

The sound of the report in the tiny cabin was deafening. Jackson jumped between them going for the gun that Sarah still gripped in her hands. The silence after the gunshot was shattered as Allie began to scream.

Jackson fought to get the gun out of Sarah's hands. She was stronger than she looked. Her eyes were wide. She smiled at him as she managed to pull the trigger a second time.

The second silence after the gunshot was much louder.

"Allie, are you hit?" Jackson cried as he wrenched the gun from Sarah's hand.

She looked at him, tears in her eyes, and shook her head.

For a moment all three of them stood there, then Sarah fell to her knees, Allie dropping to the floor with her, to take the woman in her arms.

"She killed herself," Allie said to Jackson. "She could have killed me, but she turned the gun on herself." Still holding Sarah, Allie began to cry.

Jackson pulled out the phone, tapped in 911 and asked for an ambulance and the marshal, but one look at Sarah and he also asked for the coroner.

Epilogue

Be careful who you marry—including the family you marry into. That had been Jackson's mother's advice when he'd married Juliet. He hadn't listened. But Allie's in-laws made Juliet's look like a dream family.

"If you want to file charges," Marshal Hud Savage was saying. "You can get your mother-in-law for trespassing, vandalism, criminal mischief…but as far as the gaslighting…"

"I don't want to file charges," Allie said. "The real harm she's done… Well, there isn't a law against it, at least not for Mildred. And like you said, no way to prove it. How is Mildred?"

After what Allie had told him, Jackson hoped the woman was going through her own private hell. She deserved much worse.

"She's shocked, devastated, but knowing Mildred, she'll bounce back," Hud said. "How are you doing?"

"I'm okay. I'm just glad it's over."

Jackson could see the weight of all this on her. He wanted to scoop her and Natalie up and take them far away from this mess. But he knew the timing was all wrong. Allie had to deal with this before she would be free of Nick and his family.

"I did talk to the psychic Belinda took you to," Hud said. "She claims she didn't know what was planned. Mildred had given her a recording of Nick's voice that had been digitally altered with Drew helping with any extra words that were needed. She alleges she was as shocked as anyone when Nick said what he did."

"I believe her," Allie said.

"As for who shot your horse up in the mountains…" Hud rubbed a hand over his face. "I've arrested Drew for that. I can't hold him for long without evidence, but he does own a .22 caliber rifle and he did have access to the ranch."

"So that whole family gets off scot-free?" Jackson demanded.

Hud raised a brow. "I wouldn't say scot-free. I'd love to throw the book at Mildred and Drew, believe me. But neither will see jail time I'm afraid. Their justice will have to come when they meet their maker." Hud shook his head and turned to Jackson. "I heard Austin is recovering fine."

"It was touch and go for a while, but he's tough. The doctor said he will be released from the hospital in a week or so, but he is looking at weeks if not months before he can go back to work. He might actually get up to Montana to see the Texas Boys Barbecue joint before the grand opening."

"I suppose you're headed back to Texas then?" Hud asked. "Dana said Ford will be starting kindergarten his year?"

Jackson nodded. "I suppose I need to get a few things sorted out fairly soon."

Allie couldn't face the cabin. She had nothing but bad memories there. So she'd been so relieved when Dana had insisted she and Natalie stay in one of the cabins. All but one of them was now free since Laramie had gone back to Texas, and Hayes and McKenzie had bought a ranch down the highway with a large house that they were remodeling. Only Jackson and Ford were still in their cabin, not that Ford spent much time there since he was having so much fun with his cousins.

The same with Natalie. Allie hardly saw her over the next few days. She'd gotten through the funerals of Sarah and a second one for Nick. Mildred had tried to make her feel guilty about Sarah's death. But when Mildred started insisting that Natalie come stay with her, Allie had finally had to explain to her mother-in-law that she wouldn't be seeing Nat and why.

Of course Mildred denied everything, insisting Sarah had been a liar and blamed everything on her poor mother.

"We're done," Allie said. "No matter what I decide to do in the future, you're not going to be a part of my life or Natalie's."

"I'll take you to court, I'll…" Mildred had burst into tears. "How can you be so cruel to me? It's because you have all my Nickie's money now. I can't hold my head up in this canyon anymore, my husband is divorcing me, Drew is selling out and leaving… Where am I supposed to go?"

"I don't care as long as I never have to see you." Allie had walked away from her and hadn't looked back.

"I don't want Nick's insurance money," she'd told Dana the day she and Natalie had moved into one of the ranch cabins.

"Use just what you need and put the rest away for Natalie. Who knows what a good education will cost by the time Nat goes to college? Then put that family behind you."

But it was her own family that Allie was struggling to put behind her, she thought as she saw Megan drive up in the ranch yard. Megan had been calling her almost every day. She hadn't wanted to talk to her. She didn't want to now, but she knew she had to deal with it, no matter how painful it was.

Stepping out on the porch, she watched her half sister get out of the car. Natalie, who'd been playing with the kids, saw her aunt and ran to her. Allie watched Megan hug Natalie to her and felt a lump form in her throat.

"We can talk out here," she told Megan as Natalie went to join her friends.

Allie took a seat on the porch swing. Megan remained standing. Allie saw that she'd been crying.

"I used to ask about you when I was little," Megan said. "I'd seen photographs of you and you were so pretty." She let out a chuckle. "I was so jealous of your green eyes and your dimples. I remember asking Dad why I got brown eyes and no holes in my cheeks."

Allie said nothing, just letting her talk, but her heart ached as she listened.

"I always wanted to be you," Megan said. "Dad wouldn't talk about your mother, so that made me all the more curious about what had happened to her. When

I found out… I was half afraid when I met you, but then you were so sweet. And Natalie—" she waved a hand through the air, her face splitting into a huge smile "—I fell in love with her the moment I saw her. But I guess I was looking for cracks in your sanity even before Nick was killed and Mildred began telling me things. I'm sorry. Can you ever forgive me?"

Allie had thought that what she couldn't do was ever trust Megan again, especially with Natalie. But as she looked at her stepsister, she knew she had to for Natalie's sake. She rose from the chair and stepped to her sister to pull her into her arms.

They both began to cry, hugging each other tightly. There was something to this family thing, Allie thought. They might not be related by blood, but Allie couldn't cut Megan out of their lives, no matter where the future led them.

Allie watched her sister with Natalie and the kids. Megan, at twenty-three, was still a kid herself, she thought as she watched her playing tag with them. She knew she'd made the right decision and felt good about it.

She felt freer than she had in years. She'd also made up with Belinda. They would never be as close, not after her friend had kept her relationship with Nick from her. But they would remain friends and Allie was glad of it.

Belinda said she wanted her to meet the man in her life. Maybe Allie would, since it seemed that this time the relationship was serious.

Drew had tried to talk to her at the funeral, but she'd told him what she'd told his mother. She never wanted to see either of them again and with both of them leaving the canyon, she probably never would.

Beyond that, she didn't know. She would sell the cabin, Nick's pickup, everything she owned and start over. She just didn't know where yet, she thought as she saw Jackson coming up the mountainside.

He took off his Stetson as he approached the steps to her cabin and looked up at her. "Allie," he said. "I was hoping we could talk."

She motioned him up onto the porch. He looked so bashful. She smiled at the sight of his handsome face. The cowboy had saved her more times than she could count. He'd coming riding in on his white horse like something out of a fairytale and stolen her heart like an old-time outlaw.

"What did you want to talk about?" she asked. He seemed as tongue tied as Ford had been when he'd met Natalie.

"I... I..." He swallowed. "I love you."

Her eyes filled with tears. Those were the three little words she had ached to hear. Her heart pounded as she stepped to him. "I love you, Jackson."

He let out a whoop and picking her up, spun her around. As he set her down, he was still laughing. "Run away with me?"

"Anywhere."

"Texas?"

"If that's where you want to go."

"Well, here is the problem. You know my father, Harlan? I think he might just make a better grandfather than he ever did a father. I want Ford to have that."

She smiled. "Montana?"

"This is where I was born. I guess it is calling back my whole family. Did I tell you that my mother's new husband, Franklin, owns some land in the state? They're going to be spending half the year here. Hayes and

McKenzie bought a place up the road and Tag and Lily will be living close by, as well. Dana said we can stay on the ranch until we find a place. The only thing we have to do is make sure our kids are in school next month."

"Montana it is then."

"Wait a minute." He looked shy again as he dropped to one knee. She noticed he had on new jeans and a nice Western dress shirt. Reaching into his pocket, he pulled out a ring box. "You're going to think I'm nuts. I bought this the day Tag and I went to pick up his rings for the wedding. I saw it and I thought, 'It's the same color as Allie's eyes.' Damned if I knew what I was going to do with it. Until now." He took a breath and let it out. "Would you marry me, Allie?"

She stared down at the beautiful emerald-green engagement ring set between two sparkling diamonds and felt her eyes widen. "It's the most beautiful thing I have ever seen."

He laughed. "No, honey, that would be you," he said as he put the ring on her finger, then drew her close and kissed her. "I can't wait to tell the kids. I have a feeling Ford and Natalie are going to like living in Montana on their very own ranch, with their very own horses and lots of family around them."

Allie felt like pinching herself. She'd been through so much, but in the end she'd gotten something she'd never dreamed of, a loving man she could depend on and love with all her heart. For so long, she'd been afraid to hope that dreams could come true.

She smiled as Jackson took her hand and they went to tell the kids the news.

* * * * *

Get 4 FREE REWARDS!

We'll send you 2 FREE Books <u>plus</u> 2 FREE Mystery Gifts.

FREE Value Over **$20**

Both the **Harlequin Intrigue®** and **Harlequin® Romantic Suspense** series feature compelling novels filled with heart-racing action-packed romance that will keep you on the edge of your seat.

YES! Please send me 2 FREE novels from the Harlequin Intrigue or Harlequin Romantic Suspense series and my 2 FREE gifts (gifts are worth about $10 retail). After receiving them, if I don't wish to receive any more books, I can return the shipping statement marked "cancel." If I don't cancel, I will receive 6 brand-new Harlequin Intrigue Larger-Print books every month and be billed just $6.49 each in the U.S. or $6.99 each in Canada, a savings of at least 13% off the cover price, or 4 brand-new Harlequin Romantic Suspense books every month and be billed just $5.49 each in the U.S. or $6.24 each in Canada, a savings of at least 12% off the cover price. It's quite a bargain! Shipping and handling is just 50¢ per book in the U.S. and $1.25 per book in Canada.* I understand that accepting the 2 free books and gifts places me under no obligation to buy anything. I can always return a shipment and cancel at any time by calling the number below. The free books and gifts are mine to keep no matter what I decide.

Choose one: ☐ **Harlequin Intrigue Larger-Print** (199/399 HDN GRJK)   ☐ **Harlequin Romantic Suspense** (240/340 HDN GRJK)

Name (please print)

Address   Apt. #

City   State/Province   Zip/Postal Code

Email: Please check this box ☐ if you would like to receive newsletters and promotional emails from Harlequin Enterprises ULC and its affiliates. You can unsubscribe anytime.

Mail to the **Harlequin Reader Service:**
IN U.S.A.: P.O. Box 1341, Buffalo, NY 14240-8531
IN CANADA: P.O. Box 603, Fort Erie, Ontario L2A 5X3

Want to try 2 free books from another series! Call 1-800-873-8635 or visit www.ReaderService.com.

*Terms and prices subject to change without notice. Prices do not include sales taxes, which will be charged (if applicable) based on your state or country of residence. Canadian residents will be charged applicable taxes. Offer not valid in Quebec. This offer is limited to one order per household. Books received may not be as shown. Not valid for current subscribers to the Harlequin Intrigue or Harlequin Romantic Suspense series. All orders subject to approval. Credit or debit balances in a customer's account(s) may be offset by any other outstanding balance owed by or to the customer. Please allow 4 to 6 weeks for delivery. Offer available while quantities last.

Your Privacy—Your information is being collected by Harlequin Enterprises ULC, operating as Harlequin Reader Service. For a complete summary of the information we collect, how we use this information and to whom it is disclosed, please visit our privacy notice located at corporate.harlequin.com/privacy-notice. From time to time we may also exchange your personal information with reputable third parties. If you wish to opt out of this sharing of your personal information, please visit readerservice.com/consumerchoice or call 1-800-873-8635. **Notice to California Residents**—Under California law, you have specific rights to control and access your data. For more information on these rights and how to exercise them, visit corporate.harlequin.com/california-privacy.

HIHRS22R3

Get 4 FREE REWARDS!

We'll send you 2 FREE Books plus 2 FREE Mystery Gifts.

FREE Value Over **$20**

Both the **Harlequin® Desire** and **Harlequin Presents®** series feature compelling novels filled with passion, sensuality and intriguing scandals.

YES! Please send me 2 FREE novels from the Harlequin Desire or Harlequin Presents series and my 2 FREE gifts (gifts are worth about $10 retail). After receiving them, if I don't wish to receive any more books, I can return the shipping statement marked "cancel." If I don't cancel, I will receive 6 brand-new Harlequin Presents Larger-Print books every month and be billed just $6.30 each in the U.S. or $6.49 each in Canada, a savings of at least 10% off the cover price, or 6 Harlequin Desire books every month and be billed just $5.05 each in the U.S. or $5.74 each in Canada, a savings of at least 12% off the cover price. It's quite a bargain! Shipping and handling is just 50¢ per book in the U.S. and $1.25 per book in Canada.* I understand that accepting the 2 free books and gifts places me under no obligation to buy anything. I can always return a shipment and cancel at any time by calling the number below. The free books and gifts are mine to keep no matter what I decide.

Choose one: ☐ **Harlequin Desire**
(225/326 HDN GRJ7)

☐ **Harlequin Presents Larger-Print**
(176/376 HDN GRJ7)

Name (please print)

Address _____ Apt. #

City _____ State/Province _____ Zip/Postal Code

Email: Please check this box ☐ if you would like to receive newsletters and promotional emails from Harlequin Enterprises ULC and its affiliates. You can unsubscribe anytime.

Mail to the Harlequin Reader Service:
IN U.S.A.: P.O. Box 1341, Buffalo, NY 14240-8531
IN CANADA: P.O. Box 603, Fort Erie, Ontario L2A 5X3

Want to try 2 free books from another series? Call 1-800-873-8635 or visit www.ReaderService.com.

HARLEQUIN
PLUS

Try the best multimedia subscription service for romance readers like you!

Read, Watch and Play.

Experience the easiest way to get the romance content you crave.

Start your **FREE TRIAL** at
www.harlequinplus.com/freetrial.